Also by Jenna Hartley

<u>Love in LA Series</u>
Inevitable
Unexpected
Irresistible
Undeniable
Unpredictable
Irreplaceable

<u>Alondra Valley Series</u>
Feels Like Love
Love Like No Other
A Love Like That

<u>Tempt Series</u>
Temptation
Reputation

For the most current list of Jenna's titles, please visit her website www.authorjennahartley.com.

Or scan the QR code on the following page to be taken to her author page on Amazon.com

SCAN ME

Unpredictable

jenna hartley

ISBN: 9798385616862

Editing: Lisa A. Hollett
Cover Artwork © 2022 Indie Sage Designs

For my husband.

You're my favorite!

Content Warnings

This story contains explicit sexual content, profanity, and topics that may be sensitive to some readers.

For more detailed information, visit the QR code below.

Playlist

"When You Look Like That" by Thomas Rhett
"Good Girls Go Bad" (featuring Leighton Meester) by Cobra Starship
"Slow Hands" by Niall Horan
"Run the World (Girls) by Beyonce
"The Tide" by Niall Horan
"Too Much To Ask" by Niall Horan
"Love On Top" by Beyonce
"Blue Afternoon" by Leighton Meester
"Higher Ground" (featuring Naomi Wild) by ODESZA
"Light" (Instrumental) - ODESZA
"Just A Memory" (featuring Regina Spektor) by ODESZA
"Can U Handle It" by Usher
"Better" by SYML
"BLOW" (featuring Chris Stapleton & Bruno Mars)by Ed Sheeran
"Greenlight" by Jonas Brothers
"Come Back To Bed" by Sean Stemaly
"Make Out With Me" by Maren Morris

You can find this playlist and more at
https://www.authorjennahartley.com/playlists

CHAPTER ONE

Juliana

The water sucked me under, pulling me in. Swirling, dark clouds that forced the air from my lungs. I saw his face, and then it was gone. Felt his fingers slip through mine. Then he vanished. I kept reaching for him, screaming underwater, feeling as if my lungs might burst.

Something brushed against me in the darkness, and I tried to grasp it…

The blare of my alarm jolted me from my dream. I bolted upright, heart racing as I placed a hand to my chest. *Holy shit.* I reached over to my nightstand and fumbled for my phone, jabbing at the screen several times before finally shutting off the alarm.

My breath came in short pants, and I pulled my knees to my chest. My tank and boy shorts were damp with sweat, and my blond waves fell over my shoulders, covering my face. An image flashed through my mind, and I squeezed my eyes shut, attempting to force the memories away. It had been two years since the day that had changed everything. Two years since I'd last seen…*him.* I swallowed.

Just the thought of Ryan had tears springing to my eyes, the bands around my chest tightening as if to squeeze the air from my lungs. With an unsteady hand, I opened the drawer of my nightstand and removed the frame with our picture. I stared at the image, tracing his smile, remembering the moment as if it were yesterday. Reliving the good in an attempt to push away the bad. But tears streamed down my cheeks, especially when I caught sight of the small velvet box nestled inside the drawer.

Despite knowing it was a terrible idea, I reached for it. I held it for a moment, feeling as if I were staring at Pandora's box. Except, I knew what lay inside. I knew how much it would hurt, and yet I opened it anyway.

Unable to resist, I slid the ring onto my finger, admiring the two-carat solitaire set in a band of diamonds. I could remember the expression on Ryan's face when he'd knelt to the ground and asked me to spend the rest of our lives together.

We just hadn't realized how short our time together would be. Hadn't realized everything was about to change.

I moved my hand from side to side, the diamonds sparkling in the light like the glint of the sun on the water. A sob caught in my throat, and I wondered—as always—what had happened to him. I didn't know if I'd ever discover the answer. And that was almost the hardest part—the not knowing. The wondering. The worrying.

My phone chimed with an incoming email, and I swiped away my tears and quickly glanced at the screen. I immediately cringed. It was the organizer for a huge wedding show I was attending later in the day, and I'd almost forgotten all about it. I would've considered sending my assistant in my place, but I was the keynote speaker. And it was a great opportunity.

I pushed out of bed, forcing myself to put one foot in

front of the other. I needed to get ready, get my head on straight, and get out the door.

But when I climbed into the shower, I was assaulted by memories both good and bad. And my resolve instantly crumbled. I leaned against the wall, pounding the tile. I was a tempest, and anger, regret, and sadness swirled through me.

Finally, when I had no more tears to cry and the water was cold, I switched off the faucet. I stepped out of the shower and met my reflection in the mirror. I looked…tired, sad. But more than anything, I was lost.

To the outside world, I had it together. I was a successful business owner, a highly sought-after event planner. I delighted in managing the controlled chaos, in seeing my clients' joy on their special day. And I loved my clients—most of the time. But today…today, I just couldn't face the world.

I'll just take one day.

Surely, I deserved that. I rarely, if ever, took a day off. I'd worked my ass off to build my company. I glanced at my calendar, skimming through my appointments, quickly realizing how ridiculous the notion was. Especially when I spotted the name Amanda Jackson. She was *the* Hollywood starlet at the moment, and she was engaged to a man who had been voted "Hottest Man Alive" four times.

And she was coming in today. To talk to me about her dream wedding.

She was *not* the type of client who would look kindly on rescheduling. You canceled, and she walked.

With a deep sigh, I placed my palms on the counter and met my reflection. One of the Post-it notes on my mirror caught my attention, and I read the words I'd written so carefully.

You are stronger than you think.

. . .

I dropped my head and took a deep breath. I wanted to believe those words, but...my heart wasn't in it. At the moment, they felt like nothing more than a collection of letters on a colorful note affixed to the mirror of a woman who didn't exist anymore.

Still, I had obligations, responsibilities. Clients.

And with that reminder, I finished getting ready and drove to work. When I arrived at the office, my assistant glanced up from the front desk.

"Good morning. Coffee?" Landon stood and took my purse before handing me a mug with my logo emblazoned on the side.

I'd always been a coffee drinker, but even more so lately. I couldn't make it through the day on fewer than four cups. And as tired as I was, I often stayed up late into the night, working on projects in an effort to keep my mind occupied.

"Thanks," I said, taking a large, fortifying gulp.

"Your nine o'clock is waiting in the conference room."

"Perfect. Thank you." I grabbed my tablet and phone, then headed to the conference room where the two grooms were waiting.

"Good morning," I said, entering the room and setting my things on the table.

James and Declan stood, and each of them hugged me before kissing me on the cheek. They were two of my favorite clients—sweet, happy, decisive but not overly opinionated. They were a pleasure to work with.

"It looks like Landon already got you something to drink. Do you need anything else?" I asked.

"We're good," James said.

"Great!" I sat down, and they followed suit. "How are you guys feeling? Did you make a decision on the cake?"

"Red velvet," James said at the same time Declan said, "Cheesecake."

They turned to each other, frowned, then started talking over each other. I couldn't make out every word, but they were arguing about cakes. How cheesecake was superior or too heavy or whatever. I tried to keep my expression neutral, even as I felt a headache building.

"Guys." I held up my hands, wondering if this was really about cake or something else. So often with the couples I worked with, fights over these small decisions were merely a reflection of a deeper issue. And sometimes, they really did just fight about cake.

"Typically, there is a bride's and a groom's cake. Why don't we do two groom's cakes? Then, you can each pick a flavor."

They both seemed to relax at that suggestion. Declan nodded. "Yes. I like that."

"It's perfect." James smiled at him, and I could see the love pinging between them.

I was happy for them, but also—my heart ached. That had been Ryan and me. Planning our wedding, our future. We hadn't argued over cake flavors, but I'd give anything to see him, talk to him again. Even if it was to bicker over something as trivial as cake.

"Juliana," Declan said. "Are you okay?"

I shook my head to clear it, pushing the memory from my mind as I forced a smile. "Yes. Of course. Now—" I glanced at my tablet where my notes were displayed. I went over a few more items before asking if they had any questions.

They glanced at each other then back at me. "I think we're good," James said.

"Great." I stood, wobbling a little as I smoothed down my dress. "Then I'll see you in a few weeks for one of your last appointments before you walk down the aisle."

James clapped his hands together, and Declan wrapped an arm around his shoulder. They were such a stylish couple, such an attractive couple, but it was their love that really spoke to me. Especially when Declan pressed a soft kiss to James's hair and whispered, "I love you."

I held it together long enough for them to leave. But as soon as I was alone in my office, I burst into tears. I'd known today would be hard, but everyone had told me it would get easier with time. They'd lied.

Maybe if I could sleep without the nightmares, I'd be functioning better. But over the past month, they'd really ramped up again. Drinking wine before bed didn't help nor did sleeping pills. The only thing that seemed to work was avoiding sleep altogether.

"Juliana," Landon called through the door. "Juliana." He knocked, and I rushed to swipe away my tears without smearing my makeup.

I pushed back my shoulders and swung open the door. "Yes?"

His eyes were wide, panicked, and he kept glancing down the hall toward the lobby. "Taylor Long is here."

I frowned. "I don't remember seeing her on the calendar today."

"She's not," Landon said. "But she just came from a fitting, and she's pissed."

I pinched the bridge of my nose. I should've known better than to agree to plan Taylor Long's wedding. She was a rising pop star and a notorious diva. But the money was good, and the exposure even better—as long as she got everything she wanted. And keeping her happy was no small feat.

"Send her in," I said to Landon, dreading the emails already piling up in my inbox.

I squared my shoulders, but every click of Taylor's heels on the floor felt like a nail pounding into my skull.

I'm so freaking tired.

Even though I longed to drop my head on my desk and close my eyes, I straightened, preparing for battle.

"Taylor." I forced a smile, accepting her hug and air kiss. I tried not to roll my eyes. This woman had become the bane of my existence, and I couldn't wait for her to get married.

Fortunately, I didn't feel that way about most of my clients. But that didn't make dealing with Taylor any easier. Her demands were outrageous, and I'd honestly started to pity the poor groom. I'd also begun to wonder if this wedding was all part of an elaborate—and expensive—publicity stunt. I sincerely hoped not, but I'd continue to do my job as long as they paid me.

"Jules." The sound of her voice grated on my already-fragile nerves. "You look terrible. You're not getting sick, are you?"

For a second, I thought maybe she was genuinely concerned. But then she backed up a few inches and covered her nose and mouth with a bold-patterned scarf, the Gucci logo interspersed throughout.

"I'm fine," I said. "Promise."

"Oh good," she sighed, taking a seat in the chair across from me. Landon came in with a glass of champagne and handed it to her before disappearing once more. Her designer dog popped out of her designer purse, and I gripped my pen more tightly as he sniffed around my office.

I swear to god, if he pees on my rug...

"You know, a different color dress and some different makeup could really do wonders for your complexion. You're not bad-looking, you just have to know how to play to your strengths."

I stared at her, blinking. Was she serious?

"Even a few small changes would make a huge impact.

Then maybe *you'd* be the one getting married." She tossed her hair, her expression thoughtful.

My jaw dropped. *Wow.* I'd never been more insulted. And today, of all days.

"Okay." She perked up. "That was fun. Now, back to me. So, I went to my fitting—" She glanced down at the floor where her dog was…pissing on my rug. *Lovely.* "Fifi, don't do that. Next time you have to tinkle, tell Mommy."

She was deluded. Crazy. Why had I ever agreed to work with her? I almost wanted to laugh at how ridiculous the situation was. But I kept getting madder and madder the longer she droned on about "the fitting from hell," all in a nasal, whiny tone that made me want to strangle her. Still, I nodded at the correct intervals, listening politely.

"I understand," I said, wanting her to feel that I empathized. When really, I just wanted to get us back on track. I wanted to find a solution to the issue and then get her out of my office as soon as possible.

She sighed and took a sip of her drink. "How can you possibly understand? I mean, it's not like you've ever been married."

Never...been married.

I sucked in a jagged breath, but it didn't seem to make a difference. She was right; I'd never been married, but that was only because I'd lost the man I'd loved before we could walk down the aisle.

I stood, my fists shaking with rage. I couldn't deal with this—with *her*—right now. I took a step forward but the room spun, and I reached out for the desk to steady myself.

"Where do you think you're going?" she screeched.

"You—" I glared at her, my tone full of venom. "Do you realize how insulting your words are?" My chest tightened, vision blurring. I gripped the desk, squeezing the edge as I let her have it. "How dare you. You—"

Spots danced before my eyes, and then everything went black.

I HEARD SHRIEKING. OR WAS THAT BARKING? NEXT THING I knew, something wet hit my face, and I gasped for air. I opened my eyes to see Landon kneeling beside me. His expression was fraught with worry as I blinked up at him.

"Are you okay? Do you need your EpiPen?"

Taylor Long sat on the couch behind him, fanning herself as if she were the one who'd just fainted. I squeezed my eyes shut, wishing this were just another bad dream. But the fact that Fifi was licking champagne off my face told me it was very real.

"No." I pushed myself up to a seated position.

"I don't know that that's..." Landon said, but I waved away his concern.

"I'm fine. Apart from the fact that my face and hair are covered in champagne." I glared at him.

But when I moved to stand, my legs buckled. Landon helped me to the couch before escorting Taylor to the waiting area. I was just thankful he'd gotten rid of her before I could do any more damage. Had I really just yelled at a client? I groaned, covering my face with my hands.

"I think we should call a doctor," Landon said when he returned, handing me a towel.

I shook my head, but immediately regretted it. I pressed my temples, wondering if my headache would go away anytime soon. "Absolutely not. I'm fine, honestly."

"Mm-hmm." He crossed his arms over his chest. "Have you eaten anything today?"

I lifted a shoulder. I hadn't had much of an appetite this morning, but that wasn't surprising considering my nightmare. Up until the past month, the nightmares had mostly gone away. But then they'd come back with a vengeance. The one last night had been so vivid, so real… I couldn't seem to shake it.

"Either you tell me what's going on, or I'm calling a doctor."

I dabbed at my face with the towel, taking longer than necessary as I debated my response. Landon was tenacious—it was one of the reasons I'd hired him. He was also a good friend. I knew he'd just keep pushing, and I simply didn't have the energy to fight.

"I didn't get much sleep last night. But I'll be fine."

"Last night? Honey, you've been sporting dark circles for weeks."

He'd noticed? Of course, he'd noticed. Another reason I'd hired Landon—his meticulous attention to detail rivaled my own.

"Here's what we're going to do," he said, taking control. "One of the interns is with Taylor. She'll be fine—" He waved away my protest. "And if she isn't—well, she had it coming."

"My behavior was completely unprofessional."

He sliced a hand through the air. "We'll send her some flowers."

I wanted to laugh but knew better. If Taylor Long blabbed about this, I was screwed. I could lose a lot of business based on my outburst.

"I'll meet with Amanda Jackson," he continued, and I opened my mouth to protest. "Nope." He held up a hand. "It's that, or I call a doctor."

"Fine." I gnashed my teeth. Maybe I needed to delegate to Landon more often—he certainly knew how to take control in a crisis. I'd already been considering giving him a larger role.

"Meanwhile, you'll go home and get cleaned up, get some rest. I'll pick you up later for your speech at the wedding expo."

I sighed, knowing there was no use arguing. It was something I couldn't skip. I was the keynote speaker after all.

"Fine." I gathered my things. I hated admitting defeat, but if I was going to make it through the wedding expo, I needed to get my head on straight.

I didn't know how I would manage—being surrounded by smiling faces and some of the biggest figures in the wedding industry on the West Coast—but I would. If I could survive losing the love of my life, I could handle anything.

CHAPTER TWO

Harrison

"I'm so sorry to interrupt," a woman said, and I glanced up from the menu. "But would you mind taking a picture with me?" She held up her phone, flashing me a bright smile.

I'd selected this restaurant, hoping for some privacy, but also knowing better than to expect it. Even though I'd long since retired from the Hollywood Heatwaves, fans still sought me out for pictures and autographs. Though it could be tiresome at times, in all honesty, it was flattering. I was humbled that they remembered me for my role on the football team, as well as the work I'd done since.

I forced a smile. "Sure."

She stopped one of the waitresses and asked her to take the picture for us. I stood and wrapped my arm around the fan, smiling for the camera.

"Thank you." She grinned up at me after the waitress had returned her phone. "Thank you so much, Mr. Hayes. My son is going to be so excited when I tell him I met you today. He's a huge fan of the Heatwaves. A huge fan of yours."

"My pleasure." I smiled, and she stared up at me for a moment, in a daze.

"Think the Heatwaves will win tomorrow night's wild-card game?"

I lifted a shoulder, my lips twitching with a grin. "I guess you'll have to tune in to find out."

"I guess I will." She glanced toward the floor, and her eyelashes fluttered like the wings of a hummingbird. "I always do when you're commentating."

When she met my gaze, her neck was red as if she hadn't intended to admit that. I chuckled, no stranger to having women hit on me. Though, her bashfulness was refreshing. "Well, thank you. I appreciate it."

"Well, um. Thank *you*. For being so gracious about the picture."

"It's always nice to meet a fan."

When she lingered, I scanned the restaurant for Olivia, wondering if she'd gotten caught up in a meeting. It wouldn't be the first time since she'd started working at Harlow & Phillips. A quick glance at my phone showed no missed calls or texts from her, but I worried all the same.

"You wouldn't be—"

The front door opened, and Olivia rushed inside, waving at me as she spoke to the hostess. My smile split my face. She was always in such a hurry. Always busy chasing her goals and making her dreams come true. I was proud of her, though. So damn proud.

"Oh. *Right*," the woman said, drawing my attention once again. I'd almost forgotten she was there. "Of course. I'll leave you to your lunch date. Thank you again," she said before she made her way to the exit.

"Livie." I smiled, pulling my daughter in for a hug.

I held her close, soaking in her sweet scent. Reveling in this brief moment where she was safe in my arms. Where I could hold on to the illusion that I could still protect her from everything.

She brushed her ponytail over her shoulder, waiting while I pulled out a chair for her. "Sorry I'm late. I know you have a meeting with Talia after this."

Talia was my agent—whip-smart and a marketing genius. She ran a small but successful sports firm that had previously belonged to her father before his retirement. Much as I loved her dad and appreciated everything he'd done for me, I enjoyed working with Talia even more. She'd revamped my career at a time when it should have been winding down, helping me transition seamlessly from player to color commentator. And she'd always encouraged my philanthropic interests.

I took a seat across the table from Olivia, assessing her appearance. Her chestnut hair was smoothed back into a ponytail, her suit tailored and impeccable. She seemed happy, excited—even more so than usual. And I wondered at the cause of it.

"It's fine, really. Her office is just down the street." I smiled to reassure Olivia as the waiter came to take our drink order before disappearing again. "So, what's new with you?"

Even though we shared a meal once a week, it never felt like enough. I was grateful to have such a good relationship with my daughter, but she was busy living her own life. She had a successful career at an up-and-coming publishing house. She was dating a guy I actually liked. And even though I was busy myself, I always had time for her.

She updated me on her job but kept fidgeting with something in her lap. It wasn't until the waiter left again that she said, "Dad, I need to tell you something."

I tried to keep my expression neutral, even as my heart

raced, anticipating what she was going to say. She might be twenty-seven, but she'd always be my little girl.

She sipped her water, glancing around. Every second that ticked by was killing me. I considered myself a patient man, but alarm bells were sounding in my head.

"Olivia." My tone was firm. "What's going on? Are you okay?"

"Yeah." She straightened. "I'm great. I'm just…" She swallowed. "I have some news, and I'm not sure how you're going to take it."

I placed my hand over hers, peering into her green eyes that were so like my own. "You know you can tell me anything, I promise. Whatever it is, we'll get through it together."

"Dad." She laughed, her voice like a birdsong. Something in my chest eased, but I remained alert, nevertheless. "I'm fine. More than fine, actually. I'm great."

She placed her hand on the table, and a sparkling light caught my eye, pulling my attention to the ring on her finger. I glanced from her hand to her face, where I found a blinding smile. "Connor asked me to marry him."

I frowned, glaring at the engagement ring the size of Texas. Engaged? *Engaged?* My vision blurred, spots dancing before my eyes. She was getting married?

"Dad?" Her voice came to me as if from afar. "Say something."

I lifted my head, meeting her eyes. Eyes I'd stared into countless hours when she was a baby. She'd peered up at me with so much love and trust. I'd always been her hero, and now…

"Dad?" She waved her hand in front of my face, the diamond glittering, casting rainbows all over the fucking table. "You're really starting to freak me out."

"Married?" I spluttered, my mind struggling to catch up. "You barely know this guy."

"This *guy*?" She blinked at me, leaning back with a forced smile as the waiter delivered our meals. We thanked him, and then she asked, "You mean Connor?"

"Olivia—" I reached for her hand, but she pulled it back. "Calm down. I just want to make sure you've really thought this through."

"What is there to consider? I love him, and I want to marry him."

"For starters, you've been together less than a year."

"True, but we got to know each other before we ever met. We established a solid friendship first. Not to mention, he saved my life." She crossed her arms over her chest. "I thought you'd be happy for me."

"Marriage isn't a decision to be taken lightly. Over fifty percent of them fail." My own included.

"Yes, Dad," she sighed. "I'm well aware of the statistics, but it's a risk I'm willing to take."

"You know, your mom and I dated for two years before we ever got engaged. And we still ended up getting divorced."

"Exactly." She leaned forward, a fire in her eyes. "It doesn't really matter how long we've been together. We love each other, and we want to get married."

"You're signing a prenup, right? If you need a lawyer, I'm sure Jacob would be happy to help you draft one."

She shook her head, setting her glass on the table. "We don't need a prenup. I'm not going into my marriage preparing for divorce, because it won't happen. We love each other."

"Do you think any couple goes into marriage thinking they'll get divorced?" I ground out. "Life isn't some fairy tale like the books you read."

"God, Dad," she huffed. "I really hoped you'd be happy for me. For us."

"I just…" I rubbed my temple, trying to adopt a calmer tone. "Why are you in such a rush? You've had a lot of big life changes in a short amount of time. You sold your house, changed jobs, and moved in with Connor all in the past year."

"I know." She smiled. "It's been amazing."

I wanted to be happy for her, but I couldn't ignore the doubts and fears swarming in my mind. *Had she really thought this through?*

"And what about your job? You've been so busy, and I thought you wanted to focus on making your way up the ranks at Harlow & Phillips."

"I do." She took a bite of her meal before setting her fork aside. "And that hasn't changed. I can do all that and still get married too. The two aren't mutually exclusive." She studied me for a moment before asking, "Are you upset because Connor didn't ask for your blessing first?"

I shook my head, realizing I hadn't even thought of that. "No. I just—" I blew out a breath. "Marriage is a big step."

She glared at me from across the table. "One I'm ready for. And I'm hoping you'll walk me down the aisle."

I barked out a laugh. "Right." But then I sobered when I saw her pained expression.

"You know what? I came here, excited to tell you, thinking you'd be there to support me, like you always have. Apparently, I was wrong." She stood and yanked her purse off the back of her chair. "I'm marrying Connor whether you like it or not."

She stormed out of the restaurant like a petulant child. And it felt as if everyone's eyes followed her before turning to me. Blaming me, no doubt.

"What?" I snarled to no one in particular as I threw some bills on the table.

I marched out of the restaurant and down the sidewalk toward Talia's office, leaving my lunch half finished. *Married?* Was she out of her mind?

I took a few deep breaths before opening the door, but I knew it was going to take a lot more than that to calm me down after my lunch with Olivia. We rarely argued, but I couldn't stand by and watch her make the biggest mistake of her life. It wasn't that I didn't like Connor—far from it. It was how quickly everything was changing, and the fact that she refused to even consider a prenup.

While I waited for Talia in the conference room, I paced along the windows, staring down at Sunset Boulevard. Pedestrians passed, the palm trees swayed, and I thought back on lunch. Where had it all gone so wrong?

The door opened, and I turned to see Talia enter. "Harrison." Her smile immediately fell. "What's going on? You look stressed. Is it the endorsement contract? Because we can negotiate whatever terms you want."

I sank down in one of the chairs. "No." I closed my eyes and pinched the bridge of my nose. "Olivia's engaged."

"Aww. That's great news!" She took the seat at the head of the table, so we were close. "Isn't it?"

I shook my head. "I don't know what the hell she's thinking." I sighed, rubbing my temples. "They haven't even been together a year."

Something flitted through Talia's eyes, an emotion I couldn't place. "You don't think she's pregnant, do you?"

My eyes went wide. *Oh shit.* I hadn't even considered that possibility. I'd been too blindsided by Olivia's announcement to contemplate the possible motivations behind it.

I blinked a few times. I wasn't ready to be a grandpa. *Gramps? Pop? Grandad?*

"Harrison," Talia said, placing her hand on my shoulder. "Take a deep breath."

I did as she said, annoyed with myself for getting so worked up. If Olivia was pregnant, it wouldn't be the end of the world. She was twenty-seven, for crying out loud, older than I was when we'd had her. But I didn't want that to be her reason for getting married.

"I don't think she's pregnant. But what the hell do I know? Clearly, I can't think straight when it comes to Olivia and marriage. I kind of lost it on her when she told me." I cradled my head in my hands. I didn't care about the potential negative publicity from my little outburst; I cared that I'd hurt my daughter. "God, I'm an ass."

"You're a dad. And you're protective because you love her."

I looked up at her, knowing it was true. But that didn't make me feel any better. "Yeah, but you should've seen her face. She stormed out of the restaurant. She's never been upset with me—not like this."

"You both are upset because you care." I nodded at her words. "But Harrison, you need to accept that Olivia's a grown woman. She can make her own decisions."

"I know." I dipped my head, chagrined. But apparently Talia wasn't finished.

"And just because your marriage didn't work out doesn't mean Olivia is destined to follow the same path."

I swallowed hard, knowing she was right. *Fuck.*

I pounded my fist on the table. I was letting my own issues get in the way of my daughter's happiness. She loved Connor, and he loved her. That much I knew. Would they make it for the long haul? I hoped so.

And while I could've expressed my concern in a million different ways, I'd lost it on her. I'd ruined what should've been a special moment and twisted it into something ugly. I needed to fix this.

I tugged at the neck of my shirt, glancing side to side

before meeting Talia's gaze once more. "Do you think you can help me fix this?"

Talia folded her hands on the table, a smile playing at her lips. "What do you have in mind?"

I started brainstorming ideas. Hiring a wedding planner would certainly go a long way in proving to Olivia that I supported her and was there for her. I knew Talia had hired party planners in the past for her twin boys' birthday. If nothing else, maybe she'd be able to connect me with someone who could help.

"I think...I need a wedding planner."

"That's a step in the right direction," she said. "I've worked with an event planner in the past, and I think she and Olivia would get on well."

I exhaled a sigh of relief, knowing I was on the right track. "Great. Let's get this ball rolling so I can apologize."

Talia nodded and grabbed her phone. She tapped on the screen, then placed the phone on the table when it started to ring.

"Juliana Wright Events," said a male voice.

"Hi, Landon. This is Talia Winters."

"Hey, Talia. How are you?"

"Good, thanks. Look—" She crossed her legs, and I noticed a subtle shift in her demeanor. She was in business mode. "I have a client of mine here, and we were wondering if Juliana has any appointments available today."

"She's actually out of the office the rest of the day. And she's booked solid for the next few weeks."

I cursed under my breath. I knew there were other event planners, but I wanted someone with a personal recommendation.

"I hate to ask, but are you sure she's not available—even for a quick phone consult?" Talia pushed, and I appreciated her dedication.

A keyboard clicked in the background. "She doesn't have any openings until next month. But…she will be at the Vu Hotel for a wedding expo tonight."

Talia glanced at me, and I nodded. "He'll be there. And please let us know if something opens up."

I knew I should be grateful to Talia, but all I could think about was that I wasn't ready. I wasn't ready for my baby girl —my only child—to get married, let alone become a mother. Though, when I'd found out Camille was pregnant with Olivia, I hadn't been ready then either. But it didn't matter. Because when you were a parent, when you had a child relying on you—regardless of how old they were—you stepped up. You did what you had to do.

And so, that's exactly what I was going to do now. I would be there for Olivia, like I had been every day of her life. And I would be there for her until the day I died.

CHAPTER THREE

Juliana

"Are you drinking enough water?" Landon offered me a water bottle.

"I swear to god," I ground out, peering past him toward the crowded ballroom. "If you ask me one more time, I'm going to dump that bottle over your head."

"Okay. Okay." He held up his hands. "Geez… I'm just trying to help. Can't have you passing out in the middle of your speech, now can we?"

I glared at him.

"Are you nervous? Because you're going to rock it."

"Thanks." I took a calming breath and smoothed down my dress. I knew Landon cared about me, which was why I let it slide. That and I was a little preoccupied at the moment by the large audience. "I just get a little anxious about public speaking."

He leaned in, butting my shoulder with his. "Do you want to hear a tip?"

"If you're going to tell me to imagine the audience naked, it's not going to work."

"No." He picked at my shoulder, removing a piece of lint.

"Just be yourself. You're prepared, you're passionate, and you're going to rock this."

"Thanks." I grinned, feeling better already.

And I did feel better. After an invigorating run and a shower, I felt like a new woman. And coming to the wedding expo had been just the thing I'd needed. Interacting with so many professionals in the industry was inspiring, exciting. I'd come away with new ideas for my clients and couldn't wait to implement them.

Landon and I watched as the event organizer took the stage, walking over to the podium. She greeted the audience before introducing me. When the crowd started clapping, Landon gave me two thumbs up, mouthing "You've got this." I grinned and shook my head before making my way toward the podium.

"Thank you for joining us tonight. I'm honored to be here among so many talented professionals." My hands shook as I reviewed my note cards, but I forced myself to slow down.

As I spoke about the importance of catering to unique diets, I could feel myself growing more excited. This was my passion—helping celebrate life's events, both big and small, while ensuring that no one was left out due to their special dietary needs. It was why I'd started my business, and it was what kept me going.

When I finished my speech, the applause was deafening. I beamed out into the crowd, feeling more like myself than I had in months.

"You rocked it," Landon said, giving me a high five. "Seriously, Juliana. You had the audience captivated."

"Thank you." I grinned. "Want to go to the bar for a celebratory drink?"

"Are you sure that's a good idea after—" He gave me a meaningful look. "You know?"

"I told you. I'm fine. I went for a run earlier, ate some food, drank a ton of water."

"And you're staying here tonight, right?" He narrowed his eyes at me, hands on hips.

"Yes." As one of the speakers, part of my compensation included accommodations. It wasn't necessary, seeing as I was a local, but Landon had convinced me to accept the offered suite. He argued it would be the ideal opportunity to sample the full guest experience for our clients. I secretly hoped the change of scenery would help me finally get a good night's sleep.

"All right. All right. I'll go to the bar with you," he said it like it was a hardship, when we both knew it wasn't. "But no shots." He pointed at me, narrowing his eyes.

"Deal."

We headed to the bar, though we got stopped several times by people who wanted to congratulate me on my speech. I exchanged contact information with a few of them, and by the time we reached the bar, I was floating.

We took a seat and ordered drinks, still buzzed with excitement from the event. When they arrived, Landon held his up to toast. "To the best boss babe I know," he said with a huge grin. "You rocked that speech, girl. And you are going to rock this wedding season." He tipped his glass to mine.

"*We* are going to rock this wedding season," I said with a grin, and we both sipped our drinks. "Actually, there's something I wanted to talk to you about."

"Uh oh," he said. "That sounds ominous."

"No." I shook my head. "You really impressed me today. You kept the clients calm and business running smoothly, even when…" I cleared my throat, glancing down at the bar. "I couldn't."

"Thank you. You know I'm always happy to help where I can."

"I know," I said. "Which is why I want to give you a promotion."

His mouth fell open. "Promotion?"

I nodded. "I've been thinking about it for a while, and I want to bring someone on to handle the front desk exclusively. Which would free you up to support me more on some of the bigger events, as well as plan some of the smaller ones by yourself."

"Oh my god." He fanned himself, looking like he was going to cry. "Are you serious?"

"Yes." I laughed. "Landon, you deserve it."

"Thank you!" He threw his arms around me for a hug. "I'm so excited." He leaned back, suddenly serious. "And I promise that I will do my utmost to execute every event to your high standards."

"I know you will." I smiled.

We sat there a while longer, drinking and planning for the future, and it felt good. It felt *really* good, especially after what had happened this morning.

But when Landon excused himself to the restroom, I tried to make sense of what had gone wrong. As I sat there, staring at the contents of my glass, I tried to reconcile my behavior. Why was I so stuck in the past? Why couldn't I let go?

Maybe because I still didn't know what had happened. It had been two years—to the day—since Ryan had disappeared, and I was still no closer to answers.

For the first year, I'd remained hopeful, optimistic. I was certain he was out there and he would return to me. It was only a matter of time. But as the months dragged on, turning into one year and now two, my hope waned. In my heart, I knew it was time to move on, but I couldn't seem to take that next step.

"Life is funny, isn't it?" I mused aloud, more to my glass than anyone. "Unpredictable. Uncontrollable."

"That's part of the fun," said a deep voice to my right.

I snapped my head up, my eyes colliding with a pair of the most unusual green eyes I'd ever seen. The green of a rare emerald—clear and without imperfections. His gaze was warm, and his gentle smile formed crinkles next to his eyes. I didn't know if it was the alcohol or my grief, but he looked like an older, more muscular version of Ryan.

I sucked in a sharp breath as I took him in, feeling as if I were staring at my future husband. Despite the silver in his hair and the scruff lining his chiseled jaw, he was still very much in his prime. If anything, the years only added to his appeal. He wasn't Ryan, of course. But my heart wanted to believe he was, even if only for a moment.

"Is it?" I asked. "In my experience, change is neither good nor fun."

"Ah." His expression was knowing. "Spoken like a true control freak."

"I-I am not." I glared at him, annoyed by his assessment. His assumptions. He knew nothing about me. And yet, his comment was infuriatingly correct.

"She is," Landon interrupted.

I startled and leaned away from this strange man who had me feeling things I hadn't felt, well…not for a long time now. Things I'd never expected to feel again. I turned to Landon, glaring at him.

"Well, boss," he said, and it felt as if he was making a point of using the title. "I'm going to head out. Have fun!" He waggled his fingers, shooting me a wicked smile behind the sexy stranger's back. I waved, fully aware that he was ditching me.

As I lifted my glass to my lips, I said, "I can go with the flow."

"Can you?" The man leaned in so his breath grazed the shell of my ear. It sent goose bumps racing down my spine.

"When was the last time you did something spontaneous? Something…unpredictable?"

"I…" I frowned down at the bar.

When was the last time I'd done something unexpected? Something that wasn't part of my schedule? Not since before Ryan's disappearance.

"Just as I thought." I could hear the smile in his voice, and I turned to look at him and immediately regretted it. He was too handsome, too tempting, despite his smug grin. "You need to learn to let go."

The way his eyes pierced mine made me feel exposed, vulnerable. Though he couldn't possibly know about what had happened with Ryan, it felt as if he did.

I let out a shaky breath, surprised by my response to him. Surprised by the way this stranger made me feel as if he knew all my secrets, all my desires and fears. "I…" I swallowed. "I don't know if I can," I whispered.

"I'll tell you a secret," he said, and I placed my hand on his knee to steady myself. "Control is an illusion. It's only when you realize that you have no control—that's when you'll be free."

He made it sound so simple. Though the idea of being free was incredibly tempting. Ever since Ryan's disappearance, my life had felt chaotic. And the more I attempted to control things, the more I struggled. The only place I felt any shred of confidence and authority was at work—probably why I was so successful as an event planner.

"Maybe you're right." I sipped my drink. There was a certain logic to what he said.

"There's no maybe." He grinned.

On another man, I would've found his confidence annoying, but it suited him. He seemed so self-assured, so calm, that I couldn't help but be drawn to him. He made me want to relinquish control, to surrender to him.

He scanned up my legs, his gaze appreciative. I shifted in my seat, my libido roaring to life after lying dormant all this time. Maybe this was a sign. Maybe this delicious man was the universe's way of telling me to take that step forward.

A little over a year ago, my best friend Lauren, had challenged me to do something that scared me. Since then, what did I have to show for it? I was pretty sure putting the picture of Ryan and me in the drawer of my nightstand didn't count. Nor did the fact that I no longer wore my engagement ring. Though that was more out of self-preservation than anything else. When people saw it, they inevitably asked questions, made assumptions.

Then there was the online dating service. I'd only gone on a few dates, and it had been enough to realize I wasn't ready. I hadn't kissed any of the men I'd met, let alone slept with someone. If I was honest with myself, the idea of sleeping with another man terrified me. But the idea of sleeping with this man—this stranger—stirred something within me. Made me feel more alive than I had in a long time.

So, emboldened by the alcohol and the mischievous look in his eye, I channeled my inner Lauren. She was bold, brazen, and never hesitated to ask for what she wanted—especially when it came to sex.

I leaned forward, getting a whiff of his scent. He smelled earthy, like the embers of a dying fire. I was reminded of bonfires and good memories, and warmth spread through my limbs. It told me this was the right thing to do, not that my body needed any reassurance.

"Okay, Zen guru," I said, enjoying his bemused grin. "Show me your ways."

He leaned closer too, as if drawn to me. "Zen guru, huh? And how do you propose I do that?"

I just needed one night. One night to forget. One night to heal. One night to lose myself in a man's touch.

I released my plea into the air. "Help me forget. Help me let go."

He regarded me a moment, a muscle twitching in his jaw. "I'd love to give you the escape you crave. But I also don't want to be something you regret come tomorrow."

My stomach plummeted, and I turned away to hide my embarrassment. For the first time in two years, I'd put myself out there, I'd attempted to hit on a man, and…it had completely backfired. I'd thought we had a connection, an attraction, but I must have been wrong. My cheeks flamed, and I wished the floor would open up and swallow me whole.

"Well, that was…completely mortifying." I stood and slung my purse over my shoulder before throwing a few bills on the counter. Thank god I'd already given the bartender my room number so he could add the drinks to my bill. "Have a good evening."

I nearly tripped over myself as I tried to get out of there as quickly as possible. *He's probably right*, I thought as I sped across the lobby. Tears pricked my eyes, and I tried desperately not to cry as I waited for the elevator to arrive. I jabbed the button a few extra times, wishing it would come faster. How could I have so completely misread the signals? My shoulders slumped. Though it seemed like a fitting end to a shitty day.

I heard someone call, "Wait," as the doors finally, mercifully, opened.

I slipped inside, pressing the button for my floor while keeping my head down.

"Wait." He darted through the doors just before they closed. I looked up, realizing it was the man from the bar. And he was talking to me. My limbs tingled in anticipation.

The elevator doors closed, sealing us off from the rest of the world. It was just him and me, and he looked like he wanted to devour me. His eyes were dark, hooded. His fists clenched. He was breathing hard, and he appeared to be waging some internal battle.

"I don't normally do this," he said, closing the distance between us. "But... Well, fuck it."

He took me in his arms, and I gripped his shoulders as if bracing for the impact I knew was coming. He crashed his lips against mine, and I crumbled. He tasted like mint and bad decisions, and he kissed like he'd known me forever.

His tongue brushed against the seam of my lips, and I opened for him. Kissing him was like a homecoming and the beginning of a new adventure. It was comforting yet exhilarating. Familiar while still surprising.

I gave in to the kiss, gave in to him, and wrapped my arms around his neck. He felt so solid, so warm, and my body roared to life. It had been so long since I'd kissed a man, touched a man, and I'd forgotten how amazing it felt. I'd been so trapped in my grief, my anger, my pain that I'd forgotten what pleasure felt like.

His hands were everywhere, and I was desperate for his lips, his touch. My body hummed with anticipation, especially when his erection dug into me. I needed him.

"More," I whispered between kisses. "Need. More."

He groaned, backing me against the wall, our centers pressed together. Right there in the middle of the elevator, I let him squeeze my breasts and palm my ass, and I ground against him shamelessly.

What am I doing?

This so wasn't me—inviting a man back to my hotel room. Having a one-night stand. I knew nothing about this man other than the fact that I wanted him. I'd never felt more reckless or free, and I liked it, craved it even. This stranger made it difficult to think of anything and anyone else when he was touching me like he was.

Distantly, I registered the chime of the elevator, but I ignored it. He held out a hand to stop the doors from closing, disconnecting from my lips in the process. He grabbed my hand and tugged me into the hall.

"Which one is your room?" His hair was mussed, his smile disarming.

"I'm in 2302," I said, grabbing the key from my purse.

We couldn't keep our hands off each other as I led him toward my room. I batted his hands away when we passed an older couple, and I giggled as soon as we reached the door to my room. I was anxious and excited and a whole ball of emotions I didn't want to dissect, couldn't delve into without risk of chickening out. But overriding all of it was need. I *needed* this. I needed an escape, a release. I needed change.

I slipped the key into the slot, then stepped into the room and kicked off my shoes. As soon as the door closed, his lips were on mine, his hands on my body. And I was just as eager, just as needy. As I fumbled with the buttons on his shirt, he backed me farther into the room. He yanked off his shirt, casting it aside without his lips ever leaving mine.

Next to go was his undershirt, and I marveled at the tanned muscles of his chest. He was so beautiful, the light casting shadows on his chest and abs. I traced the divots and curves, admiring the work that surely went into such magnificence.

He was... I swallowed. God, he was even more gorgeous than I'd imagined. His tailored shirt had hinted at his powerful physique. But seeing him bare chested, pants hanging low on his waist, had me aching for more.

He spun me so my back was to him, taking his time as he lowered the zipper on my dress. Down, down it went, exposing my skin to the air, to his eyes. He slid his hands beneath the fabric, his touch both a soothing balm and a brush with fire.

As he pressed his lips to my neck, my dress fell to the floor, pooling at my feet. In that moment, with his eyes on me, I was glad I'd worn my good lingerie instead of the basic stuff I usually chose.

"You're stunning." He continued to kiss my neck, my back, everywhere. Anywhere there was bare skin, his lips explored.

I sighed, limbs relaxed. I hadn't felt this alive in months—years, if I was being honest. In the back of my mind, I knew I might regret this come tomorrow. But just for tonight, just for one night, I allowed myself to give in to the moment, losing myself in this man and his touch.

CHAPTER FOUR

Harrison

I couldn't stop kissing this woman, touching her. She'd captured my attention from the moment I'd set eyes on her in the bar. I'd come here hoping to find Talia's event planner, intent on making things right with Olivia. Instead, I'd left with a blond goddess.

When I'd walked into the bar, there she was—all long legs and soulful eyes. She was striking in both her appearance and the confidence she wore like a second skin. I was drawn to her—arrested by her beauty but captured by her downcast demeanor, which seemed so out of place on such a gorgeous creature.

I sure as hell hadn't expected her request—*help me forget*. And I hadn't planned to help her, despite wanting to. God, how I'd wanted to. I understood her pain, her need for escape. Even if I didn't know the exact reason for it, I knew how tempting it could be to lose yourself in the arms of a stranger. But it wouldn't help—at least not beyond tonight. So, I'd tried to let her down gently.

But when I'd seen the wounded look in her eyes, I'd moved without thinking. I couldn't let her walk away, not like that. Now when she thought I didn't want her. A deeper part of me—a part I didn't care to acknowledge—wanted to help her. Wanted to do whatever it took to banish the haunted look in her eyes.

I tangled my fingers in her hair, tilting her head, wanting to memorize the feel and taste of her. But it wasn't enough. So, I hooked her legs around my waist, easily carrying her over to the bed. I set her gently on the mattress, only stepping back to remove my pants. But I paused, hand on my zipper, spellbound by the sight of her sprawled out on the bed.

The bedside lamp was on, the white comforter pristine and puffy like a giant cloud. Her white lace underwear reminded me of a bride on her wedding night, and I was struck by an overwhelming urge to claim her as mine. Her blond waves fanned across the pillow, her gaze full of desire, lips swollen. I didn't know anything about her, but something in my gut told me to help her. Or maybe it was my dick, the greedy bastard wanting more of that creamy skin that smelled of flowers.

I kicked off my pants and crawled over her. Her skin was so smooth, her legs so long. I slanted my lips over hers, my cock seeking her heat. She sighed in response as I mapped her body with my hands, exploring the rise of her breasts, the valley of her stomach. Goose bumps dotted the surface of her skin, following the path I'd laid. She shuddered beneath my touch, and my dick twitched in response. It had been hard since I'd charged after her in the lobby, and I was aching for release.

"Tell me your name," I whispered in her ear. I licked the shell, nipping at her skin, but she merely shook her head. Then I asked, "Do you know mine?"

She met my eyes, searching my gaze, studying my features, no doubt. "Should I?"

I shook my head and smiled to myself, loving her perplexed expression. She clearly wasn't a football fan. But judging from her toned legs and flat stomach, she worked out. With every new discovery, I became more intrigued.

"I don't need to know your name, but I do need to know you want this." I gestured between us.

As desperate as I was for this woman, I wouldn't take it any further without hearing the words from her lips.

She gripped my shoulders, pulling me closer, close enough to whisper in my ear, "I'm clean and have an IUD. I want this."

That was all the confirmation I needed. "Good. I'm clean, and I have a condom."

I kissed my way down her chest, peeling back the lace of her bra to suck on one nipple then the other. She arched her back, letting out a frustrated sigh as I made my way southward. I'd never met a woman so responsive, so attuned to my touch. My chest swelled with pride, knowing I'd had this effect on her.

I continued my descent, brushing my lips against her stomach, lavishing her skin with attention. Her arousal scented the air, and I was eager to taste her. I smoothed my hand down her stomach, caressing the skin over her hips, until a raised area on her side gave me pause. I retraced the route, curious about her past, about her scars. Though, I got the feeling from the way she tensed that I wouldn't be getting answers anytime soon.

So, I did what she asked—I made it my mission to help her let go. I threw myself into the task of giving her pleasure and forgot anything but this moment. The past didn't matter. The future didn't matter. The present—this woman and her pleasure—were what mattered.

"Oh god." She hummed when I nuzzled her through her underwear.

I pulled the lace scrap aside, and she bucked her hips when I circled her clit with my tongue. She tasted amazing—sweet and fruity, and I lapped her up. When I sucked her into my mouth, she clenched the sheets. And when I added a finger, she writhed, grasping the sheets as if they'd help her. I pressed a hand to her stomach to hold her in place.

Her orgasm came on quickly, and in what felt like record time, she was shuddering from my touch. I gave her a moment to catch her breath, while I stripped off my boxers and tossed them aside. Then, I peeled off her underwear and bra, leaving us both completely bare.

I stood at the foot of the bed admiring her as I sheathed myself. She was younger than me, but that wasn't why she was so appealing. She was just… I didn't know what it was about her, but there was just something that spoke to a part deep within me. It sounded absurd, but I felt a connection I'd long been missing. Some spark I hadn't had with any of the other women I'd been with, maybe ever.

"What are you waiting for?" She smirked, scanning my body.

"Just taking a moment to admire the view." I rubbed a hand over my chin.

She was magnificent, especially now that she was more relaxed. Her cheeks were pink, her lips swollen, and her limbs loose. *I'd* done that to her. I'd made her feel good. I'd helped her forget. I'd chased the haunted look from her eyes, even if only briefly. And I'd continue doing it if I got another smile like the one she was currently flashing me.

"Which brings me to my next lesson," I said, settling over her.

"What's that?" She hushed out a breath, and my skin ignited from her touch.

"Stop to admire the view." I lined myself up with her

entrance, dragging myself through her folds. I stared at our connection, entranced.

"Mm." She grinned, eyeing my chest greedily, her hands grazing over my skin. "I think I'm going to ace this one."

"I had a feeling you'd be a model student." I pressed my lips to hers briefly.

I eased into her inch by inch, amazed by how snug she was.

"You okay?" I asked when her features pinched with pain.

"Yeah." She forced a smile and let out a slow breath.

"You're just…big," she swallowed, meeting my smile. "And it's been a while."

I nodded, my chest swelling with pride from her comment. And even though my cock urged me to speed up, I took it slow, leaning back to play with her clit and tease her nipples, wanting it to feel as good for her as it did for me.

When I was fully seated, we both let out a sigh of relief. I began to pump, loving the feel of her breasts brushing against my chest.

"I forgot how amazing this feels," she sighed, which only sparked more questions.

Her eyes were closed when she said it, and they remained closed even as I continued to touch her. I wanted to ask her what she meant. But more than that, I wanted her to look into my eyes.

"Look at me." I needed to know she was here—with me. Not thinking about something—or someone—else.

She shook her head, seeming to squeeze them shut more tightly. In that moment, I regretted not insisting on knowing her name. I rolled us so she was on top, which had the desired effect.

I grabbed the back of her neck, forcing her attention to me. The moment our eyes locked, her blue ones flared. She was close. It hadn't taken much to set her off with my hand

and my mouth, and I could sense it in the way she bit her lip —she was on the edge once more. She swiveled her hips, her blond waves flowing around her. She really was a goddess.

"Oh god." She held in a breath, then let it out slowly. "That feels… Holy shit."

She threw her head back, hair wild, eyes closed in ecstasy. Her muscles clenched around me. *Thank fuck.* I wasn't sure how much longer I could hold out. Not when I had a front-row seat to one of the hottest shows I'd ever seen. Her tits were bouncing, lips parted, and the only thing that would've made it hotter was looking into her eyes.

I pressed my thumb to her clit, and her jaw dropped on a gasp. "Yes. Yes. Yes," she chanted.

I continued circling her nub, using my free hand to caress her hips, her breasts, her lower back. God, she was something. Glorious, uninhibited, and stunning. But I wanted her to give in, to give over to me completely. I wanted her to surrender.

"Let go," I commanded. "Let go," I said again, more forcefully.

She finally went over the edge, giving in to her release. I followed a moment later, and with a final thrust, I exploded.

She flopped back on the bed beside me, draping her arm over her forehead. "Wow. That was…" She didn't finish her statement, but she didn't need to.

I smiled at her as I got up to dispose of the condom. I wasn't gone long, but by the time I'd returned, she'd already passed out. I considered leaving, but I decided against it. I wasn't ready for my time with her to end, and I had a feeling there was more we could learn from each other. So, without giving it much thought, I switched off the lamp and climbed beneath the covers.

I must have dozed off, because I awoke at some point in the middle of the night. The clock showed it was sometime after two, and I extracted my arm from beneath her, careful not to wake her. Maybe we could go for another round when I got back, but first, I needed to piss. I was returning to bed when she reached for me. Her eyes were still closed, her voice groggy with sleep.

"Ryan," she said. Or at least that's what I thought she said into her pillow. "Don't go."

I stilled. *Ryan?* I mouthed. Who the fuck was Ryan? Was he the man she wanted to forget? And if so, why was she asking him, *me,* to stay?

She hadn't been wearing a ring at the bar, but what did I really know about her? I didn't know her name. I didn't know if she was married or not. Or who the hell this Ryan guy was.

I remained there a moment, debating what to do. But then the covers slid down to reveal her amazing breasts, and I couldn't resist. She beckoned me back to bed, and I willingly did her bidding. I might regret this come tomorrow, but I couldn't help myself. She wanted to forget, but I was intent on giving her a night to remember.

CHAPTER FIVE

Juliana

The following morning, I slid out of the car and rushed inside the restaurant. I glanced back to check my skirt for stray toilet paper, but there was none. Though I'd checked my reflection countless times since I'd left the hotel, I still felt like I'd missed something. Or maybe that was just my guilty conscience talking.

Lauren flagged me over from across the restaurant, and I pressed my lips together as I weaved through the chairs. Finally, I reached the table where my best friends, Alexis, Lauren, and Harper, were already seated with drinks and menus. *Crap.* I was even later than I'd feared.

"Hey, sorry." I sank down into the empty seat, hoping they wouldn't make a big deal out of it.

But I didn't fail to miss their raised eyebrows and questioning glances. I was never tardy. I was the friend you could always count on to be at least ten minutes early. And here I was, over twenty minutes late to a standing weekly brunch date.

"Everything okay?" Lauren asked.

She looked stylish as ever in her cobalt dress and sky-high heels. Her dark hair was straight today, her lipstick a bright pop of pink. She always looked fabulous, and she ran her interior design business with confidence.

Then there was Alexis. Her caramel strands hung in waves, a light smile playing at her lips. She seemed relaxed, happy—despite the fact that she ran one of the most successful brokerage firms in LA. In the past few years, though, she'd focused more on family than work. And I was happy for her.

And finally, Harper. Her chestnut hair grazed her collarbone, her recent cut a bit edgier than her norm, stylish yet practical. She was always traveling for work—always jet-setting to scout locations for films. I knew her job wasn't as glamorous as it sounded, but she absolutely loved it.

"Juliana?" Lauren prompted, reminding me that she'd asked a question.

"Yeah. Great." I flashed her a bright smile. "I'm starving."

I opened a menu and studied it like a seating chart for one of my weddings—with unwavering focus. I focused on that menu as if my job depended on it, even though I wasn't actually absorbing any of the information on the page.

"It's just weird that you're late. You're never late," Lauren said, always the one to call us on our bullshit.

I kept my eyes focused on the offerings. "I'm human. Shit happens." Though I was referring more to my impulsive decision to sleep with a complete stranger than my tardiness.

Conversation resumed, and I felt my shoulders relax as we brainstormed gift ideas for Alexis's husband's birthday. She wanted to do something special, something memorable for Preston. As we sat there, debating the options, my mind drifted to last night. My memory was a bit hazy, but I hadn't forgotten how amazing my sexy stranger had made me feel. The way his lips brushed against my skin, the way his large hands scaled my body. I hadn't felt so alive in—well, over two years.

But my elation quickly turned to unease, and a deep sense of guilt twisted through my gut. *Oh my god. I cheated on Ryan.*

"Jules?" Lauren's voice came to me as if from afar.

My three best friends watched me with matching concerned expressions. It was then I realized I'd said the last part aloud—I cheated on Ryan.

My cheeks flushed with heat, and my eyes stung. I glanced between them, but instead of judgment or disgust, I saw only love and concern reflected back at me. That was why I adored these women—our lives, our goals, our outlooks might be very different, but we were always there for one another. We always supported one another.

Lauren placed her hand over mine, her eyes swirling with emotion. "Do you want to talk about it?"

"I, um…" I'd already confessed, I might as well get the rest off my chest. "I slept with someone last night."

They were all quiet, listening patiently. Lauren brushed her hair over her shoulder. Alexis watched me with rapt attention, her hands folded in her lap. And Harper leaned back in her chair, crossing one leg over the other.

"He was—well, he reminded me of an older—" I clamped my lips shut before I could say "hotter." Ryan and my one-night stand were both handsome in their own right; there was no need for comparison. I shifted and cleared my throat. "More muscular version of Ryan."

Harper's hand flew to her mouth to cover a gasp. "You don't think it was him, do you?"

After the tsunami, Harper had leaned on her contacts in the area to help search for Ryan. I'd managed to survive, but many hadn't been as lucky. I didn't want to believe that Ryan was among them. To this day, she was one of the few people who hadn't given up on finding him. My parents, my sister, and even most of Ryan's family accepted he was gone. But they hadn't been there; they hadn't let him slip through their fingers.

The first year, everyone had been supportive. But then one year had turned to two, and it felt as if everyone had moved on. Had given up. Everyone but me, until now.

Oh my god. What have I done?

My chest squeezed, and everything around me seemed to shrink away. I shuddered, trapped between memories of that day and my guilt over last night.

"Jules," Lauren said. "Hey." She placed her hands on my face, forcing me to look at her. "Just breathe. It's going to be okay."

I shook my head slowly. Tears pooled in my eyes as the panic crested, and a wave of guilt slammed into me. "No. I slept with another man. I betrayed Ryan."

"Let's get one thing straight." Her tone was commanding as her eyes blazed with emotion. "You did not cheat on Ryan. Okay?"

"But—"

"No." She shook her head, her expression stern as she removed her hands and sat back. "You did nothing wrong."

Alexis and Harper nodded their agreement. But they didn't understand. They'd rallied around me after the tsunami, and they continued to check in and love me even now. But I was tired of feeling like a burden—not that they ever made me feel that way. Still, I saw the pity in their eyes, and it made me want to break something. And my life was already broken enough.

"But we're engaged, and I—"

Harper was the one to speak up this time. "Jules, I know you love Ryan, but it's been two years. Even if he miracu-lously returns at some point, I don't think he could fault you for what you did."

I twisted my napkin in my hands. I wanted to believe her, but I knew that was only because it would make me feel better. Whether it was the truth was an entirely different matter.

"Let's say roles were reversed," Alexis said, ever pragmatic. "And, gosh forbid, something had happened to you instead. Would you want Ryan to be lonely, missing out on life while he waited for you to maybe someday come back?"

I considered it a moment, but I already knew the answer. "No."

"Right. You'd want him to be happy."

I nodded. "Of course I would."

"Even if that meant he was with someone else?" she pushed.

The idea of Ryan happy with someone else pained me, but I agreed. Had I been the one to disappear, not him, I wouldn't want him to be sad. I would want him to live. Something in my chest eased.

"I know, but—" I lowered my voice and said, "I used this man, and then I totally passed out on him. I passed out with a complete stranger in my hotel room." I scrunched up my face, bracing for their reactions. "He could've been an ax murderer for all I knew."

Lauren lifted her shoulder. "Well, clearly he wasn't, or else you wouldn't be here this morning."

I narrowed my eyes at her. "Seriously?"

I appreciated her blasé attitude toward sex, even if it was a foreign concept to me. I'd been with the same man for five years. Before that, I'd had a few boyfriends but never a one-night stand. This was the first, and that was after a two-year dry spell. A dry spell I hadn't once been tempted to break—until last night.

"Stop beating yourself up," Lauren said. "I'm sure he was

happy to be of service. And you'll probably never see him again."

"God, I hope you're right," I said, though a voice in the back of my mind whispered that was a lie. "But I feel terrible about it."

"Yeah, but was the sex terrible?" She waggled her eyebrows.

All three of my friends leaned in as if I were sharing the secrets of the universe. I glanced between their matching eager expressions and considered lying before finally confessing, "It was amazing."

And now that I'd admitted it, I couldn't stop myself from saying, "He did this thing with his tongue—" My eyes rolled to the back of my head, and I clenched my thighs together. "Oh. My. God."

And the way he'd commanded me to let go. It was as if he'd understood exactly what I needed. I'd asked him to help me forget, and he'd actually accomplished it. For the first time in nearly a month, I'd slept. And it had been a restful, dreamless sleep that left me feeling refreshed. At least until I'd found his note on the nightstand and remembered what I'd done.

"You said he was older?" Harper asked. "How much older are we talking?"

I pursed my lips, inventorying his features in my mind. Though silver lined his jaw and temples, his body was fit. More than fit—it was all chiseled muscles and sculpted abs. And that V…

"If I had to guess, I'd put him in his mid- to late-forties. He had laugh lines." I'd had no idea laugh lines could be so sexy. At least, not until him.

"Wow. That's unusual in LA," Alexis joked, though we all knew it was true.

"Right?" I felt lighter now. I was still a tumult of emotions, but I didn't feel as guilt-ridden as I had a few minutes ago. "But it was hella sexy on him."

"And you're sure you don't want to see him again?" Harper asked.

I shook my head. "It was one night. It was nothing more than meaningless sex."

Though the way he'd looked at me with those emerald eyes felt weighted with meaning, with promise. And not just for a night of fun.

"Hey! Meaningless sex can be fun," Lauren said. "Not now." She rolled her eyes when we all turned to her. "Before Hunter."

"I just—" I rolled my bottom lip between my teeth. "Is it wrong that I enjoyed it so much?"

"The sex?" Lauren asked. "Fuck no. I sure as hell hope you enjoyed it after a two-year hiatus."

My cheeks heated as nearby diners turned to look at us. "Will you keep your voice down?" I hissed.

"Sweetie, it's okay," Alexis said, patting my hand. "No one's judging you."

"The problem is, I'm judging me." I hung my head. "I feel like a spoiled brat for saying this, but I'm not happy with my life."

There was a collective exhale, as if they'd been hoping I'd say those very words. Waiting, even. I glanced between them, wondering what I was missing. Suddenly wondering how much they'd been holding back the past two years.

"You know what Preston's mom always tells me?" Alexis asked. "If something's not working, change it."

"I'm not sure I know how." I stared at the table, feeling as if I were admitting the truth for the first time in two years. For two years, I'd buried myself in my grief and my work. I'd focused on building the wedding planning side of my busi-ness, while still offering birthday parties, engagement parties, and more. And while it had taken off, my personal life was a disaster. "I've been frozen."

I dropped my head to my chest, taking a few deep breaths. I could feel the panic rising, trying to consume me. My heart squeezed in my chest, stopping and starting and trying to continue beating.

"And I can't do this anymore," I finally admitted.

"Can't do what?" Harper asked.

"Live with one foot always in the past. It's breaking me. And…it's affecting every aspect of my life, even my work."

Within the span of twenty-four hours, I'd yelled at an A-list client, collapsed in my office from exhaustion, and slept with a complete stranger. I was a hot mess.

"Hey," Lauren cooed, rubbing circles on my back. "There's no manual for navigating grief. You have to do what's best for you."

I stared at the napkin in my lap, toying with the edges as I wished for answers. "Sometimes, I just wonder—what's the point? I've already met my soul mate. I've already had my one great love. I was lucky to experience it, even briefly."

"Bullshit." Lauren's tone was sharp, and I jerked my head up.

"Yeah, you heard me." Her gaze was intense, her eyes blazing. "That's bullshit. You're young, sexy, successful. You deserve to be happy. There's someone out there for you—I know it."

Harper and Alexis nodded their agreement. But I was thrown by Lauren's words, her conviction. Of the four of us, she'd always been the most cavalier, especially when it came to men and love.

"Geez. When did you become such an optimist? Such a romantic?" I teased.

"Juliana." She leaned forward, her expression serious. "Listen to me—I know it's hard to believe now, but one day, you will be happy again. One day, you will smile without having to think about it. You will breathe without feeling as if your chest will crack. You will love again."

"How can you be so sure?" I asked, wishing I shared her confidence.

Losing Ryan had rocked my world, shaken my beliefs, and made me question everything.

"Because I know you. And if someone like me—jaded, distrustful, sex-crazed—could find someone to love and trust, you certainly can. You plan weddings, for crying out loud. The universe owes you a fucking happily ever after."

Alexis and Harper laughed, but I could tell they agreed. I wanted to believe Lauren; I did. But…I just didn't see how it was possible.

"Do you want to know what I think?" Alexis asked.

I nodded. She was wise, and I trusted her advice. I knew she, like Lauren and Harper, only wanted the best for me.

"You're not frozen. Last night proved that. You're trying, but you're scared. And that's okay."

I nodded and glanced toward the ceiling. My emotions, like the truth, were pouring out of me. All this time, I'd tried to put up a good façade, and it was crumbling like the beach town Ryan and I had been vacationing in that fateful January day.

"I can't keep living in my house, surrounded by his things." Tears were streaming down my cheeks. Now that I'd opened the floodgates, the words—like the tears—were pouring out of me.

"Okay, then," Lauren said. "Sell the house."

I swallowed hard. "I've considered it."

She seemed surprised by that, but I hated going home to an empty house. An empty house that was filled with memories of the past and promises of a future that would never happen.

"Do you think you should talk to someone?" Alexis asked, concern evident in her tone. "Do you remember how depressed I was after Blair was born? And you guys, Preston especially, encouraged me to talk to a specialist, and it really helped."

"I don't know." I wasn't necessarily a fan of the idea. I'd attended some counseling when I'd first returned from Thailand, but it hadn't really made a difference. And I'd done nothing since. Maybe it was time to revisit the idea.

"Or you could try to find a grief support group," Lauren said.

I arched an eyebrow, which prompted her to say, "After my mom died, I attended one. And when my dad passed away last year, I went to a different one for a while."

That surprised me. Lauren always put up such a tough front that I was shocked she'd even consider attending a grief support group. If she was willing to go, it definitely made me reconsider my stance.

"Whatever you decide," Harper said with a warm smile, "we're here for you."

"Thanks, guys," I said, and I meant it. These women had been my rock, my support. And I didn't know what I'd do without them.

Their encouragement gave me hope. Hope that if they could survive the things they had, I'd survive this too. They'd moved on, and maybe it was time I did too. I'd never stop loving Ryan, but I couldn't keep living like this.

CHAPTER SIX

Harrison

"I can't believe you scored an appointment with Juliana Wright," Olivia said as we walked down the sidewalk toward the wedding planner's office. "I mean, she's like *the* event planner for celebrity weddings."

I scoffed. "What? Am I not a celebrity?"

She knew I was teasing. But I was grateful Olivia had accepted my apology and peace offering—a meeting with the exclusive event planner. I still wasn't sold on the idea of marriage, but my relationship with my daughter was more important than my personal reservations. Besides, her relationship with Connor was different from Camille's and mine. And Talia was right—just because my marriage hadn't worked out didn't mean Olivia's was doomed to fail.

"Dad." Olivia rolled her eyes, but her lips curved upward. "You know what I mean."

"I don't know, do I?" I sniffed.

"Oh please. How could I forget that my father is a football legend, one of the greatest players of all time, the man who led the Hollywood Heatwaves to victory four years in a…"

"You're really laying it on thick," I teased, relieved we were back on solid ground.

"Well, it is Juliana Wright." If Olivia hadn't been wearing a dress and heels, I swear she'd be skipping down the sidewalk. When I'd called her to tell her about the appointment, she'd nearly busted my eardrum with her shrieks of excitement.

"So you said." I watched her, warmth filling my chest. Anything to make Olivia happy. "What's so special about Juliana Wright?" I affected a posh accent.

"What's *not* special?" Olivia asked. "She's made a name for herself offering eco-friendly events that cater to those with special diets."

I hmphed. "You mean like the actresses who only eat potatoes on Tuesday."

Olivia rolled her eyes with a smile. "Probably. But I was referring to food allergies like mine. Juliana caters to clients with celiac disease, nut allergies, vegans, you name it."

"Is being a vegan a disease?" I teased, though I'd eaten a heavily plant-based diet for years when I was training for the Heatwaves and even after.

"You know what I mean, Dad," Olivia said.

"Yeah, and she probably charges through the nose for it."

"Probably." She shrugged. "But you know it's not cheap to eat high-quality, plant-based food. And she's organized a number of events raising awareness and funding for celiac disease and other causes."

"Really?" I asked. "How do you know all this?"

"There's this thing called the internet. You should try it." She stuck her tongue out at me.

I butted her shoulder with mine. "And who's still carrying around an iPhone 6?"

Despite the fact that I'd offered to buy her the latest model, she still wouldn't let go of the old one. The only reason she'd agreed to let me give her my old Land Rover was because I'd wanted to get a new car.

"Yeah. Yeah." She shielded her eyes from the sun, glancing up at the building. "This is it."

I held the door open for her. "Where's Connor again?"

She pressed the button for the elevator. "Virginia. He'll be back on Friday."

"And you're sure you don't want to wait to meet with the wedding planner until he can be there?" I asked as the doors opened and a few people filed out. Though, honestly, I had no idea how long that would be. I hadn't connected with Juliana at the hotel like I'd hoped. And Olivia and I had been lucky to get this appointment after someone canceled.

Olivia barked out a laugh and stepped into the elevator, pressing the button for the eighth floor. "And miss the chance to meet with Juliana Wright?" She shook her head. "No way."

"You know this isn't a done deal, though, right?" I asked. I didn't want to burst her bubble, but I felt the need to caution her. I'd hate to see her disappointed. "I don't know if she's even available for your date or if you'll like her or…"

"Dad." She placed her hand on my arm. "As a wise man often likes to remind me—it will all work out."

Leave it to my daughter to throw my own advice back at me. But she was right. I considered myself a laid-back guy, but I struggled when it came to my daughter's happiness. Still, I knew that whether it was this wedding planner or another, we would make her dream wedding happen.

"Thank you again for setting this up. It means a lot to me."

"You're welcome." I draped my arm over her shoulder, and she wrapped hers around my waist. "I'm sorry for over-reacting the other day. I know how important this is to you, and I'm honored to be included."

"I'm glad to have you here with me. And I'm sorry too. I'm

stressed about work, and you know how grumpy I get when I'm hungry."

"I do." I gave her shoulder a quick squeeze before releasing her. "All right. Let's get this over with."

"*Dad!*" she said, dragging out the word.

"Okay. But I just… Keep an open mind. She's not the only wedding planner in LA."

"Okay." The elevator chimed, and the doors opened to our floor. "But—" she backed into the hallway and cupped her mouth "—it's Juliana freaking Wright," she whisper-yelled.

I smiled despite myself, more curious than ever to meet *the* Juliana Wright. Olivia rarely got excited about celebrities. She'd been surrounded by them thanks to my career, and she often interacted with famous authors in her line of work. So, for her to get this excited about a wedding planner… Well, I was certainly intrigued.

And I was kicking myself for not looking her up ahead of time. Considering the amount of research I put into football —both as a player and now as a color commentator—it was surprising. But I'd been so busy preparing for the wild-card game, then there'd been that night with the woman at the wedding expo, and a photo shoot, that there hadn't been much time to research Olivia's wedding planner. I'd just been grateful to get an appointment. And I'd never expected for Olivia to ask me to come with her.

I adjusted myself at the reminder of the night of the wedding expo. I'd gone there on a whim, hoping to catch Talia's contact. I still didn't know my mystery woman's name, but if I closed my eyes, I could trace every slope and curve of her body. I could recall all the ways I'd made her come and envision all the ways I still wanted to. If only she hadn't been so hung up on her ex…

Perhaps it was for the best that it would never happen

again. I didn't have any way to contact her. And much as I might want a repeat of that night, I couldn't give her what she needed beyond a brief escape.

"Here we are," Olivia said, bringing me back to the present.

She pushed open the frosted glass door with an interlocking J and W etched in a cursive font. I hesitated a moment, trying to get my brain to catch up with reality. This was happening. My baby was getting married.

"Welcome to Juliana Wright Events," said a man at the front desk. He smiled at Olivia, but his eyes lingered on me, scanning me from head to toe with an appreciative grin, a knowing grin. "Do you have an appointment?"

He looked familiar, and I frowned as I struggled to place him. I shook away the thought—he was probably just another fan or something.

I shoved my hands into my pockets. "Harrison Hayes. Talia Winters referred me."

The office was clean and stylish. Everything was blush pink and gold and white—definitely feminine. But also... welcoming.

He glanced at his computer screen. "Yes. Harrison." He smiled at me and rounded the desk to shake my hand. "Welcome. And...?"

"Olivia." She held out her hand.

"Landon." He shook her hand. "Right this way." He led us to a conference room, though he kept glancing back at me. All the while, I couldn't shake the feeling that I should know who he was.

Framed photographs lined the hall, happy couples smiling as they said their "I Dos," a child blowing out her birthday candles, a glowing mom-to-be embraced by her girlfriends. The conference room had a wall of windows overlooking LA. A large pair of orchids rested in the middle of the glossy table, surrounded by a few leather-bound books.

"Can I get you something to drink?" Landon asked once we were seated. "Water, champagne?"

"I'd like a water, please," Olivia said before turning to me. "Daddy?"

Landon coughed into his hand.

"You okay?" I asked, and he nodded. "I'll take a water, thanks."

I picked up one of the leather albums from the table and thumbed through it. More smiling couples. More weddings and parties. All elegant, extravagant, and…expensive, I was sure.

I didn't think much could faze me considering the life I'd led, but staring at some of the parties, I realized I was wrong. Cirque du Soleil at a five-year-old's birthday party? I shook my head and closed the book, afraid to see what else it might contain. I had no idea what Olivia had in mind for her wedding, but I didn't think a flock of albino peacocks was on her must-have list. At least, I hoped not.

"Oh my god," Olivia said from beside me. "That is stunning."

I furrowed my brows, glancing between the album and her. The wedding looked fit for royalty.

"And those flowers. I love hydrangeas."

"Hydrangeas?" I asked, to which she just laughed.

I had a feeling I was in for a long afternoon. When Landon returned with our waters, I began to second-guess my decision not to request alcohol.

"And here she is now." Landon turned toward the door and smiled as if amused by something.

A phone rang in the background, and I looked up when I heard the click-clack of a woman's shoes against the marble floor. A familiar blonde with legs for days entered the room, her eyes on her tablet. Olivia and I stood, both of us smiling, albeit for different reasons. *Well, well, well.* Talk about life being unpredictable.

She looked the same as that night at the bar—well-dressed, polished, fucking stunning. Her fuchsia dress and pumps were professional, but they only made me want to undress her. I wanted to pull her hair from the bun she wore and watch the waves tumble over her shoulders. I wanted to—

"Hi, I'm…" She glanced up, and when our eyes met, she faltered. She quickly composed herself, masking her surprise with a smile. "Juliana Wright."

And suddenly everything made sense as the pieces fell into place. Juliana was my mystery woman from the wedding expo. And Landon had been with her at the bar when we met. His eyes were currently ping-ponging between Juliana, Olivia, and me.

Olivia extended her hand to Juliana. "Olivia. So nice to meet you. Thank you for squeezing us in."

"Of course." Juliana smiled, though her gaze was questioning when she focused on me.

I wrapped my hand around hers, encasing her delicate fingers with my callused hand. The sight of her skin against mine sparked a wave of fresh memories. Her hand around my cock, pumping. My palm sliding down her spine as she released a shaky exhale.

My lips curled into a smile, and without thinking, I stroked my thumb over her skin. Again, I felt that spark. That…pull. "Harrison."

She frowned down at our hands, quickly pulling hers away. I didn't understand her reaction. Was she embarrassed about the other night? I studied her expression for clues, but she quickly turned for the door, putting her back to me.

Maybe she was mad that I'd vanished? But she'd been

sleeping so peacefully, I couldn't bear to wake her. Besides, what had she really expected? We both knew it was nothing more than a one-time thing, even if I did want a repeat. And I hadn't been a complete ass—I'd left a note.

After Landon excused himself, Juliana closed the door, her palm pressed against the surface for a moment longer than necessary. When she faced us again, she wore a mask of professionalism. She took a seat at the table, composed, calm.

"First of all, congratulations." She smiled. "So—" She glanced down at her tablet. "I see we're on a tight schedule."

Olivia nodded. "Yes. My fiancé and I would like to get married this fall, preferably in September."

"Okay." She shifted, returning her attention to her tablet, where I presumed a calendar was displayed. "It looks like I have some availability—at least, the third, maybe the fourth, weekend."

Out of the corner of my eye, Olivia nodded. But my attention remained focused on the blonde sitting across from me. I knew what she looked like when she came, and I couldn't get the image out of my head. And now I finally knew her name.

I missed the next part of the conversation. Something about dates and venues and pricing. All the while, Juliana kept her attention focused on Olivia, only glancing to me when absolutely necessary.

"If you don't mind my asking, why the rush?" Juliana asked.

"We've been together for almost a year. When you know, you know. Right?" Olivia laughed, but Juliana didn't.

"A—" She swallowed. "Year." Her face blanched.

I frowned, the tension in the room rising. "I'm sorry, but why is this information necessary?"

"I, um…" She stared at her tablet. "I like to know the backstory of a couple. It helps me get a better picture of their personalities and style." When she met my eyes again, hers blazed with anger. A challenge. "Though, really, how well can you ever know someone?"

I crossed my arms over my chest, enjoying the way her eyes darted to my biceps. "I don't know. I think you can know someone pretty well, even after just one night."

Juliana's breath caught, but Olivia was so busy looking through the notes on her phone, she missed it. Juliana's skin flushed with color, creeping up her neck and staining her cheeks. I smirked.

"One night can make *or break* a relationship," she ground out, and I wondered if she was referring to an ex. Clearly, he'd done a number on her.

Olivia's phone buzzed, and she glanced at the screen. "I'm sorry. I have to take this."

She held the phone to her ear, talking in a hushed voice as she darted toward the door. Juliana stood and tried to escape, but I was faster. I placed my hand on the door, stopping her.

"What do you think you're doing?" she asked, skin flushed. Her chest rose and fell, her breasts nearly brushing against me.

"Stopping you from running away." I was so tempted to reach out and touch her, to place my hands on her hips. To physically restrain her from running away from me, even though she was completely and emotionally unavailable.

She swallowed, her eyes darting everywhere but at me. "I-I—" she stammered. "You shouldn't be here."

I furrowed my brow. This woman perplexed me. "Why? Because we slept together?"

"Yes," she hissed, her eyes darting toward the door, toward Olivia.

I leaned in, getting a whiff of her floral scent. She looked polished, just as she had that night in the bar. And just like that night, I wanted to muss her up. I wanted to get her to let her hair down, live a little.

"Last time I checked, picking up a stranger in a bar isn't a crime."

"It is if one of the parties is engaged," she shot back.

I frowned. "Engaged?"

So that's who Ryan was—her fiancé? Fuck. I never would've slept with her if I'd known they were still together. I thought he was the bastard who'd broken her heart. I figured her night with me was a rebound or revenge. She hadn't been wearing a ring then, and I glanced down to confirm she wasn't wearing one now.

She moved past me and started pacing. "You shouldn't be here. And there's no way I can plan this wedding. I just—" She stopped, looked at me, then started again. "I can't. You need to tell Olivia."

"What?" I jerked my head back. "I'm not telling Olivia we slept together. That's none of her business."

Her mouth fell open. "She's the bride. Of course it's her business." She shook her head. "I can't believe I slept with such a…such a—"

I crossed my arms over my chest, trying to understand her reaction. "Such a what?"

"Such a—"

The door swung open, and Olivia breezed in. "Sorry about that."

Juliana swallowed back her words and glared at me. What the hell was her problem? If she'd cheated on her fiancé, that was her decision, not mine. I wasn't happy about it, but I didn't see why we needed to involve my daughter.

"Where were we?" Olivia asked, completely oblivious to the tension that had settled like a thick fog over the room. "Right. Guest list." She took a seat.

Juliana and I continued our stare off a moment longer

before she took a seat. She tapped aggressively at the screen of her tablet, and I wondered if she was angrier with herself or me.

"We're thinking around two hundred guests," Olivia said.

My attention snapped to her. "Does that include all your coworkers and their spouses? And what about my former teammates?"

"I'd really like to keep it small." She placed her hand over mine.

"You know what?" Juliana jumped out of her seat like her ass was on fire. "I, um—" She backed toward the door. "I just remembered something. Something I wanted to show you. I'll, um—" She grabbed the doorknob, twisted, and stepped into the hall. "I'll be right back."

I stared at the door a moment, debating whether or not to go after her.

"So...?" Olivia asked. "What do you think?"

"About what?" I asked, dazed.

"Juliana, silly."

How to answer that? Juliana was...beautiful, haunted, complicated. And even though everything told me I should let her walk away, I wasn't sure I could.

CHAPTER SEVEN

Juliana

Oh my god. Oh my god. Oh my god.

Alone in my office, I paced the floor as my mind raced. What were the odds? What were the odds that my one-night stand was now the groom and my new client?

It was probably about as likely as being in a freak accident—a tsunami. So, really…I didn't know why I was so surprised. LA was huge, but the universe seemed to have it in for me. Was this a cosmic joke? Ha-freaking-ha.

But as I'd sat there, staring at my one-night stand and his *fiancée*, I couldn't breathe. I'd already felt bad enough for betraying Ryan, though my girlfriends convinced me that wasn't the case. But Olivia was the living, breathing proof that my night with Harrison was wrong.

She'd smiled and talked about their wedding. And he alternated between watching her with a doting smile and eyeing me hungrily. I covered my face with my hands.

The door swung open, and I jolted upright.

Landon halted when he saw me. "Hey, boss."

"Shut the door," I hissed.

He did as I asked. "What's going on?"

His concerned look wasn't lost on me. Nor was the fact that I was totally freaking the fuck out. I never freaked out. Not when the bride got cold feet and nearly made a run for it. Nor when the mother of the groom decided to make an unexpected, and unwelcome, appearance. Torrential rains, no big deal. Regardless of what happened, I was normally unflappable. I had a backup plan for the backup plan. I could roll with the punches without breaking a sweat. But that was business; this was personal.

"We need—" I swallowed. "I need you to go in there and tell them I can't plan the wedding."

"What? Why not?" He pulled his brows together, hip cocked to the side.

"The… I… I just need you to, okay?" I turned away.

"Because you slept with Harrison." It wasn't so much a question as a statement.

My cheeks flamed with heat, and I wished I could hide beneath my desk.

Oh. My. God. Talk about mortifying. I'd slept with the groom, and my employee knew it. So unprofessional.

"Mm, girl." He snapped. "I knew there was something between you two that night at the bar. That man is fine."

My eyes widened. "He's also taken."

Landon suppressed a smile. "You sure about that?"

"Pretty sure." I clenched and unclenched my fists.

I had the irrational urge to swipe everything off my desk. To dismantle my neat and orderly space. I had no right to be so angry. We hadn't exchanged names or any information about each other, but I'd naïvely assumed he was single.

"He's here to plan his wedding to a woman half his age," I said, still trying to wrap my head around that fact.

"She's his daughter."

I resumed pacing, warring with myself. "Oh my god. You're right. She is young enough to be his daughter."

"No, Jules." He grabbed my biceps, forcing me to stop. To look at him. "Olivia *is* Harrison's daughter." He enunciated the words slowly, as if I didn't understand English. Though at the moment, I wasn't sure I understood anything.

I started laughing, the sound slightly hysterical. *Daughter.* Olivia was Harrison's daughter. *Not* his fiancée.

"Are you sure?" I finally asked, swiping away a tear.

"Completely. He used to play for the Hollywood Heatwaves, and he's now a color commentator on the local network."

"How do you know all this?" I asked.

"While you guys were discussing venues and flowers, I looked them up." He settled his hip against my desk. "So…tell me more about you and Harrison."

I shook my head. "There's nothing to tell. It was one night. I wasn't supposed to see him again. I didn't even know his name until this morning."

"Ooh. Kinky." He smirked with a shimmy of his shoulders.

I closed my eyes and pinched the bridge of my nose. "Not kinky. Reckless. Impulsive."

The one time I'd thrown caution to the wind and had a one-night stand, it just had to come back and bite me in the ass.

"How was the sex?"

I squeezed my eyes shut before opening them once more. Landon and I were friends, good friends. But he was still my employee. And I didn't want to talk about this, not with him, not with anyone. I was still grappling with my feelings about sleeping with a man who wasn't Ryan. It didn't matter how I tried to justify it to myself, I still felt bad about it. Like me sleeping with someone else meant I'd given up hope for his return.

"Okay." I gripped the edge of my notepad. "Let's get this conversation back on track. I can't plan his daughter's wedding."

"You can, and you will. Besides, you probably won't see much of him after the initial meeting."

"True." I pursed my lips. Maybe Landon was right. Maybe I was being rash. I straightened, annoyed that I'd allowed Harrison to ruffle my feathers—again.

"And if you do, would that really be such a bad thing?" He arched an eyebrow as if challenging me to disagree.

"No. Yes. I don't know." I covered my face with my hands. I couldn't stand it when clients were indecisive, and now I was falling into that trap. I was Juliana Wright, and I was better than this.

I uncovered my face and straightened. I marched toward the door, head held high, shoulders back. I'd slept with the father of the bride—so what? I could be professional.

I marched down the hall with newfound confidence, at least until I opened the door to the conference room. The way Harrison's eyes swept over me made me feel exposed, vulnerable. But it also made me feel alive. Made my body tingle and awaken in places that had long lay dormant. I faltered, poised on the threshold momentarily.

"Did you find it?" Olivia asked as I took a seat across from them, my mind still trying to reconcile everything.

"Hmm?" I shook my head to clear it. "Oh, um, no." I'd completely forgotten about my fabricated excuse. There had never been anything to find. "I'll email it to you when I do," I said, hoping she'd forget all about it. "Now, where were we?"

I tried to ignore Harrison's bemused smile, turning my attention to the checklist on my tablet. Olivia's wedding. We were here to plan his daughter's wedding.

Now that I knew Harrison wasn't engaged to Olivia, I viewed him in a completely different light. He was no longer a sleazeball groom with a wandering eye. He wasn't taken or off-limits. He was the sexy, mature, father of the bride.

Exactly how old was he? I hadn't put him past his mid-forties, but he had a daughter—a daughter who was old enough to be getting married. I continued working my way through my list, gathering information—though not the answers to the questions I really wanted to ask.

While I could've just emailed them the paperwork and had them fill it out ahead of time like some of my competitors, that wasn't how I did business. I strove to give my clients a hands-on experience. Plus, there were a number of benefits to meeting in person. It was easier to gauge their reactions, to understand the dynamics of the couple's relationship, and to build rapport. My clients were entrusting me with one of the biggest days of their lives—not to mention a significant chunk of money. It wasn't something I took lightly.

Finally, after we'd finished, Olivia said, "Thank you. That was a lot of really good information, and I feel like I have a clearer vision of what I want."

"Good. I'm glad. I feel like I have a clearer vision of what you want too." And I did. A timeless, elegant wedding. Preferably at a venue with a historic feel. I already had a few ideas for the location, but I needed to check availability.

"I really wish Connor could've come today," Olivia said, referring to her fiancé. Harrison squeezed her shoulder. "Next time."

"Yes." I smiled, relief flooding me at the realization that I wouldn't have to sit through another meeting with Harrison. Relief and a twinge of regret that I promptly ignored. "I look forward to meeting him."

At the reminder of their relationship, I smiled to myself. I couldn't help it, laughter bubbled out of me.

"What's so funny?" Harrison asked.

I shook my head, embarrassed by my outburst. "Nothing. I'm sorry." But then I started giggling again, unable to stop.

"Now you have to tell us," Olivia said with a smile.

My cheeks heated, and I knew they weren't going to let it go without some explanation. "I'm sorry. I, um, it's just, for a good chunk of the meeting, I thought the two of you were getting married."

They glanced at each other then back at me before Olivia burst out laughing. "I can't believe you thought he was my fiancé." She hooked her thumb at Harrison.

Harrison leaned back in his chair, one leg crossed at the ankle. I tried to assess his reaction, but the only word to describe it was amused. "I mean, I'm flattered that you think an old guy like me could snag someone as young and beautiful as my daughter, but no. Besides, I'm not the marrying kind."

"Dad!" Olivia turned to him with wide eyes.

"What?" He shrugged.

She lowered her voice, but not enough that I couldn't make out what she said. "Your attitude is kind of insulting to someone who plans weddings for a living."

He turned to me. "I didn't mean to offend you. I'm honestly a bit overwhelmed and in awe of what you do. I can understand how difficult it might be at times to let go."

I tried to ignore the meaningful glance he threw my direction, but it was impossible to avoid. He wanted me to relax, unwind, and I had. But now we were back in professional mode, and I was in control. This was my domain.

I smiled, some of the earlier awkwardness dissipating. "No need to apologize. Marriage isn't for everyone, and it's definitely not something to be taken lightly."

Still, his comment lingered. Why didn't he see himself as the marrying kind? Was he having too much fun flitting from one woman to another like a bee pollinating flowers? I cringed at that thought, at the idea that I was just one in a bouquet of many. I preferred to think that he simply hadn't met the right person. But maybe he was just against the institution on principle.

"Is that why you aren't wearing a ring?" Olivia asked, and I tensed.

"Now who's being offensive?" Harrison elbowed her, though I couldn't ignore the way his eyes darted to me as if desperate to know the answer.

"I'm just curious," Olivia said. "I mean, you run a successful event planning business. Surely, you have visions of a perfect wedding."

I did, I thought.

Once upon a time, I *had*.

But those dreams had died with Ryan. And while I usually fielded this question better, brushed it off, my emotions were still raw after the events surrounding the two-year anniversary of the tsunami. That and the fact that I still wasn't sleeping. The only time I had slept was when I was with Harrison. I sighed.

"I'm sorry," Olivia rushed to add. "I shouldn't have said anything. It's really none of my business."

"It's fine." I forced a smile. "And my idea of a perfect wedding is giving you a beautiful, stress-free day. Now—" I turned my attention back to my tablet, more than ready for a change of topic. "If everything we discussed sounds good to you, Landon will send over my contract."

Olivia turned to Harrison. "Dad?"

He shook his head as if to clear it. "Sounds good."

"Great. Take some time to glance over it, and let us know if you have any questions. Please send Landon any other inspiration you have, and we'll set up an appointment to tour some venues. Sound good?"

They nodded, so I stood, signaling an end to the meeting. When Olivia excused herself to the restroom, Harrison stayed behind.

He stepped closer, lowering his voice, his words intended only for me. "I'm sorry if Olivia's question upset you."

"It's fine. I'm used to it." But then I realized my response came off as brusque. I felt bad, considering how genuinely contrite he seemed, so I forced a smile. "But thank you."

His hand brushed against my lower back, and he leaned in even farther. "I've been thinking about you. About that night."

"I—" I wanted to say, *So have I*. But I wasn't ready to face my feelings. Wasn't prepared to move on, despite what my body said. So, I swallowed back those words and said, "You should forget that night ever happened."

His emerald eyes blazed with heat. "I'm not sure I could, even if I wanted to. Can you honestly tell me you can?"

I glanced away. "I already have."

He scoffed. "Let's try that again. Look me in the eye and tell me the truth."

I met his eyes, steadying myself with a deep breath. I couldn't say I'd forgotten about it, nor that I ever would, so I settled for something that was true. "It won't happen again."

"The problem is," he said in a gruff voice, "I think we both want it to."

Damn him for being so perceptive. I guessed that was part of the territory of having a daughter. But holy Batman, the words he used coupled with the gravelly tone of voice made me quiver with anticipation.

"You ready?" Olivia peeked her head into the conference room.

I took a few steps back, feeling as if I'd been caught doing something I shouldn't. Harrison smiled as if unaffected, and I tried my best to ignore Olivia's questioning gaze. If we were going to pull off this wedding, there was a lot that needed to be done. Lusting over the father of the bride wasn't one of the items on my checklist.

CHAPTER EIGHT

Harrison

"That's amazing news," Reg said after I told him Connor had proposed to Olivia.

I sank down on the grass next to him, still trying to catch my breath. The man was a beast. And I was glad we'd continued our Sunday morning runs, even after all these years. He'd been one of my best friends since he'd joined the Heatwaves, and he was Olivia's honorary uncle. He was like a brother to me.

"I guess. Why do you not seem surprised?"

He took a swig of water. "Why are you surprised? That boy is head over heels for your daughter. Surely you see that."

"Yeah. Of course. But…don't you think it's a little fast?"

He leaned toward his foot. "Is it? It feels like they've always been together."

"Less than a year." Even though I was supportive of Olivia, it was fast.

He laughed. *As if this were a joke.*

"Reg." I scowled. "I'm serious. And to make matters worse, they're practically running to the altar."

"Well, Olivia's not one to rush into anything, so she must have a good reason."

"True, but this isn't like her, and I feel a bit blindsided by it all. She tells me she's engaged, and then we're meeting with the wedding planner a few days later. Setting dates. Making plans. I'm sure I looked like a fucking deer in the headlights." I took a swig of water, needing to cool down. Problem was, it was going to take more than a few gulps. Even now, days later, I was still thinking about Juliana.

"I would too," Reg said, and I realized I'd zoned out. "God, I remember when Jas and I were planning our wedding." He shuddered. "Too much money. Too many decisions. But, hey, you have it easy—you just have to foot the five-figure bill."

"Six."

"Six?" His eyes went wide, and he choked on the word. "Holy shit. Six figures?"

I laughed, grateful that money wasn't a concern. Grateful that I could shell out six figures on a wedding for my daughter without so much as batting an eye. And that was why I'd worked so hard all these years—for her. Everything I did was for Olivia; she was my heart.

"I can't believe our baby's getting married," Reg said, and I knew come wedding day, he'd be bawling.

He'd been there with me since the beginning. While most of our teammates were out partying, doing stupid shit, we'd stayed home with Olivia. He'd attended dance recitals, graduation, and now…her wedding.

"I know," I said. "I can't believe it either."

"So, who are you going to take as your date? Because you know Cam's going to be there with her latest boy toy." He rolled his eyes.

I frowned, knowing he was right. And knowing my ex, she wouldn't just bring her latest boy toy but also her usual circus of drama. I let out a deep sigh, hoping that maybe, for once, Cam wouldn't try to make it all about her. Still, that didn't change my answer.

"No one." I pushed off the grass, the rising sun casting my shadow over him, making me appear larger than life.

"Oh." He pointed to his nose and gave me a knowing grin. "I see. You're going to hook up with someone there."

I shook my head. "I'm not hooking up with anyone, Reg."

"I know." His expression turned serious. "And that's the problem."

"It's not a problem."

He stared at me, slack-jawed, before shaking his head. "I know you have the hots for me," he teased. "But I'm taken." He flashed me his wedding band.

"Even if I were interested in you—which I'm not—I'm terrified of Jas."

He held a hand up to the side of his mouth and whispered, "Me too."

We both laughed, even though we knew it was true. Jas was one of the best people I'd ever met, but you did not want to piss her off. Like, ever.

"What about Elena?"

I shook my head. "Not this again. I told you, I'm not interested in Elena—not like that." Our friends had been trying to hook us up for ages. She was nice enough, but I didn't feel anything for her. There was no zing. No spark. It was nothing like my feelings toward Juliana.

Whoa. Where did that thought come from?

"Who, then? Take your pick," he said, glancing around. "No fewer than six women have stopped to ogle you. One nearly ran into a palm tree because she was watching you instead of where she was going."

I chuckled, wiping my hand over my face. "You want to hear something funny?"

"What's that?" He lifted his shirt, using the hem to wipe his forehead.

"Juliana, the wedding planner—she thought I was the groom." I laughed, recalling her face when she'd discovered the truth. Her cheeks had flushed with color, reminding me of a rose in bloom. Reminding me of when I'd made her come. "Can you believe she thought I was marrying a woman twenty years younger than me?"

"And that surprises you *why?*" Reg asked, and I stared at him like he had three heads. "You're handsome. Well-mannered. A former NFL player. Rich. And as if all that wasn't enough to make a woman's ovaries explode, you're a single dad."

I scoffed. "Yeah. Okay. I wasn't being modest. But thanks for the ego boost."

He shook his head and laughed, pushing off the ground as well. "I can totally see you with a younger woman."

"You can?" My mind immediately jumped to Juliana. She was younger than me, beautiful, successful. I shook my head to clear it. "Because I'm not sure I can picture myself with any woman, let alone a younger one."

"Maybe that's the problem," Reg said as we walked down the sidewalk. "You need to open up your mind to the possibilities."

"Nah. I'm good."

"Alone? In that big-ass house?" He frowned, and it felt like he was disappointed in me. "You don't even have a dog, man."

"So?" I shook it off. "I like my solitude."

It wasn't like I hadn't been with women over the years—I wasn't a saint. But there had never been time for dating; I'd never made time for dating. What was the point? Most women wanted marriage, children—things I couldn't give them. And I refused to be like Cam—every event, she had a new man at her side. Olivia would never admit it, but I could tell it embarrassed her.

"You're so full of shit." He nudged me with his shoulder. "Don't tell me you honestly believe that."

I shrugged. "I don't want some woman taking over my house. How would Livie feel?"

"*Livie* is a grown-ass woman with a house of her own. Stop putting your life on hold and start living for yourself."

"I'm too old for this shit."

"For what? Love? Companionship? A relationship? With the way you take care of yourself, you could live another forty years. Do you honestly want to spend it alone?"

Well, when he put it that way…

"Honestly?" I asked, and he nodded. "I'm not opposed to the idea of a relationship, as long as we have separate hous-es." He elbowed me in the side, and I clutched my stomach, feigning injury. "And bank accounts."

He shook his head. "Cam really did a number on you."

"Whatever, man." I flipped him off. I hated talking about Cam. It had been over twenty years; I'd moved on. But that didn't mean I was willing to repeat the same mistakes. I'd never failed at anything, except my marriage.

"Let's say you were looking for a relationship," Reg said, unwilling to let the matter drop. "What would you look for in a partner? Just humor me," he added when I opened my mouth to protest.

I huffed, already knowing the answer, even if I didn't want to admit it. "Someone who's independent and confi-dent." With every trait listed, I thought of Juliana. "Someone who's kind, generous, and passionate. Someone who…" *Has long blond hair the color of sunshine and eyes that sparkle like the ocean.*

"Someone who what?" he prodded.

"Oh, um." I cleared my throat. "Someone who takes pride in their body and shares similar interests."

He nodded, considering. "What about kids?"

Was he joking? I was pushing fifty-one, well past the age to consider having a baby.

"I have a kid, and she's great. But I can't imagine starting over again at this point in my life. I'm too old for those late nights."

"That shit is no joke," he said. He and Jas had five kids, and I had no clue how the hell they did it. Though most of their kids were older now, the youngest was in middle school.

"Which is a big reason why a younger woman is out. No biological clock's ticking here."

He laughed. "I get that. I think Jas would go for number six if I agreed."

"You don't want to add another to your brood?"

He shook his head. "Our house is loud enough as it is. And chances are, the baby would be another girl, and I'd be even more outnumbered."

Reg had four daughters. He was seriously outnumbered as it was. But I knew he loved it.

I patted him on the back. "Better start saving for those weddings now."

"Uh-uh. Nope." He shook his head. "I'm putting them through college. They can pay for their own damn weddings."

"Right…so, when Izzy comes to you, batting her eyes, and asks for the wedding of her dreams…"

"I'll tell her to get a job." His expression, like his tone, was stern.

"Oh, please. I don't buy that for a minute. You—like me—would do anything for your daughter."

"Damn straight. And I would do anything for my wife."

"What's with all the wife and marriage talk today?" I asked.

He shrugged. "Our twentieth anniversary is coming up. I guess it's got me feeling all nostalgic and shit."

I laughed. "What are you going to do to celebrate?"

"Not a fucking clue. But I know it has to be something special."

I nodded, thinking about my own failed marriage. It felt like a lifetime ago. I would've said it was my biggest regret, but it had given me Olivia.

"You should talk to Juliana. Olivia's wedding planner," I added, when I saw his perplexed expression. "I bet she'd have some great ideas for your anniversary."

His shoulders relaxed at the suggestion. "What's she like —uptight, high-strung? I'm sure that's a lot of pressure. Plus…needy clients."

Not after her night with me. I thought of unraveling her, undoing her. I liked her put together and mussed up. She might be guarded and closed off, but I'd never describe her as uptight or high-strung.

"She's actually very calm, considering her profession. Maybe she's freaking out on the inside, but she never lets the clients see it. She's poised, graceful." *Beautiful,* I didn't add.

"Hmm. Interesting." He was scrutinizing me.

"What?"

"That look." He pointed at my face, being an obnoxious ass. "You like her."

I rolled my eyes, feeling a bit like I was back in middle school. "I do not. I respect her. Actually, if she weren't a wedding planner, I think she'd make a good athlete. She's disciplined, stays calm under pressure."

Landon had invited us to attend one of her weddings over the weekend, and I'd certainly been impressed. Everything ran smoothly, and the event was wonderful—or maybe that was just the event planner. Juliana had been in her element, and though I'd barely gotten to see her, she'd seemed happy.

"She sounds perfect for you."

My eyes widened. "Do you really think I'm dumb enough to get involved with my daughter's wedding planner?"

"Yes."

I sighed. "Reg, just drop it, will you?"

He narrowed his eyes at me. "Oh shit."

"What?"

"You already are involved with her."

"I'm not—" I pinched the bridge of my nose. Reg had a big mouth, and I did not need this getting back to Olivia. But I knew I couldn't lie to him either. "I slept with her—once. Before I knew she was going to be Livie's wedding planner."

He covered his mouth, though nothing could muffle his booming laugh. "This keeps getting better and better! Man, next thing you know, she'll be planning *your* wedding."

I rolled my eyes. "She's more likely to run away than run to the altar."

He stopped laughing and frowned. "What does that mean?"

I thought back to the night we were together and the way she'd begged me to help her forget. And at our meeting, she'd shut down when Olivia had asked about her dream wedding.

"Something's holding her back, weighing her down."

"What do you think it is?"

I blew out a breath. "Not what, but who."

He arched an eyebrow, but his lack of comment was most telling.

"You better not say anything to Livie." I glared at him. "I don't want to pull a Cam and take away from her special day." Luckily, Olivia had forgiven me for my outburst at the restaurant the other day. Scoring an appointment with *the*

Juliana Wright had certainly gone a long way to getting me back in her good graces. I wasn't going to fuck it up now.

"Dude. I'm not telling Livie her dad's boning the wedding planner."

"Jesus, Reg. I'm not 'boning the wedding planner.' We slept together once. I'd like to see her again, but she's…" I settled on, "Skittish."

"So, what you're saying is that she doesn't fall all over you like most women?"

"It's part of the reason I like her," I admitted.

"You always did love a good challenge."

I shook my head, giving his shoulder a hearty shove. Juliana was more than a challenge; she was a puzzle. I shouldn't want to know more about her, but I couldn't seem to say no when it came to this woman.

"GOOD NEWS OR BAD?" OLIVIA ASKED A FEW WEEKS LATER.

We'd arrived early for our appointment with Juliana and were currently seated in the conference room. Though I'd attended several appointments, I mostly left the wedding planning to Olivia. But for some reason, she'd insisted I attend again today, and I wasn't going to complain. I'd leaped at the chance to see Juliana. She'd been nothing but professional since the first meeting, never giving me a chance to be alone with her. She seemed intent on maintaining that distance, and we were always so busy touring venues, meeting with vendors to talk about anything but the wedding.

I frowned. "Um. Bad news, I guess."

"Wrong answer. Let's go with the good." Her tone was

matter-of-fact, and I would've laughed at the serious expression on her face were I not concerned.

"Uh oh. The bad must really be bad, then," I said, trying to make light of it.

She grimaced but quickly covered it with a bright smile. "I got a promotion."

"Another one?" I teased. She'd only been with the company a few months and had already been promoted once before.

"Yeah. Well, the perks of working for a small start-up. Long hours but fast-track to promotion."

"That's great, honey." My chest filled with pride and happiness for my daughter. "And so well deserved. You work your ass off, and I'm glad they recognized that."

"Thanks, Dad."

"So, what's the bad news?"

She let out a short huff. "They want to send me to one of the other offices for training."

"New York?" I asked, tracking Juliana's fantastic legs as she crossed the office to speak with Landon. She was alluring, as always. Her floral-patterned dress was a tailored style that nipped in at her waist and ended before her knee. It showed off her slim figure, full breasts, and—my favorite part—long, smooth legs.

"London," Livie said, the word landing like an anvil and bringing me back to the matter at hand.

My eyes went wide. "London? As in London, England?"

"The one and only." She looked nervous, fidgeting with a pen on the table. But she also seemed excited, like she was holding back a smile. She'd always wanted to travel.

"For how long?" I had a feeling I wasn't going to like her answer.

"Three months."

"Three." I swallowed. "Three months? What about the

wedding?" Forget the wedding, how the hell was I going to handle the distance for three months? When she went off to college, she was still a quick flight or relatively short drive away. Not…a continent, an ocean, apart.

"Well…I was kind of hoping maybe you'd plan it?" She scrunched up her nose and squeezed one eye shut as if bracing for a negative reaction. As if I could ever say no to her. But still…

"Me?" I scoffed. "I don't know the first thing about planning a wedding."

"But Juliana does. Just think of yourself as a project manager, with some seriously good perks—like cake testing."

Too bad I'd rather sample the wedding planner. I shook my head, my gut telling me this was a bad idea. How could Olivia expect me to plan her wedding?

"What about Connor? Why can't he do it?" I asked, thinking he was the more obvious solution. He was the groom after all.

"He's crazy busy at work. He has several trips coming up as well."

"Well, then maybe we should postpone the wedding, considering how busy the two of you are."

If they couldn't make time to plan their wedding, how would they make time for each other? I knew better than anyone how ambitions could get in the way of a healthy, loving relationship. I didn't want that for my daughter. I wanted someone who was one-hundred-percent devoted to her.

Besides, we were two months into planning. Despite the relatively short timeline, I had a feeling we could still get back most of our deposits. And even if we couldn't, if Olivia wasn't ready, the money wasn't as important to me as her happiness. I'd hate for her to feel like she was being rushed into something.

"Dad," she huffed, and I could tell she was genuinely upset. She'd never been good at hiding her emotions, especially from me. "I thought we'd moved past this."

"We did. I'm just...I'm still not sure I understand the rush." I wasn't trying to upset her, but I wasn't going to bury my feelings on the matter. Marriage was a big step, and I wanted to be sure she was taking it for the right reasons.

"Why do I need a reason apart from the fact that I love Connor and want to be with him?" she asked, and I sensed she was holding back tears. "Last year, one of the guys at Connor's office nearly died. I just want to celebrate life and love."

I placed my hand over hers, wanting to comfort her. She was too young to have lost so many friends. And it made me realize that perhaps she'd given this decision more thought than I'd realized. That perhaps she was more prepared for marriage than I was willing to admit. Besides, I knew Connor was devoted to her. He was a man of duty, of service. He was a good, upstanding man. A former navy SEAL who now worked for a Hudson Security—a company that specialized in executive protection. Basically, high-end bodyguards, though they did other stuff as well.

"I'm sorry." I squeezed her hand, hoping she'd feel the love and strength flowing through me and into her. "I promise to be nothing but supportive from here on out."

"Thank you." She sniffled, and it nearly broke my heart. "So—"

The conference room door swung open before Olivia could finish her sentence. Juliana breezed in like a breath of fresh air. Her smile was warm and inviting, and she really was stunning. The vise on my neck loosened, and for a moment, I forgot about the bombshell my daughter had just dropped as well as the heavy conversation it had led to.

"Good afternoon." Juliana gave Livie a hug, then shook

my hand. Her gaze darted between us, but if she had questions about what she'd walked in on, she was professional enough to act like nothing had happened.

I lingered a moment longer than necessary, loving the feel of her soft skin against mine. But then it was over. I waited for Livie and Juliana to be seated before joining them.

"How are you doing?" Juliana glanced between Livie and me. When neither of us answered, Juliana said, "Guys, is everything okay?"

"Well…" Livie hesitated. "I got a promotion, and I'm being temporarily relocated to London."

If this news alarmed Juliana, she didn't show it. She seemed completely unfazed, but I could tell her mind was whirring with activity. She was the calm in the storm, the eye. When everything was swirling around her, complete and utter chaos, she was stillness, serenity.

"What does that mean for the wedding?" she asked.

Livie turned to me. "We were just discussing that, actually. I was hoping the two of you could handle it."

Livie's eyes were pleading, but I had my reservations. This was her wedding day after all, not mine.

"Honey." I placed my hand over hers. "You know I'd do anything for you. But…well, I'm not sure I'm the best person for this. What about Alyssa?" I asked, referring to her best friend and maid of honor.

She shook her head. "No. It has to be you. I trust you, Dad. You have excellent taste and love chick flicks. Besides, you *know* me, and Juliana knows what she's doing."

I held a hand up to the side of my mouth and stage-whispered, "You weren't supposed to tell anyone about the chick flicks."

Juliana laughed, and the musical sound spoke to something deep in my soul. Though she often smiled, I rarely heard her laugh. At least, not a genuine laugh like this one.

I already knew the answer before I said it. I was such a sucker when it came to my daughter. I might have been strict when it came to discipline growing up, but she knew she could have almost anything she wanted.

"Yes. Fine." I turned to Juliana and found her watching me with a bemused smile. "As long as that's okay with you."

She opened her planner and smiled. "I'm sure we can handle it. Now, let's talk dates…" She dove into the logistics, and by the time we were done, I felt both more and less over-whelmed.

CHAPTER NINE

Juliana

I stood on the sidewalk outside the boutique, watching the sun as it descended over downtown LA. Olivia and Harrison would be here any minute, and I was still trying to wrap my head around the fact that this was one of the last times—apart from the surprise engagement party this weekend—I'd see Olivia in person until a few weeks before her wedding. She wouldn't be my first long-distance bride, but this was the first time I'd be planning a wedding with the father of the bride.

The hairs on the back of my neck stood on end, and I felt Harrison's presence before I saw him. He and Olivia were walking down the opposite side of the street, his head thrown back, laughing at whatever Olivia had said. He looked so sexy, carefree, and it made me wonder for the millionth time why a man as hot and successful as him was single.

I wasn't the only one who'd noticed. Across the street, a woman stopped for a double take. And who could blame her? Between the dark jeans that highlighted his muscular thighs, and the T-shirt draped over those broad shoulders, he was impossible to ignore. But it was more than that—it was the way he carried himself, with effortless poise that belied his strength. Unwavering confidence that spoke of control and discipline.

I waved when he spotted me and watched as he and Olivia crossed the street to join me. They were similar in looks and temperament, and seeing them interact made me wish I was closer to my own father. But he'd never understood my career. He'd always thought parties, weddings, were frivolous and extravagant. According to him, I didn't live in the real world.

"Olivia, Harrison, great to see you." I hugged Olivia, and then an awkward moment passed where I couldn't figure out what to do with Harrison. I reached out to shake his hand; he leaned in as if to hug me and ended up kissing me on the cheek.

"Thanks for, um, meeting me here." My skin felt like it was on fire from that brief contact. And I resisted the urge to cup my cheek as if to capture the feeling of his lips on my skin.

No matter how many times I'd told myself to be cool, act calm, my façade crumbled any time he was near. I told myself it was because he'd seen me naked, but I knew it was more than that. All he had to do was smile and my knees turned to Jell-O.

I gestured to the store. "I asked you to meet me here because Evelyn is a talented designer who creates gorgeous custom gowns. Also…she can work within our short timeline."

"That's fantastic." Olivia smiled, and her shoulders visibly relaxed.

I knew how important the wedding gown was to most brides, and I wanted to be sure Olivia would love hers. I also knew we had limited options, and I was grateful Evelyn was available. When she wasn't designing, she was often traveling for dance competitions where she helped with costumes and competed. She was close to Olivia's age, gorgeous, with long dark hair, and I had a feeling they'd hit it off.

"My maid of honor, Alyssa, is coming. But she got stuck in traffic," Olivia said.

"Great." I smiled. "I look forward to meeting her."

Fortunately, Connor didn't need to be fitted for a tux, nor did his groomsmen. Most of them—like the groom—were current or former SEALs and would be wearing their dress uniforms. Though, I still had yet to meet the man.

"Are we waiting on anyone else?"

I didn't want to come right out and ask about her mom, but I was curious. Olivia and Harrison had mentioned Camille briefly in passing, but that was the extent of it. She never attended the appointments, but I'd half expected her to come today. Trying on wedding gowns was a rite of passage for most brides.

"Just us," Harrison said with a tight smile as he held open the door.

A bell chimed overhead as the three of us entered the shop. It wasn't your typical wedding boutique, not that I thought Olivia wanted typical. Instead of the sparkling chandeliers and damask wallpaper, there were concrete floors and exposed beams. It was rustic and functional and not without its charm. But it definitely didn't scream "bridal."

Evelyn joined us, and I made the introductions before returning my attention to Olivia. "Why don't you take a look around and see if anything catches your eye? You're in good hands."

Olivia nodded, then tucked a few strands of hair behind her ear. I'd already given Evelyn some information on the type of dress Olivia was looking for, as well as some suggestions for what I thought might look good on her.

When they moved over to a rack of dresses, I turned my attention to Harrison.

"I'll just be over there." He hooked his thumb in the direction of a sofa, clearly expecting to wait while his daughter tried on dresses.

"Not so fast." I tugged on his arm, preventing him from sitting.

Olivia giggled. "Oh good. He definitely needs all the help he can get." She turned back to Evelyn.

"What?" His jaw dropped, but Olivia merely shrugged, and she was soon immersed in chiffon and tulle.

"You're coming with me," I said to Harrison, curling my hand around his bicep. I should've let go, but instead, I continued to cling to him like a lifeline.

He flashed me a wicked grin. "I like the sound of that." He leaned in and lowered his voice. "I've been wanting to see if I can break my record from that night at the hotel."

"Harrison," I ground out, tightening my grip as if I could control the situation. "You promised not to mention..." I lowered my voice to a whisper. "That night."

"No." He lifted a finger, pointing it in the air. "I promised not to mention that night *to Olivia.* I never promised not to mention it to you."

I rolled my eyes, releasing him. "It was implied."

"You're a stickler for details," he said. "I'm sure someone as meticulous as you would've mentioned it."

I couldn't help but smile at his compliment, even if I was annoyed that he was twisting my words. "Now—" I straightened, forcing myself back into professional mode. "We're getting you fitted for a tux."

He crossed his arms over his chest, biceps bulging. A sudden vision of our night together flashed before my eyes. His body hovering over mine, his biceps straining as they bracketed my head. His chest brushing against mine as he...

"I already have one." He wore a bemused expression that contradicted his intimidating stance.

"Yes." I swallowed hard, forcing back the image. "But the father of the bride deserves to wear something special too. You're the one walking her down the aisle. You're the one giving her away. Would you really want to do that in a tuxedo you've worn countless times for far less important occasions?"

He closed his mouth and shook his head, confirming what I already knew. When it came to his daughter, Harrison would do anything. At least if I was going to have to plan Olivia's wedding with him, I knew how to get him to cooperate.

"Lead the way." He swept his arm wide.

One last glance at Olivia confirmed that she was smiling, talking with her hands. Evelyn nodded and smiled back, listening intently to whatever Olivia said. I couldn't wait to see her selections. Even more, I couldn't wait to see Harrison's reaction to them.

I led him over to the men's section where a number of tuxedos in various cuts and fabrics were on display. They were all appealing, but I had a specific one in mind for Harrison. It was a classic cut, made of the highest quality fabric, and I knew he'd look incredible in it. I'd already had the tailor pull one from the racks and hang it in the fitting room.

"Here you go." I held back the velvet curtain.

"This is the one?" He arched an eyebrow, inspecting the material as he studied the garment.

"It is," I said. "Try it on. Trust me."

He disappeared behind the curtain, and I stood there a moment, frozen as I heard the hiss of his zipper. The way his belt buckle jangled as it fell to the floor. I swallowed hard and took a few steps back so I wouldn't be tempted to join him.

Ever since that night, I couldn't stop thinking about him. The way he'd touched me, the way he spoke. The way he made me feel—sexy, powerful, alive. I felt all that and more any time he was near, but usually Olivia was with us. Soon, that wouldn't be the case, though. Olivia would be off in London, and it would just be Harrison and me. *Alone.*

I busied myself with checking my emails, but I couldn't ignore the grunts coming from behind the velvet curtain. "Everything okay?"

More sounds of a struggle, then he said, "I could use a hand."

"Mm-hmm." I crossed my arms over my chest. "Likely story."

"No, really. The jacket's stuck."

"Okay." I sucked in a breath. "I'm coming in."

I slipped behind the curtain, unable to contain my laughter when I saw his predicament. His face was red, and his arms were bound. His biceps were too thick for the sleeves, and he looked like he was caught in a straitjacket. Actually, as he spun, glancing over one shoulder then the other, he looked like a dog chasing his tail.

"You can stop laughing now." He glared at my reflection in the mirror.

"I'm sorry." I pressed my lips together, trying to contain my laughter. "It's just—" I tugged on the jacket, doing my best to free him without damaging the expensive material. "You just—" I finally got it over his forearms and tugged to release him. Laughter spilled out of me the entire time.

"Just what?" He pinned me with a gaze, and I stopped laughing, stopped breathing.

"Nothing."

I couldn't think straight. I needed to get out of there—away from those kissable lips and questioning eyes. Away from this man who saw too much and demanded too much. A man who made me want things I shouldn't.

His eyes darted between my eyes and my lips, and it was then I realized how close we were standing. Our chests nearly brushed against each other, the air between us filled with our shared breaths.

"Have dinner with me," he rasped. It was more of a demand than a question.

Despite asking him to forget that night. Despite asking him to leave it be, leave us be. He wouldn't give up. It was both flattering and exasperating—to be the sole focus of his attention.

I shook my head. "I can't."

"Does this have something to do with Ryan?"

It felt as if the wind had been knocked out of me, and I stumbled backward as if I'd been struck. "What do you know about Ryan?"

Harrison closed the distance between us, grasping my chin in his fingers. His eyes searched mine, and I felt more exposed than I had the night we'd had sex. "Did he hurt you?"

I swallowed, intimidated by the burning look in his eyes. My heart thumped out a beat that raced then stilled, as if it didn't know how to react. I didn't know how to react. He'd caught me off guard with his question about Ryan. And then he'd sent my body into overdrive by crowding me, by filling my lungs with his scent and my body with his warmth. My head spun, but his touch grounded me.

"Not in the way you'd expect." I closed my eyes briefly, not wanting to get into it.

He frowned, his eyes darkening. "What does that mean?"

The seconds stretched on, and a muscle in his jaw twitched. "Juliana?"

I shook my head and backed away, my eyes stinging with

unshed tears. "Drop it." He opened his mouth as if to protest, and I gripped his hand. "Please."

"If he hurt you—if he's hurting you," he revised. "Tell someone. I don't care if it's me or a friend or even a stranger. Just please tell someone."

"He's…" I huffed, angry that he was forcing me to explain. This wasn't any of his business. My heart clenched, and my insides were a tumult of emotions. I waited to respond until I thought my voice wouldn't shake. "He *was*—" I swallowed. "My fiancé."

Confusion made way for compassion. He opened his mouth to say something, but then Olivia called, "Dad? Juliana?"

I knew he had more questions, but I wasn't ready to answer them. So, I darted out from behind the curtain, grateful for the excuse to escape.

"We're over here," I called, forcing a smile when her eyes met mine over the racks of dresses. "Come give us your opinion."

The tailor fitted Harrison with a more appropriately sized jacket, while I attempted to regain some of my composure. How the hell did Harrison know about Ryan? And what did he know? Not much other than Ryan's name, if his questions were any indication. Still…I racked my brain.

But when Harrison emerged from behind the velvet curtain, all other thoughts fled my mind. Never had a man looked as handsome in a tuxedo as Harrison Hayes, and it wasn't even tailored. He wasn't even wearing a button-down shirt or a bow tie. Just a plain gray T-shirt. But damn, did he look good.

Olivia whistled as Harrison stepped onto the dais in front of the mirrors. "Wow, Dad. Lookin' good."

"Thanks," Harrison said. "Juliana, what do you think?"

I avoided his gaze, keeping my attention fixed on the length of the pants, the fit of the jacket. "It looks very nice."

He stared at me in the reflection in the mirror, but I studiously avoided him. Harrison was too perceptive, and he seemed to see right through me. I couldn't handle his scrutiny or his questions. I made a few suggestions, all without ever meeting Harrison's gaze.

"Come on, Olivia," I said, while the tailor finished taking Harrison's measurements. "Show me what you found."

She floated over to the bridal side of the shop, and I knew I'd made the right decision in bringing her here. She wasn't the type of bride to get hung up on labels, and she wanted something unique.

"Not many girls share this moment with their dad. You guys are close, huh?"

She grinned, and I could see the resemblance to Harrison in that expression. "Always have been, especially after my parents divorced."

I nodded. And even though I knew I'd regret it, I found myself asking, "And your mom?"

Olivia admired the beading on a gown. I felt like I was holding my breath; this afternoon had gone from one difficult conversation to another. Though usually, I wasn't so invested in the whereabouts of the bride's mom.

"She had to work." There was a bitter undertone to her voice.

She wasn't the first bride who had a strained relationship with her mother. But I didn't want anything to mar her excitement over trying on dresses. And I felt like my question had cast a shadow over the whole affair.

I placed my hand on her shoulder. "Well, I know your dad's happy to be here. And if you want, I can take pictures of each dress so you can send them to your mom."

"Whatever." Her eyes remained on the dress. "I mean,

she's probably more concerned with her dress for the wedding than mine."

I cringed but tried to hide it. Instead, I absorbed myself with the veils, trailing behind Olivia as she admired the various styles—lace, beaded, cathedral.

"Sorry," she said. "I'm not usually so snarky. I'm just stressed about London and the wedding. And I'm going to miss Connor like crazy."

I nodded. "I bet. But you know what? You don't have to worry about the wedding. Your dad and I have it covered. And it's going to be beautiful."

"I know." She glanced up at me and smiled. "I trust you. You and my dad make a good team."

I wondered if she was hinting at more. Or if she knew about our tryst. Surely not, but I tugged at my shirt, feeling like she sensed something between us. So, I changed the subject.

"You guys have a good relationship. I'm jealous."

"I'm lucky," she said, fingering the lace edge of a veil. "Despite my dad's hectic schedule, he's always made me feel like I'm number one."

My throat was clogged with emotion, so I merely nodded.

Everything I learned about Harrison only made me like him more. And that scared me. We had a connection that went beyond lust. And as much as I wanted to ignore it, I wasn't sure I could.

CHAPTER TEN

Harrison

"Harrison." Juliana's voice rang out through my house, and I closed my eyes and took a deep breath. "Harrison?"

She'd arrived a little early, though I should've expected that. I'd always been known for my punctuality, but she took being on time to a whole other level. I'd made it a sort of game, trying to beat her to a destination, but she always arrived first. Which was why I'd been about to jump in the shower when she and her team had arrived to set up for Connor and Olivia's surprise engagement party. I'd since showered and dressed and was about to put on my tie when she'd called for me.

"In here."

"Oh, um." She stopped just short of coming in the room. "Sorry. I, uh, didn't realize this was your bedroom."

Her eyes swept up my figure as mine did the same, drinking her in. She looked professional, as always. But now that she was in my home, standing at the threshold to my room, I couldn't help imagining her in my bed. I clenched and unclenched my fists, knowing I needed to get my thoughts under control before my erection became painfully obvious.

When her eyes lingered on my chest, I glanced down, wondering if I'd missed a stain or something. "Is this... appropriate?" I asked, knowing how much emphasis Juliana had placed on my appearance for the wedding.

"Yes." She swallowed. "You look great. Though—" She furrowed her brow. "I'm not sure about that tie with that shirt."

"What's wrong with this tie?" I asked, holding it up for inspection. It was a tie with a subtle pattern, and I often wore it with this shirt. "It's one of my favorites."

"So, wear it." She lifted a shoulder. "You should wear something you feel confident in. Even if it clashes with your shirt," she added.

"Clashes?" I frowned, glancing down at my shirt and tie. "It's blue on blue. How can it clash?"

Sure, I wasn't known for my sense of style. But that wasn't entirely my fault. For years, I'd hired a stylist for big events. Even now, the station handled my wardrobe. I cared about comfort and quality more than what was on trend, but Juliana's opinion mattered to me.

"I just think you could pick a color combo that pops a little more. Or one that complements the decorations."

I tugged on her hand, pulling her in the direction of my closet. "Come with me."

She laughed, though there was a nervous edge to her tone. "Um. Where are you taking me?"

"My closet. I want to see what you'd pick."

Surprisingly, she didn't fight me on it. I switched on the lights and led her over to the drawer where my ties were stored. When I glanced back at her, she was spinning around, taking it all in. I'd never had a woman in my closet other than the organizer I'd hired when I'd bought the house, and I liked seeing Juliana here. Watching her in my space. I wanted to keep her there.

"What about this one?" she asked, indicating a lavender button-down.

I frowned, thinking of how rarely I wore it. "That one?"

"Yeah." She took the hanger off the bar and held it up to my chest. "Lavender really suits your skin tone and hair color."

I started to unbutton my shirt, enjoying the way her eyes darkened.

"I'll give you a minute to change." She averted her eyes, but she couldn't hide the pink tint of her cheeks.

"It's not like you haven't seen it all before," I taunted.

"Still." She spun, putting her back to me.

I stripped out of my shirt and tossed it aside before stalking over to her. I reached around her for the lavender shirt, letting my hand brush against her arm in the process. She shivered but didn't lean away. If anything, she seemed to gravitate toward me.

"Thank you," I whispered, wanting so badly to kiss her. But I wouldn't. After the day at the gown shop, it was clear she was still hung up on her ex-fiancé.

"Something's been bugging me," she finally said, spinning to face me.

"What's that?" I asked, not entirely sure what to expect.

I started buttoning my shirt, watching as she studied the contents of my tie drawer intently. As she debated the options, her long, delicate fingers caressing the ties, she asked, "How did you know about Ryan?"

Speak of the devil.

I threaded the next button through the hole. "I thought you didn't want to talk about him."

I certainly didn't want to talk about him, especially now that we were finally alone. But I also wanted to know where they stood. Did she want him back? Did I even stand a chance?

A chance? I shook my head. Since when did I even want a chance?

"I don't, but...well," she huffed. "It's bugging me. Did Landon say something to you?"

I shook my head. "No."

"Okay." She dragged out the word, holding up one tie and then another to my chest, all without looking me in the eye.

"You told me not to mention—" I leaned in and lowered my voice "—that night."

She pulled her brows together. "That night? I don't understand."

I let out a deep breath. "The night we were together, you said his name in your sleep. You called out for him."

Her eyes went wide. "I did? Oh my god. That's—" She covered her face with her hands. "Mortifying." The word was muffled.

"Hey," I soothed, placing my hands on her shoulders. "I knew what I was getting into when I went back to your room that night."

"Did you?" she asked, but her voice wavered.

"You asked me to help you forget. It was clear you were running from something."

"Yeah, but..." She uncovered her face and sniffled. "You didn't deserve that."

"Juliana." I stared at her lips, wanting to kiss away her pain even though I knew it was a bad idea. A bad idea, but a tempting one, nevertheless. Finally, I asked the question that had been plaguing me since that night. "I—are you wanting to get back together with Ryan?"

She glanced down at the floor, rubbing her ring finger absently. *Interesting.*

It felt like an eternity before she finally said, "I can't. He's, um—well, he's missing."

"Missing?" I frowned. Of all the things I'd expected her to say, that wasn't one of them.

She nodded, finally forcing her eyes to mine. "I..." She drew a shaky breath. "I know it's silly, but a body was never found. So, I prefer to think of him as missing, not..."

I nodded, understanding dawning on me. All this time, I thought they'd split up, that maybe he'd broken her heart. Now, I understood it was so much more complex than that. He was missing, and she was grieving him.

"How long has it been?" I asked.

"Two years." She swallowed. "You're the first person I've slept with since...him."

I took her hands in mine, trying to process her words. I was the first guy she'd slept with in two years? *Holy shit.*

"I'm honored."

"I'm sorry." She sniffed and used a finger to pull at the corner of her eye. "I— This is completely unprofessional. Guests will be arriving any minute. You should be focused on your daughter's engagement party, not comforting the wedding planner."

"I'll let you in on a little secret," I said, lowering my voice to a whisper. "The party was just a pretense to spend time with you. Actually, the entire wedding is. Olivia isn't getting married. I made it up to get close to you."

She studied me for a moment before throwing back her head and laughing. "Very funny. Those checks you wrote were very real. And from everything I've heard, so is the love between Olivia and Connor."

"You're right. But, damn, it's good to see you laugh." I smiled.

Her cheeks turned pink, and she was so beautiful it stole my breath. I knew she was here to do her job, but I wanted her by my side, talking to my friends. I wanted to get to know her—and not in these stolen interludes between appointments or tucked away in my closet.

"I like you." I hadn't meant to say it, but it was true. And the more I got to know her, the more I liked her. The more I respected her. She was hardworking, honest, fair, but also friendly, kind. A calm resolve blanketed me with the admission.

"I'm… I like you too," she said, finally looking me in the eye. But unlike before, her blue eyes were clear, her face calm.

I pressed my lips to her cheek and tried to ignore the way her scent infiltrated my nostrils, pumping through my veins. It filled my mind with memories I was trying to ignore, when all I wanted to do was relive them, repeat them.

Still, I knew she wasn't ready, and I didn't want to push her. Besides, I didn't want anything serious. I'd been down that road before and been burned. And I got the feeling that a woman like Juliana didn't do casual, despite our night together. We liked each other, respected each other, but we wanted different things.

"So, is that the winner?" I indicated the tie clutched between her fingers.

She looked down at it, as if surprised to see she was still holding it. She nodded, and I expected her to hand it over to me. Instead, she draped it over her shoulder, reaching up to flip the collar of my shirt. With deft fingers, she looped the tie around my neck, bringing us even closer. I watched her lips, listened to the sound of her breathing, and wondered if she could hear my heart drumming against my ribs. It was impossible to deny the attraction between us, but this close, it was even more difficult to ignore.

She kept her attention on my tie, executing the Windsor knot with the precision and care I'd come to associate with her. Her jasmine scent was like a drug, and unable to resist, I settled my hands on her hips.

She stilled, and her eyes flicked to mine before returning to the tie. This close, I could see the faint smattering of freckles on her cheeks, the dark flutter of her eyelashes. I tipped my forehead to hers, our breath mingling as I struggled for control.

I groaned, tightening my grip on her hips. Her chest rose and fell, brushing against mine. My dick jerked in response; surely, she could feel her effect on me.

"This is…" She rasped. "A bad idea." She placed her hands on my chest, but it felt more like she was clutching me to her rather than pushing me away.

"Why?"

I knew she was right, but I still wanted to hear it. Wanted to know why I couldn't taste those lips or do any number of things I wanted. Because at the moment, my body was over-riding my brain.

"Because…" Her lips parted, and I wanted to take them in mine, claim them.

"Because…?" I leaned in, a breath away from kissing her.

The doorbell rang, and she jolted. "Because the party's about to start. Excuse me."

Right. She was here for a job, and I was hanging on her every word.

"Of course. I'll go with you."

I placed my hand on her lower back, needing to maintain some connection. We stepped into the hallway and nearly collided with Reg, who was jogging up the stairs.

"Hey, man." He paused, glancing between Juliana and me. "I was just coming to get you. Jas texted. They're headed this way."

Jas was responsible for running interference with Connor and Olivia. She was supposed to pick them up and "take them to dinner," then reroute to my house before they ever made it to the restaurant. So far, everything seemed to be going according to plan.

"Great," I said, trying to ignore his questioning gaze. "Reg, this is Juliana. Juliana, this is my best friend and former teammate, Reginald Hawkins."

Reg rolled his eyes at the use of his full name and held out his hand. "Juliana, huh?" He grinned, and I glared at him, silently pleading with him to keep his big mouth shut for once. "Nice to meet you. You're the wedding planner, right?"

"Yes." She smiled, though I detected a hint of nervousness on her part as she shifted from one foot to the other. "I was just updating Harrison on the progress of the preparations. And now I'm headed back downstairs."

"Actually," he said. "I was hoping to talk to you…" He paused, and my heart stalled out momentarily. "About planning a twentieth-anniversary surprise for my wife."

"Sure." Her shoulders relaxed, and mine did too. "I'd be happy to help. Let me grab one of my business cards, and we can set up a time to talk."

"Great." Reg smiled.

She rushed downstairs as if eager to escape. I moved to follow her, but Reg put his hand to my chest. "What was that about?"

"What was what about?" I asked, feigning ignorance.

"'Preparations'?" He nudged me with his elbow, his tone rife with insinuation.

"It was nothing, Reg."

"Mm-hmm." He crossed his arms over his chest. "I saw the way you two looked at each other, and that was definitely not nothing."

"Yeah, well, it was one time. And nothing more is going to happen." Nothing had happened in the weeks since then.

Despite several meetings, a flurry of texts, flirting—nothing had, in fact, happened.

"Why not?"

I blew out a breath. "Look—it's complicated."

Despite her attraction to me, she was still grieving her fiancé. She was in love with another man, but I didn't want to get into the details out of respect for Juliana.

He frowned. "Okay. But clearly, she's interested."

"Just…drop it," I ground out. "I'm not getting involved."

"The problem is, I think you already are."

He was right, but I wasn't going to admit that. I was so in over my head when it came to this woman.

CHAPTER ELEVEN

Juliana

"Surprise!" the guests shouted as Olivia and Connor walked through the front door.

Olivia's answering smile was huge, and Connor took the opportunity to take her in his arms, dip her low, and kiss her. The guests cheered, and I joined in, so excited for this adorable couple.

They made their way through the crowd, accepting congratulations as I checked on the food. Everything was running smoothly, and I returned to the living room to see if anything else required my attention. Olivia immediately came over to join me.

"This is…" Olivia smiled. "Breathtaking. I mean, *wow*."

I followed her gaze, taking in the candles, the photo display, and the hydrangeas. It was romantic and intimate, and I was thrilled by her reaction. When Harrison had approached me with the idea of a surprise engagement party, I'd been hesitant. Olivia was busy getting ready for her move, tackling her new position at work, and saying goodbye to her fiancé, all while planning a wedding. It was a lot.

But Harrison had been right. She absolutely loved it.

Which only confirmed what I'd suspected—he knew his daughter. And I was beginning to feel that he knew me. Already, I'd shared things with him that I hadn't with anyone else. I'd opened up to him; I'd let him in. And that terrified me.

"Don't thank me." I smiled, feeling calmer now that everything was running smoothly and the bride was happy. "This was all your dad's idea."

I glanced over to where Harrison was standing. He looked sharp in the lavender shirt and patterned tie I'd selected for him. And I secretly reveled in the fact that he'd accepted my advice. That he seemed to want to please me.

Perhaps sensing my gaze, Harrison caught my eye and smiled. Warmth filled my limbs, flooding my body with a sense of happiness I felt anytime he was near. I couldn't stop thinking about that almost-kiss in the closet earlier. The way he'd looked at me—with such reverence and desire. The way my body roared to life from his attention. And even though I knew it was probably for the best that nothing had happened, I couldn't help wishing it had.

"No," Olivia said, bringing my attention back to her. "I'm pretty sure I know who's responsible for the beautiful hydrangeas, and it isn't my dad."

"Don't be so sure. Your dad wants to make you happy. He really loves you."

She nodded. "He's the best. And even though I know he isn't thrilled about my move to London, he's still super supportive. You know…" She leaned in, lowering her voice. "I was actually wondering if you could help me with something."

"Anything," I readily agreed, assuming it had something to do with the wedding.

I really did like Olivia, and not just because I was

crushing on Harrison. She was sweet and passionate about her job. And she had the best book recommendations.

"You guys are heading up to Ojai next Saturday to visit the venue, right?"

I nodded, wondering where she was going with this. We were supposed to attend a menu tasting at the inn in Ojai, though I'd considered staying overnight since it was a two-and-a-half-hour drive each way.

"I was hoping maybe the two of you could make a weekend of it. Explore the area and check out some of the local restaurants and attractions. You know—for the guests," she added, though it seemed like more of an afterthought.

The idea was tempting, but a weekend trip in Ojai conjured images of a romantic getaway for two. Olivia's smile was hopeful, and I had the flitting thought that maybe she was trying to set me up with her father. I shook my head at the ridiculous notion.

"Think of it as a gift," she said. "To thank you and my dad for all your hard work planning the wedding."

"That's not necessary," I said, and I meant it. "It's my pleasure."

She placed her hand on my forearm. "Seriously. It's the least I can do to show my appreciation."

I could tell she wasn't going to relent. *Like father, like daughter.*

Besides, it was never a bad idea to acquire local knowledge of the area. I'd been wanting to check out venues away from the city, and this was a great place to start.

"That's so nice of you, but I'll expense my part as a business trip."

"Excellent." She beamed, and I wondered if she suspected anything between Harrison and me. "It's settled, then."

"What's settled?" Connor approached, wrapping his arms around Olivia's waist.

His dark hair was buzzed close to his scalp, and he exuded strength and masculinity. Despite his size, he seemed to soften when it came to Olivia. I got the impression he was a big teddy bear—at least with her.

He pressed a kiss to her neck, and she giggled. I glanced away as I was hit with a potent wave of longing. I wanted that—connection, love, someone to wrap me up in their arms. Not just someone, though—Harrison.

"Juliana," Olivia said before I could digest that thought. "This is Connor, my fiancé."

He stepped out from behind her and held out a hand to shake. "It's a pleasure to finally meet you."

"Same," I said. "I've heard a lot about you."

"All good things, I hope." He grinned.

"Of course," I said. "Though your work ethic seems to rival my own."

Olivia beamed up at him when she spoke, her hand resting on his chest, her engagement ring sparkling in the light. "I'm so proud of you."

He smiled down at her, dropping a kiss on her nose. They were too freaking adorable. "I'm proud of you too, Goody."

"Yeah, but I'm not protecting people and saving lives," she said.

"Your job is equally important—sharing stories with the world, bringing people hope."

Connor surprised me. He fit the build of a navy SEAL, but he was so sweet, so gentle with Olivia. They were cute together.

"You're a navy SEAL?" I asked, knowing he'd be wearing his dress uniform for the wedding.

"Was. I work for an executive protection company now," Connor said. "Before retiring from the SEALs, I considered going back to law school and applying for the JAG Corps, but a desk job wasn't very appealing."

"I can imagine."

"Considering his interest in the law," Harrison said, coming to join our group. "Connor, of all people, should know how important a prenup is."

"Dad," Olivia hissed, glancing around to make sure no one had overheard his comment.

I wondered if I should excuse myself or try to defuse the conversation. Luckily, none of the other guests seemed to notice what was going on. Everyone else was drinking and laughing, enjoying the food as music played on in the background.

Despite Olivia's tense posture, Connor kept his arm draped loosely on her shoulder. "With all due respect, sir, a prenup is a personal decision. Olivia and I have discussed it at length, and we both agreed it wasn't something we wished to pursue."

"With all due respect," Harrison ground out, leaning forward. "My daughter is in a position to inherit a considerable amount of wealth."

"Oh, Harrison," sang out a woman with a melodic voice. She traipsed over, but her light air seemed even more at odds with the tension that had settled over the small group. "Don't spoil what should be a happy occasion."

She kissed him on both cheeks, her dark brown hair glossy and curled. Her dress was one I'd seen in the latest Diane Von Furstenberg spring collection, and it wrapped around her perfect figure. She looked vaguely familiar, but I couldn't place her.

"Hello, darling," she said to Olivia as she gave her a gentle hug.

"Mom." Olivia forced a smile, and I stiffened. *Mom? This was Olivia's mom? Harrison's ex?* "I'm surprised you came. I thought you were in New York."

She lifted her nose in the air and sniffed. "And miss my only daughter's engagement party? Absolutely not."

"Says the woman who missed her only daughter's wedding dress fitting," Harrison muttered. "Which reminds me—" He turned to me. "I don't believe you've met Juliana. Juliana, this is Olivia's mom, Camille."

"Juliana is planning the wedding," Olivia added, drawing my attention to the fact that Harrison hadn't indicated my title.

Camille turned to me with a smile that looked more like a sneer. "Lovely to meet you. Now, would you be a dear and find me a seltzer?"

She spun back to the group, and I didn't miss the way Harrison clenched his fists. I was no stranger to the entitled and elite, but her demand grated on me more than something like that usually would. Maybe because I knew she was Harrison's ex.

"Of course." I forced a smile. After all, keeping guests happy was my job. And it was a good reminder that no matter how close I'd grown to Harrison and his daughter the past few weeks, I was here as the wedding planner, nothing more. "Can I get anything for anyone else?"

Olivia shook her head as did Connor, though they both looked uncomfortable. Connor seemed to lean forward as if to shield Olivia, while she seemed ready to step in and play referee between her parents if necessary. I wondered if this was how it always was between them, though I sensed Camille wasn't the easiest person to get along with. Even from our brief interaction, she seemed snobbish, spoiled, attention-seeking. Basically, the complete opposite of Harrison.

"Let me help you," Harrison said, taking a step forward.

Camille placed a hand possessively on his arm. "I'm sure Julie will be fine. It is her job, after all."

"It's Juliana," he ground out.

His eyes flickered to mine, and I spun away before he could protest. As I headed toward the kitchen, I heard Camille's laughter ring out over the group. Landon shot me a questioning glance from across the room, but I merely shook my head.

When I returned with Camille's seltzer, she accepted it with a dismissive, "That will be all."

"Camille," Harrison chided, the furrow between his brows deepening.

"What?" she asked.

"You could at least say thank you."

"I said thank you, didn't I?" She held a hand to her chest in a false display of modesty, and I began to wonder what he'd ever seen in her apart from her looks. She then proceeded to turn to him without ever actually saying the words to me.

Her attitude reminded me of some of the other celebrities I'd worked with. It was the type of thing I despised, the type of attitude someone like Taylor Long was known for. And in that moment, I was even more grateful to be planning the wedding with Harrison, not Camille.

"Oh, Harrison, you always did love to point out my shortcomings as a wife and a mother," she sighed, though she didn't seem all that affected. "Perhaps our marriage wouldn't have failed if you'd been a bit more complimentary."

As I watched it all play out, I still couldn't imagine the Harrison that Camille described. Because from what I'd seen, he'd been nothing but supportive and complimentary. Though, who knew the real story.

A muscle twitched in Harrison's jaw, but Olivia interrupted before he could say anything. "Mom." Olivia looped her arm through her mother's. "Can you come with me? I was actually hoping to get your opinion on the, um…"

"The bridal party's dresses," I offered.

"Yes, well, of course." Camille set her seltzer down on a side table, untouched.

Connor excused himself a moment later, leaving me alone with Harrison. Well, as alone as we could be in a house full of guests.

Harrison rubbed a hand over his forehead, chagrined. "I'm sorry about that."

I glanced toward the floor. "You don't need to apologize."

"I can't tell you how many years I spent apologizing for her behavior," he sighed.

I wanted to know more, but this wasn't the time or the place. When Harrison was drawn into conversation with some of the guests, I excused myself to the kitchen.

Landon glanced up from his phone when I entered. "Hey, boss."

"Hey." I took a sip of water, the weight of the day settling over me. Guests had already started to leave, but our work was far from done. "Everything okay?"

"Yep. Just catching up on some comments on Instagram." He studied me with a furrowed brow. "Are you feeling okay? You're a little flushed."

"I'm—actually, it is a little warm in here." I pulled my dress away from my skin, wishing I had something to fan myself with.

"Why don't you go outside?" He gestured to the door off the kitchen, the one that led to the backyard. "No one's out there."

I considered it a moment before relenting. After my brunch with the girls, I'd started seeing a therapist, and I knew Lindsay would encourage me to take this moment to de-stress. It was part of our plan. And though I'd been sleeping better, sometimes the nightmares struck without warning. Last night, I'd woken up, my limbs twisted in the sheets, my heart pounding. I'd felt…off most of the day, and I could use a breather.

Besides, Landon had it covered, and if he needed me, he knew where to find me. I slipped outside, staying in the shadows close to the house. Harrison's backyard was amazing, and it was one of the things I liked best about his property. The slate patio overlooked a lush green yard, pool and cabana, and trees beyond. It was a peaceful haven.

I closed my eyes and drew in a deep breath.

"Needed to escape?"

Startled, my eyes popped open, and I placed a hand to my chest. "God, you scared me."

"Name's Harrison." I could hear the smile in his voice as he came to stand beside me. "But it wouldn't be the first time you've referred to me as a god."

I smacked his bicep then had to shake out my hand. *Dang.*

"Are you always so cocky?" I teased.

A smirk played at his lips. "What can I say? You bring out the best in me."

If I'd thought it was warm inside, it was a million degrees hotter out here. His eyes devoured me, his lips parting as he shifted closer. My nerve endings tingled with awareness, but I tried to ignore it. To push it away.

My core heated, and I needed to change topics. "It's beautiful out here."

"Yes." He cleared his throat, shoving his hands in his pockets as he peered out over the yard. "It is. I half hoped Olivia would want a backyard wedding, but—" He lifted a shoulder, indicating it wasn't meant to be.

"It would be a great location." I could easily envision it. "Chairs over there." I gestured to a section off the pool. "Leading to a floral arch. Flowers scattered over the pool."

"Sounds pretty perfect to me," he said, and I could feel him watching me intently.

I squirmed a little, my skin heating beneath his perusal. I wasn't sure he was talking about Olivia's wedding anymore, but I quickly shook away the thought. Harrison wasn't the marrying kind.

"But we don't always get what we want, do we?" he asked, to which I nodded.

The conversation was taking a personal turn, and as much as I craved that connection with him, it scared me. Besides, as Camille had so painfully reminded me—I was here to do a job.

"Speaking of wedding venues," I said. "We have the menu tasting at the inn next Saturday."

"Looking forward to it."

"And—" I shifted on my feet, suddenly anxious "if you don't have other plans, Olivia was hoping we could go for the weekend. She wants us to scope out some restaurants and attractions for the guests."

"*Olivia* wants us to go for the weekend, huh?" His arched brow belied his skepticism, so I merely nodded. "So…you're saying I get an entire weekend alone with you?"

His words sparked my desire and ignited my core. "It's strictly a business trip," I insisted, not sure who I was trying to convince more—him or myself.

The corner of his mouth tipped into a grin, and I glanced away. A weekend away with Harrison… I shook my head. It was going to be difficult, if not impossible, to keep things professional.

CHAPTER TWELVE

Harrison

"I was thinking we could kick off the weekend with a winery tour." Juliana glanced down at her tablet, where I was sure a detailed, color-coded schedule was displayed. I merely watched her, a smile playing at my lips as she continued to list her plans for us. "Then dinner at a local restaurant downtown. It's within walking distance to some shops. Then…"

"Juliana." I crossed my arms and leaned against the porch railing.

A breeze picked up, swirling the air around us, giving me a hit of her floral scent. And then there was her dress, which bared most of her tanned, toned shoulders. I rubbed my hands together, wishing I could rub them over her skin. I couldn't get her out of my head.

"Hmm." She hummed absently, her attention still focused on the screen.

I admired the resort's lush garden, lifting my hand to shield my eyes from the sun. The mountains rose up in the distance, and I didn't intend to waste our weekend alone by filling it with local attractions. She seemed intent on staying busy, when all I wanted to do was slow down, soak her in. Explore the landscape and her body.

When she continued to ignore me, I pushed off the rail and went over to her. She was so immersed in her schedule, she didn't notice my approach. I wanted nothing more than to imagine that we were here together and not because of something to do with my daughter's wedding. I wanted to see my Juliana again—the one I'd spent the night with. The one who ditched the strict schedule and knew how to have fun. So, I tugged the tablet out of her hand.

She jerked her head up. "Hey! I need that."

"Nope." I tucked it behind my back. "What you need is to let go, *relax*."

"But…but—" she sputtered, attempting to reach behind me for the tablet. "This is a business trip. I'm here to explore the area for the bride—your daughter—as well as future clients."

"And I'm here to help you lighten up. Have some fun. Though I'm beginning to wonder if you know what that is."

She placed her hands on her hips and narrowed her eyes at me. "I know how to have fun."

"Oh yeah?" I arched an eyebrow. "Prove it. Ditch the tablet. Ditch the schedule. And let's see where the wind takes us."

"Where the wind takes us?" she asked with a laugh. "Who are you—Pocahontas?"

"Can't say that was one of Olivia's favorite movies growing up," I said, though I was familiar with the song "Colors of the Wind."

"Lucky. I mean, it's not terrible as far as kids movies go. But it's not my first choice."

I studied her. "And you watch a lot of kids movies?"

"My sister has young children, as does my best friend

Alexis. So—" she held up her hands "—I babysit from time to time."

"Ahh." I tilted back my head. "Do you ever wish you had your own?" I immediately wished I could take it back because I wasn't sure I wanted to hear the answer.

"A few years ago, my answer would've been yes."

"And now…?" Why couldn't I just let the matter go?

"Now…" She scrunched up her face. "Now, I'm not so sure. I think…what if something happened to me or my partner? Who would take care of our child then?"

I nodded. "As a parent, it's one of the most difficult things to contemplate."

"Yeah. I just think I'm getting a bit old to consider having children."

"Old?" I barked out a laugh. "You're not old."

She leaned her hip against the railing. "Well, thank you. But in terms of getting pregnant and having children, I am. I'm thirty-seven."

My heart was racing as I quickly tallied our age difference. *Fourteen years.* I was fourteen years older than her.

"That's not old. Trust me. Besides, you don't look a day over thirty."

She rolled her eyes. "You're just being nice."

"I'm being honest."

She leaned forward, and I was distracted by the sight of her glossy pink lips. I wanted to kiss her. Fuck, I wanted to kiss her.

We were alone, outside the city, for the entire weekend. The sky might be cloudless and sunny, but the current forecast included lots of cold showers for me.

She brushed past me, momentarily distracting me. But I was faster. I tightened my grip on the tablet and held it away from her grasp.

"Sneaky, sneaky," I said with a disapproving shake of my head.

"Harrison." She jumped up on her toes, arms stretched above her as she reached for the tablet. I was getting hard from watching her attempts to reclaim it. "Give that back!"

"I'll give it back," I said, and she relaxed slightly. "At the end of the weekend."

She growled and lunged for it. She landed against my chest with a thud, and I let out an "oomph."

"You're vicious." I chuckled, slightly winded.

She seemed dazed, but then shook her head. "I'm determined. Now, give it back."

I arched a brow, amused by her attempt to threaten me. She was tall, but I still had six inches on her. Not to mention, I was a former professional athlete. I'd gotten paid to evade lineman twice her size. If I could avoid their efforts to tackle me, I could certainly handle Juliana.

"I'll tell you what," I said, holding the tablet out over the railing. I wasn't going to drop it into the flower bed below, but the threat was enough to make her pause. "Let's go for an adventure—no devices. And when we get back, you can have your tablet."

"Fine." She straightened, shimmying her hips so her skirt fell back into place.

I wondered what she was up to. Why she was suddenly okay with it.

"Okay." I eyed her as I glanced toward the front door to the inn. "Did you bring workout clothes?"

She nodded. "Where are we going?"

"You'll see. Meet back here in ten?"

She glared at me but ultimately turned and marched toward the door. Ten minutes later, I jogged down to the front porch, only to find her waiting for me as she typed something on her phone. I stilled, raking my eyes over her curves. A turquoise sports bra hugged her breasts, revealing her flat stomach. Her hips were encased in compression leggings, and I nearly let out a groan at the sight of her ass.

I strode over to her, swiped the phone from her hand before shoving it into my front pocket. "Nope. Remember what I said. No devices."

"But my work—"

"Can wait," I said in a firm tone that left no room for argument.

I admired her drive, her dedication, but I sensed it was more than passion for her career. She used her job as an excuse for avoiding life, and I was determined to change that.

She stuck her tongue out at me as we headed for the car. "Okay, Dad."

I backed her against the side of my Range Rover, caging her in with my arms. It trapped the air between us, making me even hotter for her. "Trust me, Juliana. The thoughts I have toward you are definitely not paternal."

She sucked in a jagged breath, but I merely reached around her to open the passenger door before the temptation to kiss her became too much to resist.

"Now, get in." My tone was gruff.

"Mm. Someone's bossy today." I heard the smile in her voice, and I remembered how much she'd liked my bossy side during our night together.

I smirked and closed the door, rounding the car to the driver's side. This woman drove me crazy in the best possible way. And if I could just get her to let go for a while—to drop work and the pretense of this being a business trip—I had a feeling she might actually enjoy herself.

As soon as we were out of the parking lot, I rolled down the windows. I expected her to protest, but if anything, she seemed happy. Her blond ponytail fluttered in the breeze, and a smile played at her lips. It took everything in me to tear my eyes away from her and return my attention to the road.

It was cooler beneath the shade of the trees, and the scent of fresh mountain air swirled through the car. We drove mostly in companionable silence before I pulled off the road into a dirt parking lot. The tires rumbled beneath us until I put the car into Park. I hopped out and jogged around to open the door for her.

"Ready?" I slung a backpack over my shoulder.

"I am if you are." She grinned, one hand on her hip, water bottle in the other.

We headed up the trail, the gravel path crunching beneath our feet. When she stopped to tie one of her shoes, I stared at her heart-shaped ass a moment before shaking my head to clear it. What had I been thinking, bringing her on a hike? Between the leggings and the sports bra, this woman was going to be the death of me.

I glanced down the trail, wondering how far she'd make it. Wondering if she would last past the first mile, or if she was too much of a city girl to enjoy nature. But as we passed the first mile and then the second, I was impressed. We talked every so often, about work, family, life. And it was nice—easy.

When we stopped for a water break, I took a seat on a nearby rock ledge and dug in my backpack for some of the snacks I'd brought. "Hungry?"

"Maybe." She took a sip of her water. "What do you have?"

I held out several options, all gluten free and some that were vegan. Her eyes lit up when she saw them. "I love Emmie's cookies. Thanks."

"You're welcome."

I'd noticed she kept them around her office, so I'd picked up some before our trip.

I watched as she opened the package and popped one in

her mouth. Her freckles were more pronounced today, and her blond ponytail hung down her back, tempting me to wrap it around my fist.

Instead, I took a bite of my apple, the juice dripping down my chin before I wiped it away. "You surprise me."

"Yeah?" She tilted her head to the side. "How so?"

"I don't know." I shrugged. "I guess I figured you were too much of a city girl to enjoy hiking."

She laughed from her perch nearby. "You might be surprised what I enjoy."

I leaned in, aching to be closer. "Tell me more," I murmured, my voice gravelly with need.

She elbowed me. "Harrison."

"What?" I sat back, fighting a grin as I attempted to maintain an innocent expression. "You said I'd be surprised, so I asked for more information."

"Mm-hmm." She crossed her arms over her chest, which had the effect of pushing her breasts together. "I think we both know you weren't referring to recreational activities."

"Well, I was. I just had one very specific activity in mind." I smirked.

She rolled her eyes and looked away, but she couldn't hide the effect my words had on her. It was clear in the rise and fall of her chest and the pink color creeping up her neck.

"So, tell me about your other interests," I said, wanting to know more about her. "Do you like sports? Cooking? Art?"

"Are you going to strand me here if I say sports isn't high on the list?" She cringed as if bracing for impact.

I merely laughed. "Perhaps."

"Harrison." She tossed her wrapper at me as we stood. I caught it, shoving it into my pack.

We resumed our hike and soon approached a bridge.

"Do you like any sports?" I asked.

Juliana hung back, and I stopped, realizing she was no

longer behind me. "It's getting late. Maybe we should head back."

I glanced at my watch and frowned. "We have plenty of daylight. Certainly enough time to hike to the falls before we leave. Come on."

I made it halfway across the bridge before I realized she still hadn't moved. "Juliana?" I tilted my head to the side, assessing her. She seemed frozen in place, her eyes wide. "Are you okay?"

She shook her head. "Yeah." She swallowed, placing her hand to the rock face as if to steady herself. "I'm, uh—" Her skin paled. "Fine."

She didn't look fine. She looked like she was going to pass out. The rosy bloom of her cheeks had faded to a pallor that alarmed me.

"Are you afraid of heights?" I took a few steps closer.

Again, she shook her head, but she kept staring at the bridge. She wore a dazed look that ratcheted up my anxiety. This far out, there was no cell reception. I'd seen a few other people on the trail, but not in a while.

Think, Harrison. Think.

"You're not diabetic, are you?"

I'd known a few guys throughout my career who were, and though her reaction was similar, I didn't think that was it. Besides, we'd recently had a snack and water. If it wasn't a blood sugar issue or a fear of heights, what else could it be?

"I need to see the package." Her breathing was labored, and I tried to stay calm.

"What?" I glanced around. "What package?"

"The..." she gasped. "The Emmie's."

She reached for my backpack, and I sprung into action. I rummaged through the contents, finally discovering another cookie like she'd eaten at the bottom.

"Here." I held it out to her, hoping she didn't notice the way my hands shook. "Here."

She flipped it over and looked at the ingredients before reaching for something in a pocket in her leggings I hadn't noticed. Her face was going red, and I felt helpless. She pulled out a plastic tube, removed a blue cap, and then swung it toward her thigh. She held it there a few seconds, counting to three before her hand fell to the side. She closed her eyes and leaned her head back against the rock wall.

"Juliana?"

She held up one finger, but her response was far from reassuring. I took her hand in mine, wanting to comfort her —to do...*something*. Selfishly, I needed to know she was okay.

After what felt like an eternity but was probably no more than a minute, her eyes fluttered open. Her breathing seemed more normal, her skin color more regular. But I wasn't a doctor, so what did I know?

"Are you okay? Do you want some water?"

She nodded, and I held the bottle to her lips. She took a sip, some of the liquid dribbling down her chin. "Thank you."

I checked my phone again—no service. "We need to get you to a hospital."

She shook her head. "Just...give me a minute. I'll be fine."

We sat there for a few moments before she said, "I should've read the package. I always read the package when they change the label." She didn't attempt to remove her hand from my grasp. It was nice—apart from the fact that she'd nearly given me a heart attack.

I frowned. "I don't understand."

"I've had these cookies before, but when the label changes, companies often change ingredients too. I'm allergic to coconut."

I tilted my head back, feeling like an idiot. How had I not realized she was having an allergic reaction? My own daughter carried an EpiPen for her nut allergy, though thankfully, she'd never had to use it.

"I'm so sorry I didn't realize…"

"You didn't know. How could you have? I'll be okay." She slid her hand from mine. "I'm ready."

"Are you sure?"

She nodded and attempted to stand, but her knees buckled. I immediately reached out to steady her.

"It's okay. I've got you."

"Don't say that." She shook her head. "Don't." She closed her eyes as if pained.

"All right," I said, hefting her into my arms without giving her a chance to protest.

"Harrison!" she shrieked, but it was weak. "Put me down."

I shook my head and started down the trail. I didn't care what she said; I wasn't letting her go.

CHAPTER THIRTEEN

Juliana

"Have some more water," Harrison said from the lounge chair next to me.

We were hanging out by the pool, a slight breeze ruffling the umbrella above us. After returning from the hospital, he'd insisted I take it easy. *Take it easy?* I wanted to laugh. There was no way I could take it easy sitting next to the hottest man I'd ever seen. His bare chest was on display, showcasing a mouthwatering eight-pack. And he somehow managed to have evenly bronzed skin even though it wasn't yet summer. *Ugh.*

I rolled my eyes beneath my sunglasses. "I'm going to have to start calling you Landon. He can be such a nag sometimes."

He narrowed his eyes at me, and I flashed him a smile. I held out a moment longer, finally taking a sip of water before reclining against the chair.

"I'm not even sure we should be out here," he said.

It didn't matter how many times I'd told him I was fine, he insisted on taking care of me. I'd never forget the way he'd scooped me into his arms, carrying me down the trail. I wasn't sure anyone had ever treated me like that—like I was something precious. In all honesty, it was nice to feel taken care of. Cared for.

He'd stayed by my side the entire time, supporting me while ensuring the doctors took good care of me. And he'd been insistent that I get a new EpiPen immediately. Though my body's response to coconut was swift and scary, I'd reacted quickly and so had he. His reaction was especially impressive for someone who had never experienced something like that. Harrison hadn't batted an eye; he was simply there—right where I needed him to be.

But it was more than that. More than his looks. Clearly, he was hot—that was a given. And a good father—kind, caring, and compassionate. He was also generous, involved with a number of charities in the city. And he'd asked me to help plan one of their annual events. He was also smart, attentive, and patient. Despite not knowing anything about weddings, he was interested and invested in planning this one with me.

I stood, removing my sunglasses and setting them on the table beside me. "The doctor said to take it easy. I'd say lounging by the pool is about as easy as you can take it."

I headed for the pool, eager to cool down. Harrison was… He was too close. He saw too much. And the way his eyes devoured me made me want to give in.

"Where are you going?"

"For a dip," I threw over my shoulder, gratified by the fact that his eyes were glued to my ass.

He stood, growling my name. "Juliana." It was a warning.

"Some Zen master you are," I teased, descending the stairs to the pool. The water was cool against my skin, refreshing after the long hike and the hospital visit. It was just what I'd needed.

If I'd thought the hike would help me clear my mind or in

some way lessen my attraction to him, I was wrong. Despite his spontaneous, carefree attitude, he'd been thoughtful and prepared. And it didn't hurt that his backpack had been full of some of my favorite snacks.

He followed me with his eyes, and I relished the feeling of being watched. Of being wanted.

"If you're so concerned about my well-being, maybe you should join me." I spun away so I wouldn't have to see his reaction.

"Is that an invitation?" he rasped.

I didn't answer, letting him read into my silence what he wanted as I paddled around the pool. I felt the water shift before I saw him. He swam beneath the surface, popping his head out just before he reached me. His hair was darker, water sluicing down the hard planes of his face.

"You couldn't just sit by the pool, could you?" he teased.

"You took away my tablet. And my phone. What was I supposed to do?" I pouted.

"Relax. *Be.*" He smoothed his hair away from his face, his green eyes more intense than usual.

"I'm not sure I know how," I admitted. "But I'm working on it."

"Good." He placed his hands on my shoulders. His skin was warm, his grip firm. It was comforting, yet… His touch sparked something in me—awoke a desire. "Juliana, you scared the shit out of me."

It was the first time I'd really looked at him since the incident, and his concern was clear. It was etched into his face, evident in the tightness in his grip.

"I'm sorry. I rarely have a reaction that severe, fortunately." I wasn't going to admit how scared I'd been for a moment. My throat closing in on me, feeling dizzy and weak.

"Hey." His voice was soothing as he smoothed his hand down my arm. "Are you okay?"

"You heard the doctor," I said, unable to bear the intensity of his gaze—this moment—any longer. "I'm fine. I didn't mean to scare you. I also didn't mean for you to carry me down a mountain. I'm not some damsel in distress." I stuck my tongue out at him, needing to lighten the moment.

"I know you're not. But you can't blame me for wanting to protect you." He pulled me into his chest without another word, holding me tight to him. His body was wet but warm, and his heart beat a steady rhythm.

For a moment, I let myself give in. I closed my eyes and wrapped my arms around his waist, and I allowed myself to *feel.* I allowed myself to imagine what it would be like to open my heart again. What it would be like to love someone again. And while I wasn't sure if Harrison was that person, it certainly felt like he could be. He was kind and compassionate. He was courageous and selfless. And he was good at helping me let go, at getting me to relax.

His skin was so smooth, and I was tempted to get lost in him. Surely, he could feel my nipples pebbling against the thin material of my swimsuit. I could certainly feel his arousal poking my stomach. But instead of pushing for more, he backed away. His eyes darted to my chest, and my nipples seemed to harden even more under his gaze.

"So..." He cleared his throat.

"So," I said.

"I guess I now know why you cater to clients with specialty diets." He rested his arms on the edge of the pool.

I ached for his touch, craved it. And yet I knew it was for the best that he'd put some space between us.

I nodded. "Having food allergies isn't easy, especially as a kid. I can't tell you how many times kids made fun of me or I had to miss birthday parties or social events because of it. My parents did their best, but it wasn't easy."

"I bet. Kids can be vicious. I was lucky most of Olivia's friends were nice."

"Awareness of food allergies is also a lot better than it used to be."

He nodded, and we fell into an easy silence. I leaned back against the edge of the pool and closed my eyes, tilting my head toward the sun. Soaking in the rays as the water lapped at my skin.

"This is…" I sighed, feeling a sense of contentment. "I didn't realize how much I needed something like this. I love my job, but it can be stressful."

"That's why it's so important to take time for yourself to recharge," he said.

I nodded, peering at him from across the pool. The sun reflected off the water, glinting in those green orbs. "Everyone keeps telling me that."

"Maybe you should listen." He inched closer but still gave me space. "Maybe you need to let go. Do something unexpected."

I narrowed my eyes at him. But it was difficult to remain focused. He slicked back his hair, and I watched as a rivulet ran down the hard plane of his chest. "I remember what happened the last time you asked me to let go."

"Then you'll also remember the handful of orgasms that accompanied it." His eyes sparkled with mischief, but underlying that, I saw something that told me I could trust him.

"Keep your voice down," I hissed, whipping my head around as if someone might overhear us.

But we were alone. The other guests were out on excursions, and no one knew us here.

"Bottling up your emotions isn't healthy either, trust me."

"Yeah?" I sensed there was more to the story.

He let out a deep sigh, scrubbing a hand over his face. "After things fell apart with Cam, I tried to hold it all together. I was away a lot for games, but I tried to be there for Olivia. I was trying to act like everything was normal, like everything was fine, and it was…a lot of pressure."

I nodded, encouraging him to continue.

"One of my teammates—this guy who loved to push my buttons—made a comment one day. I lunged for him and got in a few punches before Reg pulled me off. If it weren't for Reg, I might have been kicked off the team."

He glanced over at me and I sensed trepidation on his part, but I understood. Perhaps better than he knew.

"I get it. And I probably shouldn't tell you this, but I lost it on a client recently. And mid-rant, I sort of fainted," I blurted. "God, it was mortifying."

He jerked his head back. "You what?"

"I know…" I sliced my hand through the air. "It was so unprofessional."

"No." He stepped closer, grasping my arms. "You fainted?" I nodded. "Recently?"

I lifted a shoulder. "Um, it was a few months back. Actually, the morning of the wedding expo."

"Juliana." He peered into my eyes as if searching my soul. I squirmed beneath the intensity of his gaze. "You have to stop."

"Stop what? Planning weddings?" I shook my head, my blood pressure rising. The weddings, the stress of my job weren't the problem. My memories, the nightmares that came out of nowhere, drenching me in sweat, were the issue.

"I love my job," I said. "She just… Ugh. You can't tell anyone this, but she's the kind of client that makes me regret planning her wedding."

"I'm sure you've had your fair share of bridezillas," he said, dropping the matter—and my arms—at least for now.

"Most clients are great, but everyone has something they get hung up on. Cake flavors, the song for the first dance, honeymoon destinations. Which reminds me—have Olivia and Connor settled on a destination?"

He blew out a breath. "They're leaning toward Virginia Beach."

"And you don't approve."

He shook his head. "Olivia deserves…everything. Virginia Beach feels like, I don't know, settling."

"Do you feel like she's settling by marrying Connor?" I asked, wondering if that was the real issue.

He furrowed his brow then shook his head. "No. Connor's a good man. He's good to Olivia. Good *for* Olivia."

I nodded. "I agree. Even in the brief time I've spent with them, it's clear they love each other."

"But is love enough?"

"I'd like to think so." I swallowed, wondering if I should stop myself from pressing further. "Can I ask you a personal question?"

He lifted a shoulder, but I saw the tension he carried there. "Sure."

"Why are you against marriage? Is it because of what happened with Cam?"

He groaned. "Do I really have to answer that?"

"What?" I placed my hands on my hips. "You can push me on my personal life, but I can't do the same to you?"

He grimaced. "Fine. And yes. It's because of what happened with Cam. Neither of us was without fault, but our divorce was nasty. I don't ever want to go through something like that again."

"I can understand that." My circumstances might be different, but I was afraid to risk my heart again.

"It's getting late," I said, noting how the sun was dipping lower in the sky. "We should head in to get ready. I don't want to be late for the tasting."

"Should I bring a notepad to keep track of everything?" he teased.

"Just your appetite. They don't skimp on portions, despite the fact that it's a tasting menu."

"I'm always hungry." He patted his stomach, though his eyes spoke of a different type of hunger as I ascended the pool stairs. The type of hunger that spelled trouble. "What? You don't believe me?"

"You can't eat whatever you want and have a body like that."

"A body like what?" He waggled his eyebrows, watching me as I walked along the edge of the pool. "Are you finally admitting that you find me attractive?"

I rolled my eyes and tossed him a towel when he exited the water. "I never denied it. I just said we shouldn't talk about it."

"In front of Olivia."

I glared at him, wrapping a towel around my waist. "We shouldn't talk about it at all."

"Why? Don't you know I just *love* talking about me?"

But I knew it wasn't true. Considering who he was and all that he'd accomplished, Harrison was incredibly humble. He was confident, but he carried himself with a sort of grace that I admired.

"Honestly..." I paused, then shook my head. "Never mind."

"Wait—" He grabbed my arm, forcing me to look at him. "I want to know."

"It doesn't matter." I stepped away from his touch. I shouldn't tell him what I was thinking. He was emotionally unavailable—a risky choice when my heart had already been broken.

"Your opinion matters," he said. "It matters to me."

"In this line of work... Well, I see it all. I'm no stranger to working with celebrities and professional athletes, but you're…" I cocked my head to the side. "Different."

"Different how?"

I shook my head, lips sealed. I'd already said too much. "Just different." He opened his mouth as if to say something, but I started walking, forcing him to follow. "Come on. We don't want to be late."

"Are you ever late for anything?" he teased.

"It's rare, but it does happen."

He held a hand to his chest, gasping in mock horror. "You mean, you're not perfect?"

I rolled my eyes. "I never claimed to be."

"You're pretty damn close." His voice was low but still loud enough for me to hear. "Will we be tasting cakes too?" he asked hopefully as he opened the door.

I shook my head and pushed past him. "Appetizers and entrees. I doubt you'll have room for dessert by the time we're finished."

"I wouldn't be so sure about that." He flashed me a wicked grin, and a bolt of desire shot to my core as I pretended not to hear him.

We were playing a dangerous game. He was getting too close, and I was getting too comfortable. I wanted to let him in, but I was scared. Scared that my already-fragile heart couldn't take much more.

CHAPTER FOURTEEN

Harrison

Juliana was right. By the time we finished tasting the options for the reception, I was stuffed. Full of good wine, good food, and good conversation. It hadn't been all about the wedding either. I sensed that after today's events, she was letting me in a little more. And the more time we spent together, the more captivated I was by this stunning woman. Everything about her was alluring, from the way the light flickered off her bare skin to the sparkle in her eyes.

I held the door open for her as we exited the building housing the restaurant and made our way back toward the one with our rooms. She brushed past me, and her scent lingered in the air, enveloping me with memories of our night together. I was so tempted to touch her, kiss her, inhale her. Or at least take her hand in mine as the gravel crunched beneath our feet.

When we'd toured the property with Olivia weeks ago, it was beautiful. But at night—with the stars overhead and a warm breeze blowing through the trees, it was magical. Or maybe that was the company. Despite what had happened on the trail today, Juliana seemed lighter this evening, more relaxed. And I liked it. If getting out of LA meant getting to see this side of her, I was going to have to do it more often.

"This is…" I glanced around, taking it all in, from the white lights to the lush garden beyond. "It's beautiful. And the food was delicious. I think Olivia will be very happy."

"How's she doing? Is she settling in okay?" Juliana asked.

I held out my arm, pleased when she took it. "She's doing great. Me—not so much. I suspect that's why she asked me to come to Ojai this weekend. To keep me distracted."

"Aww. You miss her." She gripped my arm, leaning into me as I steered us toward a bench. I wasn't ready for the evening to end. I wasn't ready for my time with Juliana to be over.

I nodded. "I'm so proud of her and happy. She's always wanted to travel, so this is a dream come true for her. But she's my only daughter, and I worry."

"I can see that. I think it's really…" She seemed to search for a word. "Sweet."

I rubbed a hand over my face. "Sweet? You think I'm sweet? You're going to ruin my street cred."

"First of all…" Her lips twitched as if she were holding back a smile. "The fact that you said 'street cred' tells me you have none."

I opened my mouth to protest, but she continued talking. "And secondly, it's not a bad thing to be sweet. I love that you're close to your daughter. If anything, it makes me wish I had a relationship like that with my father."

"You aren't close?"

She shook her head. "He's…old-fashioned. A bit chauvinistic, if I'm being completely honest."

I frowned. "What does that mean?"

"He thinks my career is a joke. Parties are…frivolous and

silly. His words, not mine. It was a big reason why he liked Ryan so much. His job was stable, traditional."

Ryan. I was surprised she'd mentioned him, and I wondered what was responsible for this shift. I wanted to dive more into the Ryan issue, but I was trying to respect her wishes. She'd asked me not to bring up him or our night together, but she was the one who'd mentioned his name. I wasn't sure what was or wasn't safe for discussion.

So, I settled for a different topic. "Well, I think your dad sounds like an ass."

She nearly choked on a laugh. "He definitely can be."

"I just—" I shook my head. "I can't even imagine. My parents have always been supportive. Olivia's very close to them, so I'm grateful they'll get to attend her wedding."

She gave me a warm smile. "Grandparents are so important. My nana is ninety-one, and I credit her with my love of entertaining. She was always cooking, hosting big parties."

It was nice to know that Juliana shared the same family values that I did. She might not have the best relationship with her father, but it was clear she still loved him.

"I think I ate too much." Juliana smiled, though it quickly turned into a yawn.

"Come on." I stood and held out my hand, tugging her to stand. "Let's get you to bed."

She arched her brow, and I grinned. "I'd certainly be happy to join you. But it's been a big day."

She nodded, letting my comment slide. "You're right. I'm exhausted."

I placed my hand on the small of her back, escorting her upstairs. My room was just across the hall, and I lingered for a moment outside her door. She was so appealing in her floral dress, hair the color of sunshine. Unable to resist, I leaned in and pressed my lips to her cheek. Anything to prolong the moment.

"Good night, Juliana." My breath fanned against her skin.

I pulled back ever so slowly. If I'd moved an inch to the right, our lips would be pressed together. Her eyes fluttered open, and her smile was relaxed when she said, "Good night, Harrison. Thank you for a nice day."

"A nice day?" I barked out a laugh, drawing the attention of a staff member walking past. "You had an allergic reaction and ended up at the hospital."

"Yeah. And apart from your nagging, I really enjoyed myself." She grinned.

"What can I say?" I leaned in, pressing my hand to the doorframe, caging her in. "You bring out the best in me."

She laughed, placing a hand to my chest. Her touch singed me through my light shirt, and I wondered if she was just as affected. Judging from the way her eyes widened, I'd say so. Even though it was complicated and a bad idea, I wanted to taste her again, devour her. But she was still grieving Ryan, and I didn't think she was ready for anything more than friendship. Fuck me. This was going to be a long weekend.

"You know…" I leaned in to whisper in her ear. "I only nag you because I like you."

She grinned. "You sound like a kid on the playground."

I tucked some of her hair behind her ear. "You make me feel young again."

She rolled her eyes, though she leaned into my touch. "You *are* young, Harrison."

When she yawned again, I stepped back, giving her space to open her door. Who was I kidding? Just because I felt young with her didn't mean I was. The reality was that I was an old fool, lusting after a much younger woman.

She was young, gorgeous; she had a whole life ahead of her. She deserved someone who would want the same things that she did—marriage, children. Not a man who was fourteen years her senior. A man who'd been burned. A man who couldn't give her—or anyone—his whole heart. And to ask for anything more than friendship would be selfish.

I waited until she'd closed her door to make my way across the hall. Juliana might only be a few feet away, but it felt like we were miles apart. I paused with my hand on the doorknob, tempted to turn back. She shouldn't be alone, not after what had happened on the trail. But would she let me stay even if I offered to sleep on the floor?

I shook my head. I was being ridiculous, overprotective of a woman I had no right to be. As she'd so clearly told me— she wasn't a damsel in distress. So, I pushed open the door to my room, ignoring the nagging feeling in my gut. If she needed me, I was just across the hall.

I stripped out of my clothes, brushing my teeth before grabbing my Kindle. Olivia had sent me another book to read, and I was hoping it would be a good distraction. My legs were restless, my mind wandering, and I considered going for a run. My stomach protested the idea, and I frowned down at it. Maybe if I hadn't eaten so damn much.

A glance at the world clock on my phone told me Olivia would be headed to work soon. And talking with Juliana had made me realize how much I was missing my daughter. It felt like I hadn't seen Olivia in weeks, even though it had only been days. I sent Olivia a text, wishing her a good day.

I was surprised when the phone rang a second later, her name flashing across the screen. I grinned, tucking the phone between my shoulder and my ear. "Hey, Livie."

"Hey, Dad."

"You headed to work?"

"Soon. I'm eating breakfast. This jet lag is murder. What are you up to?"

"I'm in Ojai."

"That's right." She laughed. "God, I'm so confused on my days. How's it going?"

"Good." I blew out a breath, wishing it would release some of my pent-up tension. "The weather has been gorgeous, and I'm pleased with the service at the venue."

"That's good." I could hear the smile in her voice. "And Juliana…?"

"What about Juliana?" I asked, hating how defensive I sounded.

"How's it going with her?"

I briefly wondered if she was implying something about my relationship with the wedding planner. I brushed the thought aside. "Great. I really like the hotel, and the food is delicious."

"Good. Anything else I need to know?"

"No," I answered quickly, too quickly if the silence on the other end was any indication. I stood and started pacing at the foot of the bed. "How are you doing? How's London?"

"It's good. I miss Connor. But the city is amazing, and so are my colleagues. The hours are crazy, but I'm still hoping to venture out and really experience the city."

"That's great." I smiled, sincerely happy for her.

"Yeah." Despite her enthusiasm, I sensed she was a little down. "I'm just not sure how I'll make it six weeks without seeing Connor."

"I thought he was coming to visit sooner?"

"He's too busy at work."

Too busy to make time to see my daughter, his fiancée? I gnashed my teeth, not liking that answer. I knew how difficult long-distance could be, but I also knew that he was going to have to put in the work if he wanted to be with my daughter.

"That's no excuse."

"Dad." She laughed. "I'm doing the same thing. And we're trying to save up vacation time for the honeymoon."

"Mm-hmm." I stopped pacing and sat at the foot of the bed.

"What?"

"Nothing." I didn't want to ruin her day, but I intended to have a little conversation with my future son-in-law.

"Hey, have you talked to Mom lately?" Olivia asked, interrupting my thoughts.

"No. Should I?"

"She has some thoughts on the seating charts. I told her to take it up with you."

"Gee, thanks."

"She also told me she intends to bring her new boyfriend, and she'd like for him to be in the photos." She sounded surprisingly calm, considering.

I scrubbed a hand over my face. *You've got to be fucking kidding me.*

"The family pictures? Do you think they'll even still be together by the time the wedding rolls around?" I asked but immediately regretted it. I didn't want Olivia to feel caught between her mom and me. And I didn't want to disrespect Cam in front of our daughter, even if my ex drove me nuts at times.

She laughed. "Who knows. I seriously hope not—he's practically the same age as me. I mean, what can they possibly have in common besides the obvious?"

I grimaced, thinking of Juliana. Though I wasn't old enough to be her father, she was significantly younger than me. How would Olivia feel if Juliana and I were together? Would she be as disgusted by the idea?

"Dad?" she asked. "You still there?"

I shook my head to clear it. "Don't worry. I'll sort it out." I didn't want anything to ruin Olivia's day.

"Thanks." She cleared her throat, and I wondered if there was something more. Then she said, "I have a favor to ask."

"Another one?" I teased. "I'm not planning your bachelorette party."

"Ew. No." She laughed. "Alyssa's got that covered. But since I'm out of town, I was wondering if maybe you could invite Connor over for family dinner every so often even though I'm gone. I really want you two to get along since he's going to be my husband."

I frowned. "We get along."

"I know, but… Well, I think he feels like maybe you don't like him."

How much of that was thanks to my continued badgering to get a prenup?

"I like him," I said, hoping to get out of it. It wasn't that I didn't like him. I just didn't feel the need to make both of us suffer through a weekly meal together.

"Please," she begged. I was grateful we weren't on Face-Time. Judging by her tone, I would've already caved by now.

I let out a deep sigh. "Isn't it enough that I'm planning your wedding?" I was only half teasing. I'd secretly been hoping that alone was worth a lifetime of "get out of jail free" cards.

"Dad," she chided. "It would mean a lot to me. And Connor. He's going to be part of this family soon. I really want the two most important men in my life to get along."

"Fine," I huffed dramatically. "Anything else you'd like? A new car? A million dollars."

"I think I'm good." She laughed, likely knowing I would gladly give her anything she wanted. "Crap. It's getting late. I gotta go, Dad. Let's catch up soon."

"Sounds good. I love you."

"Love you too."

I disconnected the call and flopped back on the bed in my

boxer briefs, tucking my arm behind my head. I knew she was right about getting to know Connor, but I still dreaded the prospect. If I didn't get to know him, then I wouldn't have to like him. I opened my Kindle and started reading, not wanting to think about it.

I must have fallen asleep at some point because I awoke to a woman's scream. *Juliana.* I bolted upright. The lamp was still on, and the bedside clock indicated it was nearly two in the morning. I stilled, wondering if I'd imagined it, but then I heard it again.

I threw open my door and sprinted across the hall, knocking on her door. "Juliana?"

No answer, but then sounds of a struggle. A moan.

"Juliana!" I called out again. "I'm coming in."

I backed up a little then rammed my shoulder into the door. It flew open, light from the hallway streaming into the room. I glanced around, looking for signs of an intruder, but there were none. The window remained closed, and nothing was out of place save for the bedsheets, which were twisted in a mass around Juliana. I stepped closer, the door shutting behind me.

"Juliana," I called, not wanting to startle her. But considering her distress—and the fact that she didn't respond, not even after I'd barged in—I assumed she was in a very deep sleep.

Her eyes were closed, but she kept mumbling something, throwing her head from side to side. The sheets were wound about her, providing me with tantalizing glimpses of bare skin. The top of her thigh. A sliver of her flat stomach. She was breathtaking. I switched on the bedside lamp, not wanting her to mistake me for an intruder in the dark.

"Juliana. Hey." I shook her gently. "Juliana. Wake up."

CHAPTER FIFTEEN

Juliana

ater swirling. Pulling. Drowning.

I couldn't breathe.

"Juliana." Harrison's voice called as if from a distance. "Juliana." He shook me. "Wake up."

My eyes popped open, and I jolted upright.

"It's okay." He placed a hand on my back. His touch was calming, and it grounded me. "You're safe."

My breath came in short pants. And I didn't realize I was crying until he wiped the tears from my cheeks.

"Hey." He lifted my chin to meet his gaze. "You're okay. It was just a bad dream."

I shook my head and scooted back. I wrapped my arms around myself, keeping my eyes focused on the shadows the moon cast on the floor across the room.

"How—" I swallowed, glancing toward the closed door. "How did you get in here?"

"I heard you crying out, so I broke through the door. Must have been some dream."

I shook my head. "It wasn't."

"Wasn't what?" He tilted his head to the side.

I swallowed. "It wasn't just a bad dream."

I shivered, ignoring the concerned look in Harrison's eyes. My brain was so…confused. As was my heart. The more time I spent with Harrison, the more I liked him. But I lacked closure. How could I move forward with Harrison—or any other man—when I still didn't know what had happened to Ryan?

In all likelihood, I would never know.

Even though his family and I had done everything to find him, it was difficult to accept the truth. Difficult to accept that he was gone. And as much as I told myself that I needed to move forward, to be thankful I was alive, sometimes I just wondered…why him and not me?

Harrison rubbed his hand up and down my back, the warmth of his skin seeping into me. "Do you want to talk about it?" he finally asked.

I swallowed back tears, meeting his emerald eyes, which were calm. Nothing like the turbulent storm raging in my heart.

"You don't have to," he added. "But I've been told I'm a really good listener." He leaned in, butting my shoulder with his. "I've also been told I'm a really good kisser. You know—" he smirked, and I rolled my eyes "—in case you need a distraction."

I laughed, feeling a little lighter. He could drive me crazy, but he always knew how to make me smile.

"Are you trying to take advantage of me when I'm in a vulnerable state?"

"Vulnerable?" He scoffed. "I'm the one who's vulnerable. How can you expect me to control myself when you're wearing—well, that?" He pointed at me.

I followed his gaze as it scanned my body. The thin camisole that clung to my breasts. My peaked nipples, begging for attention. The matching silky boy shorts.

"You're one to talk." I crossed my arms over my chest, which only drew his attention there. "Mr. 'I strut around in boxer briefs with my fabulous abs and fantastic chest.'"

He chuckled, his eyes sparkling in the darkness. "Oh, you noticed that, did you?"

"Kind of hard not to."

"So, tell me about this dream…"

I blew out a breath. Was I really going to do this? And where did I even start? I wasn't sure I'd ever told anyone the story, except for Harper.

"Two years ago," I began, my voice shaky. "Ryan and I were on vacation in Thailand. It was the trip of a lifetime. Paradise." I could just imagine his gorgeous smile, the feeling of his hand in mine. "He had just proposed, and we were taking one last walk on the beach before heading to the airport and home."

Harrison took my hand in his, swiping his thumb back and forth over my skin.

"The tide was low, really low. But there had been a full moon, and no one seemed alarmed. I only learned later that can be a sign of an impending tsunami."

"Oh shit," he said under his breath.

"Yeah." I laughed, though the sound was devoid of humor. "Oh shit is right. The next thing I knew, people were running inland. And when I turned toward the ocean, I understood why."

I closed my eyes, overwhelmed by the onslaught of memories. It didn't matter how much time had passed; I'd never forget that day. Harrison gave my hand a gentle squeeze, grounding me in the present. But nothing could erase the past.

"Ryan and I started running, but we were sucked under by a wave that towered over buildings. I tried to reach out for him, hold on to him, but it was complete and utter chaos. I was swept under the water, something pressing on my lungs. I couldn't breathe. Couldn't think. Every time I tried to crawl toward the surface, it was only to be pushed back down. It was…hopeless."

I remembered thinking I was going to die. Debris drifted around me, polluting the water, making it toxic. But I let go. Let go of everything, accepting my fate. And then, there was a shift. I was weightless, lighter than air. The universe bounced around and through me in the wake of my surrender.

"By some miracle, I was pushed above the surface. The world I saw seemed familiar yet strange. The water was being sucked back into the ocean, dragging everything with it, including me. People were screaming—shouting for loved ones or pleading for help."

He sucked in a sharp breath, but I focused on the comforter as if it were a lifeline. I remembered reaching for a palm tree as I drifted past, only to miss. I passed another one, and that time, I grabbed hold, clutching the trunk. All I could do was wait and hope.

"I survived by clinging to a palm tree for hours. I called out for Ryan until my voice grew hoarse. I didn't know where he was or if he was alive. But he was a strong swimmer. Surely, he'd survived—he had to."

At least that's what I'd told myself as I clutched the tree for hours, my body racked with pain. That's what I'd told myself when the paramedics arrived and took me to the hospital. And that's what I'd told myself weeks later when I was finally discharged from the hospital, doing my best to repair the damage to my body as well as my heart.

"It's been over two years, and there's still been no sign of him." I hung my head, unable to stem the tears.

Harrison pulled me into his arms, holding me close, giving me strength. He sat with me, giving himself for as long as I needed. And when my sobs finally quieted to hiccups, I felt a sense of calm I hadn't before. As awful as reliving the memory was, telling someone was cathartic.

"I'm so sorry," he said. "I'm sorry for your loss. And I'm sorry you had to endure something so horrific."

"Thank you." I wiped away my tears. So many people had uttered similar sentiments in the wake of the tsunami. But for the first time, I felt like Harrison actually understood— that he connected with me on a deeper level.

"And you're a wedding planner? Shit." He wiped a hand over his mouth. "I already suspected you were a bit of a masochist for dealing with bridezillas, but now…" He shook his head. "How the hell do you plan weddings after…" He trailed off, and we both knew the words he couldn't bring himself to say.

After losing the man you were supposed to marry.

I lifted a shoulder. "It's my passion. And celebrating life's biggest moments became even more important to me in the wake of his…loss," I said, still unable to say "death."

"It might seem silly or trivial, but it's important to celebrate the good," I said. "To be grateful for every moment because you never know what will happen."

He nodded, and a look flashed through his eyes that I couldn't quite decipher. An owl hooted in the distance, the quiet peace of the country blanketing the room. I wanted to push my bad dream aside and soak in the tranquil environment, but spending time with Harrison was bringing so many feelings to the surface. Feelings I wasn't prepared for. Some I hadn't even realized I had.

"You…" He peered into my eyes with a look of such admiration, of reverence, it stole the breath from my lungs. "You are an incredible woman, and I'm honored to know you. Thank you for sharing your story with me."

"You know," I said, needing to lighten the moment. "You are a good listener."

"And a good kisser." He gave me a mischievous grin. "Don't forget that."

I couldn't have, even if I'd wanted to. The memory of our kiss—our night together—was seared into my brain. His lips on mine, his hands canvassing my skin. I was hit with a pang of desire.

"I'm good at other things too," he said, bringing me back to the present.

I gave him a playful shove, and he fell off the bed with a grunt. I laughed, but when he didn't immediately get up, I leaned over to check on him.

"Are you okay?" I asked, noting his pinched expression.

Before I realized what was happening, he tugged my hand. I gasped, tumbling from the bed and into his arms. He tickled me, and I batted away his hands, even as I laughed and squirmed.

"Stop," I cried out, though I really didn't want him to. Especially not when he pulled me on top of him, my legs bracketing his waist. His hard-on seeking me out, nudging my center through the silk of my shorts. Making me even wetter.

"Harrison." I was breathless with laughter, and I couldn't remember the last time I'd laughed so hard.

I leaned forward, my blond waves cascading over his face. With one hand still firmly planted on my waist, he lifted the other to tuck a strand of hair behind my ear. In that moment, everything stilled. My heart slowed, my stomach bottoming out. He curled his hand around the back of my neck, applying gentle pressure to pull me toward him. He hadn't needed to—I was drawn toward him like a magnet, unable to resist the allure.

Our foreheads kissed, our noses brushing against each

other, his breath fanning over my skin. Apart from that night at the wedding expo, this was the closest I'd been to a man in years. And this time, there was no alcohol clouding my judgment. No excuses. Nothing to blame my actions on, other than raw desire.

Just when I thought he was going to close the distance and press his lips to mine, he groaned. "I really want to kiss you."

My body screamed that it was ready, but I was emotionally drained after my nightmare and then the retelling. The memory and Ryan weighed heavily on my mind. And the idea of kissing Harrison while thinking about Ryan didn't seem fair to either of them.

"But I won't." Harrison's voice was gravelly, eyes dark with need. "Not yet."

I nodded, resting my head on his chest, listening to the steady beat of his heart. I wasn't sure whether I was relieved or disappointed. A bit of both, I supposed. But I also wasn't ready for him to leave.

"Stay with me?" I whispered.

"I don't know if that's a good idea." His erection dug into me as if to prove his point.

I lifted my head, peering into his eyes. "Please? I don't want to be alone."

"Just to sleep."

I nodded, and he let out a heavy sigh, a muscle twitching in his jaw. "One day, you'll be ready for more than just sleep. And when that day comes—" He gripped my hips tighter, shifting so I could feel his hard length. I gasped, clutching his shoulders, the feel of my nipples brushing against the silk negligee so erotic. I'd forgotten what it was like to be intimate with someone, to feel their skin against mine. Their heart beating in time to mine.

"When that day comes...?" I breathed, reveling in his closeness, his scent.

"When that day comes..." he rasped, "there will be no turning back. You *will* be mine."

His words, the hooded look in his eyes, his touch—everything made me realize just how much I wanted to be his. How badly I wanted to move forward—with him. And despite my hesitation, despite my fears, I wanted to take that next step.

He went over to the door and opened it, glancing out into the hall.

"What are you doing?" I asked, afraid he'd changed his mind.

"Just making sure my door's closed." He crouched down to inspect my door. "And the lock's broken on your door. I'll sort it out in the morning."

"Oh." He was so incredibly thoughtful, always watching out for me.

He dragged one of the armchairs over to the door, and I watched in awe at his strength. Then we climbed between the sheets, and he turned out the light. I stared at the ceiling, lying as still as possible. When I'd begged him to stay, I hadn't really considered the consequences. What it would be like to lie in bed next to this man. What it would feel like to have heat radiating off him, while knowing I needed to keep my hands to myself.

"Do you believe in a higher power?" I asked.

He shifted, the sheets rustling beneath him. "I don't know. But I do believe that everything happens for a reason."

"Really?" I turned to face him, both of us lying on our sides.

"If I didn't—" he smoothed his thumb over my cheek "—I might not be here with you. And that's an outcome I'd rather not imagine."

I melted beneath his touch, softened at his words. He was incredibly compassionate, and he never made me feel bad about my emotions. And he was right. I could dwell on all that I'd lost, or I could focus on what I'd gained. The past was filled with pain, regret. But I couldn't say I regretted this weekend with Harrison. Or this intimate moment we shared.

"I'm glad I'm here with you too."

His hand was whisper-soft on my cheek. "Go to sleep, Jules."

My eyes fluttered closed, my muscles relaxing at that simple command. At his use of the nickname only those closest to me used. Somehow, Harrison always seemed to know just what I needed. And having him here with me, watching over me, helped me relax. I drifted off to sleep with a smile on my lips, at peace for the first time in months.

CHAPTER SIXTEEN

Harrison

The scent of jasmine filled my nose, and I smiled with my eyes still closed. *Juliana.*

Our legs were intertwined, her body pressed to mine, my arms wrapped around her as if to prevent her escape. I exhaled through my nose, not wanting to blast her with my morning breath. I snuck a glance. Her eyes were still closed, lips parted in sleep. She was so beautiful. So strong.

Last night, she'd bared herself to me, sharing her innermost secrets and fears. Revealing the tragedies of her past. I finally understood what had happened with Ryan, and I hated that she'd gone through something so horrific. She was too young, too kind, to have experienced such a traumatic event.

I knew I should move, should release her, but I couldn't bring myself to do it. I told myself it was because I didn't want to wake her, but I knew that wasn't entirely true. I didn't want this to end. I wanted to bask a little longer in the fantasy that this was real, and she was mine.

I hadn't meant to say that last night. But when the words left my mouth, I knew they rang true. Because despite what

I'd told Reg at Olivia's engagement party, this thing between us—whatever it was—wasn't "nothing." I could feel it in the way Juliana looked at me, in her smile. And I knew, deep down, there was a reason our paths had crossed when they had. At least, I wanted to believe that was true.

I admired the slope of her cheek, the golden color of her hair. Those pillow-soft lips. My fingers ached to reach out and touch her, but I didn't want to move for fear of waking her and ruining the moment.

She was… God, she was enchanting, and I was completely captivated by her. And it wasn't just her body. She embodied all the characteristics I'd tried to instill in my daughter. Juliana was kind and smart, caring. Above all else, she was resilient. She had a mental toughness that many of my former teammates would've killed for. And though she'd been through her fair share of heartache, she remained optimistic and hopeful.

After what she'd told me, I couldn't blame her for being unable to move on. She'd been stuck in limbo for two years. *Until me.* That was the part that stood out in my mind. The fact that I was the first man she'd slept with since Ryan. That had to mean something, right?

"You're staring," she said, finally opening her eyes. The blue color was clear, like a perfect, cloudless sky. She looked surprisingly rested considering the events of the past twenty-four hours.

"Hey." The corner of my mouth tilted into a grin. "How are you feeling?"

She blinked a few times as if to clear the sleep from her eyes. "Pretty good, all things considered. Thanks for staying."

I released her, forcing myself to put some space between us. Last night, I'd wanted to kiss her—badly. I'd wanted more than that. And the need had only intensified after spending the night in bed together.

"I should—" I rolled away, shifting myself in a futile attempt to hide my hard-on. There was no way she could ignore the steel rod poking her thigh. "I should go before I do something stupid."

"Wait." She placed a hand on my arm, and I closed my eyes, trying to ignore the effect such a simple touch had on me. "I—" She swallowed. "Please stay," she said, echoing her plea from the night before.

I took a deep breath, plagued by conflicting thoughts. I wanted her. I wanted to heal her, to save her from any pain. But I couldn't. And I'd never settle for being a consolation prize.

"I don't think that's a good idea," I said, repeating my words from the night before. But this time, I meant them. I wouldn't sleep with her until she was ready, until I knew her heart belonged to me.

I shook my head, taken aback by the idea that I wanted her heart. But the more I thought about it, I realized it was true. I didn't want just her body; I wanted everything. This weekend—last night—had clarified my feelings for Juliana. This was definitely more than a fling, and I was coming to realize just how much she already owned my heart.

"Because you're my client?"

I chuckled, turning to face her. It was a mistake. I was weak in the face of this woman. "No. Because being here—with you—and not being able to touch you, to have you, the way I want is torture."

She blinked owlishly up at me, and I would've laughed if it weren't taking everything in me not to join her in bed. Not to strip her naked and make her scream my name.

"And I don't think you're ready for that," I said.

She tilted her head to the side, an innocent expression on her face. Her skin was devoid of makeup, and she was hands down the most gorgeous woman I'd ever seen.

"What?" she asked.

"You're beautiful," I blurted. I was tired of fighting my feelings for this woman.

The corner of her mouth lifted. She parted her lips to say something, but I placed a finger to them, silencing her.

"Don't." I shook my head. "I don't want to be someone you use to run away. I want to be the man you run to. Do you understand?"

She nodded, and though I should've lowered my hand, I caressed her bottom lip with my thumb. She opened her mouth, inviting me inside. She sucked my digit between her lips, and I was entranced by the way she made it disappear. Her mouth was warm and wet, enveloping my skin and making my head spin.

"Juliana," I growled in warning. "What are you doing to me?"

She swirled her tongue around my thumb, just like I wanted her to do to my cock. Any remaining blood in my head rushed to my groin.

"Fuck," I groaned then shook my head. No, not fuck. We needed to talk.

"Harrison." Her eyes were dark, liquid need. She pushed up on her knees. "I'm ready."

Her words gave me hope.

"And I'm finally doing what you asked." She reached for the hem of her camisole, pulling it over her head. "I'm letting go." She dropped it on the floor before shimmying out of the matching shorts.

My brain short-circuited as I drank in her naked form. She was just as stunning as I remembered, and I couldn't stop myself from scanning her head to toe. The dusky, pert nipples, the curve of her hips, that thatch of hair at the juncture of her thighs. And those legs—damn.

"Fuck me." I bit my fist, my eyes glued to her luscious tits, begging me to touch them.

I was used to being in control. But right now, this woman was stripping me of all my power.

She grinned as if she knew what she was doing to me. My cock strained against my boxer briefs, aching for release. This was such a bad idea. This was… *Ah. Fuck it.* I stripped out of my boxers, grabbing Juliana and tossing her on the bed. She claimed she was ready. Who was I to disagree?

"Hi." She giggled, peering up at me. Some of her earlier bravado seemed to have faded, and I found her sudden shyness incredibly endearing.

"Hi." I hovered over her, electricity arcing between our naked bodies. Until my dick jerked, pressing between her legs, seeking entrance.

"Harrison," she rasped, arching her back so her hips met mine. No turning back now.

"Yes…" I swiveled my hips, taunting us both.

"What are you waiting for?"

I ground against her, dry humping her like a horny teenager. But that's how she made me feel—insatiable. She closed her eyes on a sigh, and I froze.

"Don't stop." She pouted, finally opening her eyes, blinking those bright baby blues up at me. "Why'd you stop?"

My chest squeezed at an unwanted memory, and I did my best to push it away. Juliana wasn't Cam. But the more I told myself that, the more my vision blurred. This was why I'd avoided intimacy. Because when you let someone in, when you opened your heart—you were likely to get burned.

"Harrison?" Juliana's tone was rife with concern.

I rolled to the side, draping my arm over my forehead.

"What's wrong? Oh my god." She held her fingers to my neck, taking my pulse. "Are you having a heart attack?"

"What?" I jerked my attention to her. "No. Cam cheated on me."

Nothing like talking about your ex to kill the mood. I dragged a hand through my hair and stared at the ceiling. Juliana propped herself up on her elbow. I hadn't meant to confess that, but now that I had, I owed her an explanation.

"We were both…busy with our careers, traveling, raising a child. She…" I swallowed. "At one point, she got pregnant again. I was overjoyed, but she wasn't as enthusiastic."

Juliana linked her fingers with mine, silently giving me her support. I continued to stare at the ceiling, unable to meet her eyes.

"Cam lost the baby, and I blamed her. I was drowning in grief. And even though I knew it wasn't her fault, I…pushed her away. I pushed her into the arms of another man." I squeezed my eyes shut, remembering it all so vividly. The pain of the loss never faded, but sometimes it was more pronounced than others.

"I'm so sorry, Harrison."

My chest ached. I fucking hated talking about this. But for some reason, I felt compelled to share with Juliana. Maybe it was because she'd opened up to me. Maybe it was because I wanted her to realize everyone had their struggles. Whatever the reason, I knew I could trust her.

"Which is why—" I turned to face her, sucking in a deep breath. "Which is why I want you to look at me, to see me."

She nodded, her expression thoughtful.

"And while I know what you and I are doing isn't wrong," I said, needing to get it all out in the open. I wasn't going to move forward without addressing the elephant—or the ghost —in the room. "I can understand why you'd have mixed feelings."

"Harrison," she sighed, and I tried to ignore the warmth

of her body, the fact that she was naked. Lying next to me, her tits pressed against my arm.

Fuck me. If we didn't have sex after this, I was certain my balls were going to fall off.

She trailed her finger along my collarbone, down my chest, and I squeezed my fists to resist touching her.

"What are you doing, Juliana?" I clenched my jaw, closing my eyes briefly as she continued to tease me.

"I want to move forward. I want to take the next step..." she said on a shaky exhale. "With you."

That was all the confirmation I needed. I pulled her into my arms, crashing my lips against hers. She tasted as sweet as I remembered, though there was a hint of saltiness too. She was delicious, addictive, and I couldn't get enough of her.

I caressed her back, her ass, pulling her into me. My skin was on fire everywhere she touched, my body coming alive in a way it hadn't with anyone else. I was already so close, and I needed to be inside her.

"You feel amazing," Juliana said as I slid my cock between her legs.

"So do you," I murmured between kisses. I was light-headed as I kissed my way down her neck, brushing my lips over her collarbone. "I need you."

She tilted her head back, moaning. The walls weren't soundproof, but I didn't care who heard us. I wasn't usually this reckless, and I blamed it on the gorgeous creature cradled in my arms.

"I need you. I need this." Her eyes were intent on mine, her determination unwavering. "I want to be with you and only you."

I slid my hand down her stomach, gliding easily over her clit. She was ready, and I wasn't sure how much longer I could hold out. It seemed like an eternity since we'd last been together. Weeks of dancing around our attraction.

Months of pent-up desire that was finally allowed to burst free.

She arched her back as I teased her center, sliding inside her channel with one finger, then another. I curled my fingers, capturing her moan with my mouth. She was writhing beneath my touch, and I couldn't wait to be inside her.

"Fuck. So sexy," I said as I watched her unravel. When she came, it was fast and hard, and I milked every ounce of pleasure from her.

I pressed my lips to hers, gratified when she uttered my name like a plea. "Harrison."

That one word set my heart and mind at ease. Unlike the last time we'd been together, I knew that she was here—with me.

"Yes?"

She swallowed, her eyes taking everything in. My chest puffed with pride, knowing she liked what she saw. "You're stunning."

I grinned, pleased by her compliment. "I could say the same."

I fisted my cock, ready to plunge inside her, when it hit me. "Shit. I don't have a condom."

We stilled at the realization. Fuck. How could I have been so unprepared?

"I'm clean, and I have an IUD. More than anything, though, I trust you." Her eyes were filled with sincerity and desire.

I swallowed hard. The idea of being with her, with no barriers, was so incredibly tempting. "So am I, but are you sure?"

"I've been stuck in the past for far too long. And while I don't know what will happen in the future, I know that I want to move forward—with you."

I kissed away her confession and my fears, gobbling up her words as if they'd protect us. Protect my heart.

"Thank fuck." I gathered her to me, my cock brushing against her, seeking entrance. "You don't need to consult a spreadsheet first?" I teased, kissing my way down her neck, teasing her nipples with my breath, then my tongue.

"I think..." Her breath hitched, chest rising as she attempted to push her nipple into my mouth. "I think I have all the data I need."

I grinned to myself, determined to leave no doubt in her mind. My lips closed around her, sucking, biting, and flicking the rosy bud with my tongue.

"I'm glad to hear it." I rolled so she was on top, the sound of her throaty laugh going straight to my cock. I brushed her hair away from her face, drowning in her eyes.

She lowered herself onto me, and it took everything in me not to come right then. Her scent, her breasts bouncing—it was... I swallowed. *Holy fuck.* And her pussy. It had been so long since I'd had sex without a condom. And Juliana was warm and wet, drawing me in deep with every pulse.

She placed her hands on my cheeks, leaning down to kiss me. "Harrison."

"Yes," I sighed. Every time she said my name, it felt like a victory. It felt like she was finally letting her walls down, letting me in. She couldn't guarantee she was over Ryan, but it was enough for now that she was trying.

I was frantic with need for her, touching, kissing her everywhere I could reach. I shifted, sitting with my back against the headboard so our chests brushed against each other. My need for this woman was overpowering. I'd never clicked with anyone like this, never had this deep and intense connection. With every thrust, every kiss, I came closer to release. And I sensed she was close too if the way she clutched the headboard was any indication.

"Let go," I whispered into her ear, repeating my words from our first night together.

Her smile had me grinning in return. And she pressed her lips to mine at the same moment she found her release. Her walls clenched around me as she cried out, and I quickened my pace, a shiver racing through my entire body.

"Yes," I hissed, exploding inside her a moment later.

Finally, spent, she slumped against me. "Wow."

"Yeah." My heart was still racing and not just from the sex.

I was falling for her.

I'd told myself to take things slow, to give her time. I couldn't change the past. But I could help her focus on the future—on a future with me.

CHAPTER SEVENTEEN

Juliana

I tugged on my hair, my eyes darting around the closet. Clothing was piled up around me like a fortress, but I felt more like a damsel in distress than the queen of the castle. After returning from my weekend in Ojai with Harrison, I was more determined than ever to move forward with selling my house. I'd slowly been cleaning it out, preparing it to list. But I finally felt ready to tackle Ryan's side of the closet.

Because of Harrison. He gave me the courage to take that next step, to prove to him—and more importantly, to myself—that I was ready to embrace our relationship. Even if we were keeping it a secret from Olivia for the time being.

"Hello?" Alexis called. "Anyone home?"

Was it already four? A quick glance at my phone confirmed that it was, indeed, four. Where had the day gone?

"Up here," I said, pushing off my knees to stand.

Harper had always had a spare key to my house. But after the tsunami, I'd given Alexis and Lauren ones as well. I was used to the three of them letting themselves in, though they usually only did so when invited.

Alexis appeared in the doorway to the closet but frowned when she saw the mess that I'd made. *Or maybe the mess that I was,* I thought as I caught sight of myself in the mirror. My hair was knotted on top of my head, a scarf holding it back. I was wearing workout gear, and I hadn't showered or done my makeup. Still, I knew Alexis would never judge me.

"Thanks for coming over." I dusted off my hands. "Let's —" I lunged to step over one of the piles of clothing and nearly tripped. "Get out of here."

She held out her hand, and I accepted it, practically leaping toward freedom.

"So, what's up?" she asked when we made it to the kitchen. "I know you're a fanatic about spring cleaning, but this seems extreme even for you."

I grabbed some supplies for mojitos and started mixing them as I tried to gather the courage to speak. "I want to sell the house." Even though sweat beaded along my forehead and my heart was racing, I knew it was the right decision.

Her brows inched toward her forehead. She blinked a few times, then asked, "You're sure?"

"I need... a change."

She nodded. "Do you know where you want to move?"

I honestly hadn't gotten that far. And now that she'd asked, I felt a bit foolish.

"I was hoping you could help me with that, but it's not a priority. Harper has an extended trip coming up, and she offered to let me stay at her place for as long as I need."

She sipped her mojito, expression unreadable, and I wondered what she was thinking. Alexis was honest but tactful, diplomatic. It was part of what made her such a good mom and real estate agent.

"Okay, but are you sure you're ready to list?" She brushed her hair away from her face. "You've always been adamant about staying here."

I understood her concern, and it touched me that she cared. For two years, I'd stood firm on my decision to stay here. But over the past few months, I'd realized I was holding on to a dream that didn't exist, a life that didn't exist. Spending time with Harrison had only cemented what I already knew—it was time to move on.

"I know." I swallowed. "But I've had a change of heart. And Lindsay helped me realize that was okay."

Alexis took my hands in hers. "I'm so glad she's been able to help you."

I'd continued my sessions with Lindsay. She was helping me process my grief over losing Ryan, as well as any guilt I had about my feelings for Harrison. I wished I'd started seeing her years ago.

I nodded. "Living here—" I glanced around the house where I'd spent the past five years, three of them with Ryan "—was wonderful. But…" I blew out a harsh breath. "Honestly?" She nodded. "It's become suffocating, being surrounded by so many memories of Ryan and the life we had."

She squeezed my hands before releasing them. Just because I was ready to move forward didn't mean it was easy. "Do you want to consider a redesign instead?"

I shook my head, struggling to imagine the place any other way. It would always be Ryan's and my home. "No. I need a fresh start."

"What are you going to do with his things?"

"His parents don't have the space for much, so most either has to go in storage or be donated."

"Are you okay with that?"

I lifted a shoulder, the bands around my chest tightening at the idea of saying goodbye to my few remaining links to him. I knew it was just "stuff," but it had been his stuff. "I'm trying to be."

She leaned forward, resting her arms on the counter. "I'm here to help, so put me to work!"

I laughed. "I invited you over because I miss you. But I'd also hoped you'd be willing to list it for me."

"Of course. So...let's do a walk-through, discuss what needs to be edited. And then we can get to work on some of Ryan's stuff."

"Alexis...I..." I didn't know what to say, so I settled for, "Thank you."

"Let me just text Preston, and then we can get to work." She smiled.

"You sure he won't mind?"

She dug in her purse for her phone. "Not at all. He's been encouraging me to spend more time with my friends now that Blair's sleeping better at night."

"I'm so glad." My shoulders relaxed.

Just talking to Alexis about her family made me feel more at ease. I loved hearing about Sophia's adventures and what baby Blair was learning and doing. Though, she wasn't that much of a baby anymore. She was one now, and she was walking and babbling—such a happy little girl.

"I can't believe she's one," Alexis said, echoing my thoughts. "*One.*"

"Where does the time go?" I asked, thinking as much about her girls' lives as my own.

Two years had passed—at times, both fast and slow. Waiting to hear news of Ryan was agonizing, but during that time, my business had taken off. My clients, their events, had become my life.

Which was part of the problem. I had been so focused on my business, I hadn't given myself any time to grieve and find myself again. But Harrison was helping with that, helping me realize that it was okay to respect the past while embracing the present.

"I don't know," she sighed. "My babies are growing up way too fast. The other day, Sophia came home and started baking cookies by herself."

"That sounds pretty awesome." I grinned, loving her daughter's ambition. Sophia was sassy, smart, and so self-assured.

"It would be—if she hadn't been making them for her boyfriend." She cringed.

I laughed. "Oh my. I don't envy you that. How did Preston take it?" I asked, knowing how protective her husband could be of his girls.

She laughed. "His eyes nearly bugged out of his head. But he handled it calmly. And after she told him why she liked the boy and what it meant to be boyfriend/girlfriend, he helped her make the cookies."

I smiled, thinking of sweet Preston baking cookies with Sophia. "He's such a good dad."

Alexis smiled. Before I could ask what it meant to be someone's girlfriend at the age of eight, she clapped her hands together. "Let's do this!"

I flashed her a bright smile and clapped my hands together, mimicking her. "I'm so excited!"

Her brows pulled together. "I'm not sure if you're being serious or sarcastic."

I laughed. "More like, trying to psych myself up for the task. I once read an article that if you were dreading something, you should smile and say, 'I'm so excited,' even if you aren't. Try to trick yourself."

She laughed. "How's that working out for you?"

"Enh." I lifted a shoulder. "Not so well."

She wrapped an arm around my shoulder, pulling me in for a hug. "I'm proud of you, Jules. I'm sure this isn't easy. And not to compare in any way, but after I divorced Cal, moving out was hard. Necessary and a long time coming, but still hard."

I nodded, appreciating her encouragement. "I was so proud of you for standing up for yourself. For doing what was best for you and Sophia."

The corner of her mouth lifted, and the sadness that used to lurk in her eyes was no longer there. "Me too. And now it's your turn."

I glanced around, finally admitting that I was ready. I wanted to move forward. I wanted to reclaim my life and my happiness. And while I wasn't naïve enough to think that selling my house and moving would solve all my problems, I knew it was a huge step in the right direction.

"Let's start at the front," Alexis said, interrupting my thoughts.

I followed her to the front door. She walked outside, down to the curb. She tilted her head as she assessed the exterior, and I waited anxiously to hear what she had to say.

"Front looks great. Maybe a fresh window cleaning and some pots by the door."

I made notes on my phone. So far, not too bad. But it wasn't the curb appeal that concerned me; it was the work that needed to be done on the inside. Because the exterior was gorgeous and inviting, but the inside was a wreck. Not that it was disorganized—more that I had a lot of emotional baggage to shed if I was going to leave this home. But I finally felt like I was up to the challenge.

We passed through the family room, and she paused by the windows overlooking the backyard. "This is a huge selling point. A tranquil oasis in the big city."

Ryan and I had spent hours and poured a lot of sweat and money into the fountain, white lights, and patio. I'd dreamed of having our wedding here, surrounded by our closest family and friends. I let out a heavy sigh, thinking of how that would never happen. This backyard that had held so many hopes and dreams. But there would be no wedding, no lazy Sundays spent lounging on the outdoor bed, no children running across the grass barefoot. At least, not for me.

Alexis turned to me. "You okay?"

I nodded, not wanting to discuss it. If I stopped to consider what I was doing, what I'd be leaving behind, there was a very real possibility I'd chicken out. And while the idea of selling my home with Ryan made me slightly nauseous, it also gave me a sense of freedom. For the first time in a long time, I felt empowered—like I was taking back control over my life.

"What else?" I asked.

I had to keep moving forward. It had become my mantra since the new year—keep moving forward. I'd taken down all my sticky notes and started over. I'd been putting inspirational quotes or mantras on my mirror for so long, I couldn't remember when I'd started the habit—maybe college. But there were just three now. One said, "You are stronger than you think." The other was "Keep moving forward," and I intended to do just that. And the last one was inspired by Harrison. "Control is an illusion."

"You'll want to remove any valuables, as well as any personal items and minimize the number of framed photographs."

I glanced toward the fireplace where pictures lined the mantel. Ryan and me on his thirty-fifth birthday. The two of us in Hawaii. So many incredible memories.

"People want to imagine themselves living here," Alexis said. "They don't want to think about someone else's toenail clippings in the carpet."

"Ew." I cringed, turning away from the photographs. "That's disgusting."

She smirked. "Just telling it like it is."

I laughed, feeling a bit lighter. "Do you think we should have Lauren stage it?"

She leaned her hip against the couch. "Might not be a bad idea. Lauren has a great eye and knows what buyers want."

I nodded. "Agreed."

She glanced around. "I'm guessing it wouldn't take much—mostly a few decorative items."

"Great. What else?" I asked, feeling more excited about the prospect now that we were working on a task list.

I'd always loved a good to-do list. And maybe by the time I'd completed the items on it, my heart would be more aligned with my head. If nothing else, it was a good distraction from the reality of what I was doing.

We continued through the kitchen and dining area, then on to the bedrooms. Finally, we returned to where we'd started—the master closet.

"So…" Alexis said. "You want some help going through his clothes?"

I lifted a shoulder. "It's nice of you to offer, but it's getting late. I'm sure you have better things to do with your time."

"Are you saying that because you think you should? Or because you're trying to tell me you want me to leave without coming out and saying it?" Leave it to Alexis to ask.

I considered it a moment. "A little of both, I guess."

"If you want to be alone, just say so. But I'm more than happy to help."

When I hesitated, Alexis made the decision for me. "Come on." She hooked her arm through mine. "I can just sit and keep you company. And if you want my help, I'm here."

I nodded, crossing the threshold into the disaster zone. Clothes were everywhere, and the piles alone made me anxious. But the idea of actually going through them was even more daunting.

We sat on the floor and started sorting through everything. We devised a system, and the time passed quickly. The first few items had been easy enough; they didn't hold much sentimental value. But when I got to the next stack, it was a different story. The shirt he was wearing when we met, his soft baseball T-shirt I loved wearing to bed. A single tear slid down my cheek as the memories washed over me. And when I held the garment to my nose, inhaling deeply, I couldn't find any traces of his scent.

I set those in the keep pile, grateful when Alexis didn't comment. I picked up another one and started to place it in the keep pile when Alexis laughed.

"Seriously—his Hawaiian shirt? I thought you despised that thing. I believe you once said you'd burn it if you could."

I laughed, remembering it all too well. The luau-themed party, and his shirt that had become a running joke.

"Girl, you need to let that one go. To the bonfire," she teased.

"I know. You're right. That's what Harrison's always telling me. To let go." I bit my lip, only realizing my mistake too late.

"So, this whole house-selling thing…" she hedged.

"Yeah?"

"It doesn't have anything to do with Harrison, does it?"

"Harrison?" My voice came out high-pitched and airy.

Just saying his name sent my pulse skittering. After our weekend in Ojai, something had shifted. And it wasn't just because we'd had sex again. We'd finally opened up to each other, baring our souls as we connected over the tragedies of our pasts.

My girlfriends knew about him—knew I was now planning the wedding for the daughter of my one-night stand. But I hadn't told them about our weekend in Ojai. And I didn't want Alexis to think my decision to sell the house was influenced by him.

"Yes. The silver fox father of the bride you seem to be spending a lot of time with lately." She arched an eyebrow.

"I-I'm helping him plan his daughter's wedding." I stumbled over the lie.

"You know, if that wasn't all you were doing, that would be okay too."

"Alexis," I gasped, holding a hand to my chest. "Are you *encouraging* me to mix business with pleasure?" I teased.

Ever since she'd started publicly dating Preston, it had become a sort of inside joke. She'd always been so opposed to mixing business with pleasure, and then she'd fallen for her daughter's nanny.

She laughed and tossed a shirt at me. "Whatever. My situation with Preston was different, and you know it."

"How?" I folded the shirt. "You're a single parent, and so is Harrison. You both hired someone younger to do a job."

"First of all, Harrison may be a single dad, but his daughter is getting *married*. While her opinion factors into the equation, it's different from my situation. Also…you slept with him before he ever hired you. Not that it really matters."

"I might have slept with him again." I squeezed my eyes shut, bracing for her reaction.

"I knew it!" She flashed me a big grin, a smug one. "So… was it as good as the first time?"

I blushed, thinking back on last weekend and the way he'd made love to me. We'd spent Sunday morning in bed, having sex, ordering room service, and nearly missing our check-out time. "It was amazing."

She grasped my hands. "I'm so happy for you, Jules—so *proud* of you."

"Thanks." I dipped my head, feeling as if her praise was unwarranted.

She took my hand in hers. "I'm sure it isn't easy. I get it—

sort of. Just...don't blow what you have with Harrison because you're scared."

I nodded. "Thanks. But...it's hard, you know? Moving on after being so invested in someone else."

"I get it." She folded a shirt and placed it in the donate pile. "It was hard to trust after Cal. And I was so scared of what I had with Preston that I almost lost him."

The trouble was, I was fearful. I'd already lost one man I loved, and I was falling for Harrison. He made me happy. He was supportive and caring. Everything he said and did told me this was more than just sex for him. I wanted to love him, but that meant putting my heart on the line again. And it scared the hell out of me.

CHAPTER EIGHTEEN

Harrison

"So…" Reg said, leaning against the bar. The lights of the skyline reflected in the aqua pool of the hotel. "How's it going with the wedding planner?"

Reg had wanted to get drinks. And since Juliana had asked me to meet her here after work, I figured I could kill two birds with one stone.

"Pretty good," I said. "We've got the menu nailed down, and Olivia seems happy with everything so far."

He tilted his head back to take a sip of his beer. "Not what I meant. But I'm glad the planning is going so well."

I scanned the crowd, eager to evade his questions. Women sauntered around, scantily clad in tiny bikinis, tottering on high heels with their runway-ready hair and makeup. I almost felt overdressed in my jeans and button-down, but I didn't care. The only person I wanted to impress was Juliana. And I'd taken great care to select a shirt I thought she'd like.

I glanced at my watch, knowing it would be another hour until she was done. One of her clients had gotten married here earlier in the day, and I couldn't wait to see her.

Couldn't wait to take her up to the hotel room I'd gotten for the night and undress her. Reg nudged me, and I realized I'd zoned out, envisioning all the ways I wanted to make her come.

"So, what are we doing here? Because this isn't your usual scene."

He was right. I usually preferred something with a more laid-back vibe. Somewhere I was less likely to be recognized. We'd already had one person stop to ask us for a picture, and if the women prowling toward us were any indication, they knew who we were. I let out a deep sigh, turning my back to the crowd, hoping it would be enough to deter them. I wasn't interested in any woman but Juliana.

"I'm meeting up with someone after this."

He arched his brow. "Someone, huh? This 'someone' wouldn't be a certain blonde who also happens to be planning your daughter's wedding, would it?"

I took a sip of my drink. I wasn't giving anything away, but Reg knew me well enough that I didn't have to say anything. A knowing grin spread across his face.

"Not getting involved, my ass." He slapped his knee with a loud chuckle. "Man, you're so fucked."

"Yeah. Yeah." I waved my hand through the air and took another drink.

I didn't want to think about it. Didn't want to think about what might happen if this went south and the shit hit the fan. Regardless of my feelings for Juliana, I was determined to give Olivia the wedding of her dreams.

"So?" He elbowed me. "Are you going to have to change your Facebook status from 'single' to 'in a relationship'?"

I rolled my eyes. "It's—" How did I describe what Juliana and I were doing? We were having sex—amazing sex. And she seemed to be moving forward, but I still had my concerns. "Complicated. She's…" I rubbed the back of my neck. "I like her. A lot."

He frowned. "You make it sound like that's a problem."

"I'm just not sure where her head's at. The sex is—god, it's fucking amazing. But she's still hung up on her fiancé." *There. I'd said it.*

If I didn't talk to someone, I was going to explode. And I sure as shit couldn't bring it up with Juliana.

"Whoa. Hold up a minute." He placed a hand to my chest. "She's engaged?"

I barked out a laugh, though it lacked humor. "Yes." I shook my head. "No. Sort of." I rolled my eyes.

"So that's why you said it was 'complicated'? Shit, man." He swiped a hand down his face. "After what happened with Cam, this was the last thing I'd expect."

"No." My eyes went wide. "Oh god, no. She isn't cheating on him with me. At least—" I tilted my head to the side, considering the circumstances. Trying, like always, to think about how I'd feel in her shoes. In his shoes. My stomach clenched. "He's missing."

Reg gaped at me, while I gave him a quick overview of the situation. "Oh fuck. You weren't joking. Complicated seems like the understatement of the century."

I nodded, taking another sip of my drink. "Yep."

"But you like her." I wasn't sure whether he intended it as a question or a statement. He seemed distracted, likely trying to process it all.

I nodded all the same. I didn't just like Juliana—I was falling for her, but I wasn't going to tell Reg that. I could barely admit it to myself. I was afraid to admit it for fear of losing her.

My phone buzzed, and I pulled it out of my pocket to see a new text message.

. . .

*JULIANA: **WRAPPING UP, BUT IT MIGHT BE A LITTLE LATER THAN I thought.***

*HARRISON: **I'M HERE. ALWAYS.***

I SLID MY PHONE BACK INTO MY POCKET, ONLY TO FIND REG watching me. "Was that her?"

"Yeah. I have to go soon." I polished off the rest of my drink before setting the glass on the counter.

"I'm sure it's nice to get laid after a fifty-year dry spell." He smiled, but it didn't quite reach his eyes.

"Ha-fucking-ha." I rolled my eyes and stood, needing to see her whether she was ready or not.

"Do you think you like her because it feels safe?"

I jerked my head back. "What?"

"Well, she's not going to want marriage, right? Not after what happened."

I shoved my hands deep into my pockets, focusing intently on the ground. "I don't know. I hadn't really thought about it."

"You might want to." He stood and slapped me on the back.

I walked to the elevators, a bit dazed from my conversation with Reg. Was I playing it safe? Did I like Juliana because I assumed she'd never expect more than—well, this?

I frowned and made my way toward the ballroom. My frown deepened to a scowl when I saw Juliana standing across the ballroom with a man in a tuxedo. He had his hand on the wall, preventing her exit. And his body language said he was into her. She was smiling and laughing, and it felt like a punch to the gut—witnessing their intimate conversation.

Mine, my body roared. *Mine. Mine. Mine.*

I watched for a moment longer before I couldn't take it anymore. I stalked over to them, looping my arm around her waist.

"Hey, baby." I pressed my lips to her temple, staking my claim.

I'd never considered myself a possessive person or even a jealous one. Despite what had happened with Cam, I hadn't been jealous when I'd found out she'd cheated on me. It was more of a deep sense of betrayal. But when it came to Juliana, things were different. I was different.

She jolted, relaxing when she realized it was me. "Hey." She smiled, and she looked beautiful but tired.

"Are you—" the douchebag across from me stuttered. "Harrison." He blinked a few times, and I would've laughed had he not just been hitting on my girl. "H-Harrison Hayes?" He swallowed.

I grinned, a predatory one that said this woman was mine. "I am." I turned my attention to Juliana. "You ready?"

She glanced around one last time. "I think so. Trey, it was a pleasure to meet you."

He nodded, still gaping at me. We barely made it down the hall before I was attacking her with my lips, my hands.

"Harrison." She giggled. "What are you doing?"

"Kissing you." I dove back in, kissing her neck as she continued with those breathy sighs that turned to moans. I grabbed her hand, glancing behind us to confirm no one had followed.

"Where are you taking me?"

I tried a door, and it was locked. The second one opened easily. Even though we had a suite upstairs, I couldn't wait. Didn't want to wait.

"Here." I ushered her inside, my hands on her hips as we shuffled through the door. It closed behind us with a snick.

The room was dark, and I could make out various shapes

in the shadows—chairs and tables, other supplies for a big event. It was a storage room, and we were alone.

I slanted my mouth over hers, roaming her body with my hands. I was like a man possessed—intent on branding her. I'd never felt so frenzied. She sighed into my mouth when I cupped her breast, cried out when I pinched her nipple through her bra.

"What on earth has gotten into you?" she teased as I lifted her skirt, dipping beneath her underwear to tease her, touch her.

"You're mine," I growled, sounding feral, possessive.

I didn't know who I was trying harder to convince—her or myself. Because after my conversation with Reg about Ryan, and then seeing her with Trey, I had to know. I needed to know that she was mine. Despite our pasts, despite the fact that we were keeping this a secret, despite everything—She. Was. Mine.

"Yes," she sighed, angling her head back against the wall as I teased her clit.

Her voice seemed louder in the darkness, every sound, every sensation intensified. I could smell her arousal. And when she touched me, I nearly lost it.

She unbuckled my pants, sliding her hand inside to grip me. *Fuck me.* I was going to explode if she kept doing that, her smooth hand gliding over my hard cock. But first—I needed to hear it from her lips.

I gripped her chin in my fingers, forcing her gaze to mine. My eyes had adjusted to the light, and though it was dark, I could still make out her lips, her eyes. "Say it."

She hesitated a moment, regarding me, perhaps sensing how serious I was. She swallowed, and the air between us grew tense as I waited for her to respond.

Finally, she pressed her lips to mine, then smiled. "Take me. I'm yours."

"Yes," I growled, hefting her up, her back to the wall.

My jeans fell, pooling at my ankles, as I slid her underwear aside and pushed into her. I was acting like an animal, and I didn't care. At the moment, I only had one thought. One word. *Mine.*

When I was fully seated, I let out a satisfied sigh, tilting my forehead to hers. "Fuck. You feel so good."

She dug her heels into my back, spurring me to move. "Harrison, *yes.*"

The moment was intimate and raw, and I sensed Juliana felt it too. Her eyes were clouded with lust, but also something that looked a lot like love. And with every brush of her hands, every kiss from her lips, I hoped it was true. Because the more time I spent with this woman, the more I fell for her. The more I wanted from her.

Our kisses were fervent, our movements jerky and hurried as we raced to the finish. I'd never been so desperate for someone.

"Harrison!" My name rushed out of her in the dark. A moment later, she was coming, gripping me so tight, I was ready to explode. And finally, I did, detonating inside her.

With her forehead still pressed to mine, we struggled to catch our breaths. I wasn't sure I'd ever done anything so reckless, and I chuckled to myself.

"What's so funny?" she asked, sliding down my body.

I bent down to grab my jeans, pausing a moment to caress and kiss her legs. She shivered, letting out a laugh.

"I just—" I grunted, tugging on my jeans. "You drive me crazy, in the best possible way."

She smiled, cupping my cheek. "That was..." She swallowed. "I've never done something like that."

"Like what?"

"I'm such a rule-follower. I've never had sex somewhere I

could get caught. Never even considered that it could be anything but nerve-racking."

"I'd never do anything to put you in a compromising position." I tucked her hair behind her ear.

"Even so, that was hot."

"Yeah?" I grinned, pulling her against my chest and kissing her temple. "You're hot."

She wrapped her arm around my waist and squeezed. She turned her face up to me, those pouty lips glistening, begging to be kissed. So I did. And then I kissed her again, tangling my fingers in her hair, tilting her head to deepen the connection.

"Let's go upstairs," I said. "I got us a room for the night."

"Wait. What?"

I laughed. "What, what?"

"You dragged me in here to have sex, even though there's a perfectly good bed waiting upstairs?"

I lifted a shoulder. "I couldn't wait."

She laughed, rolling her eyes. "You couldn't wait the five minutes it would take to get upstairs?"

I stepped closer, tugging on her lower lip. "No."

Even now, I was tempted to turn her around, push her thong aside and thrust into her again. When it came to this woman, I was insatiable. An animal, apparently.

"I thought you were the Zen guru," she teased.

If she only knew how *not* Zen I was when it came to her. For all my talk of letting go of control, I wanted assurance that we had a future together. But I couldn't tell her that. At least, not yet.

"I am. Didn't I just show you a valuable lesson?"

"What's that?" Her gaze showed her skepticism.

I smirked, wrapping my hand around her neck and bringing our lips close before whispering, "Seize the moment."

CHAPTER NINETEEN

Juliana

"Juliana!" Sophia squealed, rushing toward me. Her footsteps echoed off the marble floor of my office, ponytail swinging from side to side.

"Hey, kiddo." I leaned down, wrapping my arms around her. She was getting so big! I grinned at her, those blue eyes so full of wonder and mischief.

She pushed her ponytail over her shoulder, and I wanted to laugh. "I can't wait to tell you about all the ideas I have for my birthday party!"

I ruffled her hair. "I'm excited!"

Alexis walked through the front door to my office a moment later, Blair resting on her hip. My friend looked gorgeous, seeming to easily juggle motherhood and her real estate brokerage firm, all while looking flawless.

"Hey." I hugged her, dropping a kiss on Blair's head. "Hi, sweet girl."

Blair giggled, her head whipping around as she checked out my office—likely considering what she could play with first.

"Hey," Alexis huffed. "Sorry we're late." Her eyes darted to

Sophia, who was currently paging through a bridal magazine with Landon, wearing matching animated expressions. *Oh my.*

"No worries. You want a drink?" I asked, leading them over to the conference room. Sophia followed us after giving Landon a hug.

"I hadn't planned to bring Blair too." She set her purse down on the table, shifting Blair to her other hip. Blair smiled and babbled, though it was mostly unintelligible, and I grinned back at her before grabbing some toys from my secret stash.

"Is everything okay?" I handed Blair a toy, enjoying the way her eyes widened at the colors and sound.

"Yeah. Preston had something come up at work, so she got to come along."

"Well, I'm always happy to see her."

Alexis smiled, pulling a snack out of her purse for Blair before taking a seat.

"So…birthday. What are you guys thinking?" I asked, knowing that when it came to Sophia, she usually had a lot of ideas. Little girl, big plans.

She darted over to the table, taking a seat across from me. She placed her hands on the table before her, a stern expression on her angelic face. "I want a unicorn party. Pink and purple."

"Ooh. I love it." I nodded, considering her suggestion. "Pool party?"

"Hmm." She tapped a finger to her lips, and it took everything in me not to laugh at how serious she was. "I don't know. Do you think that's too similar to my mermaid party?" When Blair started fussing, Sophia turned to her. "Here, baby." She handed Blair her water bottle.

This kid. As an only child, Sophia had always been mature

for her age. But now that she was a big sister, it was a role she took very seriously.

"Not if we do different decorations and games, but it's up to you. And with a unicorn theme, a rainbow color palette could be a lot of fun."

"Yes!" Sophia's face lit up, and she bounced in her seat. "And we can do one of those surprise rainbow cakes covered in rainbow sprinkles."

"Great! What else?" I made a note on my tablet.

"A… What about a rainbow of snacks?"

"I love it. Perfect."

We brainstormed a little more before Alexis said, "Those all sound like great ideas, Soph. Jules, didn't you say you could use her help with something?" Alexis gave me a meaningful glance, and I sensed that she wanted to talk to me without little ears listening in.

"That's right." I turned my attention to Sophia. "Some of the interns are assembling goody bags. Do you want to help?"

"Heck yes!" I knew the answer before she jumped out of her seat, but it still made me smile.

"Go find Landon. He'll get you set up."

"Okay." She grinned before turning to skip down the hall to his office.

"What's up?" I asked, smiling at Blair and taking some of her goldfish, pretending they were swimming.

"We got an offer on your house."

I glanced up at Alexis, my eyes wide. "Already?" We'd barely listed my house. And even though it was "selling season," according to Alexis, I'd expected it to take longer than a couple of weeks. "How does it look?"

"They offered $15,000 over list price. Cash. And—" she grinned "—they want to close by the end of July."

My jaw dropped. "July? That's…that's soon." I glanced at

the calendar on the wall, confirming it was only a few weeks away.

She nodded. "It's more than enough time to move, but only if you're ready."

I considered it a moment, dreading the idea of moving mid wedding season. Perhaps sensing my hesitation, Alexis said, "I'm not trying to pressure you, but you're probably not going to get a better deal than this. Plus, they're willing to pay closing costs."

"Holy..." I blinked. "Wow. They must really want the house."

She nodded. "They do. It's their dream neighborhood. Great schools. Cute family."

I swallowed, struggling to process it all. I'd gotten an offer on my house. One I'd be an idiot to refuse. But in saying yes, a new family was going to move in on my dreams. I shook my head— dreams I'd once had. Now, I had new dreams. And as difficult as it would be to say goodbye, I was ready. I was going to accept.

"Let's do it," I said.

"Are you sure you don't want to sleep on it?" Alexis asked.

I shook my head. "I'm ready. I'm actually kind of excited."

Alexis grabbed my hand and squeezed. "I'm so happy for you. I know this hasn't been easy, but it's so nice to see you happy again."

I tilted my head to the side, a soft smile curving my lips. "I am happy."

Incredibly so. For the first time in years, I was sleeping well. Living life. I was doing a job I loved, spending time with a man I loved. *Whoa. What?* I stilled. Did I love Harrison?

"You okay?" Alexis asked.

"Yeah." I tried to shake away the question, but it wouldn't leave me be.

Blair reached out to me, babbling and smiling. "Juju."

I opened my arms, grateful for the distraction. "Come here, Blair bear."

I grinned down at her, filled with so much joy and love. She was such a sweet little girl, and I laughed as she played with my cheeks. Alexis and I talked a little more about Sophia's birthday party, until we were interrupted by a knock at the door.

"Oh, hey," Harrison said when I glanced up. "I didn't realize you were with a client. I'll be in the lobby."

"No," Alexis stood. "It's fine. We were just wrapping up. I need to get Blair home for her nap."

"Alexis, this is Harrison. Harrison, this is one of my dear friends, Alexis. And her daughter, Blair." I bounced her on my hip.

He shook hands with Alexis before launching into the most adorable, heart-melting game of peekaboo with Blair. "Aren't you a cutie?"

"You're a natural," Alexis said, grinning at me as the two continued their little game.

But I couldn't tear my attention away from Harrison. He was so sweet with Blair, and I could imagine him with Olivia as a little girl. But as great of a father as he was, I still didn't want children.

"I'm out of practice," Harrison said. "My daughter is about to get married."

Alexis pretended to cover her ears. "No! I'm freaking out that my almost-nine-year-old has a boyfriend. I'm not ready to think about her wedding."

Harrison chuckled. And when he smiled, small creases lined the corners of his eyes, only adding to his charm. "They grow up way too fast. Enjoy it while you can."

Alexis smiled. "I fully intend to. It was nice to finally meet you."

"Bye, Blair bear." I squeezed her close, and she giggled when I kissed her neck.

Once they'd gone, Harrison crossed the room, placing a kiss on my cheek. "Hey. How are you?"

"Good," I sighed, falling into his touch. "Better now that you're here."

"It was nice to finally meet one of your friends," he said, placing his hands on my hips. "She seems nice. Did she just stop by for a visit?"

"I'm planning her daughter Sophia's birthday party."

"Ah." He tilted his head back. "You looked happy—holding the baby."

"I love her girls. Sophia is sassy and smart. And Blair—" I shook my head, my lips curling into a smile. "She was an unexpected surprise. And she's such a sweet baby."

"Oh boy." He chuckled, pulling me into his side. "Do I have to worry about you getting baby fever?"

I narrowed my eyes at him. "I can admire a baby without wanting one for myself."

"You sure?" His eyes searched mine. "Because it suited you. Motherhood would suit you."

I turned away, busying myself with some papers on the conference table. "I told you. I wanted kids, once upon a time. But not anymore."

"Juliana." His tone was solemn, asking me to take notice. "Just because I don't want to have more children doesn't mean you shouldn't have them if you want them. I don't want you to miss out on something by being with me."

I spun and met his gaze, mine unwavering. "I'm not missing out on anything."

I knew what it was like to miss out on life. I'd spent the past two years missing out.

I was happy now, fulfilled. At one point, I'd wanted kids; now, I didn't. My outlook on life had changed, as had my goals. I was fulfilled and content with my job, myself. In my friendships and my relationship with Harrison.

"Yeah, but…have you given this enough thought? I'm… older. Significantly older than you. Men often die before women."

"Stop." I marched over to him and pressed my lips to his. "Please." My heart accelerated at his words, at the prospect of losing him. And it only made me realize just how much I cared about him. "I don't want to talk about it."

I didn't want to think about it. If I did, I'd go back to being alone. Closing off my heart again because I was afraid. And I didn't want to be miserable anymore.

"I think we should—" he brushed my hair over my shoulder "—talk about it if we're going to be together."

I pursed my lips, trying to understand where this conversation had come from. Was it just about kids, or was there something more going on? "What happened to Mr. 'we can't control the future'?"

"I'm not trying to control the future. I'm trying to be realistic."

"Realistic?" I scoffed. Was it realistic to think you'd lose the man you loved while on vacation? Was it realistic to imagine that we'd only have a few years together instead of a lifetime? I shook my head. "If the tsunami taught me anything, it's that there are no guarantees. I could be struck by a car tomorrow. You could well outlive me."

"Juliana." He cupped my cheek, his eyes pleading. "Don't talk like that."

I closed my eyes briefly, willing myself to stay calm. I understood where he was coming from; I did. But I didn't want to think about the possibilities. I didn't want to contemplate losing him.

"There's only one thing I need to know." I stared into his

eyes, feeling the weight of the moment. "Do you want to be with me?"

"Of course." He leaned his forehead to mine, our breath mingling.

"I want to be with you," I said, holding his gaze, letting him know there was no one else for me. "And since when do you get hung up on future what-ifs?" I teased, thinking about all the times he'd told me to let go.

His shoulders relaxed. "You're right. I just—I want you to be happy."

He pulled me into his arms, holding me close. We were a perfect fit, and I knew that I was where I was meant to be. I inhaled his scent, listened to the beat of his heart, and I surrendered to the moment. To this man. To the realization that I loved him.

"You okay?" He rubbed my back.

"Big day."

"Yeah?" He backed away, sliding his hands down my arms, letting me know he was still there. "Want to tell me about it?"

"I accepted an offer on my house."

He blinked at me a few times. "Really?"

I nodded, trying to gauge his reaction. But the next words out of his mouth were the last ones I'd expected. "Move in with me."

All the air whooshed out of me in a rush. "What?"

He took my hands in his. "Move in with me."

I shook my head, struggling to keep up. Move in with him? We hadn't even told his daughter about us. I hadn't even signed the papers on my house. And he wanted to move in together? It was a big step. Was I ready for it? Were *we* ready for it?

"Why not?" he asked. "You already spend most nights at my place."

"Yeah, but..." I paused. Why was I hesitating? I loved

Harrison, and I wanted to be with him. "It's… That's quite the commitment. Are you sure?"

"Yes." His gaze was pinned to mine, sincere but intense. "Yes," he said again, as if to prove his earnestness. "I'm tired of you shuffling back and forth between your place and mine, and I'm sure you are too."

"Well, geez." I placed my palm on his chest. "Aren't you romantic?" I teased.

"You want to hear the truth?" he asked, and I nodded. He pulled me to him, his movements—like his voice—gruff. "I can't bear to be apart from you for even a night."

I stilled, surprised by the intensity of his movements, his words. He was agile, yet strong. A true athlete.

"What about Olivia?" I asked, knowing how important her opinion was to him. I'd never want to do anything to jeopardize their relationship.

He waved a hand through the air. "We'll tell her—after the wedding."

"So, you want me to move in, but we're going to continue to keep this a secret?" I screwed up my face. "Are you sure it wouldn't just be better to tell her now?"

He shook his head. "No. Cam always makes everything about her. I'm not doing that to Olivia. I want her wedding to be perfect."

He watched me, his intensity unnerving. All the while, I made a list of the pros and cons in my head. "Come on, Juliana. Do something unexpected with me."

I rolled my eyes, but I couldn't help grinning despite myself. "You always say that when you want me to do something that's likely a terrible idea."

"And it always turns out to be a great idea." He was so cocky, so sexy. I couldn't resist anymore. I didn't know why I'd ever thought I could.

This man made me want to be spontaneous and carefree.

Made me want to relinquish all my lists and just see what happened.

It had all started that night at the bar, with our one-night stand. He continually pushed me to give in, to let go. And I found that I was enjoying myself, perhaps more than ever. Besides, he was right—so far, everything really had turned out great.

"Okay."

"Okay?" He dipped his head so our eyes were level, his gaze searching.

"Yes." I nodded. "I'll move in with you."

He pulled me closer and held me tight, his chin resting on my head. "You have no idea how happy you've made me."

So was I. I'd gone from staring at my Post-it notes and thinking they'd never happen—I'd never move forward. And now, I was finally doing it. I was letting go of my past and embracing my future.

CHAPTER TWENTY

Harrison

"Connor? What the—" I glanced between him and the back door Juliana had walked through a few minutes ago. "What are you doing here?"

My heart was pounding, even as I tried to remain calm. My son-in-law had nearly caught me having sex with the wedding planner in the pool. For all I knew, he might have witnessed our intimate moment. He'd practically appeared out of thin air, nearly giving me a damn heart attack. Even now, my pulse was still skittering, struggling to settle into a more normal rhythm.

His posture was stiff, his eyes hidden behind his sunglasses. Giving nothing away. "The better question would be—how did I get in?"

He loomed over me from the slate patio, his large form casting a shadow across the water. The fence surrounding my home was ten-feet high. And he didn't appear to have come from the extensive property behind the house. Which meant he'd likely scaled the gate or come through the house. Without a key. I frowned.

I glanced toward the house, unable to see Juliana—to

warn her. I shook my head. Fuck. Why was I acting like a teenager who'd been caught by his parents? *I* was the parent. This was *my* house.

"How did you get in?" I hopped out of the pool, splashing water along the tile as I headed for my towel.

I knew why he was here—obligatory family dinner night. I couldn't believe I'd forgotten. But in the excitement of Juliana moving in, I guessed it wasn't all that surprising.

He crossed his arms over his chest, and I straightened. "You should really consider hiring Hudson."

I frowned, wrapping the towel around my waist. I'd paid for a top-of-the-line system. And he'd somehow managed to get past all the cameras, the sensors, completely undetected. It was an unnerving realization. And I wondered if he'd done it before. If he'd snooped around my house. I wouldn't put it past him; I'd certainly done some digging on him.

"Your company's safeguards were a joke," he scoffed. "Maverick is going to love hearing about this."

Great. Connor's boss—Maverick Hudson—was a billionaire who owned Hudson Security. I'd met him a few times, mostly at fundraisers.

"I can show you my suggestions. Or I'd be happy to walk your company through their shortcomings."

I smoothed back my hair as I considered his words. Though part of me was unsettled, a greater part was thankful. Connor had revealed the weaknesses in my current system, and I'd much rather he break in than someone who wanted to harm me or my family. In his own weird way, he was showing that he cared.

"I appreciate it. I assume you've already reviewed the security at your place?"

He nodded. "Of course. Before we ever moved in, I made sure it was safe for Olivia. And Hudson offers free monitoring for employees."

I nodded, grateful for Connor's background. For the fact that he was looking out for my daughter and would do anything to protect her. When she was younger, I'd contemplated getting her a bodyguard, but she wouldn't hear of it. Maybe having Connor around wasn't so terrible after all.

"Let's go inside." I gestured toward the back door when there was still no sign of Juliana. "I'll run through the shower, and then we can eat."

He nodded, glancing around as he followed me inside. Though he'd been here before, I tried to imagine my home through his eyes. My future son-in-law. Olivia hadn't told me much about his background, but she'd told me enough. He'd had a difficult childhood, nothing like the pampered luxury Olivia had grown up in. Both of his parents had died, though he'd never had much of a relationship with his father.

Despite the obstacles Connor had faced, he'd made something of himself—joining the navy SEALs, getting a college degree, now working for an elite executive protection company. He was a good man, and Olivia loved him. Considering his own lack of family, I was determined to be a positive figure in his life.

"Do you have company?" Connor asked, glancing around.

I cringed when I saw two glasses on the counter, one lipstick-stained. It was too late to hide the evidence.

"I, um—" I was on the verge of saying no, when a toilet flushed in the distance. "Yeah." I glanced around, anywhere but at him.

Connor was a human lie detector. Which meant I needed to tell some version of the truth. And it needed to be convincing. I didn't want this to get back to Olivia.

"Juliana's here." I rubbed the back of my neck. "I thought we could go over some wedding details during dinner."

"Sure." He rocked on his heels, glancing toward the source

of the sound. He didn't say anything more, but he didn't have to. We both knew I looked guilty as fuck.

His eyes shifted to something behind me. "Hey, Juliana."

I turned, silently trying to communicate with her as she made her way toward us.

"Oh." She shifted, looking around, I presumed for something to cover herself, seeing as she was still wearing her bikini. "Hey, Connor."

Connor glanced between the two of us, his gaze searing, questioning. *Shit.*

"I didn't realize wedding planning involved swimming." His tone was rife with insinuation, or at least, it certainly felt that way.

"Yeah." It was meant to be a statement, but with the way my voice pitched toward the end, it came out as more of a question.

If I hadn't been watching, I would've missed the ever-so-subtle lift to Connor's brow. I needed to get this back on track before it spiraled even more out of control.

"Let me just throw on a sundress, and then I can get out of here," Juliana said, even though she now lived here.

Unease pricked my veins. In trying to protect my daughter, I was betraying the woman I loved. I didn't like sneaking around. And I didn't want Juliana to feel like my dirty little secret. But I couldn't just drop this news on Olivia, especially not while she was over five thousand miles away.

Before Juliana could dart off, I said, "Actually, we were going to discuss the wedding plans with Connor. Remember?"

"Oh." She glanced between the two us then flashed us a bright smile. "Right. That's right. Be right back." She darted off, and I wasn't sure whether to be relieved or not.

The only sounds in the room were my heartbeat whooshing in my ears and the air conditioner cycling on.

Connor was silent, scrutinizing me. And I held his gaze, determined not to break.

"So." I turned for the fridge, unable to handle it anymore. "How's work?"

"Good." He accepted a glass of water and took a few gulps. "Busy. How's the wedding planning going?"

"Good." I smiled, thinking of Juliana as I pulled out the ingredients to prepare the meal.

"I know I haven't been very involved—certainly not as much as I'd like. But work has been insane lately."

I nodded, still not entirely certain what level of danger his job entailed. Sure, he worked for Hudson Security. And they specialized in executive protection, but was he doing recon from a command center or actually out in the field? There was a big difference between pushing paper and kicking asses. Though, if you took into account his hours, travel, and physique, my guess was that he was involved with the latter.

"Just so long as my daughter is your first priority."

"She is—always." He tightened his grip on the knife, chopping the vegetables as I prepared the fish. "But there was another reason I thought you should be the one to plan it."

"Oh yeah?" I arched my brow, surprised by this revelation. "Why's that?"

"Well, considering it's your money—and a lot of it—I thought you might prefer to be the one making the decisions."

I nodded. I'd never really considered that angle before. But it made me realize that Connor respected me by having respect for my finances.

"Besides, if it were up to me, we would've already eloped."

I glared at the spatula and opened my mouth to respond. Before I could say anything though, Juliana returned.

"So, Connor—" She dropped her elbows on the counter,

smiling, and I envied her ease. "I'm not sure I've heard the story of how you and Olivia met."

"Really?" He chuckled, leaning his hip against the counter. He told her about the Spines for Soldiers program.

Olivia had developed it while working at Igloo Books as a way to help current and former military personnel. It was a sort of reading buddy program, matching people from across the world and giving them access to free books. And more importantly, someone to talk to. When Connor and Olivia had been matched, they'd initially butted heads. But then something had changed; they'd bonded over their love of books. They'd found something in each other that made them feel understood, *seen*. I found that I actually enjoyed hearing the story from his perspective, and it revealed just how much he cared about my daughter.

When he finished, Juliana smiled. "Wow. That's quite the story."

"Yeah." He rubbed the back of his neck. "I figured she would've told you by now."

"We had to focus on accomplishing as much as we could in the short time we had before she left."

He nodded. "I wish I could be more involved."

"Well..." She grinned. "Here's your opportunity. We can walk you through the plans so far and see if you have anything to add."

"I'd like that," he said as we sat down to eat.

Juliana launched into an outline of the events. As she listed everything we'd done, I was honestly impressed by all we'd accomplished. We made a good team, and I enjoyed working with her. Connor listened intently, occasionally asking a question. Until finally, Juliana asked, "So, what do you think? Any suggestions or requests?"

"You've got white hydrangeas. That's super important to Olivia. I, um—" He cleared his throat, tugging on the neck of his shirt. "I'd really love it if we could find a way to honor my mom."

Juliana nodded, her expression thoughtful. "You could have a song played in her honor, or a poem or scripture read."

Connor shook his head. "Those are all nice, but I guess I was hoping for something…I don't know. More personal."

"Of course." Juliana furrowed her brow, considering it. "Well…" She tapped a finger to her lips, drawing my attention to them. Her skin was sun-kissed from our day outside, and I wanted to suck her lips into my mouth. To trail my tongue along her body. "This is just one idea, but we could reserve a seat for your mom."

Connor's face relaxed. "Yeah. I like that—saving her a seat at the table."

Juliana was getting excited now, if the way she was bouncing in her seat was any indication. She needed to stop because the way her breasts were swaying made my cock stand up and take notice. I pressed against it beneath the table, needing it to calm the fuck down.

"And I recently saw this sweet idea to do picture charms on the bouquet." She grabbed her phone, typing something before showing us the screen.

Connor nodded, as did I. "Olivia would love that," he said before turning to me. "We could include a photo of Grandma Marian too."

I nodded, appreciative of the fact that he wanted to recognize someone so important to Olivia. She'd been incredibly close to Cam's mom before she'd passed. Grandma Marian had encouraged her love of reading and baking. And I knew Olivia was sad Grandma Marian wouldn't be at her wedding.

We talked for a while longer, enjoying our dinner before

Juliana took over cleanup. While she busied herself in the kitchen, I invited Connor to my office.

"Before you go—" I grabbed an envelope from my desk and handed it to him.

He glanced down at it, brow furrowed. "What's this?"

"Open it."

He pulled out the slip of paper and stared at it. "Is this…" He jerked his head back. "Is this what I think it is?"

I nodded. "An open-ended ticket from LA to London."

"But—business class?" His eyes widened. "Holy shit."

I couldn't help the grin that split my face. I'd always enjoyed being generous, especially when it came to my daughter and her friends. And while I hadn't shown that side to Connor until now, it was clear how truly appreciative he was.

"Olivia misses you. And I want her to be happy." It was as simple as that.

He nodded, slipping the ticket confirmation back into the envelope. "Thank you, sir." There was something in his gaze, some question unspoken. "Is this hush money?" he finally asked.

"Hush money?"

"Well, I assume you haven't told Olivia about Juliana, given that she's never mentioned it to me."

"Mentioned what?" I feigned ignorance, even as a bead of sweat slid between my shoulder blades.

He crossed his arms over his chest. "Oh, come on. We both know you're sleeping together."

"Keep your voice down," I hissed.

I glanced over my shoulder to where Juliana was wiping down the kitchen counter. I was momentarily struck with the rightness of it. Of *her*—not just in my home, but in my life.

"Oh man," Connor said, and my attention snapped to him.

He was watching me with a soft gaze, head tilted to the side. "You've got it bad, don't you?"

I clenched my fists. I was not discussing my love life with my future son-in-law. And maybe if I kept my mouth shut, he'd drop it.

"Olivia likes her, you know."

I pinched the bridge of my nose. Olivia did like Juliana—as her wedding planner. She respected her as a professional.

"Which is why you can't tell her about this," I said, hoping he'd assume I was merely referring to the swimming.

Though, considering the fact that Connor had successfully broken in to my house—completely undetected—I had no idea the true extent of his knowledge of my relationship with Juliana. Had he seen Juliana's sticky notes on the bathroom mirror? Her thyroid medication resting on the nightstand in the master bedroom?

Shit. I'd been caught red-handed by my future son-in-law.

"Olivia and I don't keep secrets from each other," Connor said, which only made me respect him more. Even if he was thwarting my goals.

"Just this once…" I swallowed, hating myself for having to ask this. But Olivia's happiness was more important than anything—even my pride. Even the truth.

"I don't know," he hedged. "I don't like it. I don't like lying to her."

"Neither do I, but it's for the best. Just until after the wedding."

"And then you'll tell her?"

My shoulders relaxed slightly. I was so close to getting him to agree. "I promise."

"Fine." He let out a heavy sigh. "But if this blows up, I am not taking the fall."

"Geez. What happened to no man left behind?" I teased.

Something shifted in his eyes. "My loyalty lies with Olivia."

I stepped closer, patting him on the back. "Good man. Now, I believe you have some packing to do."

"I do." He grinned, this time a genuine smile, as he shifted from foot to foot. "Thank you. This is—" he dipped his head before meeting my eyes again "—incredibly generous."

"You're part of the family now," I said, and I found that I finally meant it.

"Thank you." He cleared his throat. "That's all I've ever wanted—to be part of a family."

I nodded, sensing this was difficult for him. In all the time I'd known Connor, he'd never really opened up to me. Olivia had told me bits and pieces about his childhood, but the PI I'd hired when they started dating seriously had filled in the details. I'd never told Olivia, of course.

From the file, I knew that his mother was dead. His father had died only recently, but he hadn't been part of Connor's life for years. After his mother's death, he'd lived with his aunt Lucy.

Despite Lucy's continued presence in Connor's life, he didn't have any other family. At least not beside Olivia. My daughter loved Connor, saw something in him that made her want to marry him. And after today, I felt like I finally under-stood. The knowledge had been there all these months. I'd always liked Connor, but I finally felt like I respected him— as a man, as my equal.

"Go," I said, unwilling to delve further into my emotions. This was enough for now.

He nodded. "Tell Juliana goodbye for me."

I walked him over to the French doors off my office, opening them to let the warm night air breeze through. He started down the path toward his car when he paused, turning back. "Harrison."

"Yeah?"

"Olivia wants you to be happy."

I knew she did. But would she be happy about my relationship with Juliana? And if she wasn't, then what would I do?

CHAPTER TWENTY-ONE

Juliana

Alexis's heels clicked against the wood floors, the only sound in the house apart from my breathing. I'd signed the contract, packed everything up, and we were doing one final walk-through of my house before Harper and Lauren came over for drinks to celebrate.

I pressed my hand to the wall, lingering as a memory washed over me. Ryan and me on Christmas morning. We'd waited too long to go tree shopping and were stuck with a pathetic excuse that would barely support an ornament. Instead of being sad at the reminder of our Charlie Brown Christmas tree, though, I smiled. I was grateful for the memory. Grateful for the time I'd shared with such a wonderful man, brief as it was.

"What's this?" Alexis asked, drawing my attention from the living room.

She plucked a piece of paper from the back of the built-in bookshelves. Somehow, I'd missed it—the white paper blending in with the painted wood. She handed me the envelope, and I could tell there was something in it. But it wasn't addressed to anyone, and I figured it might have belonged to the previous owners. I opened it, never expecting what I'd find inside.

I gasped when Ryan's familiar scrawl greeted me, my heart pounding as I stared at my name written at the top.

"What is it?" Alexis asked.

"It's—" I let out a shaky exhale. "A letter from Ryan."

"Oh my god," she whispered.

I sank to the floor as I read the contents—shocked by the discovery, by his words.

JULES,

HAPPY 34TH BIRTHDAY. I HOPE YOU KNOW HOW MUCH I LOVE you. I hope you always remember just how happy you make me.

REGARDLESS OF WHAT THE FUTURE HOLDS, I'LL ALWAYS BE cheering you on. Loving you. Be happy, Jules. That's my greatest wish for you.

LOVE,
  Ryan

BY THE TIME I'D FINISHED READING IT A SECOND TIME, I WAS sobbing. It was a rush of emotion—happiness, sadness, gratitude, relief. It felt as if he were speaking to me from wherever he was, watching over me. Giving me his blessing.

Alexis joined me on the floor, hugging me as she read the letter over my shoulder.

"Holy shit," she whispered. "That's got to be some sort of sign, right?"

I nodded, convinced it was. All this time, I'd hoped for closure. And it had been there all along, waiting to be revealed until I was ready. I swiped away my tears, a smile forming on my face.

The doorbell rang just before the door opened.

"Hello," Lauren called, her voice echoing in the empty entryway.

"Guys? Everything okay?" Harper asked.

I shook my head, fingertips pressed to my lips.

"Alexis? Juliana? What's going on?" Lauren dropped her purse on the counter, along with two bottles of champagne.

I was grateful when Alexis answered for me. "We found a letter from Ryan."

Harper gasped, her eyes immediately wet with unshed tears. "Seriously?"

I nodded.

"What does it say?" Lauren asked, and I passed it to her to read aloud.

When she was done, silence settled over the room, blanketing the house with the gravity of this moment.

"It's totally a sign, right?" Harper asked, echoing Alexis's earlier sentiment.

"It certainly feels like one," I said.

"And how does reading it make you feel—better or worse?"

I stared at the floor. "A bit of both, I guess. But on the whole—" I straightened "—better."

"Good. Let's talk about it while we drink champagne and eat expensive cheese," Lauren said, offering a hand to help me up.

We headed outside. The new owners had wanted to keep the patio furniture, and I had no use for it, so it was staying at the house. We took a seat around the fountain; the sound of water rushing over rocks was soothing. It was definitely something I missed at Harrison's house. Otherwise, I'd found the adjustment to living at his place surprisingly easy. It was closer to my office, larger, and my backyard—nice as it was— couldn't compare to his large treed lot with a pool.

"Crap," Harper said as Lauren popped the cork on the champagne. "I totally forgot glasses."

I laughed. "It's fine. We'll just drink from the bottle."

"You first," Lauren said, holding it out to me.

"Okay." I laughed, accepting it.

I was about to take a sip when she said, "Wait. We have to make a toast."

"Oh. Right." I lowered the bottle. "But I'll be drinking to it alone." I pouted.

Alexis grinned and mimed raising an imaginary glass to toast. Lauren and Harper joined her. "To Juliana."

"To new beginnings," Harper said with a warm smile.

"And hot men," Lauren added, which only made us laugh, even as we all said, "Here, here."

I took a swig and passed the bottle to Lauren before grabbing a cracker and a piece of cheese. "Thank you, guys."

"Of course," Harper said, wiping her mouth with the back of her hand. "Another thing I forgot—" She rolled her eyes. "Napkins."

I tilted my head to the side. Now that I was paying attention, Harper seemed distracted. She rarely forgot anything. It was part of the reason she excelled as a film location scout— she seemed to have a photographic memory.

"Everything okay, Harp?" I asked.

"Yeah." She flashed me a bright smile. "It's been a hectic week at work."

"Ugh. Work." Alexis flopped back in her chair. "That's the last thing I want to think about right now."

"Wolfe is being a pain in the ass about an investment property," Lauren said by way of explanation.

"When is he not a pain in the ass?" Alexis asked.

"True." Lauren popped a cheese cube in her mouth. "But he brings you a ton of business. So, he can't be that terrible."

Alexis nodded. "Speaking of terrible, Sophia is driving me crazy about her birthday."

"Uh oh." I took another drink. "What now?"

"She wants to invite every kid from her culinary summer camp."

"So?" I shrugged, handing her the champagne. Clearly, the woman deserved a drink.

"That's like two hundred kids."

"Oh." I laughed. "Okay. Well, how about just the ones from her class?"

Alexis pushed her hair away from her face. "I suggested that, but you know how stubborn she can be. Maybe I should have Preston try."

I nodded. "She'll listen to him. Otherwise, we're going to have to rent out an Olympic-sized pool."

We all laughed.

"Riley would have a field day," Lauren said, referring to her labradoodle. "All those kids running around."

I shook my head. "Oh dear lord."

"How's Hunter?" Harper asked.

"Great. He's got some exciting new apps in the pipeline. So, he's happy," Lauren said. "Actually, I've been meaning to call you, Juliana." She turned to me. "I have a party I'd love your help with."

Before I could inquire about the occasion, Alexis leaned in as if sharing a secret. "Guess who's pregnant?"

"You?" I teased, but I knew she and Preston were done having kids. One surprise baby was enough. I turned my attention to Lauren, eyes wide. "What? You're pregnant?"

As much as Lauren loved kids, I didn't think she'd ever want to have her own.

"No." Lauren waved her hands in front of her as if to ward off any fertility mojo. "Not me." She glared at Alexis. "Kate."

"Aww. Really?" I asked, and she nodded. "How does Hunter feel about the fact that his baby sister is knocked up?"

"Surprisingly happy." She smiled. "He's already spoiling the kid rotten."

"So, you want to host a baby shower. And you want my help."

"Hunter and I, actually."

I arched a brow. "Wow. A co-ed shower. How much persuading did that take?"

"None." She took a swig from the bottle then tipped it upside down, frowning. "Empty."

Harper shot out of her seat as if her butt were on fire. "I'll grab another one."

"Are you sure?" I moved to stand.

"No. No. Sit." She gestured wildly, her smile a little watery. "I'll get it."

"Okay. Thanks." I sat back down, kicking off my shoes. I waited until I was certain she was out of earshot to ask, "Is Harper okay?"

Alexis lifted her shoulder, but Lauren screwed up her face. "Oh shit." She covered her face with her hands. "I shouldn't have mentioned Kate's pregnancy in front of her."

"Oh." Alexis shook her head. "I'm so sorry. It's all my fault. I wasn't thinking."

"Neither was I." Lauren placed her hand on Alexis's shoulder. "Let's just—maybe we won't bring it up again in front of her."

I nodded, knowing how badly Harper wanted to be a mom. "Should I go check on her?"

Lauren shook her head. "Maybe just give her a minute."

A few minutes later, Harper returned, but her eyes were rimmed with red. My heart sank, and I felt terrible that my friend was hurting. Ever since the talk of Kate's baby shower, she seemed to have lost some of her spark.

"Harper," I said, turning to her, wanting to distract her. "Anything new with you?"

Something passed through her eyes, and then it was gone. I frowned, wondering what was going on with my friend. I'd been so wrapped up in my own life that I hadn't been there for her like I should've been. Like she'd been there for me. That was going to change.

"I'm going to Thailand to scout some locations soon."

I nodded. "That's good." Neither of us mentioned the tsunami or Ryan, though I was positive we were both thinking about it.

"How's Harrison?" she asked.

"He's…" I smiled. "He's good. He's in Oregon for a photo shoot for an outdoor gear company."

There was a collective "Ooh" from my best friends, and I merely laughed. "You guys are ridiculous." I grabbed a piece of prosciutto.

"I was kind of hoping I'd finally get to meet your hunky pro athlete," Lauren said.

"Yeah," Harper chimed in. "Alexis told us he's a hottie."

The corner of my mouth lifted. "He is."

"You didn't want to go with him to Oregon?" Harper asked.

I shook my head, taking another sip of champagne. With every round, the bottle got lighter. "Between wedding season ramping up and closing on the house, I couldn't."

She nodded. "How's it going—living together?"

"It's good. Really good, actually."

"Aww. Yay," Harper said. "I'm so glad."

"So, here's the real question," Lauren said, leaning in. "How does he feel about the sticky notes?"

"Or have you not put them up on the mirror yet?" Harper teased.

I ran a hand through my hair, the strands brushing against my back. "I did put them up—I only have three right now. But I find a new note on the mirror every morning from him. Sometimes it's an inspirational quote or a compliment."

"Aww." Harper held a hand to her heart. "That's so romantic."

"I thought we might have a bumpy adjustment. I mean—he's been a bachelor for so long, but…" I lifted a shoulder. "It's been great."

"And the sex?" Leave it to Lauren to ask.

"Ah-mazing," I said. "A few weeks ago, he took me in a hotel storage room."

My cheeks heated at my admission. I couldn't believe I'd done that, let alone confessed to it. Alexis and Harper gaped at me, and Lauren merely smirked.

"The thrill of being caught makes things even hotter," Lauren said with a far-off look in her eye.

"You all right there?" Harper teased, and Lauren started fanning herself. She'd always been the most sexually adventurous of the four of us.

Lauren shook her head as if to clear it. "Yep." She swallowed then grabbed the champagne from Harper to take a swig. "I'm good."

"It was hot, but—" I scrunched up my face.

"But what?" Alexis asked.

"Well…sneaking around is fun and all, but we're living together. And we still haven't told anyone about us." I dipped my head.

Lauren patted my hand. "You told us. That's got to count for something, right?"

I nodded, but my heart wasn't in it. "I guess."

"I get it," Alexis said. "Sneaking around can be fun, but it gets old."

"I just… Do you think it's weird that he hasn't told his daughter about us? I mean, I'm living in his house. That's going to be kind of difficult to hide when she comes back from London. He already has Connor lying for us."

"The fiancé?" Lauren asked.

"Yeah. He came over one day—broke in to the house."

"Wait. What?"

"No. No." I waved my hands before me, laughter bubbling out of me. "That came out all wrong." I explained what had happened. And when I was finished, the mood was decidedly different.

"Hmm." Lauren crossed her arms over her chest. "Yeah. That's weird."

"Right?" I grabbed the bottle as the three of them nodded their agreement. "Thank you." I lifted it before gulping down some.

"Though, as a parent," Alexis said, "I get it. At least, to some degree."

"Can you help me understand, then?" I asked, my tongue —like my limbs—feeling looser from the alcohol. "Because I've sold my house, moved in with this man. And it kind of feels like I've made all these changes—huge changes—but he still won't tell his daughter about us."

My eyes burned, and I tugged at the corners so I wouldn't cry—*again*. "Is he ashamed of our relationship?" *Of me.*

I failed. Tears streaked down my cheeks, my face hot with embarrassment.

"Oh, honey," Lauren said, scooting closer so she could

wrap her arm around my shoulder. "I'm sure that's not the case."

I knew it wasn't, but I was feeling overly emotional. Closing on the house, the letter from Ryan, the champagne—it was making it difficult to think clearly.

"How far away is the wedding?" Alexis asked.

"Four weeks. But that's not the point." I dried my tears.

"I know it's not." Her tone was gentle. "But…I guess, are you concerned he won't follow through on telling Olivia after the wedding's over?"

"I don't know." I massaged my temples. "Maybe."

Harper frowned.

"I'm trying to be understanding," I said. "I mean, I get that he loves his daughter and doesn't want to take away from her wedding day. But this isn't just a fling. We live together, and I'm—" I shook my head, swallowing back the words.

"You're not going to like what I have to say," Alexis said.

"What's that?"

We all turned to her, curious. "He makes you happy. And he's the one who asked you to move in—that has to count for something."

"True."

"And telling your child about someone you're dating is hard—no matter what age they are. Harrison has a great relationship with his daughter, and I know you don't want to come between them."

"You're right." I slumped. "I know you're right." And she was. I certainly didn't want to ruin Olivia's dream day or her relationship with Harrison.

"It'll work itself out," Alexis said. "You'll see."

I nodded, and the conversation turned to other matters. We stayed out there until all the champagne and most of the cheese was gone. Hunter came to drive us all home, and I paused at the front door, preparing myself for this moment. The final goodbye.

"You ready?" Alexis asked.

I nodded, removing the house key from my key chain and placing it in her palm. I closed her fingers over it, lending the moment a sense of finality. With one last glance at the kitchen and backyard, at the home I'd lived in for the past five years, I closed the door.

"Thank you for all your help," I said as we headed down the sidewalk toward Hunter's car. "And thanks for coming today for the final walk-through."

"Of course. And you're sure you got everything? Took all the pictures you wanted?"

"Yes. I'm good."

Surprisingly good, in fact. I felt—lighter somehow. Like I'd shed the weight of the past few years. Shed the emotional baggage I'd been holding on to. Now I felt as if I could truly move on with Harrison, without Ryan looming over me. I just needed him to get with the program and tell his daughter.

CHAPTER TWENTY-TWO

Harrison

"Mm. Good morning." I nuzzled into Juliana's neck, inhaling her sweet scent.

She pressed her ass into my hard-on, making it impossible to think. We'd been living together for almost two months now, and I was still ravenous for her. It was a wonder we got any sleep.

"Mm," she moaned as I slid my hand up her stomach to tease the underside of her breasts. "Morning."

I continued to touch her as she ground against me, our breathing becoming labored, bodies rocking against each other. Her skin was smoother than the organic cotton sheets enveloping the bed, her body warm and inviting. She turned her head, kissing me over her shoulder as I continued to explore her body.

She reached between her legs, pressing me to her center.

"You feel so good," I rasped.

I tweaked her nipple, eager to slide inside her. I was on the verge of doing just that when her alarm went off.

She groaned, reaching over to the nightstand to switch it

off. She turned, pecking my lips before rolling over, away from me. *Oh, hell no.*

I grabbed her around the waist, hauling her back into bed. "Where do you think you're going?"

"To work," she said. "I have the Steadman engagement party."

"Right," I said, distracted by the way our bodies pressed together, her soft against my hard. "*Later.*"

"Harrison." Dark circles lined her eyes, making the blue seem even more vibrant. She'd warned me that wedding season could be brutal, but I hadn't been prepared for just how busy she'd be.

"I haven't seen you in days."

"I miss you too." She smoothed a hand over my hair. "But this is just how it is this time of year."

"Twenty minutes," I said, kissing my way down her neck. Maybe if I distracted her, she'd forget she had to leave. "Just give me twenty minutes."

"Ten," she countered. "And we'll do it in the shower to save time."

I chuckled and threw the covers aside. "I can live with that."

She shook her head, her blond waves swaying over her naked back. I stared after her a moment before following. The clock was ticking.

She was already in the shower by the time I got in there, steam billowing out. I stepped inside, my eyes glued to her naked form. She was all curves and legs, and she had the most fantastic set of tits I'd ever seen. Her eyes darkened when she saw me, scanning my body hungrily.

Water sprayed over us, and I was glad I'd purchased a house with what my real estate agent had referred to as a party shower. At the time, it had seemed ridiculous. Who needed five shower heads? But with Juliana, I'd come to appreciate just how much fun we could have.

A waterfall shower head rained over us. Several came from the wall, ensuring no one was cold. It was heaven after a workout—and even better with Juliana. Everything was better with Juliana. I hadn't realized how much I'd been missing before she came along.

"What?" She tilted her head to the side.

I stepped closer, cupping her cheeks. Her nipples brushed against my chest, and my cock jerked in response. "I love you."

Her lips curved up into a smile, and for a moment, I wondered if the water running down her cheek was a tear. "I love you, Harrison."

I pressed my lips to hers, tongues tangling as our bodies fit together like two puzzle pieces. I smoothed my hands down her back, over her ass, pulling her to me. She lifted one leg, resting her foot on the shower seat before taking me in hand.

"I need you." Her blue eyes sparkled with emotion, with love and desire.

We both looked down, fascinated by the way I disappeared inside her, two becoming one. But the coupling was more than physical, it was so… I sighed, tilting my forehead to hers as I began to move. The way we came together was transcendent, often taking us to a higher plane.

"I love you," I whispered, our eyes locked.

"I love you," I said again, enjoying the look of pure ecstasy on her face. Her walls clenched around me as she cried out.

"I love you," I grunted, spilling inside her like the words were spilling from my lips.

She collapsed against me, her breath shaky. And as we came down from the high, I washed her body and whispered words of love.

Finally, I stepped out of the shower and wrapped a towel around my waist before holding one out for her. She switched off the water and stepped into my arms. "Thank you."

"For the sex or the towel?" I teased.

"Both." Her shoulders relaxed, and she wore a dazed smile.

Her phone chimed from the counter, and she leaned over to glance at the screen. "Oh shit. It's even later than I thought."

I gave her a kiss and headed downstairs to make us both some coffee. When I returned to the bathroom, she was standing at the sink doing her makeup.

"Here you go." I placed a travel mug on the counter in front of her.

"Thank you." She grabbed it and took a sip before returning to her eye shadow.

Watching her get ready was fascinating and strangely relaxing. I'd often sit on the sink or the edge of the tub, talking with her while she put on her makeup or curled her hair. That would likely change a bit once football season started back up, but I was intent on spending as much time with her as possible.

"Tonight's family dinner," I said. This would be the first one since Olivia had returned from London.

Juliana dropped the eye shadow brush and picked it up with a huff. "Yep. Just text me when you're done, so I know when to come home."

I knew it bothered her that we were keeping our relationship a secret. It bothered me too. The wedding was in a few short weeks, but I didn't like lying to my daughter. It was one thing to keep this hidden when she was living an ocean away. It was another to ask the woman I loved to pretend she didn't live here. And after talking with Reg—and some input from Jas—I realized maybe it was time to tell Olivia. Far better that she hear the news from me than someone else. At least that way, I could control the narrative, as Talia liked to say.

"Actually…" I paused, picking at the edge of my towel. "I was thinking maybe you should come."

"I thought you already made that happen this morning." She grinned.

I chuckled. "I meant to dinner."

She stilled, her blue eyes piercing mine in the reflection of the mirror. Then something shifted, and she grabbed her mascara and started applying it. I didn't know why she even bothered with that stuff—her beauty was striking.

"As the wedding planner." Her tone conveyed her disappointment loud and clear.

I walked over to her, wrapping my arms around her waist and resting my chin on her shoulder. "No. As the woman I love."

She set her mascara down and spun in my arms. "Are you serious?"

"Yes." I gripped her chin. "I love you." I slanted my mouth over hers. "I love you, and hopefully, Olivia can accept that."

"And if she doesn't?"

I lifted a shoulder, trying to convey nonchalance despite my concern. "We'll cross that bridge when we get there."

"Or…" Juliana paused, placing her hands to my chest. "I'll pretend to have another allergic reaction, and she'll feel so bad for me, she'll forget about being upset."

I groaned, covering my face with my hand. "Please don't. I don't think my heart could handle it."

She draped her arms over my shoulders. "So, tonight…"

I nodded, opening her robe and taking a peek inside. Fucking perfect. "Tonight."

She stepped away, heading for the closet. "Good. I can almost forgive you for making me late."

"So, you'll be on time for once. Big deal," I called after her as she retreated into the closet.

"To be on time is to be late. To be—"

"Ten minutes early is to be on time," I said, completing her sentence.

"That's right." She appeared in the doorway, fully dressed.

"Mm." I licked my lips, appraising her cobalt dress. It was professional—of course. But also undeniably sexy.

"You like?" She shifted from side to side, modeling it for me.

"No." I shook my head, stalking toward her. "I love."

Her lips tilted upward. "I love you too."

CONNOR AND OLIVIA WERE SET TO ARRIVE ANY MOMENT, AND Juliana wasn't home. I sent her a text message and frowned at the screen when there was still no response ten minutes later. I busied myself with setting the table, anxious about the evening ahead, when the doorbell rang.

I took a deep breath and opened the door with a smile. "Olivia."

She threw her arms around my neck. "Dad! I missed you."

"Missed you too, sweetie." I pressed a kiss to her hair.

"Connor." I held out my hand.

"Sir." We shook hands, and then they followed me inside.

"Dinner's almost ready," I said, the aroma of marinara sauce and cheese wafting out from the oven.

My phone chimed, and I turned away to glance at the screen. I frowned when I saw a new message.

. . .

*J*ULIANA: *I* DON'T KNOW WHEN *I'*M GOING TO BE HOME. *Y*OU *should start without me.*

"EVERYTHING OKAY?" OLIVIA ASKED.

"Yeah, um…" I hit the power button to darken my screen so Olivia wouldn't see who I'd been texting. "Nothing important."

Connor glowered at me, which I promptly ignored. He'd wanted me to tell Olivia about Juliana from the beginning. And now—when I was finally going to—she was MIA. Choosing her job over me, just like Cam had chosen work over family, time and time again.

I thought this was important to her. I thought *I* was important to her. And while I understood that stuff came up at work, I knew how much Juliana hated keeping our relationship a secret.

"Are we waiting on anyone else?" Olivia asked with a glance at the table. I'd set it assuming Juliana was coming.

"I don't think so."

"Oh, okay," she said, setting a platter of cookies on the counter. She was always baking—at least when she wasn't reading.

Connor gave me a meaningful look, but I shook my head firmly.

Dinner was relatively uneventful. Olivia did most of the talking, telling us all about her time in London. And I was excited to hear about her adventures, even if I was distracted.

Juliana and I tried to have dinner together every night, at least when I wasn't out of town for a photo shoot or she wasn't occupied with a wedding. We lived busy lives and we both loved our jobs, but we always made time for each other.

With Cam, it had been so different. We'd both been so young, so self-absorbed. I'd learned from my mistakes, but I also just wanted it more. I wanted to be with Juliana more than I'd wanted anything in my life—even a championship ring. And it made me more willing to put in the effort. To know that things wouldn't always be easy, but being with her was worth it.

I was disappointed that she couldn't make it, but I had a choice. I could stew over it and be angry about something out of her control. Or I could do something to help lessen her burden. If I loved her like I said I did, I needed to step up.

After Connor and Olivia left, I decided to call Juliana.

"Harrison, hey," she answered on the third ring, sounding winded. "I'm so sorry, but I can't really talk right now."

"I know," I said, not wanting to add to her stress. "What can I do to help?"

She blew out a breath, and the music in the background faded a little. "Give me a clone. No. Three clones. God, I'm going to be here forever."

"Where are Jen and Vanessa?" I asked, referring to her interns.

"Oh, they're here. It's the caterer who fucked up." I knew she must really be livid if she was cussing. "They're short-staffed. And now we're bussing tables and refilling drinks."

"I have to go," she said and hung up before I could say goodbye. But a plan was already taking shape in my mind.

I changed into black slacks and a white shirt with a simple tie. Fortunately, I knew the event was at an arboretum nearby. I sped there, wondering if she'd be pissed or pleased to see me. I weaved through the gardens to where the engagement party was being held. Most of the guests were on the dance floor or mingling, too busy to notice me. Which suited me just fine. I was here to help Juliana, not sign autographs or pose for pictures. It was a roped-off event, but I waltzed right in, completely unnoticed.

Juliana was off in the distance, smiling as she bent over to refill someone's drink. Her cheeks were flushed, but she looked happy. Despite how exhausted and frazzled she might be, she never let it show. At least, not with anyone but me.

I grabbed a tray and started stacking dishes, mimicking what the other servers were doing. I'd loaded several glasses when Juliana approached.

"Harrison?" she kept her voice low, likely so as not to draw attention to us.

I glanced up at her and smiled. "Hey, babe." I returned my attention to my task.

"What on earth are you doing here?"

"Helping. Now, put me to work."

"Put you to—" She shook her head. "Absolutely not. Though I appreciate the offer. Come on," she said, trying to pull me toward the exit. "You shouldn't be doing that."

"Why?" I turned to her. She was exhausted—running all the time, trying to make everyone's dreams a reality.

She leaned closer, lowering her voice to a whisper. "Because you're Harrison freaking Hayes. You don't—" she waved a hand through the air "—bus dishes. People do this kind of thing for you."

I stilled, placing my hands on her shoulders. "Juliana. When have you ever seen someone do this for me? I don't have household staff. I have someone who comes in and cleans once a week. And a guy who mows the grass and maintains the pool."

"Yeah, but—"

I shook my head. "I'm here. I'm happy to help. And the sooner we finish, the quicker we get to go home and get in bed."

Her shoulders relaxed, and I sensed I was going to win

this argument. "Aren't you concerned someone will recognize you?"

"Nah." I gave her shoulders a squeeze then grabbed the tray. "No one would ever believe I was a waiter."

"Thank you." She pressed her lips to my cheek. "I'm sorry I missed dinner. I really wanted to be there."

"I know. It's okay. We'll tell her another time."

Her face fell, but she quickly recovered. She shook her head, forcing a smile. "Yeah. You're right."

"One more thing," I said, not ready for her to walk away. Not when I sensed her sadness.

I leaned in, my lips close to her ear. "I love you, and we're in this together."

"I know. I can't tell you how much it means to me that you showed up." She gave me a watery smile.

It was then I knew I'd made the right decision. And I vowed that I would show up time and again for this woman. I would put in the effort, and I wouldn't let our relationship fail.

CHAPTER TWENTY-THREE

Juliana

"Please make sure the hydrangeas are over there. I want fresh vases in the bathrooms, and we need to double-check the list of guests with food allergies." Landon and the rest of the staff nodded as I went through my checklist for the rehearsal dinner.

Olivia and Connor were getting married tomorrow, and Harrison and I still hadn't told her we were dating. Not just dating—living together. There simply hadn't been time. Our schedules hadn't matched up, and now, it was time for the wedding.

I'd arrived at the venue early in the morning to oversee setup for the rehearsal dinner. Landon and I had been running around all day, making sure welcome baskets were in place and everything was perfect, even the weather. It was a gorgeous sunny day with a light breeze.

Most of the guests were lounging by the pool or enjoying the local attractions, and I envied them. I wanted to relax poolside with Harrison, even go for a hike. But that would have to wait for another weekend. With one last glance at the dining room, I confirmed that everything was in place.

"Hey, boss," Landon said, joining me in the back area where I was checking the desserts. Landon had already done it, but I felt the need to busy myself.

"Hey," I said, glancing up at him. He looked sharp—like always. And the past few months, he'd really flourished in his new role.

"Everything looks great. Just verified the allergy list again myself."

"Great. Thanks." I didn't meet his eyes, couldn't.

He stepped closer and lowered his voice. "You okay?"

"Yeah. Of course. I just want to make sure everything is perfect."

He placed a hand on my shoulder, forcing me to look at him. "Juliana—it's more than perfect. It always is. What's really going on? Does this have something to do with Harrison?"

I wanted to say no, but a bigger part of me wanted to say yes. I was afraid if I didn't talk to someone before the weekend started, I'd go insane.

"It's just—no one knows about Harrison and me, apart from you and Connor. And…I don't know. It's weird, okay? Attending the wedding of his daughter as an outsider." Harrison had become much more to me than a client. And by default, Olivia had too.

This wasn't the first event I'd attended for family or friends as a party planner, but it was the first one where the distinction had bothered me. For once, I wanted to enjoy the wedding. I wanted to sit at his side and show the world we were together.

He squeezed my shoulder. "I can't imagine how you feel. But just think—once this is over, you can tell her, right?"

I nodded. Landon knew all about the failed dinner. I closed my eyes and shook my head, wishing I weren't going into this weekend with a sense of dread. "True."

"It's going to be great. You'll see."

Everyone kept telling me that, but it was difficult to believe.

Someone called for me, drawing my attention. "Be right there."

Preparing for the wedding was a good distraction, at least for a while. If I didn't think about it, I could pretend this was for any other client. But then Harrison entered, and it felt as if all the air were sucked from the room. He was so handsome, and judging from the looks other women were giving him, everyone knew it. His gray suit was flawless, and he looked amazing in the shirt and tie I'd picked for him.

Me—his girlfriend. The woman he was in love with. Yet I wasn't on his arm, parading around the room with him like Cam. No, I was a sweaty mess, trying to maintain a professional demeanor as I ground my molars. I was the outsider looking in.

Harrison met my eyes from across the room and smiled, but it didn't quell the unease churning through my gut.

"Juliana," Landon said, drawing my attention away from them.

"What's up?" I asked, soon pulled in to help with various tasks.

As the evening dragged on, I was so busy, I barely saw Harrison. Though I caught glimpses of him—smiling at Olivia, dancing with Cam…

I shook my head. *I need out.*

"Hey, Landon," I said after dinner was finished and most of the guests were on the dance floor.

"What's up?"

"If you think you've got it covered, I'm going to head out." I pressed my fingers to my temples. "I've got a horrid headache."

We both knew I was lying, but I didn't care. I just couldn't stay—I couldn't stand there, watching Harrison work the room, while I worked.

Landon's brow rose, but he didn't say anything. "Sure. I've got it covered."

I could think of only one other occasion where I'd ducked out early. I always stayed until the end, well past when all the guests had left. I was the first to arrive and the last to leave.

I returned to my room, smiling at guests I passed along the way. When the door finally closed, I let out a sigh of relief. I took a long shower and had just changed into pajamas when my phone rang. Harper's name flashed across the screen.

"Hey." I tucked the phone between my ear and shoulder. "What's up?"

"Hey." Her voice sounded off, funny somehow. "I, um, are you at home?"

I switched the phone to my other ear. "No. Harrison's daughter is getting married this weekend, so I'm in Ojai."

"Oh." When she hesitated, I frowned. She was acting really weird. "Okay."

"Hey, are you okay?"

The silence seemed to drag on, and then she said, "Yeah. I'm fine. Look, let's meet up to talk after the wedding."

"Sure. I'd love that."

"Great. Are you free Sunday night?"

"Um…" I put my phone on speaker and navigated to my calendar. "Yeah, but I'm going to be wiped out after this."

"Monday, then?"

I frowned, wondering why she seemed so insistent to talk to me. "Are you sure everything's okay?"

"Yeah. I'm just really missing my friend. Monday night— my place?"

My shoulders relaxed. "Same. I'm looking forward to it."

"Mm," she hummed, and I wondered if she was distracted.

"Harper?"

"Yeah. I'll see you then."

We said goodbye and disconnected the call. I fell back on the bed, my arm over my forehead. How on earth was I going to survive tomorrow?

THERE WAS A KNOCK AT MY DOOR, THE ABRUPT SOUND PULLING me from my sleep. I blinked my eyes open, squinting against the glow of the bedside lamp. I pushed myself up to a seated position, only then realizing I'd passed out on the foot of the bed.

With a frown, I reached for my phone. *Who the hell was knocking on my door at midnight?*

Whoever it was knocked again, and I stumbled off of the bed. I smoothed my hair away from my face and glanced through the peephole to discover Harrison standing in the hall. His green eyes were piercing, and it felt as if he could see me standing there. His tie was loose around his neck, his jacket discarded.

I cracked open the door. "What are you doing here?" I hissed.

"I had a question about the ceremony." He glanced left and right, then grinned. He lowered his voice. "Now, let me in."

I opened the door and let him into my hotel room. He immediately placed his hands on my hips, and I wanted to sink into his touch, especially after the long day I'd had.

The rehearsal dinner had gone smoothly, but I hated watching from the sidelines, hated not getting to truly be a part of this special day for Harrison and his daughter. *Just a few more days,* I told myself. Soon, Olivia would know, and Harrison and I would no longer have to hide our relationship. I could do this.

"I missed you." His voice was gruff.

I smiled, softening into his hold. "I missed you too. But—" I placed my palms to his chest. "We have a big day tomorrow, and we both need our rest."

I patted his chest and tried to step out of his arms, but he tightened his grip, reeling me in. "But I sleep better with you in my arms."

I melted at his words, but I knew I had to be strong—for both of us. He sprinkled kisses over my skin, weakening my resolve. And even though everything in me was calling out for this man, I shook my head. "We can't."

"Juliana." The sound of my name from his lips as he brushed my negligee aside made me crazed with desire. He kissed over my clavicle, down my cleavage. His touch was featherlight, yet the biggest tease of all, and I nearly caved.

"What if someone comes looking for one of us?" I tipped my head back, giving him better access. "God, I'm so sick of sneaking around." I sighed as he smoothed his hand over my shoulder, taking the strap of my negligee with it. The silky material slid down, revealing my nipple.

His eyes were liquid heat, focused solely on me. "I know. But it's only for a little while longer. We just have to make it through tomorrow."

I swallowed back a moan as his lips clamped around my nipple. "And what about—" I let out a shaky breath as he moved to my other breast. "Tonight?"

"Tonight," he said, meeting my gaze. "You're mine." He all but growled the words.

"I'm always yours." I cupped his cheeks, bringing his mouth to mine for a searing kiss. Despite his laid-back attitude, I sensed he needed the reassurance.

He slid the other strap from my shoulder, and we watched as the gown fluttered to the floor. He yanked his tie over his head, quickly shucking his shirt and pants before kissing his way down my torso. Then came my panties—dragged slowly, agonizingly down my legs.

"This is a bad idea," I said, but my protest was weak. *I* was weak when it came to this man. But he also made me strong.

He pulled my leg over his shoulder, and I reached for his shoulders, steadying myself. When he licked my slit, I nearly came undone. Especially when he plunged one finger inside me, then another. I was close, so close, my leg shaking as I struggled to remain standing.

"Do you know how hard it was, watching you from across the room? Not being able to touch you? Kiss you?" He kept teasing me with his fingers, his lips wet with my desire.

I nodded, exploring his shoulders with my hands. Anything within reach, I wanted to touch. And there was nothing but smooth, hard granite beneath my skin.

"You think I enjoyed watching other women throw themselves at you?" Cam included, though I didn't mention her specifically.

He growled, picking me up and tossing me onto the bed. "You're mine, Juliana." He crawled on top of me, a crazed look in his eyes. "And I'm yours."

I nodded, pulling him to me. I needed to touch him, kiss him. Needed reassurance that this wouldn't end. That nothing and no one would ever come between us.

But he couldn't give that to me; no one could. So, I tried my best to let go. To surrender to this feeling of vulnerability. To lean in despite my fears.

And with every brush of his lips, every caress, I felt the strength of his love. He proved it to me daily with both his words and actions. And regardless of what the future held, I wanted to be with him, give myself to him.

"Juliana," he grunted, his body blanketing me with heat.

I snapped my eyes to his, knowing how important it was to him that I was present. That I was focused solely on him.

"Let go." He thrust again, this time hitting that magical spot that transported me to another place. "Let go of your worries and your fears. Give them to me. And just," he grunted with another pulse. "Let. Go."

I was overcome with the sensation of being weightless, as if I were watching us from above. And I let go. I surrendered to this moment and this man.

CHAPTER TWENTY-FOUR

Harrison

I stared at my reflection in the mirror, admiring the custom tuxedo Juliana had selected. I'd been hoping to steal a moment with her all day, but she'd been so focused on the wedding. So determined to make it the blissful day my daughter wished for that I couldn't complain. Juliana had gone above and beyond—completely transforming the venue into Olivia's dream wedding.

And being back at the historic Ojai inn only brought back memories of the last time we were here. Of the weekend that had changed everything. I smiled at my reflection, eager to see her, when there was a knock at the door.

I smoothed down my tie and called out, "Come in."

My face fell when Cam strode through the door, her skintight dress leaving little to the imagination. She'd never been one for subtlety. And last night, she'd been hanging all over me. I blamed it on the alcohol and the fact that our daughter was getting married, but with the way she was eyeing me now, I wasn't so sure.

"Looking good, Harry." She winked at me. "Your stylist did well."

My eye twitched. She knew I hated it when she called me Harry. And I resisted the urge to correct her about my "stylist."

I tugged at my collar, shifting uncomfortably. "Don't call me Harry."

"You know I only do it because I enjoy seeing you all riled up." Her lips curled into her seductive smile, though it did nothing for me.

I clenched and unclenched my fists. "Can you just behave for once? For this one day—can't we at least pretend to get along?"

"Darling…" She placed her hand on my lapel, smoothing her hand down.

At least until I grabbed her wrist and pulled it away. "What are you doing?"

She peered up at me with blue eyes, though they weren't the ones I loved. Not anymore. "I've missed you."

I shook my head. "Why are you doing this? Why today? Are you intent on ruining our daughter's wedding?"

"No." She pouted and spun away. "I'm just… This wedding has brought back so many memories. What about all the good times we had?"

I shook my head. "Memories are in the past and should stay there. We didn't work before, and we wouldn't work now."

"We were happy though, weren't we?" Her eyes filled with tears, and for once, I didn't think she was acting. But with Cam, you could really never know.

"Yes." I took her hands in mine, wanting to comfort her. I didn't love her—not anymore. But I would always care about her. Time had mellowed my feelings toward the divorce, toward Cam. I no longer resented her. "We were."

She started crying, and I hesitated a moment before wrapping my arms around her. "What's wrong?"

"I can't believe our baby's getting married." Her voice was muffled by my chest.

"I know." I rubbed circles on her back, the feeling of having her in my arms both foreign and familiar.

There was a knock at the door, and it swung open. I pulled away from Cam just as Juliana's eyes darted between my ex and me. Surprise flashed across her face, and then it was gone. I was positive I looked guilty, but I'd done nothing wrong. I gnashed my teeth.

"I'm sorry," Juliana said, immediately glancing away. She pressed a button on her headset. "She's not with Harrison."

"Who's not with Harrison?" I asked, heading toward her. I needed to fix this before she got the wrong idea about what she'd walked in on between Cam and me.

"Olivia," she said, barely glancing at me. "Have you seen her?"

I shook my head. "No, but I was about to go speak with Connor before swinging by to get her."

"Great. You have ten minutes. Max." Juliana glanced down at her tablet.

She was stunning. Her pale pink dress clung to her curves, hinting at the amazing body beneath. Her hair hung in long waves down her back, and I had a vision of pushing her dress up and wrapping her hair around my fist.

The corner of my lips curled into a grin. Oh, what I wouldn't give to have ten minutes alone with her. To muss her hair and obliterate her schedule.

"Harrison?" Cam asked, and I'd nearly forgotten she was in the room.

I shook my head to clear it and strode toward the door—toward Juliana. "Cam, I'll see you out there. And while you're here," I said to Juliana, "I had something I wanted to ask you."

"Sure. But I only have a minute. I need to get the wedding

party in place. Ms. Howard, you should probably take your seat."

Cam pursed her lips but said nothing as she marched past. I closed the door behind her, pulling Juliana inside before caging her against the wall.

"What did you need to ask me about?" She was all business, her expression so stern. Was she upset about Cam and me?

I brushed her hair over her shoulder, pushing it aside to reveal her neck. I pressed my lips to the skin behind her ear, grazing the shell with my teeth. "You look beautiful."

She shivered. "Thank you."

"Cam's emotional about the wedding."

"Emotions always run high on wedding day." She attempted to push past me, but I trapped her there.

I dipped so my eyes met hers. "Juliana, are you upset?"

"No." She shook her head, finally meeting my gaze. "I trust you. And I know there's nothing between you and Cam —at least, not on your end."

I furrowed my brows. While I was distracted, she pushed past me and made her way toward the door.

"Wait—" I grabbed her wrist.

"What?" she huffed. "I'm kind of busy."

I stepped closer, placing my hands on her shoulders. "Will you save me a dance for later?"

She pulled her lower lip into her mouth. "I'm not sure—"

I shook my head. "Nope. After tonight, you're no longer my daughter's wedding planner. You're mine."

She softened, sinking into my touch. "I already am yours."

"You know what I mean." I slid my hands down her arms. "I can't wait until we don't have to hide this anymore."

She opened her mouth to respond then held up a finger, listening to something in her earpiece. "Just a second."

I let out a deep sigh at the interruption.

"Yes." She spoke into the mouthpiece. "Please send the photographer to the bridal suite. Father of the bride will be there soon."

She grinned, returning her attention to me. "Guests are in place. Go talk to Connor. I'll find Olivia."

I dropped a kiss on the top of her head before making my way toward the study where Connor and his groomsmen were getting ready.

"Hey." I peeked my head inside after knocking. "Are you…" I glanced around, noting that he was alone. Though I could've sworn I'd heard him talking to someone. "Is every-thing okay?"

"Yeah." His voice was higher than usual, and I blamed it on nerves. Maybe he'd been practicing his vows.

"I just wanted to take a moment to share a drink with you —and perhaps some wisdom—before the wedding."

He poured us each a whiskey, and we toasted to Olivia.

"You know, I had my reservations at first," I said, opting for honesty as I studied the contents of my glass. "But you really are the only man I can imagine marrying my daughter."

"Thank you, sir."

"I see how devoted you are to her, and I hope that will continue throughout your lives."

"Of course, sir."

"Olivia's—" I stared at the wall of bookshelves before turning my attention to Connor. "Olivia's my world, and now she's yours too. Love her, cherish her, protect her."

He nodded, his expression solemn. "I take my role as her husband very seriously. I love Olivia with all my heart, and I will *always* put her first."

I downed the rest of my whiskey and stood. Connor rounded the desk to meet me.

"I only want her happiness." He held out his hand to shake, but I tugged his hand, pulling him into a hug.

"Welcome to the family, Connor. You're a good man." I patted him on the back.

It felt as if I was passing the baton in a way. I'd raised Olivia, always been there for her—always would be. But he was her world now. He was her hero. And that was exactly how it should be.

"Thank you, sir." His voice was strangled, and I knew I needed to get out of here before we both teared up.

"All right." I released him. "I'll leave you to it. Juliana will have my balls if I fuck up the schedule."

He chuckled. I opened the door, then paused. "Hey. Have you seen Olivia?"

He shook his head, and I frowned. I couldn't imagine her getting cold feet. But where the hell was she?

I glanced in every room I passed. As a result, I was dragged into a few conversations with some of the guests. By the time I made it to the bridal suite, Olivia had returned and was ready to go. Landon had the bridesmaids file out into the hall, giving me a moment alone with my girl.

I stared at her reflection in the mirror, marveling at this incredible woman. My daughter.

"Olivia." My voice was scarcely above a whisper. "You look… Wow. You're radiant."

She smiled, turning to face me. The cream lace of her veil framed her face, the gown draping over her curves like a cloud. She looked elegant and…

"Don't cry, Dad." She gave me a watery smile. "You can't cry, or else I'm going to cry. And then my makeup is going to be ruined, and Connor won't want to marry me."

"Don't be ridiculous. Connor is so in love with you. You could wear a paper bag, and he'd still want to marry you."

"I know." She sniffled, peering up at the ceiling as if to

keep her tears at bay. "Thank you for this day. Thank you for being supportive of Connor and me."

I smiled. "I really want to hug you, but I'm afraid to mess anything up."

She laughed, walking into my open arms. "I love you, Daddy."

"I love you too, Livie." I gave her a squeeze, knowing this was the last time I'd hug her as Olivia Hayes. Soon, she'd be Connor's wife—Olivia James. "Now…let's get you married."

She pulled an embroidered handkerchief out of the pocket of her dress and used it to dab at the corners of her eyes. "Okay." She smiled, tucking it back inside and grabbing her bouquet from the vanity. "I'm ready."

I held out my arm. Good thing she was ready because I wasn't sure I was. Happy as I was for my daughter, I still saw her as my baby girl. And I was struggling to get my heart to catch up to reality.

"Dad?" She peered up at me with the same look of trust and love she always had. "You okay?"

I shook my head to clear it and forced a smile. "Absolutely. Let's do this. And there's…something I want to talk to you about later. After the wedding."

"Is it about Juliana?"

I jerked my head back. "What about Juliana?"

"You guys are together, right? That's why I saw you sneaking out of her room early this morning."

I gaped at her. "You what?" I was so stunned, I couldn't even try to deny it.

"You know…" She smiled. "I totally sensed there was something between you two."

"You did?" I furrowed my brow.

Olivia nodded. "Since the first meeting."

"Seriously?"

"Yep." The "p" popped as did her smile.

"And you're not… I don't know. Upset?"

She frowned. "Why would I be upset?"

"Because she's your wedding planner. She's younger. She—"

Olivia cut me off before I could continue. "Dad." She placed a hand on my shoulder. "I'm happy for you. Juliana's amazing. Plus—" she grinned as if an idea just occurred to her "—I'd have a guaranteed spot on her calendar for all future parties. This is awesome!"

"Future parties?"

"Yeah. Baby shower, my kids' birthday parties…"

I didn't hear anything else after that, and I fumbled to sit. "Are you…are you pregnant?"

She shook her head, covering her mouth to stifle a giggle. "No. Not yet. But one day, Connor and I hope to have kids. And I absolutely want Juliana to plan all their parties."

I shook my head with a laugh. "Don't you think you're getting a bit ahead of yourself?"

"No." She placed her hands on her hips. "Connor and I are about to walk down the aisle after all."

"Not about the kids," I said. "About Juliana and me."

She was thinking years ahead—at least, in my head. And while I knew how I felt about Juliana, the worry was always in the back of my mind that she'd find someone better, someone younger, someone…who wasn't me.

Olivia barked out a laugh, sweeping her train behind her. "No. Now, come on. We're going to be late."

I stood, smoothing my hands down my pants. "Why do I feel like you're the parent and I'm the kid right now?"

She laughed, hanging on to me as we emerged from the bridal suite. Her bridesmaids were already all lined up, waiting to enter the chapel. One of the flower girls came up to us, her eyes wide as she admired Olivia.

"You look like a princess."

Olivia smiled down at her. "Thank you. I feel like one." She reached out and bopped the little girl on the nose. "You look *so* pretty."

"Okay." Landon clapped his hands together, getting everyone in the correct order. Olivia and I were at the back of the line, and Juliana joined us.

"I love you," I mouthed, excited to tell her about Olivia's reaction to the news of our relationship.

She mouthed back, a big smile on her face, "Love you too."

For a brief moment, it felt like we were a family. My incredible daughter and the woman I loved. Olivia had been nothing but supportive, and I was excited about the future, about the wedding. And I wasn't just thinking about my daughter's. I was going to marry this woman.

CHAPTER TWENTY-FIVE

Juliana

We stood behind the closed doors, a rustle of silk, a whisper of conversation. The guests were in place, and Connor and the groomsmen had just walked in. They looked stunning in their dress uniforms, a variety of medals glinting from their chests. And any minute now, the doors would swing open and the bridesmaids would walk through, followed by Olivia.

Landon stood at the front of the procession, coordinating with one of our interns inside the chapel. I was at the rear with Olivia and Harrison. I fluffed her skirt, making sure the train laid perfectly. Evelyn had done an amazing job with her dress—showcasing Olivia's curves, which were outlined with lace.

I smiled up at her, noting how calm she seemed. Her bouquet didn't shake, and she radiated happiness. For once, I wasn't sad or even envious. I was overjoyed. I was so happy for Olivia and Connor.

"You look absolutely stunning," I said, adjusting the ends of her veil.

Her gown was a cascade of lace and flowers, shimmering

when she turned in the light. It was romantic and fit her like a dream. As always, I was impressed by Evelyn's design. It was striking, and it was going to photograph beautifully.

"I forgot something," Harrison said, stepping aside. I frowned at his back, wondering what couldn't possibly wait. We were already two minutes behind schedule.

"Thank you," Olivia said, distracting me momentarily. "For everything. This dress, the venue, planning the wedding with my dad."

I smiled. "My pleasure."

She surprised me, pulling me in for a hug. "I'm so happy."

I beamed. My client's satisfaction and happiness were always important to me, but even more so for Olivia. "I'm so happy with how the wedding turned out, and I'm glad you are too."

"I am, but I was actually referring to you and my dad."

I stilled just as Landon called, "It's time."

"How did you…?" I shook my head. Now wasn't the time. The quartet had started playing *Canon in D*, the signal for the bride to start her walk down the aisle.

"That's your cue," I said. "Harrison."

"Just a minute," Olivia said, turning to me. "I see how happy my dad has been the past few months. And I'm so glad you're the reason."

I just stood there, dumbstruck, until Harrison returned and handed Olivia a small pin. He secured it to the bouquet. "Almost forgot—Grandma Marian's brooch."

They smiled at each other, then Landon asked, "Ready?"

Harrison gave me a warm smile, and I returned it, stepping to the side to grab the other door. "Ready," I said to Landon, and we opened them at the same time.

This was always my favorite part of the wedding—the anticipation and then the moment when the couple saw each other for the first time. A quick glance at Connor—who was gazing at Olivia with such love that it stole my breath. And then it was time to shut the doors.

"She looks amazing," Landon said after they were closed.

I nodded, walking quickly as we headed to check on the cocktail hour and set up for the family photos. "She does."

"And Harrison," he said.

"Yeah, that was a good call on the tux." I busied myself with the flowers, making sure every detail was just right.

"Just admit it," Landon said. "Your boyfriend looks hot."

"He does, doesn't he?" I grinned.

"You seem awfully happy." He arched an eyebrow, following me as I made my way around the tables, straightening any menus or grabbing any dropped flower petals.

"Olivia knows." He stilled, but I continued talking. "Just before the ceremony, she pulled me aside and told me she was happy for us." I was both relieved and overjoyed by her reaction.

He squealed, clapping his hands together. "That is so exciting. So…when are we planning your wedding?"

I swallowed and shook my head. "No. I mean…Harrison doesn't want to get married again."

"Are you sure?"

"Pretty sure." I laughed. "In our first meeting, he flat out said as much."

"Yeah, but…that was then. I mean, would you want to marry him if he were interested?"

"I—" I faltered, stilling at his question.

Did I? I hadn't really given it much thought, but now that Landon had asked, I was forced to evaluate my feelings on the matter. And I had to admit that the idea was appealing. I loved Harrison. I loved him, and I wanted to spend the rest of my life with him. Whether that meant we were married or just in a committed relationship, I didn't care. He was my life, my love.

"Aww. Yay! You totally do," Landon said, as if he could read my thoughts.

"I don't care about the wedding," I said. "But I do want to spend the rest of my life with him."

Landon pulled me into a hug, squeezing me tight and twirling me around. "I'm so happy for you, Jules."

"Thanks." I laughed, adjusting my dress when he finally set me back down. I glanced at my watch. "Come on. The ceremony should be about done, and we have work to do."

He saluted me. "Yes, ma'am."

We worked in silence, seamlessly executing the plan for the wedding as a team. That was why I loved working with Landon—he'd worked with me long enough, knew me well enough, that I often didn't have to say anything. As I watched how he handled Olivia's wedding, it made me even more grateful that I'd decided to promote him.

The doors opened, and the happy couple filed out. The photographer was in place, and everything was running smoothly. Connor wrapped his arms around Olivia, pulling her in for a hug. She laughed and squealed as he dotted kisses all down her neck. They didn't seem to mind—or maybe even notice—they had an audience. I smiled. They were so in love, so in their own little bubble...

I was so busy watching them, I didn't notice Harrison approach. He placed his hand on my lower back, leaning in to whisper in my ear. "Olivia wants a picture with us."

"She does?" I asked, searching his gaze.

I didn't want to get my hopes up. It was one thing for Olivia to give us her blessing. But to ask for a photo together, especially on her wedding day... It felt as if she was giving me her seal of approval. My eyes watered, overcome with happiness.

"Yep. Come on." He tugged on my hand, and I didn't fail to notice the way Cam was glaring at me.

We posed with Connor and Olivia, and then it was back to work. Though my steps were lighter now. Now that Olivia knew and had given us her blessing. I knew how important her opinion was to Harrison, and I was more relieved than I'd expected.

Dinner, the speeches, it all flew by in a blur. Harrison's speech was incredibly touching, and I teared up listening to him speak of his love for his daughter. As soon as the guests took to the dance floor, Harrison was at my side. "Dance with me."

"I…" I shook my head. "How would that look? I can't."

"It wasn't a request." He tugged on my hand with a wry grin.

I allowed him to lead me out to the dance floor. It felt like everyone was watching us, but when I glanced around, no one had taken notice. "Better" by SYML was playing, the lyrics packed with meaning. The song was about love and fate and hope. Harrison placed my hand on his shoulder, grasping the other in his.

He started swaying to the beat. "Relax, Juliana. I've got you."

In the past, I would've pushed back, I would've done the exact opposite. But I knew he had me. He was strong, compassionate, loving. I relaxed in his arms, secure in his embrace, in his love. Even though he was the one holding me, I wasn't letting him go.

"How was the wedding?" Harper asked when we'd nearly finished eating. We'd ordered takeout and were sitting on her couch with some documentary playing in the background.

"Good." I smiled, picking at a loose thread on my skirt. "Great, actually."

It had been forever since we'd spent time just the two of us. I'd missed her. Missed having girl time, but that was what wedding season was like—crazy. And any spare moment I'd had was spent with Harrison.

"I'm so glad." She smiled. "I take it that means Harrison finally told Olivia?"

I nodded. "Well, sort of. Apparently, she already suspected as much, and she was thrilled. She was so sweet about it."

"Aww. Yay. That's great news." She smiled, but it seemed guarded.

"It is. I'm glad you asked to meet up today. Attending the wedding, being with Harrison…" My heart rate picked up. "Well, it's got me thinking. You can tell your contacts to stop looking for Ryan. If they haven't found anything by now, they're probably not going to."

"That's the—" She glanced away with a pinched expression.

"You okay?"

"Yeah." She coughed, sipping some water. "So, if they'd found something…you wouldn't want to know, right?"

I stilled, gauging her expression. The closer I looked, the more I saw. The tight set to her jaw. The guarded look in her eyes. And then it hit me. "This isn't a hypothetical question, is it?"

She shook her head, her mouth set in a grim line.

My mind swam, a heavy feeling settling in my stomach as my entire world turned upside down. "They…" I swallowed. "They found Ryan?" I whispered, scarcely believing it was true.

She pursed her lips, considering her words. "Someone matching his description… It might not be Ryan," she rushed to add. "But it certainly looks like him."

"Wait. What?" I jerked my head back. "You have a picture?"

She nodded, typing on her phone. Still, she didn't show it to me. "Are you sure you want to see it?"

I nodded, my lips falling open on a gasp as she turned the phone to me. It had to be Ryan. If not, he had one hell of a doppelgänger.

"Oh my god." I cradled my head in my hands, stomach churning. "What if it is him?" I was going to be sick.

Harper had just dropped a bombshell. And while I should be overjoyed, I was…conflicted. I'd held out hope for so long that Ryan was out there. And while I still hoped that was the case, hearing those words didn't mean as much to me as I'd thought they would. Because I'd finally moved on.

"I think we should find out first whether it's Ryan or not. We'll go from there," she said. I nodded, my mouth opening and closing a few times, but words wouldn't come. "I'm headed to Thailand in a few days. Do you want me to follow up on it?"

"Yes, and I'm coming with you."

My mind spun with plans. I needed a ticket. I needed to pack. I needed to talk to Landon. We had another wedding this weekend, and I wasn't sure I'd be back in time. I'd never done something like this—never bailed on a client. I picked up the phone to call him.

"Hey, boss," he said when he answered. "What's up? Did we leave something at the venue?"

I shook my head before remembering he couldn't see me. "No. I, um, something's come up, and I have to go out of town."

"Everything okay?"

"I… Harper and I are going to Thailand. She thinks she found Ryan."

"What?" he shrieked.

"Yeah." I laughed, the sound a bit hysterical. "Pretty crazy. Look," I said, shifting to business mode. I was a planner; it was what I did. This revelation was throwing me for a loop. I had to focus on what I could control. "Do you think you can handle the Van Ness wedding?"

"Of course." He paused. "But…are you sure this is a good idea?"

"Leaving you in charge?" I deflected. "I thought that's what you wanted."

"Juliana." He blew out a breath. "I just… You're finally happy again. I don't want you to jeopardize that."

"Thanks, Landon." While I appreciated his concern, this was my decision to make.

"What does Harrison think about this?"

"He—" I swallowed. Telling Harrison should've been one of my first thoughts. At least, after I'd processed the news that Ryan might be alive. "I haven't told him yet," I whispered.

"Oh, girl. You need to talk to him." There was no judgment, just sympathy.

"I will." There was just so much to do. So much to consider.

We finalized a few more details, and when I hung up, I was surprised by how late it was. "Do you mind if I crash here tonight?" I asked Harper.

"Don't you think you should go home and talk to Harrison?"

With my hands on my cheeks and my eyes wide, I shook my head. "I don't know. Probably." I slumped, sagging beneath the weight of it all. "But I'm not ready to tell him."

"But you're going to tell him, right?" Harper's green eyes were full of concern.

"Of course I'm going to tell him." Though my stomach clenched just imagining how that conversation might go down. For all his laid-back attitude, I knew he wasn't going to like this. And I was afraid he'd try to talk me out of going.

I sighed. "I only just found out about this. I need more time to process the information." Though I wasn't sure there could ever be enough time to process something like this.

I'd moved on, and I was happy. I was living life. Now it felt as if I were dragged back in again, sucked beneath the water. And I was terrified.

CHAPTER TWENTY-SIX

Harrison

A clip of the latest Hollywood Heatwaves practice played on the TV, the linebackers in light pads, running at the opposing team. I watched number twenty-three, a new player named Xavier. He was agile despite his size, though I didn't know how he'd possibly fit all those dreads under his helmet.

My phone chimed from the coffee table, and I shook my head as I grabbed for it. Preseason games were starting next week, and I was excited. I couldn't wait to take Juliana to a game. And with wedding season winding down, we'd have more time together. Especially now that Olivia's wedding was over.

I smiled, thinking back on the past weekend. It had been…perfect. And I was so relieved by Olivia's reaction to my relationship with Juliana. Everything finally seemed to be headed in the right direction.

I glanced at my phone and frowned at Juliana's message.

> Juliana: It's getting late. I'm going to crash at Harper's tonight.

I'd really been looking forward to spending tonight with her—back in our bed, our home.

> I'll come get you.

Three dots danced on the screen, disappearing then reappearing again before a new message came through.

> Juliana: It's fine. I'll see you in the morning.

I furrowed my brow and then pressed the button to connect the call to her. It nearly went to voice mail before she answered.

"Hey."

I switched the phone to my other ear, trying to decipher her tone. Something was up. "Hey. You okay?"

"Yeah. Yeah."

"And Harper's okay?"

"Yeah." The sound was muffled, as if she were covering the speaker with her hand. "We're good. I'm just really tired after our big weekend, and I feel like I haven't seen her in forever."

I rubbed the back of my neck, feeling like an asshole. Still, my gut told me something was up.

"I'll see you tomorrow," she said.

"Sure. I don't have to be at the station until two, so we can spend the morning together."

"Great."

We'd never had such an awkward, stilted conversation. But maybe she was tired and just wanted to spend time with her friend. I knew how exhausted I was from the wedding, and I hadn't had the job of ensuring everything was perfect like she did.

I closed my eyes, imagining her smile, her blue eyes. "I love you."

"Love you too," she said, then disconnected the call.

That night, as I walked through my empty house, as I tossed and turned alone in bed, I finally understood what Reg had been trying to tell me. Before Juliana, though, the silence had never seemed so loud. The bed had never seemed so empty. But now…now, I knew what life could be like with her. And even though it was one night, it felt like an eternity.

Plus, our earlier conversation weighed on me. I suspected she was upset about something, but I had no idea what it was. I could read her better than anyone. And I got the feeling she was avoiding me, even though it made no sense.

When I finally slept, it was restless. My alarm chimed from the nightstand a few hours later, and I fumbled to shut it off. With a loud groan, I finally managed to hit the right button to silence the damn thing.

After rolling out of bed, I threw on some athletic gear and made my way to my home gym. Every rep seemed to burn more than usual, or maybe I was just pushing myself harder. I was reracking a plate when I jammed my thumb.

"Fuck," I groaned. "Fuck. Fuck. Fuck."

I dropped the plate, barely stepping out of the way in time to avoid crushing my toes.

I growled as I made my way to the kitchen, annoyed with the pain and the interruption to my workout. My thumb was already swelling when I put ice on it, and I only hoped I wouldn't have to go to the doctor.

After a shower and breakfast, my mood still hadn't improved. I was banging around the kitchen, looking for my blender, when the house alarm chimed.

I stood and spotted Juliana with her back to me. I studied her movements as she took her time removing her shoes.

"Hey." I walked over to her, my mood lightening just from her presence.

"Hey." Her shoulders were slumped, eyes puffy. Had she been crying? It looked like she hadn't slept at all last night.

I pulled her into my arms, just needing to hold her, hug her. "I missed you." I pressed a kiss to her hair. She nodded into my chest but said nothing. "Have a good time with Harper?"

She lifted her shoulder, but again, said nothing.

I cupped her cheeks with my hands. "Baby, talk to me. What's going on?"

She shook her head, unwilling to meet my gaze. Her silence was unsettling. And that coupled with the fact that she wouldn't look at me wasn't a good sign.

"I have to tell you something," Juliana said, and it was then I noticed her hands were shaking.

"Uh oh. Is this an RDT?" I teased, despite my concern.

"I, um… RDT?" Her brows pulled together.

"Relationship-defining talk." I rubbed my hands up and down her arms, needing her to relax.

"Oh." She laughed, though it had a nervous edge to it. "Um, sort of. It has to do with Ryan."

I thought I was going to be sick, but I tried to remain outwardly calm. "What about Ryan?"

She hadn't mentioned him lately, and I thought she'd finally accepted his disappearance. I'd always honor his memory, but I didn't want him to be such a looming presence as he had been. For a long time, it had felt as if there was a ghost with us, overshadowing our actions, our relationship.

"What about Ryan?" The words shredded my throat like shards of glass.

"Well," she sighed, and the wait was killing me. "Harper has some contacts in the area where the tsunami occurred."

I nodded, feeling as if my whole world was about to be obliterated. Blood whooshed in my ears, making it difficult to think.

"One of her contacts works at one of the bigger resorts, and they believe they spotted him." She finally met my gaze, her eyes searching mine.

And there it was, the explosion I'd been waiting for. *Boom.*

"Hmm." I rubbed a hand over my chin, even though all I wanted to do was punch something.

"Oh my god." Her eyes flew to my hand as she gingerly reached out for it. "What happened to your thumb?"

I shook my head, unconcerned. The pain in my thumb was nothing compared to the fucking ache in my chest. A fierce sense of protectiveness surged through my blood— protectiveness and possessiveness. She was mine. Not his.

I took a steadying breath, knowing I needed to tread carefully. I didn't want to immediately shut her down, but I also didn't want to give her false hope. The fact that Ryan would still be alive after all this time seemed incredibly unlikely.

"It's fine."

"That—" Her eyes were wide as she examined it. And I had to admit, it was pretty swollen. "That is not fine."

It was so tempting to focus on her concern for me and forget the matter at hand, but I sensed there was more. More to the whole "Ryan" sighting, if it even was him.

"Why do they think it's him? Is he going by the same name?" I needed more information.

"No." She shook her head.

"Have they seen his credit card or ID?"

"Well. No." She hesitated. "But he matches Ryan's description and build to a T."

"Do you know how many guys could fit that description?" I clenched my fists, hissing when my thumb pulsed. *Shit.*

"It's him. I know it." Her eyes were wild, and I could tell she was two seconds away from bursting into tears. "Harper had a picture."

I rubbed my temples, doing my best to stay calm. If I could keep my cool on the field, I could navigate these waters with Juliana.

"I guess I just…" I pursed my lips. "I'd be surprised if it's actually him. And I'd hate for you to get your hopes up." Though I could tell it was too late for that.

"I have to know. Either way, I have to know. And—" She drew in a shuddering breath, and I braced myself for her next words, knowing I wouldn't like them. "I leave for Thailand in the morning."

I should've expected as much, but I still felt blindsided. Her words were like a slap to the face. And though I'd tried to stay level-headed about this, I couldn't anymore. My response exploded out of me.

"What the hell are you thinking?" I roared. I began pacing, my feet pounding the tile. "Is this what it's going to be like every time you get a scrap of news? You race across the world?"

"No!" She leaned against the counter, as if it would support her. "This is the first time we've had any sort of lead in nearly three years."

"*Exactly*. It's been three years. Three fucking years. God, will you ever move on? Will you ever commit to me?"

She jerked her head back and then bared her teeth. "Move on?" She shook her head, her body coiled tight with tension, ready to explode. "How dare you."

She spun and headed for the stairs, and I raced to catch up. "Where do you think you're going? We're not done discussing this."

Her hand was poised on the banister. "I think it would be best to wait until you're in a calmer frame of mind."

I grabbed her arm, turning her roughly toward me. Her eyes were wide, anger flaring within.

"You're the one who isn't seeing things clearly. Because I —" I stabbed my chest with my finger "—*I'm* here. *I* love you."

"I know." She softened, placing her hand on my cheek. "And I love you too." Her words gave me hope and smoothed the jagged edge of my anger.

"Then don't go," I pleaded, leaning into her touch. I was prepared to get on my knees and beg if I had to.

She hesitated too long, and I knew I had my answer.

"Please," I whispered as she dropped her hand. I felt the loss of her touch keenly. I was losing her, just like I had Cam. Though the two couldn't be compared. Losing Cam was disappointing; losing Juliana was devastating.

She shook her head, eyes filling with tears. "I have to."

"Can't you have Harper check it out instead?" As soon as the words left my mouth, I felt like an asshole. *Delegate?* I tried to envision what I'd do if I were in her shoes, but I honestly couldn't. But I also couldn't imagine allowing her to walk out that door and into the arms of another man. It would break me.

She gaped at me. "Wow." She shook her head, disappointment clear.

I backed down, realizing perhaps I'd come across a bit harsh. "I don't think it's a good idea for you to go."

"Well—" she spun, climbing the stairs "—it's not your decision to make."

"This is foolish," I called, taking the stairs two at a time. I followed her into the bedroom, out of breath. And it wasn't from chasing her up the stairs.

She threw a suitcase on the bed and was already placing stuff in it. Her movements were frenetic, as if she couldn't move fast enough. Couldn't get away from me quickly enough. And I felt just as frantic to make her stay.

I leaned against the door, wishing I could prevent her from leaving. "Why?"

"What do you mean, why?" She paused, scarf in hand.

Fuck. She was leaving me.

She tossed it on the bed and walked over to me. "I have to do this. Please tell me you understand."

I did—on a deeper level, I truly did. But that didn't mean I had to like it. "What does this mean for us?"

"I wish I could give you an answer, but I don't want to lie. All I know is that I have to go. I have to find out if it's really him."

"And if it is...?" My unspoken question filled the air, swelling like a balloon of humid, oppressive tropical air.

Her eyes were tortured, conflicted. And I didn't know what outcome to hope for. If it was Ryan, if he was alive... would she choose him over me? And if he wasn't...would her grief be even worse?

It was then I realized this was a no-win situation. I needed to support her in this because I hated seeing her pain; I felt it as if it were my own. This gaping, raw wound. And in that moment, I knew I would do anything to take it away—

even send her into the arms of another man. I wanted her to find happiness, peace, more than anything. Even if that meant she wasn't with me.

So, with a deep breath, I took her hands in mine. My heart was fucking breaking. "Do what you need to do."

She swallowed back a sob, though her eyes couldn't hide her relief and sadness. "I don't deserve you."

I placed a finger beneath her chin, lifting, forcing her to meet my gaze. "You deserve nothing but happiness." I smiled a watery smile. And I hoped she knew just how sincere I was.

I rubbed my hands up and down her arms. This might be the last time I touched her, the last time I held her. The last time I called her mine. Though, could I truly call her mine when she'd always been his? Or at least, a part of her heart still belonged to him.

"Look—" I faltered. She'd been honest about what she needed, and I knew I had to do the same.

"Uh oh," she teased, perhaps hoping to defuse some of the tension. But it only filled my gut with dread.

Was I making the right decision? I knew I couldn't be with someone who wasn't fully committed to me. It had happened before with Cam. And though Juliana wasn't Cam, and our relationship was completely different, I needed to know that if push came to shove, she'd put our relationship first. Above Ryan. Above our careers. Above anything.

I was finally ready to make that kind of commitment, but...she wasn't. Seeing how she'd reacted to news of Ryan, I feared she might never be. I wouldn't settle for part of her. I wanted everything. And while I was inclined to hold on tighter, to try to convince her to stay with me, I was resigned.

I pressed my lips to hers, knowing this might be goodbye. "I love you, but I won't be a consolation prize."

Panic flared in her eyes briefly before she nodded. "You

are *not* a consolation prize, and I'm sorry if I've made you feel that way."

"You haven't." I tucked her hair behind her ear, desperate for any touch. "I hope you find what you're looking for. And if that isn't me..." I cleared my throat as if I could smother my emotions.

She opened her mouth, but I pressed a finger to her lips. "Don't." I shook my head. "Don't make a promise you might not be able to keep."

She swallowed hard and nodded. "I'm not going to make any promises, but know that I love you. I love you so much, but I also need closure—for me, for us."

For us. Her words hung in the air.

I wanted to assure her that it would be okay. That she could do this and then everything would be as it was, but my need for self-preservation won out. "Don't come back unless you're one-hundred-percent sure you want to be with me."

A tear streaked down her cheek, and she quickly wiped it away. "Okay." She sniffled. "That's fair."

She wrapped her arms around my neck, and I held her close. Bathed in her jasmine scent, I knew this was goodbye —perhaps for good.

"Thank you." Her words were muffled by my chest.

"For what?" I drew back, peering down at her. Her cheeks were wet with tears, and I dried them with my thumb. I needed to comfort her, even if my heart was breaking.

"For...for bringing me back to life." She sniffled, and I brushed her hair over her shoulder. "I love you, Harrison."

"I know." I pulled her into me. "And I love you." Which was why I was willing to let her go.

CHAPTER TWENTY-SEVEN

Juliana

To everyone else, it looked like paradise. But returning to Thailand was like my own personal hell. The trip had been relatively smooth, but I was wrung out. I'd left one man to find another, and I loved both of them. I couldn't move on, not without answers. But I also knew that Harrison wouldn't wait forever—and it wasn't fair to ask him to.

Harper and I went straight from the airport to the hotel where this man, where Ryan, was supposed to be. I could scarcely breathe the entire ride there. And when we arrived, my legs felt like lead. The thought that Ryan might actually be here, right now, was more than my mind could handle.

While Harper checked us in, my attention was caught by a man across the lobby. He had dark brown hair like Ryan's, though it was longer. He was about the same height, similar build, and for a moment, my breath caught.

"Ryan?" I whispered, scared it was a dream or a nightmare. Which, I wasn't sure.

But then he turned. There was a resemblance between the

man and Ryan, but it wasn't Ryan's warm brown eyes that greeted me. It wasn't his lopsided smile.

My vision blurred as I teetered on the verge of collapse. I was exhausted both mentally and physically.

"You okay?" Harper asked, returning to my side.

"Yeah." I swallowed, nodding. "Yeah."

Harrison was right. This was a wild-goose chase. I'd traveled halfway across the world for answers. I'd tried to anticipate every possible scenario, but I hadn't anticipated just how awful I'd feel once I got here. Whether or not I found Ryan, I'd walked away from Harrison—I'd made him feel like he wasn't enough. And while a part of me would always love Ryan, I wasn't *in love* with him anymore like I was with Harrison.

I followed Harper to our room in a daze. When I sank down on the bed, my heart was heavy. "I fucked up. I never should have come here. Ryan's gone."

It was the first time I'd admitted to myself that Ryan was probably dead. I'd known all along how likely of an outcome that was. But I'd been unable to accept the truth until now. Ryan wasn't coming back.

It was time to stop. Stop chasing after something, someone, that deep down I knew wasn't there. I stilled, shaken by the realization. The words replayed in my head. *Ryan is gone. Ryan isn't coming back.*

It didn't matter how many times I'd talked to Lindsay about it, to my friends, it had never really sunk in until now. He. Was. Gone.

She joined me on the bed, her expression drawn. "I wish I'd never told you about this lead."

"Harper." I took her hand in mine. "You were being a good friend, the *best* friend. You know how hard this has been on me—more than anyone. And you were only doing what I asked."

"I know. But you were happy. You and Harrison were happy."

I nodded. "We were, weren't we?" A soft smile played at my lips. "But it was my decision to come. You gave me the information, but I'm the one who acted on it. And I've made another decision—I don't want to meet the man your contact believes is Ryan."

She gaped at me. "You don't?"

I understood her shock. I'd spent the past few years obsessed with news from Thailand, reading online about survivors of natural disasters, miracles. I didn't want to give up hope for Ryan's sake, but I also knew it was killing me to hold on. It was destroying my relationship with Harrison.

I shook my head. "A part of me will always love Ryan, but Harrison is it for me."

She nodded. "I know he is. I can see it when you talk about him or when the two of you are together. He's... Well, we all loved Ryan. But Harrison is the type of man I always envisioned you with."

"Really?" I asked, stunned by her admission.

"Yes. And I'm kind of shocked he didn't demand to come."

"I know," I said with a humorless laugh. Despite his edict to "let go," he could be bossy at times, and it was sexy as hell.

I'd secretly hoped he'd show up at the airport and beg me not to go or demand to come along. But he hadn't. And I couldn't blame him. I knew how painful it was to watch him and Cam together. I'd never want him to feel that with Ryan and me, especially knowing about his past.

I sniffled, feeling even worse about it all. I could only imagine what he was thinking, how I'd made him feel. And my stomach clenched. "It doesn't matter now."

"But surely..."

"It certainly felt like goodbye."

We were silent a moment, the palm trees rustling in the wind.

"Speaking of goodbye," Harper said, interrupting my thoughts. "I have an idea. It's, um… Well, it might give you some closure, at least on the Ryan front."

"Okay," I said, dragging out the word.

At this point, I was over this trip. I was exhausted, and I missed Harrison. I just wanted to go home and crawl into his arms, if he'd even have me.

"What is it?" I shifted on the bed, tucking one leg beneath me.

She took a deep breath. "You know how we never had a funeral?"

I nodded, though I'd never really given it much thought. For the longest time, I'd been convinced he was missing, not dead.

"I think we should celebrate Ryan's life. We should give him a proper send-off."

"I like that." But then I frowned, thinking of the logistics, of how sad it would be. "I don't know," I hedged. "I really don't want anything depressing."

"Exactly. Which is why I was going to suggest copying some traditions from the Buddhists."

I quirked an eyebrow. "Okay. What did you have in mind?"

"Have you ever seen a Buddhist funeral?" she asked, excitement vibrating through her. I shook my head. "They're very moving. Since Buddhists believe in reincarnation, their rituals focus on celebrating the person's life. It's viewed as a way to symbolize their rebirth into their new life."

I pursed my lips, considering it. "That's… Wow. I actually really like that idea."

"Yeah?" Her mouth quirked to the side.

"Yeah." I nodded, realizing just how much I liked it. Just how much I needed it. "Let's do it."

"Maybe you needed to come back here to finally admit that to yourself. To be able to accept it and move on."

My shoulders sagged, some of my enthusiasm flagging. "Maybe…but at what cost?"

I could remember Harrison's face when I told him about Ryan. But he wasn't nearly as upset as when I told him I was going to Thailand. He'd tried to talk me out of it—begged even, but in the end, I think we both knew it was something I had to do. Now, I realized it was nothing but a big mistake.

Harper pulled me into her, and I realized I'd started crying. "It'll all work out, you'll see."

Exhausted from the jet lag and the emotional toll this trip had already taken on me, I lay down and passed out. I fell into a deep sleep, assaulted by a dream of the tsunami. I was pushed underwater. I was grasping for the palm tree, desperate for air. My lungs burned, and I reached out in the darkness. But this time, it wasn't Ryan I called out for. It wasn't Ryan I tried to clutch beneath the surface. It was Harrison.

I awoke with a start, disoriented. I called out for Harrison, but then reality crashed down on me, almost worse than my nightmare. He wasn't here.

I lay awake the rest of the night, debating whether to text him. So many times, I opened a new message, fingers poised over the keys. And so many times, I deleted it.

I scrolled through my photos, tears falling with every image I saw. Harrison kissing my cheek as we lay in bed, my hair wild on the pillow. Us with broad smiles as we posed with Olivia and Connor at their wedding. Him in the pool, arms resting on the edge, hair slicked back from his face, an intense stare tracking my every move.

My heart ached, and I wished I could go back in time. But

it was too late. And though he'd told me not to come back until I was sure, I was afraid. Afraid that even if I was certain, I couldn't repair the damage I'd done.

A few days later, Harper and I stood on the beach, watching as the waves rolled in. It was so similar to the spot where Ryan had proposed, and as the wind rustled through the trees, a sense of rightness settled over me.

There was no casket, no body, there was only the wind and the water and these friends. I wore white, as did Harper. And she'd spoken to some of the locals, who were only too willing to help. Everyone here had always been so friendly and welcoming, and this was no exception.

Many of them started to sing, and the scent of flowers perfumed the air. It felt more like a wedding than a funeral, and I found myself smiling through my tears. Though I couldn't understand much of what was said, I was overcome with a feeling of wholeness, of peace. I couldn't describe it, but it felt as if Ryan were there with us.

Finally, it was time for me to speak. I stepped forward as the music died down, and everyone turned their attention to me.

"Summing up a life in a few words seems inadequate for anyone, let alone Ryan." I smiled, though my nose stung. "He was kind and loving, generous. He was an amazing man."

I sniffled. "Some of my favorite memories of him were from our time here. And I hope—" My voice broke, and tears fell freely down my face. "I hope that wherever he is, he's happy. I hope that he's at peace."

I swallowed hard, trying to grasp the enormity of the moment. I finally accepted the fact that Ryan wasn't coming back. But instead of my chest constricting like it had in the past, instead of my stomach bottoming out, or the terrifying visions that usually came to mind, there was…nothing. I felt surprisingly free. I felt at peace.

I walked to the water's edge, mesmerized by the endless ocean. With a chain of orange chrysanthemums clasped loosely in my hands, I knew that this was goodbye. Ryan would always have a piece of my heart, but it was time to move on. He would want me to move on, and being here, returning to the place of such unimaginable beauty and tragedy, had finally convinced me of that.

And as I tossed my flowers into the ocean and watched the waves carry them out to sea, a sensation of warmth washed over me. I smiled and sent a wish to the universe that wherever Ryan was, he knew how much I'd loved him.

When I turned back toward the resort, a man caught my eye. He stood off to the side, not part of the ceremony, but interested all the same. And he looked just like Ryan. He was the same height, same build, though he was more muscular and tanner than I remembered. His hair lighter from time in the sun. My heart stopped when he removed his sunglasses, everything and everyone else stilling. The man's resemblance to Ryan was uncanny.

I squinted, wondering if my mind was playing tricks on me. I'd been duped once—yesterday in the lobby, seeing someone that wasn't him.

One of Harper's friends from the area whispered something in her ear, and she turned to me. "That's him," she said. "That's the man they thought was Ryan."

I nodded. "I can see the resemblance, but it isn't him. Ryan's gone, and it's time to let go once and for all." We'd had our time together, and it was incredible. But it was time to say goodbye.

I knew I'd made the right decision, but what happened next confirmed it. A woman joined him, and he wrapped his arm around her, leaning down to press a kiss to her temple. She was petite with dark hair, her belly round with child. And instead of a pang of longing or sadness, I was happy.

Whoever the man was, he had a bright future. I smiled and waved, silently wishing him well.

"Wow. Okay," Harper said. "I know you said you didn't want to pursue it, but still…"

I laughed, throwing my arm over her shoulder as we headed for the hotel, for home. "Maybe it's okay not to have all the answers."

She shook her head with a laugh. "Are you feeling okay? Because the Juliana I know needs answers, data."

I lifted my shoulder. "What can I say? My Zen guru has rubbed off on me."

"Oh, he's certainly rubbed *something* off on you," she teased.

I laughed, enjoying one last look at the ocean. The water had taken a lot, but it had given so much too. My heart was full despite all that had happened, and I knew with absolute certainty that Harrison was my future. And I vowed to never let him doubt that again.

CHAPTER TWENTY-EIGHT

Harrison

The doorbell rang, but I ignored it, hoping they'd go away. They pounded on the door, and with a groan, I rolled over on the couch.

"Fuck off," I muttered.

Reg's voice was muffled by the door, but booming, nevertheless. "Come on, Harrison. I know you're in there. Open up."

With a heavy sigh, I pushed myself off the couch. I plodded over to the door and opened it. Reg's eyes darted between my messy hair, stained shirt, and bare feet.

"Why don't you have your workout clothes on?" Reg walked through the house, glancing around. "Where's Juliana?" He frowned.

"I don't want to talk about it."

"Oh shit."

I shook my head, lips clamped.

"Well, my friend—" He clapped a hand on my shoulder, and I felt as if I might cave under the pressure. "You can either talk to me about it, or we can go running."

"Pass," I said, falling back on the couch.

My back was aching, but I figured it was from all the time I'd been spending on the couch lately. That and the fact that I was finally feeling my age. I'd never felt as old and tired as I had the past week since she'd left.

"Come on." He held out a hand. "Get up. Get moving. You'll feel better. You know you always do," he added when I still didn't move.

I groaned. "My back aches."

"God, you're turning into a whiny old man."

I narrowed my eyes, leaping up from the couch, despite the pain. "I can still beat your ass any day."

"Yeah?" He crossed his arms over his chest, goading me. "I'd like to see you try."

I flipped him off as I jogged up the stairs, rushing to get ready so I wouldn't have to spend any more time than necessary surrounded by Juliana's things. Her sticky notes were like a neon sign on the bathroom mirror, mocking me with their—*my*—advice.

"Control is an illusion," I muttered. "Isn't that the truth."

My latest note to her remained there. "I love your smile."

A quick glance in the mirror, and I barely recognized the man I saw. Losing Juliana had aged me. Gone was the happy, carefree, loving man of a few days ago. In his stead was a pale, lifeless, old man. Though my hair had been salt-and-pepper for years, I swore it was more salt than pepper now.

I dropped my head and turned away. I still hadn't heard from her since she'd left for Thailand. It was killing me—the silence, the waiting. But she knew where I stood. Even so, I'd been tempted to call or text her so many times. Just to know if she'd made it okay. To let her know I was thinking about her. To tell her I'd made a mistake.

I shook my head and returned downstairs.

"Let's go." Reg slapped me on the back. It was nothing out

of the ordinary, but every touch felt like I was being pounded by a jackhammer.

We drove to a local park. It was a beautiful day—not too hot. And not too crowded. The run started out all right, though I was sluggish. I blamed it on lack of sleep, but the farther we ran, the worse I felt. Without warning, I was struck with a stomach cramp that had me doubling over in pain.

"Fuck," I hissed through my teeth.

Reg's bright sneakers came into view. "You okay, man?"

I shook my head, my vision darkening at the edges. I tried to focus on his orange laces, on the way the strands were woven together. But I was fading.

"Talk to me." Reg's voice was calm. "Tell me what's going on."

"Argh." I couldn't seem to catch my breath, and I was sweating a lot more than I had been even moments before.

Several runners slowed as they passed, but most merely continued on. All the while, my gut churned. Churned and cramped, and... I jogged over to the nearest bushes and emptied the contents of my stomach.

"Whoa. Okay," Reg said, stepping back. "I'm calling an ambulance."

I let out a strangled cry, clutching my side. I was no stranger to pain or injury. In my years of playing football— first college, then professionally—I'd suffered numerous injuries. But nothing had ever felt quite like this. It was excruciating—my stomach and back radiating pain.

"No," I gasped. "No ambulance. I'm not going to the hospital."

"Okay, tough guy. Think you can walk?"

I took a few steps before I sagged, but he was there to support me. "Do you think it's food poisoning?" Reg asked as we lumbered down the path.

I threw up again.

"Fuck if I know. But I have this—" I clutched my side again. "My side fucking hurts."

He frowned. "Appendix? Can you jump?"

I glared at him. "What the hell? No. I'm not going to jump." I shook my head.

"What?" He shrugged. "I'm only trying to help. When Izzy had an awful stomachache last summer, that's what the doctor had us do."

By the time we made it to the car, Reg announced we were going to the hospital. I squeezed my eyes shut. I wanted to fight him, but deep down, I knew he was right. This pain was unreal.

A long—agonizing—ride later, I was being wheeled inside.

"I don't need—" I squeezed my eyes shut as if to ward off the pain.

"Mm-hmm," Reg said with a smug tone I didn't appreciate. "Just take the wheelchair."

Reg waited in the lobby, while I had my vitals taken and went over my symptoms with a nurse. They hooked me up to an IV, then I peed in a cup and waited. All the while, I was reminded of the day I took Juliana to the hospital after her allergic reaction. I could remember how terrified I'd been of losing her. Even now, as my mind raced with the possible reasons for my pain, my only thought was of her.

I lay back against the bed, visions of Juliana on repeat in my head. But nothing could erase the pain of her walking out on me.

There was a knock at the door, and the doctor returned.

"Mr. Hayes," he said, glancing up at me from the chart. "You have kidney stones."

"Really?" I jerked my head back. "Kidney stones? That's it?"

Kidney stones didn't sound so terrible after the scenarios I'd imagined. My dad had had kidney stones years ago, and he'd lived to tell the tale. Even though that was the prognosis, it certainly felt more like a broken heart.

"Yep. Though I'm surprised you didn't feel them until today. They're a fairly decent size."

I lifted a shoulder, knowing I had a high tolerance for pain—at least of the physical variety. Emotionally, I was shattered. But he couldn't help me with that.

"So, what's the plan?"

"We have a few options," the doctor said and began listing them.

We opted to blast them, which meant I'd be given a sedative. I texted Reg with an update and told him to go home, but he insisted on staying. I was feeling more relaxed already, thanks to the drugs. And by the time we returned to my hospital room after the procedure, I felt as if I were floating on a cloud.

There was a knock at the door, and then Reg peeked his head inside. "Hey."

"Hey." I smiled, feeling a little loopy.

He stepped inside and closed the door behind him. "You okay?"

I nodded, lying back and closing my eyes. "I'm fabulous."

"I tried calling Juliana, but her office said she's out of town. Do you want me to call her on your phone?"

I shook my head, listening to the rhythms of the hospital —the squeak of shoes outside in the hall, the steady beat of my heart rate. It was oddly relaxing. At least it had been until he'd mentioned Juliana.

"Did you guys break up?" he asked, sending my pulse racing.

"It's complicated."

He dragged one of the chairs over so it was next to the

bed. "It always seems to be when it comes to her. So, what happened?"

I stared at him, hard. "You really want to talk about that? *Now?*"

He leaned back in his chair, crossing one leg at the knee. "You got something better to do?"

I laid my head back against the pillow, the sheets stiff against my skin. He made a good point. I had nothing but time at the moment. They wouldn't release me for at least another hour.

"She went to Thailand to try to find him."

He blinked. "Come again?"

I explained everything from Harper's intel to our fight. Reg listened intently, then scrubbed a hand over his face. "Let me get this straight. She flew halfway across the world to see if it's even him?"

I nodded.

"And you haven't heard from her?"

I shook my head. What else could I say?

"Why did you let her go?"

I considered it a moment, even though I already knew the answer. Maybe I hadn't at the time, but since she'd left, my decision and the reasons for it had crystallized in my mind. And as difficult as it had been to let her go, I knew it was the right path. I just wasn't sure how to make Reg understand.

"We can't move forward until she puts the past—Ryan— to rest." Just saying his name had my blood pressure spiking.

"If you love them, you have to set them free? That about sum it up?"

"Yeah. Sure."

"Bullshit." He leaned forward, resting his elbows on his knees. "If you love someone, you don't let them go. You fight for them."

I jerked my head back. "I'm not going to compete with

another man, even if he is a ghost. Besides—" I huffed. "I did fight. I fought for her to stay."

"When that didn't work, you should've fought to go with her."

I shook my head. He didn't understand.

"Harrison," he chided. "This isn't Cam. And Juliana's not cheating on you."

"Isn't she, though? She flew across the world to be with her former fiancé."

"Did she say why?" He paused, as if waiting for me to connect some piece I was missing. "Did she say it was because she wanted to be with him? Or that she was still in love with him? Or that she wanted to marry him?"

"No, but—"

"Exactly." He clapped his hands together, and it seemed to echo off the tile floor of the room.

"If you ask me—"

"Which I didn't," I interjected.

He continued speaking all the same. "She just wants closure. Wouldn't you, were roles reversed?"

My shoulders slumped. "Yeah."

"I mean, doesn't it say a lot about her that she's still dedicated to finding him after all this time?"

I hadn't thought about it that way.

"But when is enough enough? If it's not him, when will she stop looking and commit to me?"

His expression was sympathetic. "That's a question only she can answer. But I don't think the two are mutually exclusive. She can hold out hope that he's alive but still want to be with you."

"I can't lose her." I swallowed, knowing how hard the past week had been. I didn't want to be apart anymore or ever again. "I can't."

"Then fight for her."

"How?" I croaked, feeling defeated and depleted. I wasn't sure I had any energy left to fight.

"The way you'd attack a problem on the field. You need a game plan."

I nodded. A game plan. Yes, a game plan. I needed a game plan.

The door flew open, and Juliana burst in, wide-eyed, hair wild. "Harrison," she panted. "Thank god you're okay."

I blinked a few times, certain I must be dreaming.

"Excuse me. Miss." A nurse ran into the room. "Mr. Hayes, I'm so sorry." She grabbed Juliana's elbow. "Security is on the way."

"It's okay," I said. "She can stay."

With great reluctance, the nurse released Juliana's arm. "If you're sure."

I nodded.

"Okay. But I don't want you getting aggravated. Any sign that your heart rate's up, and she's gone."

I nodded, my expression solemn. Outwardly, I may have fooled the nurse. But inside, my heart was galloping like a racehorse. I didn't care what the nurse said, there was no way in hell I was letting Juliana leave. But first, I wanted to know why she was even here.

"I'm going to go grab a snack," Reg said, following the nurse out of the room.

Juliana remained by the door, fidgeting with the strap of her purse. "Hey. Sorry about that. I think she thought I was a deranged fan."

"Meh." I lifted a shoulder. "My day has been kind of boring so far. So, I appreciate you injecting a little excitement."

She laughed, though it had a nervous edge to it. It mirrored how I felt—uneasy.

"How did you know I was here?" I asked.

"When Harper and I were waiting to go through customs, she got a local alert on her phone. I was—" Her skin paled. "God, I was terrified."

I frowned. "What did the news say?"

"That you'd collapsed during a run and had been admitted to the hospital."

"Oh fuck." I wiped a hand over my face. "I need to call Olivia. And Talia."

"They made it sound like you had a heart attack." Her eyes searched me as if checking to confirm that I was alive and in one piece. "What happened? Was it your heart?"

I shook my head, though my heart was still aching. It was stopping and starting as I tried not to get my hopes up about why Juliana was here and what it meant.

"Kidney stones."

She cringed. "Yikes. I hear those can be painful. I'm just…" She sighed. "I'm so glad you're okay." She stepped closer. "You are okay, right?"

"For the most part."

She frowned. "What do you mean, for the most part?"

"My heart's a little sore. It's been missing you." I held out my hand, reaching for her. She took it, and my body relaxed at her touch.

She perched on the edge of the bed next to me. "I'm sorry, Harrison. So, so sorry."

"Did you get the answers you wanted?" I asked, afraid to come right out and ask if she'd seen Ryan.

"It gave me the closure I needed." Both of us were skirting around the Ryan issue, but it was enough.

"I'm glad." I just didn't know what that meant for us. Even though I felt as if I might explode, I waited to hear what she'd say next.

"You told me not to come back unless I was one-hundred-percent sure I wanted to be with you." She blinked up at me, and I ached to caress her cheek, to smooth back her hair.

"And are you?" At this point, I just needed to know. Was she all in?

She cupped my cheeks. "I'm yours. Forever and always." She hesitated a moment. "If you'll still have me, that is."

I pulled her into my arms, crashing my lips to hers. The kiss wasn't gentle or timid. It was a claiming. She was mine, and I was hers.

"Of course I'll still have you," I said, slightly breathless. "Are you crazy?" I grinned, tucking her hair behind her ear. "I'm never letting you go."

And I vowed that no matter what the future held, I would always fight for her, fight for us.

CHAPTER TWENTY-NINE

Juliana

Harrison nuzzled into me from behind. It was warm beneath the covers, the sun barely filtering into the room. It had been a few days since he'd come home from the hospital, and I wasn't in any hurry to move.

"Don't you need to get ready for work?" His morning voice was delicious and gruff.

"Nope." I grinned, rolling over in his arms.

"Huh?" He arched an eyebrow, looking devilishly handsome. His jaw was lined with scruff, and I dotted kisses along his cheek, over his nose, his eyebrows.

"Mm," he sighed. "That's nice."

I grinned, shivering when he slid his hands up my sides, canvassing my skin. I was glad I didn't have to get out of bed, because there was no way I'd be able to drag myself away from this man.

"Mm, baby," he moaned when I climbed on top of him. "Yes."

My nipples brushed against the hard planes of his chest, and I slid my wet center over his erection. Though the doctor had assured us Harrison could resume normal activities yesterday, I'd waited to have sex another twenty-four hours out of an abundance of caution.

But I couldn't wait anymore. I needed this man. I needed him to fill me. I needed to reconnect, especially after all that we'd been through.

"Are you sure you don't need to get ready for work?" He settled his hands on my hips. "We both know how grumpy you get about being tardy."

I laughed, leaning forward so my hair fanned around us like a curtain. "Nothing—and no one—is more important to me than you." I pressed my lips to his.

He gripped my hips, pulling me closer, sliding me over his cock. My eyes rolled back in my head, but I quickly returned them to Harrison. I knew how important eye contact was to him, and I wanted him to feel that I was present, with him.

Suddenly overcome, I said, "I love you, and I'm sorry."

"Shh." He pressed his finger to my lips, his eyes filled with compassion and lust. "Just feel."

"Is that another lesson, Zen guru?" I teased, needing to lighten the moment.

I lifted, lining him up with my entrance. And as I sank down on him, I knew I was exactly where I was supposed to be. And for the first time, maybe ever, I believed everything had happened for a reason.

I didn't know if that man on the beach was Ryan—would never know. But I didn't need to. I was at peace in the knowledge that I was where I was supposed to be.

And Harrison was the man I was meant to be with. He was compassionate and understanding, and he'd let me go even when he wanted me to stay. While some might have seen that as giving up, I viewed it as a true testament to just how selfless he was. And though he might not have been happy about my decision to go to Thailand, he'd respected it, nevertheless. He'd given me the space to be who I needed to be and do what I needed to do. And that was one of the greatest gifts you could give to someone you loved—the freedom to make their own decisions, their own mistakes, without guilt or judgment.

"I love you," I whispered, feathering my lips over his skin. "I love you. And I'm so very grateful for you."

He held me to him, both of us still a moment—as close as any two people could be. I could feel his heart beating against mine, in sync.

"I love you." The words rumbled from his chest, and they resonated deep in my soul. "And I'm so glad you're mine."

I nodded, my eyes misting at the reminder that I'd nearly lost him. First, because of my insistence on finding Ryan, on getting closure. And then because of his kidney stone. I knew the situation with his health wasn't that dire—thank goodness. But it was a powerful reminder all the same. A reminder I shouldn't have needed in the first place. Life was short, and you had to focus on the present. On this one moment.

"What are you thinking about?" Harrison brushed my hair over my shoulder, our bodies still connected.

I smiled. "How lucky I am."

"Yeah?" He grinned, waggling his eyebrows. "Well, you're about to get even luckier." He thrust, prompting me to gasp.

I swiveled my hips, laughing when he rolled us so he was on top. His forearms bracketed my head, his body deliciously warm and heavy when he settled over me. And as we rocked together, whispering words of devotion, I fell even more in love with this man.

Higher and higher, I climbed, spurred on by the emotional connection as much as the physical one. He linked his fingers with mine, clasping them above our heads as he continued to drive into me. I wrapped my legs around his back, pulling him in even deeper, wanting to be even closer. Goose bumps rose along my skin, and I was overtaken by a powerful wave of pleasure.

I dug in my heels, spurring him on. And his movements became increasingly frantic as we lost control. With our tongues tangled and our bodies wrapped around each other like a pretzel, we surrendered.

OLIVIA AND I WERE DOWNSTAIRS, PUTTING THE FINISHING touches on the party decorations for the New Year's Eve celebration. I fussed with some of the cocktail glasses, wanting to make sure everything looked amazing. Guests would start arriving soon, and I was excited to kick off the party.

Harrison and I had hosted Thanksgiving and Christmas, but we'd spent both with Connor, Olivia, and our parents. This was the first time we'd invited everyone over—family, friends, even Cam.

"That looks great," Olivia said, standing back, and I had to agree.

We'd really outdone ourselves, and it had been fun to pull everything together with Olivia. It had given us a chance to get to know each other even better. The theme was black and white, and everything looked so crisp and formal, yet still festive.

"Take a picture with me—before everyone arrives?" She pulled her phone from a pocket in her skirt.

I smiled, grateful for the millionth time that she'd been so accepting, so welcoming. She really was the sweetest, and I enjoyed having her as a friend, as family. "I'd love to."

She held up her phone with the camera pointed toward us. I brushed my hair aside, and we tilted our heads together. We were a study in contrasts—her chestnut hair against my blond. Her green eyes to my blue. And her silk tank was paired with a champagne-colored skirt covered in sequins, whereas I wore a simple black dress.

"There." She lowered her phone, and we looked through the images.

"Will you send those to me?"

"Of course." She grinned.

"Hey, Juliana," Connor said, striding down the stairs. "Harrison asked if you could come upstairs. Something about making sure he picks the right shirt and tie."

Olivia laughed, as did I. "Sure."

I headed for the master closet but stopped when I reached the bathroom. Post-it notes covered the mirror in all colors, each one with a message written on it. I started reading, tears pricking my eyes.

You mean the world to me.

I didn't know love until I met you.

You're my favorite.

On and on, they went, all love letters from Harrison. It was beautiful and dramatic, and so incredibly creative.

I turned to find him leaning against the doorframe, watching me as he often did. I sucked in a jagged breath, in awe of this incredible man. His suit was impeccably tailored, showcasing his broad shoulders. And the black pinstripe material was striking against his green eyes.

"Wow," I whispered.

"I'll say." He grinned, scanning me hungrily. "Baby, you look—" He rubbed a hand over his chin. "Phenomenal."

"Thank you." I dipped my head.

He pushed off the doorframe and came to stand before me. "You once asked me if I believed in a higher power."

I nodded, remembering the conversation all too well. Though I wasn't sure where he was going with it. Surely… I bit the inside of my cheek.

"Do you remember my answer?"

"That everything happens for a reason," I said.

"I believe you came into my life for a reason. You showed me just how much I was missing. For all my talk of being a Zen guru, you showed me what it means to truly live. And to be loved."

He knelt to the floor, and I gasped, my heart galloping. *Oh my god, he is proposing.*

"I don't want to end this year or start another one without you. Marry me." He pulled a small velvet box from his pocket and opened it, presenting the ring to me.

"I-I—" I stuttered, my eyes darting between his and the ring. Holy smokes, what a ring it was. Dazzling perfection and so me. "I thought you didn't want to get married."

"I didn't think I did." He peered up at me. "But then you came along with your captivating blue eyes and a smile that could knock me flat."

I smiled, and he pointed up at me. "That's the one. And you changed me."

"Harrison." I tugged on his hand, inviting him to stand. "I can't wait to spend the rest of my life with you. And I would be honored to be your wife."

His answering smile was blinding, and he quickly slid the ring onto my finger before pulling me into his arms. "You don't know how happy you've made me." He pressed a kiss into my hair.

And then he was brushing my hair aside, kissing behind my ear, down my neck. I shivered.

"And how crazy you make me." His voice was gravelly as he cupped my breasts, pushing them up as he kissed me over the material of my dress. He groaned, sending a bolt of desire rushing through me.

"You're driving me crazy," I gasped as he continued to kiss any available skin, pulling my dress aside to tease my nipples. "Oh god." I leaned my head back.

The doorbell rang, and my eyes darted toward the bedroom door, which was still open. "To be continued…" I righted my dress, shimmying to get it back in place.

"We still have a few minutes. I can be fast."

I grinned and turned toward the mirror, fluffing my hair as I double-checked my appearance. I looked happy, eyes shining bright, cheeks flushed. Harrison wrapped his arms around me from behind, his erection digging into my backside.

"Beautiful." He pulled back my hair, pressing his lips behind my ear. "You're absolutely stunning. And I don't want to wait."

I shook my head with a smile, turning in his arms to pat his cheek. "You'll be fine. Plus—" I arched an eyebrow "—I promise to make it worth your while."

"Mm. I like the sound of that." He pulled me into him.

"But that's not what I was talking about. I know you plan weddings for a living, but I don't want to wait to get married."

"You know what? Neither do I." I smiled at his surprised expression. "How does March sound?"

"Wow. That's—" He blinked. "Only three months away."

"What? Are you getting cold feet?"

"No." He chuckled. "Never. I'm just surprised you can make it happen so fast, especially after seeing what went into Olivia's wedding."

"Well..." I wrapped my arms around his neck. "I was thinking something small, something in the backyard..."

"That sounds perfect." He cupped my cheeks, his gaze intense. "You're the love of my life, Jules," he murmured.

"You *are* my life." I kissed him, hoping he understood just how much I loved him. When he teased the seam of my lips with his tongue, gripping my ass, I pulled back, breathless. "Come on. We've got a party to attend."

He grinned, adjusting himself, though there was no hiding the bulge in his pants.

"Aren't you going to do something about that?" I teased, loving the effect I had on him.

"Aren't you?" he challenged.

"Later." I gave him a quick peck.

When we emerged onto the landing, everyone turned their faces upward to watch us from below. Friends, family, colleagues, they were all there.

Harrison held up my left hand, flashing them the ring. "She said yes!"

Everyone cheered, and I turned to him, stunned. "They knew about this?"

"Of course. This is our engagement party after all." He grinned.

I shook my head. "Wow. You sneaky—"

"Handsome." He captured my hand, pulling it to his chest. My engagement ring sparkled, reminding me of just how fortunate I was.

"Devil."

"Fiancé," he said at the same time, and I stuck my tongue out at him.

When we reached the bottom of the stairs, Alexis, Lauren, and Harper swarmed me. They gushed over the ring and pulled me into a group hug.

"So, so happy for you," Alexis said.

"Did you have any idea?" Lauren asked.

I shook my head. And as our friends and family hugged us and issued their congratulations, I smiled. For the first time in years, I wasn't dreading the memories that the new year would bring. I was looking forward to the future.

CHAPTER THIRTY

Harrison

T*hree Months Later*

"YOU NERVOUS?" REG ASKED, CLAPPING A HAND ON MY shoulder.

"Nah." I straightened my tie, peering at my reflection. My suit had been custom made for the occasion. Landon and Olivia had helped since I'd wanted it to be a surprise for my bride. For our wedding.

"Good." He squeezed it then released me. "Because I know you're making the right decision."

"Me too," I said, smiling as I thought of Juliana. I couldn't wait to see her. Couldn't wait for her to be mine—officially.

I'd never really considered marriage as something important to me, until her. After what had happened with Cam, it was easy to focus on the ugly parts—the fighting, the betrayal, the divorce. It wasn't until Juliana, until I wanted to show her and the world that she was my everything. And while we didn't need a piece of paper to prove we belonged together, it gave me peace of mind—knowing that if anything were ever to happen to me, she'd be taken care of. Not that she needed my help—far from it. Juliana was a successful businesswoman, financially well-off. But I wanted to give her everything because she was my everything. Without her, the house, the cars, none of it mattered.

There was a knock at the door, and Landon peeked his head inside my pool house. "It's time."

"That's my cue," Reg said, hooking his thumb over his shoulder.

Landon took his place, giving me a once-over. He tugged on my jacket, brushing imaginary lint from my shoulder. "You look…" He stepped back to admire his work. "Hot."

"Thanks." I chuckled. "How's Juliana?"

"Radiant. A knockout. The most beautiful bride I've ever seen." He gave me a watery smile.

"Hey—" I narrowed my eyes at him, wanting to lighten the mood. "That's my fiancée you're talking about."

"Oh please." He sniffed, slicing a hand through the air. "We both know I'm more likely to hook up with a groomsman than the bride."

"True." I laughed, even though Juliana and I had opted not to have a bridal party or groomsmen. Surprisingly, it had been her idea. She wanted something laid-back, relaxed. She wanted our friends and family to enjoy, and I was completely on board with that.

"Thank you again for all your help with the wedding. I know it was a lot to pull off," I said.

Now that I'd survived wedding season with Juliana, as well as Olivia's wedding, I could appreciate just how much effort went into planning one. No detail was too trivial, and Juliana and Landon excelled at their jobs. I could understand why it would be difficult for her to let go and relax, but I knew she was trying.

Following Olivia's wedding, Juliana had been spending less time working and more time relaxing. We had weekly family dinners with Connor and Olivia, and we'd settled into a nice routine. Not to say that our life was boring—far from it. I knew life could never be boring with a woman like Juliana. And it was part of the reason I loved her so much. She was like me—always striving to learn more, to be better. Individually, she was a force to be reckoned with. Together, we were unstoppable.

He nodded, his expression thoughtful. "Anything for Juliana. Now, come on," he said, leading me outside. As if I didn't know my way around my own backyard.

That said, the space had been completely transformed. The sun dipped lower in the sky, casting a pinkish hue over the surroundings. The pool was more like a reflecting pond, with white orbs floating on the water. And a harpist's music made it feel ethereal, like a dream. White chairs lined the aisle, leading to an arch of flowers. All white, all fragrant, they perfumed the air with a bouquet of scents.

I smiled at the guests as I took my spot at the front next to the officiant. Olivia and Connor sat in the first row, holding hands. Next to them were my parents. Jas and Reg were in attendance, along with Talia and her husband, and a few of my former teammates. There were maybe twenty people total, and I could feel the love and support, the joy radiating from them. We'd wanted something small and intimate, and it was even better than I'd imagined.

Juliana's parents sat opposite, as did her friends—Alexis and Preston, Lauren and Hunter, and Harper, who seemed to be perpetually single. An occupational hazard of being a film location scout, I supposed. I was distracted from my thoughts when the harpist shifted songs, and the back door to the house opened.

Everyone oohed and aahed as Blair and Sophia walked down the aisle, white rose petals fluttering behind them. When Blair got distracted by something in the grass, Sophia grabbed her hand and whispered something in her ear. I smiled at the girls, reminded of my own daughter. I glanced at Olivia, and she gave me two thumbs up and a cheesy smile, though tears were forming in her eyes. I laughed, so incredibly grateful for her support.

Then the song changed again, and all eyes returned to the house, including my own. Juliana emerged from within, and I knew it was a moment I'd never forget. Landon's description had been spot-on. Juliana was radiant and a knockout, but she was so much more besides. She was filled with joy, and her happiness spilled over to me.

Fuck, she was gorgeous. And she was mine.

Her eyes were locked on mine, greedily scanning me as I did the same. Her blond hair was curled in loose waves that cascaded over her shoulder. And her dress… I swallowed. The top of her gown sparkled, dipping low before flowing over her curves like water. The material clung to her breasts, and I wanted to kiss my way down the valley of her chest. The closer she drew, the more awestruck I was. She was elegant and sexy —her silk gown striking a balance of both timeless and modern.

When she joined me beneath the floral arch, I took her hands in mine. She smiled up at me with those beguiling blue eyes, her love endless like the ocean.

"Beautiful." I rubbed a hand over my chin, completely mesmerized. "Absolutely beautiful."

Her pink lips were ripe for kissing. Out of habit, I leaned in for a kiss. The officiant cleared his throat, reminding me that we had an audience.

"I think we're getting a little ahead of ourselves," he teased.

Juliana and I laughed, along with everyone else. Her blue eyes sparkled with love and happiness as she smiled at me. And though we were surrounded by friends and family, this woman was my sole focus. If I'd thought I was emotional at Olivia's wedding, it was nothing compared to this.

"Now, Harrison." The officiant turned to me, indicating it was time to say my vows.

I wasn't usually one for big public displays of affection, but we'd decided to write our own vows. We wanted something uniquely personal, and at the time, it had seemed like a good decision. Now, I just hoped I wasn't about to completely fuck it up. My clammy palms weren't encouraging.

"Juliana." I smiled, attempting to collect myself. She gave me a warm smile. "Thank you for trusting me. From that first night—"

Something flickered in her eyes, and I swallowed a laugh. There was no way I was going to tell our guests that our relationship had started out as a one-night stand.

"You trusted me. You trusted me enough to let go of your cares and concerns. I hope you know that I'll always be here for you. I'll always love and cherish you. And I will always put you first."

She nodded, her eyes glittering with tears.

"Whatever challenges life throws our way, I will always be here—waiting for you." I swiped away a tear, so tempted to say "Fuck it" and kiss her already.

"Juliana," the officiant said, turning to her.

"Harrison." She smiled. "I've attended countless weddings, and it feels a bit surreal to finally be the bride."

Everyone laughed.

"You are my breath, my heart, my reason for living. I

promise to never take you for granted. I promise to do my utmost to uphold the vows we've recited. And I promise that even though life may be unpredictable, you can always count on my love. I will love you without end, without cease, without fail."

I believed her. And as I slid the band onto her finger, I knew that our love was like that circle—unending and beautiful.

Juliana

The silky material of my dress swished around my legs as I climbed the stairs to our bedroom, floating about me just like I'd floated on a cloud of happiness all day. We'd done it! We were married. *I* was married to Harrison Hayes.

My groom was on the phone, and I was hoping to sneak a peek in my luggage before he finished his call.

"Now, where is it?" I mused aloud, wondering where Harper had hidden it.

When it was nowhere to be found in the guest room or in the office, I sighed. Not one to be easily deterred, I searched the back of Harrison's side of the closet until I heard footsteps approaching. I rushed to put everything back as it was and stood, pausing when I caught sight of myself in the full-length mirror.

My cheeks were pink, eyes alight with happiness, and I looked every bit the bride I was. Today had been…perfect. Like a dream. And as an event planner to the stars, a wedding planner myself, I knew that perfection was rare indeed.

But I couldn't have asked for a better day, a better celebration of our love. We'd been married in our backyard, surrounded by friends and family. And it had been everything I could've hoped for, both as a professional wedding planner and a bride. My assistant, Landon, had done an amazing job implementing my vision. The day had been seamless, everything breathtaking.

From the pool to the flowers lining the arch and the reception that had followed, the execution was flawless. In fact, I hadn't thought about the logistics at all. I didn't have to. I trusted Landon, and he had carried us through the day with grace and ease.

"Damn," Harrison groaned from behind me, and my eyes snapped to him, meeting his green ones in the mirror. "I still can't believe you're my wife."

I grinned, just from being in proximity to him and from hearing those words. But I got it. I couldn't believe he was my husband. I wasn't sure a man had ever looked more handsome in a suit, and I'd seen countless grooms. But he was all mine—Harrison Hayes. Former star football player for the Hollywood Heatwaves, color commentator, amazing dad, and one of the kindest and most loving people I'd ever met.

When he lifted his hand to run it through his hair, the light caught on the silver flecks in those strands, the platinum band on his ring finger. I could remember the moment I'd first laid eyes on him, and it felt as if it were yesterday. He was sitting at the hotel bar, drink in hand. I'd mused aloud to myself something about life being unpredictable, and he'd come back with a quip about that being part of the fun. Despite my inner turmoil, my body had been attuned to him. And then he'd made good on his promise —making me forget the past, helping me forget the pain.

"Hey," he said, bringing me back to the present. Grounding me, as he always did. My Zen guru, as I liked to tease him. He placed his hand on my upper back. His palm was warm, his touch soothing. "You okay?"

I shook away the cobwebs of my memories and smiled at his reflection. "I'm absolutely wonderful, my darling husband."

His answering grin was wide, and I could tell he liked the idea of being my husband just as much as I adored being his wife. It hadn't been an easy road we'd traveled, but it was worth it. The loss, the pain, all of it was worth it to be with this man. To have him stand by my side and take on the world.

He brushed my hair over one shoulder, and his touch sent shivers down my spine. He traced the curve with his finger, then his lips, the low back of my gown giving him easy access to a wide expanse of skin. And even though I didn't want to look away, my eyes fluttered closed, core clenching, body tingling. I finally reopened them when he leaned in and pressed his lips to my neck where it met my shoulder.

"This dress," he growled, kissing his way over my shoulder. "Were you trying to torture me?"

I smiled to myself, pleased that he liked the gown. It was an original design by Evelyn, and when I'd tried it on, I'd just known. Known this was the dress I'd walk down the aisle in, marry Harrison in. It was elegant and sexy, yet timeless. And I wasn't sure I'd ever felt more beautiful or desired. But maybe that had more to do with Harrison than the dress.

The moment I'd emerged from the back of the house and our eyes met was one I'd never forget. Friends and family were seated along both sides of the aisle, but my attention was focused solely on Harrison. He stood beneath an arch of flowers, the white and green foliage a delicate contrast to his imposing, masculine presence.

His suit fit him to a T, showcasing his athletic figure honed from years of playing professional football. When he glanced up, our eyes locking, his watery smile was full of unspoken emotion. My steps had faltered, and I'd gripped my bouquet tighter, grateful I had something to hold on to. To prove this was real; it was happening.

My dress flowed over me like water as I glided toward him. Was pulled toward him. All the while, his eyes scanned my figure, dipping down my breasts, my hips, as if he couldn't drink me in fast enough.

I'd been so nervous about saying my vows, but it had all gone off without a hitch. When a gentle breeze had blown through the backyard, a sense of peace and rightness settled over me. A certainty that I was exactly where I was supposed to be, marrying the man I loved. And now, despite all our previous heartbreak, we were husband and wife.

"My husband." I grinned, stroking his cheek.

He met my eyes, his emerald gems shining with happiness and love as he brought my hand to his mouth. When he placed a kiss on my palm, sparks raced and danced along my skin. Even with the simplest of touches, he could nearly bring me to my knees.

"My beautiful wife." He pressed his lips to my wrist, the light catching on his wedding band.

"Did you know I had your band engraved?" I asked, my heart racing.

"You did?"

His touch lingered, even after he'd released me. He removed the band from his finger to inspect the inside, then smiled as he read the words aloud. "Without end." A quick peck for me, and then he returned the band to his finger. "Just like in your vows. I love it."

"I love you," I sighed, feeling more content and joyful than I had maybe ever.

"I love you, Juliana." He guided me to him for a kiss that warmed my heart and ignited my core.

I smoothed my hands over his lapels, clutching the material when he deepened the kiss. He cupped the back of my neck, smoothing his other hand down my back to rest on my hip. His tongue sought mine out, and I leaned into him, into the kiss, the taste of mint and whiskey mingling on his tongue. I wanted to stay in this moment—live in this moment—forever.

We kissed for I didn't know how long, until he nipped my lips and released them. Even as he did so, he pulled me closer. And when his erection dug into me, I welcomed it.

"Was today everything you hoped it would be?" he asked, his voice more gravelly than usual.

I nodded. "And so much more."

He swayed us side to side as if dancing to a song only we could hear. And then, just as he had on the dance floor, he tilted me back in a dramatic dip. Though, unlike our first dance, he ran the tips of his fingers down my sternum, leaving goose bumps in their wake.

I sucked in a jagged breath, impressed by how smooth he was, though I didn't know why. Harrison was agile and graceful, an athlete through and through. He grinned, a cocky smile that told me he was pleased by my reaction. And then, without warning, he scooped me up into his arms, carrying me through the open door to our bedroom.

"What are you doing?" I giggled, light-headed from the champagne and the celebration and the love I had for this man.

"Carrying my bride over the threshold, of course." He smiled down at me, a smile full of so much love and happiness. Though beneath it was desire. *Need.* And it mirrored my own.

He set me on the bed, the comforter smooth beneath me. "And now I'm going to make love to my wife."

I watched in awe as he removed his jacket, tossing his tie aside before loosening the top two buttons of his shirt.

"I hate to be a party pooper," I said. "But don't we have a plane to catch?"

He crawled on top of me, his thighs bracketing my hips, the dark, luxe material of his suit contrasting against the cream silk of my gown.

"All in good time." His grin was enigmatic, as though he knew something I didn't.

Which—of course—he did. He'd planned the honeymoon as a surprise. He wanted it to be a wedding gift. And even though I wasn't a fan of surprises, I could tell it was important to him. That said, it was driving me crazy—the not knowing. I absolutely did not know how one of my best friends, Alexis, had lasted nine months without finding out the sex of her daughter. Though Harrison had helped me learn to let go, I was still a planner at heart.

The past few weeks, I'd done everything I could think of to extract any information out of him. I'd even asked my new son-in-law, Connor—a former navy SEAL—for tips on interrogation. He'd merely shaken his head with a laugh.

"At least tell me what time our flight is," I said, gripping Harrison's thighs. So much power and muscle beneath my hands. "You know I'll never be able to relax if I'm constantly worried we'll be late."

"You want to bet?" He smirked, obviously taking my comment as a challenge. He stripped out of his shirt, tossing it aside. My mouth watered at the sight of his toned shoulders and sculpted chest and abs.

And then I remembered what he'd said, and I rolled my eyes. "I'm serious, Harrison."

"So am I." He leaned forward, his breath fanning over my skin, then kissed me just below the ear. "And it's a private jet. They won't leave without us."

"Oh." I swallowed, distracted by the feel of his lips on my skin, kissing his way down the valley between my breasts. My nipples hardened as if reaching out, begging for his attention. But the man had the patience of a saint and continued to explore only the skin revealed by my dress. Which, admittedly, was a fair bit. As he continued to cherish me, I forgot all about the honeymoon and whether or not we'd be late for the flight.

"I love this dress—" He paused his ministrations, searching my torso, fumbling for a zipper, I assumed. "But it has to go."

When he grunted in frustration, I batted his hands away. "Chill, Zen guru," I teased, loving how riled up he was. How close to losing control, despite all his patience.

He narrowed his eyes at me, and I laughed as I stood, shaking out my curls. I pushed my hair over one shoulder and lowered the nearly invisible zipper at my side before pausing midway. Harrison watched me from the edge of the bed, mouth slightly agape.

"Where are we going on our honeymoon?" I asked.

"Juliana," he growled. "Don't make me rip that dress off you and throw you on the bed."

I glowered at him. "You wouldn't dare." He knew how much I loved this dress.

"Don't try me, baby." He pressed a hand to his crotch, and I could tell he was aching for release. "I behaved all day."

As much as I enjoyed teasing him, I was just as desperate as he was. I wanted to feel him, taste him, touch him. But I wasn't going to let him know that.

"All you have to do is tell me." I unzipped the dress the rest of the way, allowing the thin straps to slip from my shoulders while still covering my nipples. But only just barely.

"You play dirty." He rubbed a hand over his chin, and I could sense him wavering.

He surprised me by standing and unbuttoning his pants. Down they went, sliding over his powerful thighs, followed by his boxer briefs, leaving his cock bobbing toward his stomach. I swallowed hard, but when I saw the smile on his face, I snapped out of it. I allowed my dress to fall from my shoulders, silk pooling at my feet. Apart from a pair of white lace-trim panties and a strapless plunge bra, I was naked. And the moment I looked at Harrison, I knew I'd won. He stepped closer, and I licked my lips in anticipation.

"Juliana." He let out a slow exhale. "Do you trust me?"

"Yes. Of course."

"Then have faith that you'll love what I have planned for us."

I deflated at his words, shoulders drooping. *Love is trust,* I reminded myself. It was something I'd been working on. Not that I didn't trust Harrison, I did. More that, as a control freak, I needed to learn when to let go. When to rely on other people, especially him. I'd gotten better about it. At work, I'd given more and bigger events to Landon to handle on his own. And at home, I'd done the same, knowing Harrison would never intentionally make a decision that wasn't in our best interest.

"I know. You're right." I glanced up at him from beneath my lashes, only to find him watching me, brows pulled together, mouth tipped down. I owed him an explanation. "I'm sorry. I think everything has just felt so chaotic lately. Landon and I have more clients than we can keep up with, not that I'm complaining. There was our wedding to plan—in a three-month span. And…it's been a lot." I didn't mention Harper, though she also weighed heavily on my mind.

"I know, baby." He pulled me into his chest. It was warm, and he smelled so good. I felt safe ensconced in his arms, as if nothing could hurt us. He held me a moment before releasing me, then said, "Which is why it's more important than ever that we take this trip. You need to unwind and recharge, and so do I."

Football season had only ended a few weeks ago, and Harrison had been juggling color commentating and several new endorsements. We'd both been running hard, trying to get as much done as we could before the wedding. And now —he was right—it was time to sit back and relax, to reap the rewards of our hard work.

"I'm looking forward to it, I am. I just… I feel so out of control."

He grasped my shoulders. "I'll tell you where we're going. If that's what you really want." He peered at me, green eyes swirling, questioning.

I considered it a moment. And even as much as I wanted to know, I didn't want to spoil Harrison's fun. Besides, what was a few more hours at this point?

I shook my head. "Don't tell me. But—" I squeezed my eyes shut, slowly opening one. "Could you give me a clue? You know how I like to prepare my taste buds by antici-pating what we're going to be eating."

"Mm-hmm." He smoothed his hands up and down my arms.

"Well, I find that the anticipation, the planning, are a big part of the experience for me."

"Don't I know it." He flashed me a wicked grin, and I playfully slapped his chest.

"Hey! Get your mind out of the gutter."

He chuckled, placing his hands on my hips. "With you, Juliana, my mind is always in the gutter." He glanced down between us as if to demonstrate his point. His erection was aimed straight at me, hard and seeking. I stroked his length, loving his sharp intake of breath, the way his cock twitched in my hand.

"Feel good?"

He leaned his head back, exposing the long column of his throat. "Like you wouldn't believe."

"Can you just tell me—are we going to the beach or the mountains? Warm or cold?" It was March, and depending on how far you were willing to travel, anything was possible.

"Beach," he all but moaned as I continued to slide my hand along his skin, exploring.

I grinned, finally relaxing. "Thank you."

"Baby?" he said through gritted teeth.

"Yeah?"

"You're going to have to stop that. I don't want to come in your hand."

"Oh. Right." I released him. "Sorry."

"No. I'm sorry. I didn't realize how stressed you were about the honeymoon. That absolutely wasn't my intent."

"I know." I grinned, smoothing my hands down the hard planes of his chest. "You were just trying to do something nice and help me let go. Which I appreciate." When his expression betrayed skepticism, I added, "I do."

"Good. I'm glad that's settled—" he gave me a quick peck on the lips "—because I want you naked and on the bed. *Now*."

I SAUNTERED OVER TO THE BED, ADDING A LITTLE EXTRA SWAY to my hips. When I glanced back at Harrison, his eyes were dark, glittering with danger. I kept my back to him as I undid my bra before casting it aside.

When I hooked my fingers in my panties, he said, "Wait."

"Wait?" I tilted my head to the side.

"First, lie down."

I furrowed my brow but did as he requested, crawling across the bed on my knees until he said, "Turn over. On your back." I rolled onto my back, fanning my hair across the covers.

"Someone's awfully bossy tonight," I teased, growing more impatient by the moment.

"Perfect." He climbed on top of me, the weight and heat of his body blanketing me with a sense of calm only he could provide. "I got a powerful feeling of déjà vu to our first night together. Did I ever tell you I thought you looked like a bride on her wedding night?"

I blinked at him a few times, stunned by his words. "I think I'd remember something like that." I scoffed.

"Well, you did. I just didn't realize then that you were going to be *my* bride one day."

"I cannot believe you mentioned that night in your vows." I shook my head with a laugh, covering my face with my hands.

He chuckled, pushing them aside. "You act like I told everyone we started as a one-night stand."

"If you had, I might have left you standing at the altar."

"You wouldn't have." He nipped my ear. "And even if you did, you know I'll always be here—waiting for you."

"I know." My tone was solemn, and I knew he'd hold true to that promise. He already had. "But I'm yours. *Always.*"

He captured my lips, claiming me and showing me that I belonged to him. And when he explored my body, it was as if seeing it anew. His eyes and hands roamed my skin as if it were our first time. There were kisses on my neck, my chest, my nipples. He sucked each into his mouth, swirling his tongue around the tight bud. I cried out, clutching the sheets as he continued to lavish one then the other with attention.

"Harrison," I panted, arching my hips so his erection could slide along the damp material of my panties. God, it felt amazing. "I need you."

He kissed his way down my stomach, nuzzling me through my panties. "Fuck, baby."

He pulled the material aside, but I tugged on his shoulders. I wanted him to make love to me with his mouth, but I wanted him inside me more.

"Inside me. *Please?*"

The entire day had been an exercise in restraint. Every look, every touch from Harrison had only increased the anticipation until the point that I thought I might explode if he didn't make love to me.

"Can't we do both?" He pouted, mouth poised just above my most sensitive spot. Every breath from his parted lips was hot on my skin, like lava.

Harrison seemed to hesitate a moment, then slid his hands beneath the waistband of my underwear. He dragged the lacy material down my legs, but not before pressing his lips to my mound. I shivered, sensation overtaking me as he carefully removed them then kissed his way back up my calves, then my thighs.

"The only reason I agreed is because I know we'll have plenty of time on the plane for round two."

I smiled, loving him for dropping a subtle hint. Now that I'd released some of my concerns, I was less burdened. In fact, I was growing more excited about our honeymoon by the instant.

He stood at the edge of the bed, and I pushed up on my elbows so I could watch. I wanted to see where we connected as well as feel it. He lined himself up at my entrance, pushing in slowly, deliciously, inch by inch, until he was fully seated. My channel clenched around him, so full.

He shuddered, eyes locked on mine. "Don't do that again. Not if you want me to last."

I grinned, loving the effect I had on him. He pulled me closer to the edge of the mattress, and I wrapped my arms around his neck, using him as my anchor. His lips were on mine, in my hair, tracing a haphazard line down my neck. His whispered words of love and adoration just as fervent and powerful as the thrusts that accompanied them.

I dragged my nails down his back, loving the friction on my clit from his body. I was close, teetering on the edge.

"Fuck," he ground out. "You feel so good, and I don't know how much longer I can hold out."

His pace accelerated, and as out of control as it seemed, our eyes remained focused on each other. He was my constant. He was there for me, putting me first, just as he always had. Just as he'd promised in our wedding vows.

"Let go," I said, feeling my own release building.

And when the muscles of his stomach clenched, his grip on me tightening, his eyes so full of love and devotion, I followed my own advice, tumbling over the cliff with him. I cried out before smashing my lips to his, wanting to breathe his air. It was frantic and chaotic, and it was absolutely beautiful.

We stayed there a moment, wrapped up in each other, barely hanging on to the edge of the bed. My breathing was ragged, my chest brushing against his. And when he let out a deep sigh of satisfaction, I convulsed around him one last time, my nerves on edge from the surge of pleasure.

He laughed, cupping my cheeks. "I love you."

"I love you," I said just before he slanted his mouth over mine. We poured all our emotions into the kiss. All the joy, the love, the hope.

"I love you," he said again with a quick peck to my lips. "And I'm honored to be your husband."

I smiled, tears welling up in my eyes, my body bursting with emotion. There had been a time, not that long ago, when I'd been convinced I'd never be happy again. I'd never find love again. Let alone experience this kind of incandescent, all-encompassing joy.

"Don't cry, baby." He swiped away my tears with his thumbs.

"They're happy tears," I said through a smile. "I promise."

"Good." He pressed his lips to mine. His phone vibrated from somewhere in the room, and he groaned, unwilling to break the kiss.

When it continued to ring, he glanced around, pausing when he spied his pants. "Just a sec."

He dug in the pocket, peered at the screen, and then typed out something.

"Everything okay?" I asked, grabbing my lingerie from the floor before standing.

"Yep." He grinned, giving nothing away. "That was the pilot. Can you be ready to leave in thirty minutes?"

"I just need to shower and grab some carry-on items."

"Ah." He held up his pointer finger, making his way toward his nightstand. He opened the drawer and pulled out a book. "Olivia asked me to give you this."

When he held it up, I realized it was the new Meghan Hart novel—one that wasn't even for sale yet. Wouldn't be on shelves for months. I felt fortunate to have such a great relationship with Harrison's daughter, Olivia. She was sweet and kind, but savvy. She worked for a newer publishing company and always got early access to the best books, including those from my favorite romance author.

I'd been dying to read Meghan's latest book. As soon as Olivia had told me about it, I knew I needed it. A football player and the first female coach of the team? It was going to be hot, and I couldn't wait to get my hands on it. I squealed and darted to grab it from Harrison.

Harrison chuckled. "Oh my. Am I going to see you at all over the next week, or is your head going to be buried in this book the entire trip?"

"I guess that depends on how long the flight is." I smirked, setting it next to my tote that I planned to carry on the plane. I'd already added my makeup bag, a new lingerie purchase, and some other essentials like my thyroid medication and favorite snacks.

He slapped my butt on the way to the bathroom. "Come on, wife. Let's shower."

I shook my head with a laugh, following after him. Considering the glimmer in his eye, I had a feeling it was going to take more than thirty minutes to shower and get ready. *Good thing we're taking a private jet.*

"CHAMPAGNE?" PEYTON, THE FLIGHT ATTENDANT, ASKED AS soon as we'd boarded the plane and were seated.

I was still struggling to take it all in, from the tan leather to the rose-gold accents to the bedroom at the rear. It was luxury at its finest, and I'd never felt so spoiled.

When Harrison shrugged, I said, "Why not?" to Peyton. "It is our wedding day after all."

"Yes." She smiled, fidgeting with her pen. "Congratulations, Mr. and Mrs. Hayes."

"Actually—" Harrison said, and I waved my hand to ward off his comment. I might not be legally changing my last name to Hayes, but it was fun to think of myself that way, as Mrs. Harrison Hayes.

He smiled, taking my hand in his as Peyton whisked away to grab the champagne. "You ready?" he asked, rubbing his thumb back and forth over my skin.

"I'm excited."

"Good."

Peyton returned with our champagne, removing the bottle of Dom Perignon from the bucket before filling two flutes.

Harrison held up his glass, and I followed suit. "To you, my beautiful bride."

"To us," I said, the clink of the glasses drowned out by the pilot firing up the plane's engines.

"You're stuck with me now," he said, just before swallowing down some of the liquid sunshine.

I laughed, not bothered by that idea in the slightest. As I took a sip, the bubbles dancing on my tongue, I marveled once more at the beautiful and pristine interior of the jet. And I couldn't help wondering… "How much did this cost?"

Harrison leaned forward, lowering his voice. "Nothing."

I blinked at him a few times, positive I'd misheard. "Nothing?"

"It was a wedding gift from Crew." He sat back, crossing one ankle at the knee.

"Seriously?" I set my glass down on the table. "That was nice of him."

He lifted a shoulder. "I did lead the Hollywood Heatwaves to championship victory four years in a row. And I was one of the winningest, longest-lasting players on his team."

"Still…." A private jet to…well, wherever we were going, couldn't be cheap. Even for the owner of a successful national football team such as Crew Dixon.

"It's not like he *gave* us the jet. We get to borrow it for the honeymoon."

I nodded. "I'll be sure to send him an extra-nice thank-you note." I extracted my phone from my purse and opened the notes app to make a reminder for later. I was about to put my phone in airplane mode when I saw a new text message from the wedding photographer.

"I think Crew felt bad that he couldn't make it to the wedding," Harrison said as the captain came over the speaker and asked us to buckle up and prepare for takeoff.

I clicked on the link in the message, gasping as beautiful images flooded my screen.

"What is it?"

"The photographer sent me a preview." I smiled and flashed the phone at Harrison.

As we surged down the runway then glided into the sky, we scanned through the photos. I replayed the memories in my mind, knowing it was something I'd do often for the rest of my life. It had been intimate and absolutely perfect, everything I could've dreamed of. Having connections in the industry certainly helped, and many of them had insisted on providing their services for free, despite my protests. From the catering to the linens to the flowers, we'd been given so many "wedding gifts," I couldn't possibly repay all their incredible kindness.

Harrison chuckled. "Look at Reg, hamming it up for the camera."

He shook his head, amused by his best friend's antics. But my attention was on his wife, Jas. At the way her hand hovered over her stomach, as if protectively.

I turned to Harrison. "Is Jas pregnant?"

"What?" He jerked his head back then leaned in to get a closer look. "Oh damn. She might be. Want to plan their baby shower?"

"Of course." He handed back the phone. "Were they trying for another?"

He rubbed a hand over his chin. "I don't know. Reg always acted like he was done having kids. I mean, this baby would make six."

I laughed. "I can't even imagine."

"Neither can I." The crease in Harrison's forehead smoothed when he saw the next picture, his lips turning up into a smile along with mine. "One amazing daughter is all I need."

The image was of Harrison's daughter, Olivia, and her husband. She was beaming at us from the front row, Connor's arm around her. It seemed like just yesterday that we'd been planning their wedding. Though really, it had been a little over a year. So much had changed since then.

The next picture was of my parents, clapping as we'd been announced husband and wife. They were smiling through their tears, knowing what I'd gone through to get to this point.

"How sweet do Blair and Sophia look?" I asked, admiring the flower girls. Harrison nodded.

There was another picture of Preston holding Sophia on his lap, tears in his eyes. I could tell that attending the wedding had been emotional for him, and I wondered if it was because he was imagining his daughters as brides one day. The next image was of him and Alexis kissing over the top of Blair's head. Such a beautiful family.

I scrolled through a few more—Hunter and Lauren on the dance floor. Landon hugging me. I paused when I came to one of Harper, and I sighed, some of my earlier happiness dissipating. Of my three best friends, Alexis, Lauren, and Harper, I'd always been closest to Harper. She was more like a sister to me. And even though she'd smiled and put on a brave face, I knew she was hurting. It was clear from the way she held herself to the forced smile. But I kept scrolling, loving each new photo that appeared on my screen.

Reg's and Olivia's speeches. Harrison and I feeding each other cake. Sophia standing on Preston's feet as they danced. Harrison pressing his lips to my cheek. Stolen kisses. Precious moments. But still, my mind kept coming back to Harper and heartache.

"You okay?" Harrison asked, breaking me out of my trance. We'd reached cruising altitude and were flying over the ocean.

I shook my head as if to clear it and took a sip of champagne.

"Are you thinking about Ryan?" he asked, surprising me. I hadn't thought of my former fiancé all day, at least not until now.

"Actually, I was thinking about Harper."

He finished off his glass and poured another then topped off mine. "You mentioned being worried about her earlier. What's going on?"

I hesitated, knowing it might upset Harrison. But I also knew he wouldn't let it rest until I'd gotten it off my chest. I swallowed, forcing out the words. "She thought she was pregnant, and now…she's not."

His lips turned downward. "That type of loss is heartbreaking." He paused, his eyes misting over briefly before he cleared his throat and said, "But I'm glad she has the three of you to lean on. I had no one."

I squeezed his hand, hating the idea of the man I loved feeling so alone. We sat in silence a moment, the hum of the engines the only sound. At least until I blurted, "Maybe I should offer to be a surrogate for her."

Harrison coughed a few times, his face turning red as he choked on champagne. My heart clutched, but I tried to remain calm. When I asked if he was okay, he held up a hand, coughing a few more times before taking a sip of water Peyton had offered him.

"A surrogate?" He forced the words out.

"I know. I know," I sighed, dragging my hand through my hair. "Hearing it aloud, I realize how absurd that sounded." Besides, I had a feeling I wasn't the ideal candidate to be a surrogate, considering the fact that I was thirty-seven.

Harrison and I had talked about kids and didn't plan to have our own. He was fifty-one, he'd already raised one child, and he wasn't interested in having another. As for me, I was perfectly content with my life. I loved my job. I loved playing auntie to my sister's kids as well as Alexis's. And I loved my life with Harrison.

Even so, I wanted to help Harper. I *needed* to help her. It was the least I could do after all she'd done for me, especially the past few years. My chest tightened from my complete inability to do anything.

Harrison unlatched his seat belt and crouched before me, taking my hands in his. "It's not absurd to want to do something—*anything*—to help the people you love. It's admirable, and a big reason why I love you."

I softened, placing a hand to his cheek. His scruff tickled my palm, and I pulled him to me for a kiss. The connection had fire rushing through my veins, despite the orgasms he'd given me mere hours ago.

"Come on." He tugged on my hand, pulling me toward the bedroom at the back of the plane. "Let's go to bed."

"We'll be landing in a little over an hour," the pilot said over the intercom.

I blinked a few times, slowly coming to. The plane engine whirred, the white noise soothing. The sheets were smooth, and Harrison's arms were wrapped around me, his nose pressed to my back. His erection digging into me.

"Good morning, wife," he rumbled.

I smiled and stretched beneath the covers, turning over to face him. "Good morning, husband." I kissed him, lingering a moment.

Harrison kissed his way down my stomach, and I sighed, torn between wanting to stay in bed and knowing I needed to get ready before we landed. But as he inched his way toward my clit, getting ready seemed less and less important.

There was a knock at the door, and Peyton's voice wafted through the somewhat thin material. I froze, but Harrison didn't remove his lips from my skin.

"Good morning," Peyton said. "Would you like some coffee or breakfast before we land?"

"That would be lovely," I called, trying to stifle a moan when Harrison licked my clit. *Oh god.*

"What was that?" Peyton asked, and my eyes widened.

"Um. We'll be right there. Thanks." I locked my thighs around his head, doing my best to stop Harrison's movements. It felt amazing, but we didn't have time for this.

"Harrison," I hissed. "Harrison." I tugged on his shoulders when he continued to ignore me, while simultaneously making me delirious.

He popped his head out from beneath the covers, his lips slick with my desire, his hair sticking up in every direction. "What?"

"We have to get ready if we want breakfast before we land."

"I'm having you for breakfast." He ducked back beneath the covers, but I tossed them aside.

"Come on," I said, though my body felt like it might explode if I didn't let him finish. "Later."

"You said that last night." He pinned me to the mattress, his body warm and delicious as he lay on top of me. I couldn't help it; I arched my hips up into him.

"I know. But we have all week, right?" I asked, and he nodded. "And I promise I'll make it up to you."

"I like the sound of that." He pressed his lips to mine, and I could taste myself on his tongue. I lost track of time momentarily, but then I pushed gently against his chest, panting. "Breakfast."

"Breakfast." He grinned then bent forward to pull my nipple into his mouth, sucking hard before releasing it.

"You're evil." I shivered.

"You're one to talk." He pushed off the covers before standing and pulling on some boxers. "I'm going to go shower. Unless you want to go first."

I glanced at my watch, grabbing the bottle of water from the nightstand and swallowing my thyroid medicine. "Go ahead. I know you'll want breakfast, and I have to wait a little longer."

He grabbed his clothes, dropping a kiss on the top of my head en route to the bathroom. Thirty minutes—and a shower—later, I joined him in the main cabin. He did a double take at my approach, his eyes scanning my espadrilles up my bare legs to where my sundress skimmed my thigh. The white eyelet made me feel summery, bridal, but the way he looked at me had me heating beneath the material.

He gripped the armrests, and I dipped my head. The man could make me feel as if I were naked even when I was standing before him fully clothed.

"You look beautiful," he said, kissing my cheek after I took a seat.

Peyton took my breakfast order, soon returning with the

omelet and fruit I'd requested. I cupped my mug of coffee, grateful for the caffeine as I peered out the window, the world a sea of blues and greens and absolutely no land in sight. I only knew we'd been flying for nine or so hours because my watch was still on LA time. I'd slept seven of those hours in Harrison's arms, and I felt surprisingly well rested. I was still completely clueless as to our destination. All I knew was that we were going to a beach, and judging from the color of the water and remote location, it was going to be stunning.

As the plane began its descent, an island finally came into view. Turquoise water surrounded the lush haven, greenery spilling over its ridges, white sand lining the beaches. We flew over a row of bungalows that appeared as if they were floating on the water. My cheeks split into a smile, and I didn't need to know the name of the island to know it was going to be an incredible adventure.

"Welcome to Laucala," Harrison said.

I whipped my head around to face him. "Laucala? How did you—"

"Harper suggested it." He smiled, though it was tinged with sadness, likely from my revelation the night before. "And it was on your Pinterest page—one of your honeymoon recommendation boards."

"I—" I opened my mouth then closed it. Opened it again. Of all the places I had pinned and all the ones he could've selected from among them, he'd picked my top choice. My *dream* destination. "Thank you." I leaned across to kiss him just as the wheels touched down on the runway. We laughed, our bodies jostling from the impact. "Thank you."

Not long after, we stood at the top of the stairs, Harrison's palm on my lower back as I lifted my hand to my forehead to shield my eyes from the sun. Now *this* was paradise. Blue skies, puffy white clouds, dense greenery, and a chauffeur waiting on the tarmac as the crew loaded our luggage into the trunk.

"Wow." I shifted my tote on my shoulder. "I could get used to this."

"Wait until you see where we're staying," Harrison said.

I shook my head slowly. "I can't even imagine."

And I couldn't wait, even as I soaked in every detail during the drive. Tropical plants lined the road, their bright colors drawing my eye at every turn. Coconut trees, palm trees, and my favorite—the beautiful frangipani flowers with their six curved white petals and yellow center.

"Holy…*wow*," I breathed as the chauffeur pulled into the round drive of the resort.

The exterior was a traditional design with a thatched roof, but the interior was contemporary luxury. A large arrangement of orchids sat on a round table in the lobby, the warm colors and variety of textures luring me into the welcoming atmosphere. The interior design was simple yet opulent—something I could imagine Lauren gushing over. And the view…

"*Bula!*" one of the hotel employees said as he approached. "We are delighted to have you stay with us." His smile stretched from ear to ear, his presence warm like the tropical climate.

"My name is Emori," he continued. "And I'll be personally looking after you during your stay. '*Bula*' means welcome, hello, or cheers. I'd be delighted to show you to your accommodations, Mr. and Mrs. Hayes."

"*Bula*," I said. "And please, call me Juliana."

"Yes, of course, Miss Juliana. Allergies to oats and coconut. Dislikes mustard."

I stared at him a moment. "Yes. Um, wow. You are remarkably well informed." We'd barely stepped foot in the lobby, and already I was impressed by the level of service and attention to detail. I wondered if they hosted destination weddings....

"Juliana," Harrison chided, though his teasing smile told me he didn't mind the question. It was only with his comment that I realized I'd zoned out for a moment, easily switching to work mode. And also, that I'd asked the question aloud.

Emori laughed. "Yes, we do host weddings. We have one this weekend, in fact. But it was my understanding that you're newlyweds." He glanced between us as if seeking confirmation.

"We are." Harrison grinned, sliding his hand over my hip and pulling me into his side. "My wife is an event planner back in LA."

"Ah, yes. How lovely." He clapped his hands together. "Right this way, if you please."

Emori escorted us through the hotel, and the more he told us, the more awestruck I was. Not only was the resort absolutely gorgeous—situated on a private island with the most incredible scenery—but it was so much more than that. It was 100% solar powered and had a strong focus on luxury and conservation, from the soap provided in the guest rooms to its reef sustainability program.

As we passed one of the restaurants, a more upscale one with a menu heavy on seafood, Emori told us of the delicacies offered nightly. In addition to twenty-four-hour room service, every restaurant on the property served locally sourced items, all grown on the island.

"Very impressive," I said, glancing at Harrison as we continued the tour. My husband knew me well.

"And now, for your accommodations," Emori said, ushering us through an open breezeway toward the water.

A boardwalk led from the main resort over the white sand and glittering turquoise water. But we didn't head for the overwater bungalows, as I'd expected. We continued on, getting farther and farther from the main resort until we arrived at a little villa along an empty stretch of the beach.

The deck had a private plunge pool, and the doors were open, the rich wood interior blending seamlessly with the palm trees and ocean beyond. Though the overwater bungalows certainly had their charm, the villa was much more secluded and much…larger.

I turned to Harrison. "Seriously?"

He grinned, giving my lower back a gentle nudge. "Come on."

While Emori gave us a tour of our secluded villa, I felt as if I might burst from excitement. I was like a bottle of champagne that had been shaken, and all the bubbles were jostling to get out. When he finally left us to get settled in, I spun around the living room, arms wide.

"Oh. My. God." I grinned, half laughing, half squealing. "This is insane."

Harrison chuckled, his hip resting against the kitchen counter. We had a kitchen! And enough seating to have invited all of our friends.

"This is too much," I said, my heart still fluttering even as I slowed.

"You're too much," he teased.

"I mean, this view. The pool. The bed." It was all so incredible, so romantic. The white curtains draped elegantly around the bed. And the bathroom…

When I realized how quiet Harrison was, I turned to face him. "What?"

"You're even more beautiful when you let go."

Despite the fact that he was my husband, a man who'd seen me naked and explored every inch of me too many times to count, I blushed. He crooked his finger, beckoning me to him. And I went willingly. He spread his thighs, and I nestled between them, settling into his arms.

"This is amazing. Thank you."

He tucked an errant strand of hair behind my ear. "So goddamn beautiful." He pressed his lips to mine. "How did I get so lucky?"

I kissed him again, the taste of him lingering on my lips. "How did I?"

He rubbed my shoulders. "What do you want to do first?"

"Everything. Nothing." I laughed, giddiness making me light.

"How about a dip in the pool, and then we can try one of the restaurants for lunch?"

I nodded. "Perfect."

After the wedding then the long flight, I just wanted to relax and unwind with Harrison. There would be time to go on excursions, to explore, but for now, I wanted to just *be*.

With one more quick peck to his lips, I said, "I'm going to unpack and change, then I'll join you."

"Change?" He tilted his head to the side. "You mean undress?"

"Well, yeah. But I assume Harper packed me at least one swimsuit."

He lifted a shoulder, a wicked grin lighting his features. "If it were up to me, you wouldn't wear any clothes while we're here."

I laughed and turned for the bedroom with a shake of my head, when he pulled me back, crushing me to his chest. He didn't say anything, just held me a moment then released me.

"You okay?" I asked, sensing a shift in his mood.

He nodded, clearing his throat. "Just wanted to remember the moment."

I smiled, cupping his cheeks before planting a sloppy kiss on his lips. "My Zen guru."

He laughed and stripped out of his shirt before removing his pants. The doors to the pool and the beach beyond were still open.

My eyes went wide. "What are you doing?"

"Going swimming," he said, as if it were obvious.

"Yeah, but…" I glanced around as if someone would appear at any moment. "What if someone sees you?"

"It's a private beach for our villa. And none of the staff will come by unless invited."

"Still…" I hesitated, not sure I was ready to skinny-dip, despite Harrison's assurances. "I think I'll put on a swimsuit."

"Suit yourself." He removed his boxers in one swift move, tossing them at me.

I caught them just before they hit my face, his laugh echoing off the wood floors. And then all I could see was his tight, lifted ass as he prowled toward the pool. My mouth went dry, and I stared after him, completely lost in the view.

He dropped into the pool, emerging a moment later with slick hair and a deep sigh of contentment. With all the windows thrown open, outside and inside blurred together, a gentle breeze blowing in from the ocean, the scent of gardenias perfuming the air. I lingered for a moment then headed to the bedroom where my suitcase was laid out in the large closet. A garment bag hung from the rod, and I unzipped it to find a few of my favorite dresses as well as a sexy new one I hadn't seen before.

There was a note attached to the hanger, and I recognized Alexis's handwriting. "Enjoy your time together. Nothing is more important."

I smiled to myself, thinking of how far she'd come, how much she'd changed in the past few years. Preston had a lot to do with that, just as Harrison had helped me focus on what truly mattered, on being present.

In the suitcase, I found tissue paper with a ribbon tied

around it and a note from Lauren. "Have fun" was all it said, an "L" scrawled hastily at the bottom. Inside were several new pieces of lingerie, handcuffs, and a few other toys. I laughed to myself. Why was I not surprised?

Lauren had always been the most sexually liberated of the four of us. Harper and Alexis had hosted my bridal shower, but they'd left the bachelorette party to Lauren. And it had been…wild. Fun, but wild. We'd all flown out to Vegas, even the guys. At some point, we'd ended up at the same club, and Harrison and I had been so drunk, we'd started making out on the dance floor. Me in my "Bride-to-Be" sash, dick tiara, and veil, and him looking devastatingly handsome as usual. I was positive most bystanders thought I was cheating on my husband-to-be, which had only made me giggle harder.

I shook my head, a smile tilting my lips upward at the memory. I had the best friends—women who supported me, loved me unconditionally, and were there for me no matter what. The fact that they'd taken the time to add small, personal gifts to my luggage was just one more reminder of how fortunate I was.

The rest of my suitcase was well organized, and I appreciated Harper's packing skills. It wasn't surprising, considering she spent much of the year on the road as a film location scout. There was also a small waterproof point-and-shoot camera, a guide to the island, and a handwritten note from Harper with her recommendations for the top attractions. Though she did emphasize relaxing and having fun.

Beneath that were several swimsuits, including one I'd never seen but immediately fell in love with. It was a white bikini that was a little skimpier than I'd normally wear but perfect for our honeymoon. I changed into it, loving the way the bra cups covered my breasts, but only just barely. The bottom was a strip of fabric, and my tanned skin was offset by the white material. I loved the white applique flowers, and

I had a feeling Harrison was going to lose his mind when he saw it. I applied a fresh coat of lip gloss and twisted my hair up into a bun on the top of my head, grabbing my sunglasses and the camera before venturing outside.

Harrison was leaning against the edge of the pool, arms wide, eyes closed, and head angled toward the sky. I snapped a picture, and he opened his eyes.

"Sorry." I scrunched up my face, not having wanted to disturb him.

He ran a hand through his hair, though judging from his stupefied expression, I wasn't sure he'd heard a word I'd said. His green eyes glittered, the sun shining on the water and reflecting back in them. But it was the love I found gazing back at me that stole my breath. The heat, the desire, as he scanned my body from head to toe.

"I think I'm the one who should be taking pictures. Because damn, baby. That swimsuit…"

I laughed as I descended the steps to the pool, and my mind flashed back to our trip to Ojai last year. We'd been in the midst of planning Olivia's wedding, and I'd been trying—and failing—to ignore my attraction to Harrison. As we'd lounged next to the pool at a different resort, in a different time, I remembered thinking Harrison was the hottest man I'd ever seen. I still believed that.

"Where'd you go?" Harrison asked, water droplets beading on his chest.

"Ojai."

His lips curved into a knowing smile, and he waded through the water toward me. "Ah. Ojai. One of my favorite memories. Well, except the hike."

I smiled, grateful it was something we could laugh about now. "Yeah. Not the hike. Do you ever wonder—what if Olivia hadn't wanted me to plan her wedding? What if our paths had never crossed again?"

He shook his head, pulling me into him. His naked body was both hard and welcoming all at once. "I would've found you."

And I believed him.

"WE'RE ALMOST THERE," HARRISON SAID, TURNING BACK TO ME from farther up the trail.

"Where are you taking me?" I asked, sweat making my shirt cling to my skin.

The rain forest was beautiful, but the humidity was killing me. And I kept slipping on the rocks that lined the path. They were small enough that you could barely step on them but too large to walk around. And they were slick from the moisture in the air.

"Do you need a snack?" he teased.

I narrowed my eyes and growled at him. He laughed, stopping to pull something out of his backpack. "Here." He handed me an energy bar.

"Thank you." I grabbed it from him, tearing the wrapper. I took a few bites and started to feel a little less on edge. I could enjoy the scenery again, the birdsong, the swaying of the branches, and was that... "Do I hear..." I furrowed my brow. "Is that water?"

He held up his water bottle and shook it. "Yep. Want some?"

"No." I narrowed my eyes at him. "Listen."

He capped his water bottle and shoved it back in his pack before forging ahead on the trail. "Come on."

We walked a while longer, the sound of rushing water growing louder with every step. The air seemed cooler as well, and I relaxed, enjoying the vibrant hibiscus and lush forest. We rounded a bend, and a waterfall came into view. I lifted my head, glancing up to the top and watching as it tumbled and fell, plunging into a large, clear pool at the bottom.

I was so busy looking at it that I didn't notice Harrison had moved from my side. When I glanced over to look at him, I realized he was gone, standing off to the side where an elaborate picnic had been laid out on a flat patch of grass.

My jaw popped open. "Wow."

"Right?" He sat down and opened the picnic basket. "Emori outdid himself this time."

I nodded, salivating with every item he removed. I joined him on the ground, pouring us each a drink while he plated some food for both of us. We sat in peaceful silence, eating our lunch as the tranquility of the place washed over us like the waterfall tumbling over the stones.

"I think I'm putting you in charge of our vacations from now on," I finally said.

"Is that so?" He smirked, smugness creeping into his tone.

"Yeah. This has been...fantastic. Every day keeps getting better and better."

"Now you know how I feel about life with you." He brought my hand to his lips and kissed me.

I laughed. "So cheesy."

"You love it," he teased.

"I do. And I love you." I rocked on my hip, leaning toward him for a kiss.

"What's been your favorite day so far?"

"Gah. Are you really going to make me choose? I've loved it all, from snorkeling on the reef to lounging on our private beach to surf lessons. Though the tour of the island's gardens and taking the cooking class with a local chef had to be one of my favorite things."

He grinned. "I thought you'd enjoy that. I'm glad."

"What about you?" I asked. "What's been your favorite part?"

"I'm not sure I can choose," he said. "Though seeing your delight, getting to explore with you—that's probably been my favorite part."

I pushed my hair away from my face then leaned back on my elbows, tilting my head to the sky. The forest was dappled with sunlight, and I closed my eyes. I could've listened to the waterfall all day.

"I have something for you," Harrison said.

I opened my eyes, and he pulled something out of the backpack that looked a lot like a jewelry box. I furrowed my brow. "What's that?"

"I wanted to get you something to remember our time here. Something as unique and beautiful and rare as you are to me." He lifted the lid to reveal a gorgeous strand of pearls in the most amazing array of colors, from creamy white to green to chocolate brown.

"Oh my…" I held a hand to my mouth then reached out to skim the tips of my fingers along the strand. "They're gorgeous. Thank you."

I wrapped my arms around his neck and kissed him. He was the most thoughtful, sweetest man.

"When did you…?"

"While you were getting your massage," he said, and I laughed. "So that's why you skipped."

He nodded. "I hope it's okay, but I also got Olivia a necklace. It's different from yours, a pendant with a single pearl."

"Of course. I was going to suggest we get her something special. I'm sure she'll love it." I smiled.

"Good." He closed the box and returned it to the backpack. "Want to go for a swim?"

I glanced over at the pool. It certainly was clear, yet I hesitated. "Is it safe?"

He lifted a shoulder. "Emori assured me it is."

"Yeah. Okay. Sure." I stood, pushing my shorts over my hips before stripping out of my shirt, leaving me in a two-piece red swimsuit.

"Fuck me," Harrison growled.

I laughed, enjoying the way he seemed to grow more agitated with every new swimsuit I revealed on the trip. From the white bikini with applique flowers to the cobalt blue one-piece that dipped low on my chest to this red one.

I walked into the water, the cool liquid lapping at my toes. And all the while, I could feel his eyes on me, watching me. The water was borderline cold, but it felt refreshing. Before I could talk myself out of it, I dove beneath the surface, the chill a shock to my system. When I resurfaced, Harrison was nowhere to be seen. I glanced around for him, yelping when something grabbed my leg a moment later. He popped his head up, smoothing back his hair with a laugh.

"That's not funny!" I splashed him.

"I'm sorry, baby," he said, pulling me close to him.

"No, you're not."

He pressed his lips to my neck, my anger cooling as my desire sparked. I rested my head against his shoulder, water swirling around us and the falls drowning out all other sounds. It was so easy to be present, to be in the moment. His erection began to prod me, and when he slid his hands down to cup my ass, I laughed. "You're insatiable."

"Well, what do you expect when you keep parading around in these swimsuits? If I thought the white bikini was small, it was nothing compared to this—shoestring."

He smoothed his hands over my bare skin, the bottoms revealing most of my ass. My skin tingled with awareness, warmth gushing to my core where I wanted him most.

"It is pretty small, isn't it?" I leaned back and peered down at my chest. Like the bottoms, the top was a small strip of fabric. And while Harrison likened it to a shoestring, dental floss seemed a more fitting description.

His eyes followed my gaze, and the way he looked at me made me hotter than the South Pacific sun. He rubbed his thumbs over my breasts, my nipples pebbling beneath the wet material. He swallowed hard, and I suddenly found it difficult to breathe, to think clearly. My chest rose and fell in rapid bursts, goose bumps breaking out along my skin.

When he brushed the material aside completely, I gasped. He picked me up, wrapping my legs around his waist. His hard-on was insistent, brushing my entrance as he backed us toward a large shelf of rock lining the edge of the pool.

He set me down, though never losing his hold, our tongues mixing, bodies melding. Hands exploring.

"Harrison," I panted as he clamped down on one of my nipples, nudging my bottoms aside with his finger to tease my clit. "Oh god. Oh fuck." I struggled to find purchase, the water and the wind and his lips wreaking havoc with my senses.

He kept my swimsuit pulled to the side, even as he withdrew his finger. But he quickly replaced it with his cock. We both sighed in relief, and he pinned my eyes with his, linking our fingers as he continued to pump into me. I used my legs to pull him closer, fusing us together until there was no way of knowing where one of us ended and the other began.

"Don't stop," I whispered, sinking my teeth into his shoulder. "Don't...stop." And with that, I came, light bursting behind my eyelids, our movements frantic as we lost ourselves in each other.

He followed behind, with a few short thrusts and a grunt. Our breathing was ragged, and I could feel his heart racing.

He whispered words of love and pressed kisses to my hair, my temple.

Later that evening, after a delicious meal at one of the restaurants, we returned to the villa. We sat on one of the lounge chairs, watching the sunset as we had every evening since arriving. My back was to him, his legs bracketing mine, his arms wrapped around me.

I reflected back on the day, on the trip, and I marveled at everything we'd done and seen. But best of all had been the time together. Harrison was right—we'd needed this break, this alone time. And I felt more relaxed and happier than I had in years. As much as I didn't want to think about returning home, I couldn't help it.

As the sun dipped lower in the sky, casting brilliant pinks and purples throughout the clouds, I asked, "Do you ever worry that happiness like this is fleeting?"

"No." He said it with such certainty that I twisted to peer back at him over my shoulder. "Because I know it is." My heart stuttered, but he continued speaking. "Just as I know that pain, loss, unhappiness, any emotion is fleeting.

"Our relationship will go through ups and downs. That's the nature of love and life. But I will never give up on us. I will never stop fighting for us."

"Neither will I." I pressed my lips to his.

In my heart, I knew he was right. As I'd said that night at the bar, the night we'd met—life was unpredictable. But Harrison had been right too. Because that was part of the fun. He'd shown me that, and there was no one else I wanted to experience the adventure with.

Acknowledgements

I started this story what feels like forever ago, but kept getting stuck. It was more of a struggle than I wanted it to be, and it didn't help that I was attempting to write during the beginning of the global pandemic. It suddenly became too much, trying to get in the mental state to write about love after loss, to dive into some of the intense emotional scenes.

So, I jumped ship momentarily, opting to write Connor and Olivia's story, *Unwritten*, instead. It was fun and light, and it filled in the missing pieces for me. So that when I returned to *Unpredictable*, I was in a better frame of mind.

I loved the family dynamics. I loved getting to see more of both Juliana and Harrison as well as Connor and Olivia interwoven through both stories. Harrison was just such a sweetheart, and he and Juliana really balanced each other out. They restored each other's hope in love, the future, and I hope they helped restore some of yours too! They definitely restored some of mine.

Thank you for reading *Unpredictable*. I love writing for the pleasure of it, but seeing reader's reactions is definitely a highlight. To all the bloggers, bookstagrammers, and readers who get excited, who post about my stories, and who have shown me a sense of genuine community and support—thank you!

To all the authors who have been so kind and generous. Who have welcomed me into this community and answered so many questions. Not to mention all the authors who have joined me for Writer Wednesdays on IGTV. Talking to each and every one of you has been both fun and inspiring!

A big thank you to the Hartley's Hustlers and all my VIPs. You guys rock! I cannot possibly tell you how much your support means to me! I appreciate everything you ladies do to promote my books and to encourage me throughout my writing journey.

A special shoutout to Skye for coming up with the name for Harrison's former football team—the Hollywood Heatwaves. And thanks for sharing the fun tidbit about the Disney Concert Hall: when the steel walls were first installed, so much light reflected off them that nearby sidewalks hit temps of 140 degrees Fahrenheit.

Thank you to Evelyn Owen for inspiring me with your gorgeous designs. And for working with me to create a beautiful dress for Juliana's wedding. You are so talented and lovely. You can follow her on Instagram and obsess with me over all her beautiful creations.

To my editor, Lisa with Silently Correcting Your Grammar. I so appreciate your attention to detail, and your patience with my questions. You always go above and beyond. And your comments crack me up! As always, thank you for helping me create a thoughtful and well-polished book I can be proud of. Your services and advice are invaluable.

Thank you to LJ for designing such a gorgeous cover that really captures the feel of the story and characters.

Thank you to Ellen, as always. Thank you for being so supportive and positive, for being a friend. And thank you for sharing your incredible eye for detail.

A huge thank you to Kristen for being such an amazing friend. I value your judgment and honesty, and I so appreciate your support. We've been through so much together, and I treasure your friendship and advice. Seriously, I cannot thank you enough for all that you do. Thank you for holding my hand as I brainstormed ideas. For being as excited about their story as I was.

Thank you, Jade. You make me a stronger writer, and you challenge me on pacing. You are so clever and always provide great insight. I'm so grateful for your friendship, and our long chats!

Thank you to Brit! I love writing strong, badass female main characters, and you help ensure that they live up to their potential. And that the men who dare to love them do too.

A huge thank you to all my beta readers. Thank you for making me a stronger writer, for offering your unique insight and advice. You each seem to bring something different to the table, and I'm always amazed and impressed by your suggestions. I'm so incredibly honored to have you on my team!

Thank you to my husband for always encouraging me. For always supporting my dreams. You are better than any book boyfriend I could ever imagine. And to my daughter, for always putting a smile on my face. You are spirited and independent, and I wouldn't have it any other way. Dream big, my darling.

A big huge thank you to Aunt Kathie for taking such good care of our daughter while I wrote. You listened to my ideas without judgment, you encouraged me to keep going, and you enabled me to write during a stressful time.

Thank you to my parents for always being so encouraging. For reading my books. For being my biggest fans!

If this list of people shows you anything, it's that dreams are often the effort of many. I'm grateful to have such an awesome team. And I'm honored that you've taken the time to read my words.

About the Author

Jenna Hartley is USA Today bestselling author who writes feel-good forbidden romance, much like her own real-life love story. She's known for writing strong women and swoon-worthy men, as well as blending panty-melting and heart-warming moments.

When she's not reading or writing romance, Jenna can be found tending to her growing indoor plant collection (pun intended), organizing, and hiking. She lives in Texas with her family and loves nothing more than a good book and good chocolate, except a dance party with her daughter.

www.authorjennahartley.com

Also by Jenna Hartley

<u>**Love in LA Series**</u>
Inevitable
Unexpected
Irresistible
Undeniable
Unpredictable
Irreplaceable

<u>**Alondra Valley Series**</u>
Feels Like Love
Love Like No Other
A Love Like That

<u>**Tempt Series**</u>
Temptation
Reputation

For the most current list of Jenna's titles, please visit her website www.authorjennahartley.com.

Or scan the QR code on the following page to be taken to her author page on Amazon.com

SCAN ME

www.ingramcontent.com/pod-product-compliance
Lightning Source LLC
Chambersburg PA
CBHW070611300726
48975CB00006B/1779